#ilov

SOULS

A KILLERS NOVEL, BOOK 6

BRYNNE ASHER

Text Copyright

© 2022 Brynne Asher
All Rights Reserved
No part of this book may be reproduced, scanned, or distributed in any printed or electronic form without permission from the author. Please do not participate in or encourage piracy of copyrighted materials in violation of author's rights. Only purchase authorized editions.

Any resemblance to actual persons, things, locations, or events is accidental.

This book is a work of fiction.

SOULS

A Killers Novel, Book 6
Brynne Asher

Published by Brynne Asher
BrynneAsherBooks@gmail.com

Keep up with me on Facebook for news and upcoming books
https://www.facebook.com/BrynneAsherAuthor

Join my Facebook reader group to keep up with my latest news Brynne Asher's Beauties

Keep up with all Brynne Asher books and news. Sign up for my newsletter http://eepurl.com/gFVMUP

Edited by Hadley Finn
Cover by Haya in Designs

ALSO BY BRYNNE ASHER

Killers Series

Vines – A Killers Novel, Book 1

Paths – A Killers Novel, Book 2

Gifts – A Killers Novel, Book 3

Veils – A Killers Novel, Book 4

Scars – A Killers Novel, Book 5

Souls – A Killers Novel, Book 6

The Tequila – A Killers Novella

The Killers, The Next Generation

Levi, Asa's son

The Agents

Possession

Tapped

Exposed

Illicit

The Carpino Series

Overflow – The Carpino Series, Book 1

Beautiful Life – The Carpino Series, Book 2

Athica Lane – The Carpino Series, Book 3

Until Avery – A Carpino Series Crossover Novella

Force of Nature - A Carpino Christmas Novel

The Dillon Sisters
Deathly by Brynne Asher
Damaged by Layla Frost

The Montgomery Series
Bad Situation – The Montgomery Series, Book 1
Broken Halo – The Montgomery Series, Book 2
Betrayed Love - The Montgomery Series, Book 3

Standalones
Blackburn

DEDICATIONS

To Emoji,

It's a big year.
Thank you for the journey.
I can't wait to see where the future takes us.

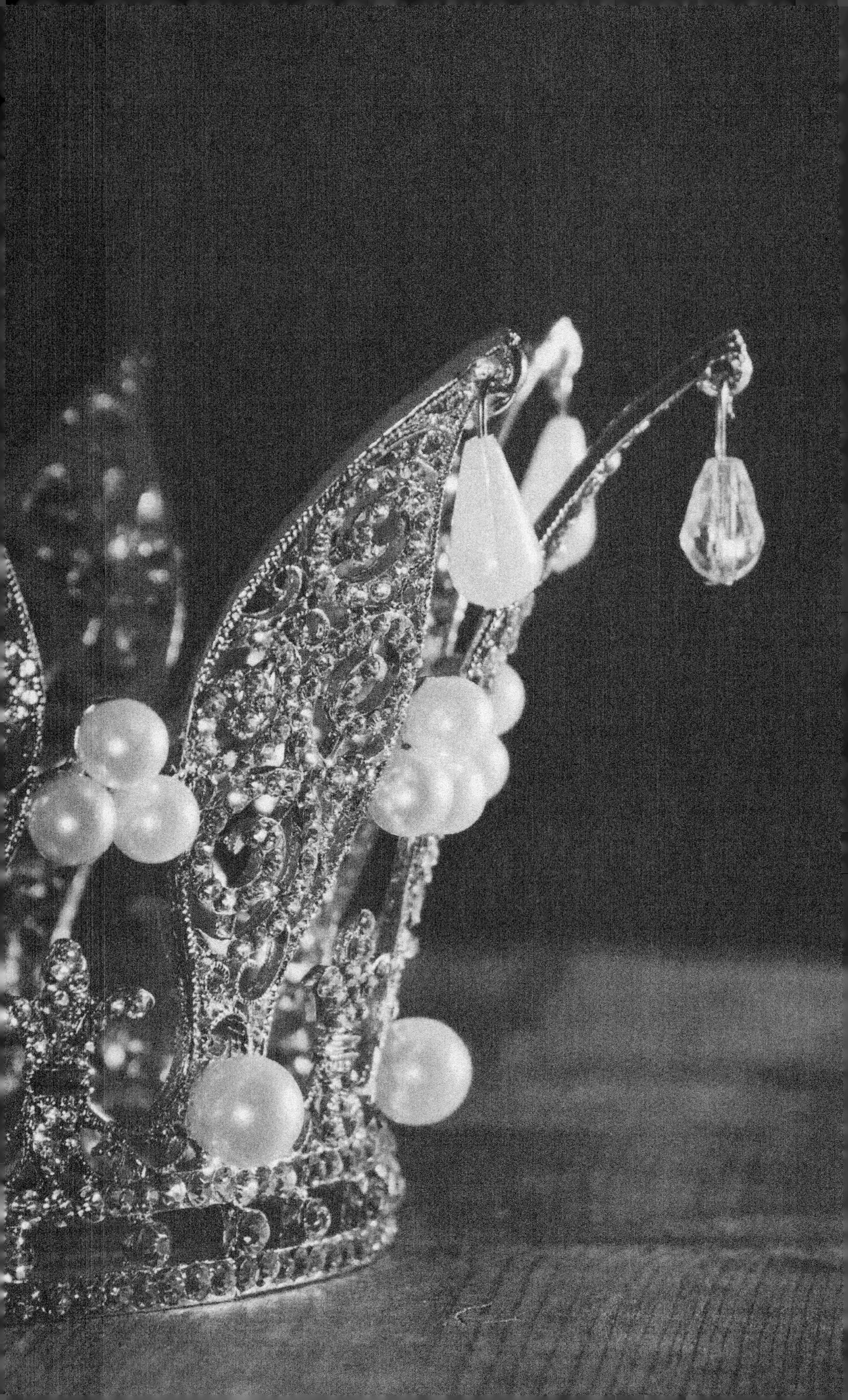

PROLOGUE

Ozzy

Choices.
They're a privilege I took for granted until they were ripped away from me.

I was pushed and pushed and fucking pushed some more. Until I was left teetering on a ledge, left to take control the only way I knew how.

Because allowing them to decide my fate is not an option.

I did what I do best. But now I've run out of choices.

Twenty-eight years, eleven months, three weeks, and six days.

I've had a good run.

I guess.

"You good?"

I don't look away from the scene playing out. "I have to be. There's no going back."

"No, there's not," he agrees. "You had no choice."

There's that damn word again. The one I took for

granted. The one I had no clue I should've valued above all else.

I hold my binoculars steady. I pulled the trigger weeks ago, but it hasn't seemed real until this moment.

"You did the right thing," he goes on. "It might not feel like it now, but you did."

I watch the casket as it's lowered into the earth. Carrying the weight of a death on my shoulders is heavier than I thought it would be. If I had access to the right kind of technology, I could see and hear everything—the way I'm used to.

Maybe I should be grateful the only thing at my disposal are basic binoculars. The sights and sounds will bounce around my empty soul and echo for eternity. The weight on my shoulders is enough to bear, not sure I can deal with the memories of anything more after what I've done.

"Let's go. This is unheard of, and Crew isn't happy we're anywhere close. We've pushed it far enough."

I sigh and take one last glimpse from afar of the terror and pain I created. I guess I need to get used to it. This is my life now. What I signed up for ... no matter how deep my guilt runs.

All it took was one tap of the finger to pull the trigger.

I can muscle the best of the best and come out the victor. I'm strong, quick, and agile, but backing that with my brains?

I've already taken Crew down. Took me exactly thirty-eight seconds to figure him out—Asa timed me. Then I took down Grady. They had to stop Jarvis and me, call it a draw.

You don't just have to be strong, you have to use your

brain to study your opponent. My mind is by far my strongest muscle.

All that ... and my index finger has proven to be the most powerful.

I lower the binoculars. I've seen enough.

"Come on. The plane is waiting."

I take one last look before I turn to Jarvis who has had my back in more ways than one lately. "Yeah. Ready."

He nods once. "You won't regret this. We'll make sure of it."

I lift my chin, but say nothing, and move past him, through the field to where we parked on the side of a dirt road.

Regrets are like choices—I lost the latter and don't have the luxury of the former. At this point, I can't afford regrets.

I can only look ahead and become the best killer I can be.

Hell, what am I talking about? I already am.

Life got messy, and I was pushed to do something I didn't want to do.

But not anymore.

From here on out, no one will control me again.

I'll do my job for Crew without blinking.

But the assholes who pushed me onto that ledge?

They won't know what hit them.

When choices and regrets are off the table, there's nothing left but revenge. It might take some patience, but I'll take down whoever gets in my way as I dish out my brand of retribution.

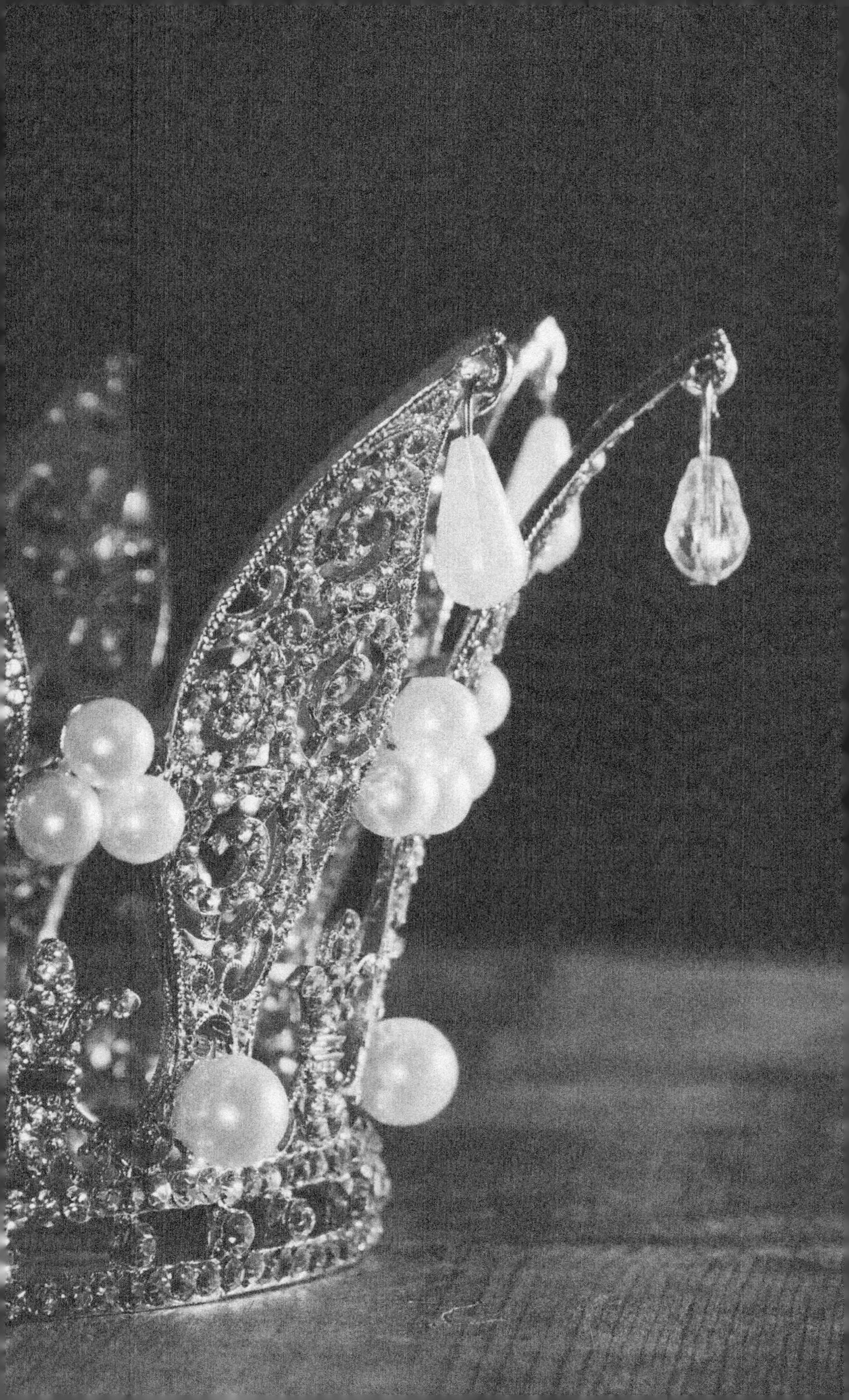

1

WANDERER

Around three years later
Ozzy

An adventurer.
　　　A voyager.
　　　An explorer.

It's who I am. What I've become. Hell, who am I kidding? Traveling is my lifeline—the only way I stay sane.

There's also the fact I'm a killer.

I've compartmentalized that part of my life into a secure place in the dark alcoves of my soul. It funds my globe-trotting and gives me life, even if it is a living hell.

At least these are the lies I tell myself.

I prefer adventurer and explorer to drifter or vagabond, which is what I've really become. I might have a home base in Virginia, but it's no home.

Perfecting the art of living and working out of a backpack might as well be at the top of my résumé.

If I had one.

Which I don't.

I'm living and breathing, which means I'm damn good at my job. I don't need a résumé to tout my skills. The moment I'm not good at my job will be the day I'm D-E-A-D in every sense of the word.

"Gracias." I take the ticket and make my way through the station in a quick jog, as final boarding for my train is announced in three different languages. I've spent the day traveling from Crew's European base in Paris. I'm cutting my connections close, but they sent me a last-minute job. I need to be in Libya by tomorrow night, which is going to be a feat in and of itself unless Asa can get my ass booked on a charter.

Private jets flown by pilots we trust in this part of the world aren't a dime a dozen—especially at a moment's notice.

Crew has my back, I know this. Hell, he treats everyone from camp as if we share his DNA. I trust him, but that doesn't mean I like last-minute jobs. I'm methodical and measured. I trust numbers and microchips more than I do people.

People—generally speaking—suck.

Give me a computer and a satellite, and I'm a content man. I don't need anyone or anything else.

I barely make it and am one of the last bodies to hop on the train. I move through the cars to my sleeper cabin. I have no desire to be close to anyone, and who knows what the next week will look like. Preparing for this job is the first priority, and some sleep would be nice too.

We start to roll, but I stop in the narrow hall. A woman with a head of hair fanned over a backpack that looks like it could explode at any moment is blocking the way. She's arguing with an attendant in English, her words hitting him rapid-fire. The poor guy can barely keep up.

"My husband ran to the dining car to pick up dinner so we can eat privately and retire early. I'm newly pregnant and not sure if I'm starving or ill. But he took off with my key. If you would kindly open the door, I need to use the restroom and freshen up. We've been traveling for two days straight."

"Madam, I cannot—"

"Yes, you can. You're simply choosing not to."

"I apologize—"

"You can apologize all day long, and it will do me no good. Apologize to my husband, who is a frequent traveler on your line. Then you can apologize to every passenger after I wet myself right here in the hall, and that's if I don't throw up all over your loafers first. You can also apologize to my doctor for not allowing me to get off my feet after the longest day ever."

The attendant pulls in a big breath.

"Now," the woman demands in a way I bet she's used to getting everything she wants. All of a sudden I feel sorry for the unknown chump tied to her because I can't imagine that's a fun gig.

The attendant glances over his shoulder to see if anyone is watching before he turns to the door and starts to mutter to himself in Spanish, mirroring my thoughts about her husband. Pulling out a master key, he holds a fob up to the door, and the moment the keypad turns green, the woman pushes through.

Despite her claims about wetting herself, she takes the time to grab the attendant by the sleeve of his shirt. For the first time, I get a look at her face. Her dark eyes are framed in lashes so long and thick, I wonder if they set some kind of record. Even though her lips are turned into an angry frown, they're still full and pink. She's not wearing a lick of makeup, but she doesn't need it. Between her dark eyes, hair, and skin, she's native to this part of the world, even though she sounds Americanized with a twinge of Brit.

In essence, she looks and sounds worldly, like she could be from anywhere and has been everywhere. There's nothing normal about this woman.

She confirms my suspicions about the worldly shit when she bites, "For the record, I speak four languages. I understood every word you just said, and, no, I do not lead my husband around by his cock."

Unlike me who had to learn five languages over the course of eight months, I bet she's been multilingual since the moment she entered the world.

The attendant turns a shade of red I've never witnessed on a human before when she calls him out for being an asshole.

"That's what I thought." She throws salt in his wounds. "Let's agree to forget this ever happened, and I won't report your foul language to your supervisor."

He gives her a curt nod. "My apologies, madam. Enjoy your night."

She steps into the cabin and slams the door in his face.

The attendant hurries off with his tail tucked between his legs and disappears into the next car. I need to find my cabin and hope I don't run into the woman who has proven to be as pleasant as a dead skunk on a hot summer night.

I start for my room when my cell vibrates. It's Crew.

I push myself against the wall to allow more passengers by and answer. "Yeah?"

"Making sure you caught your ride."

A couple with three kids, who have more bags than any five people should be allowed to travel with, pass me. I couldn't move if I wanted to. "Made it, but barely. We're pulling out of the station. I should be at the coast by morning."

"Asa is still trying to arrange for a plane once you get to Málaga. I'll let you know in the morning. Otherwise, you good?"

"Splendid."

"Reel in the smartass, Oz. You haven't been home in months. After this job, your ass is back in the Commonwealth—I don't care where you want to go or what you want to see. Consider it an order, if not by me, then my wife. You know she worries, and if ordering you back to the States will make her feel better, then I'll make it happen."

Running my hand through my hair, I grip the back of my neck and sigh. "I have plans. Tell Addy I'll try to make it for Thanksgiving."

"Fuck that. I can't hold Addison off that long. This job is a rush and you'll be done by mid-week. Your mug had better be here for The Harvest. It's the biggest event of the year at Whitetail. Hell, you can take your aggressions out on some grapes if that'll make you feel better. It's an order."

I squeeze my eyes shut. "I thought I was a contractor,

not your child. I take jobs, not orders on how to spend my personal time."

"Good luck explaining that to my wife. It's been too long since I've had everyone under the same roof. If you don't think you need time at home, then I'll call a mandatory meeting. Keep your shit tight and right, then get your ass home."

"Vega—" I start, but he stops me just as fast.

"I'm not fucking around, Oz. This job is big. No one is better suited than you. Still, get it done and get out. That part of the world is more turbulent than ever right now."

This is true. I was able to skim the background on the way from Paris. No one can carry out this job better than me.

He keeps spewing orders, as if he assumes I'll fall in line. "When you're home, we're going to have a sit down about your schedule. I'm concerned."

An elderly couple exits the room across from the pregnant grump and nods at me, before turning the other way, talking about the dinner menu in Spanish.

Crew isn't going to give up, plus I have work to do and every minute I spend standing here in the hall, I lose sleep. But there's no way I'm going back to Virginia, so I lie, "Fine."

"*Fine*," Crew echoes. "Hell, you're like the petulant teenager of the group."

"Fuck you," I spout. "I had plans to see Picasso's Museum on my way back, but I guess he'll have to wait."

"Right," he drawls. "Picasso is dead, which means he can wait an eternity. My wife is very much on my ass about you and will *not* wait."

Crew might be the brains of this fucked-up organization, but his wife, Addy, is its heart. I've done everything I can to use this job for what I need it to be, and stay disconnected, but Addy Vega makes that difficult. She's everyone's sister, mother, and best friend all rolled into one, whether we like it or not. And Crew Vega is the one who makes sure we follow her lead.

Or, everyone else does.

Addy might get her way with the rest of them, but I've kept my distance, and managed to stay away as much as possible since he let me loose to work.

"See you soon," Crew confirms the plans he thinks he can force me into.

"Grape stomping," I mutter. "Can't wait."

"The Harvest is a big deal, Oz. I'll tell Addison to reserve a place for you."

I groan as I push away from the wall and move to my cabin. "Looking forward to it already."

"I can tell," he deadpans. "Get some sleep. I'll call when Asa coordinates your connection."

"Later."

I stuff my phone in my pocket and finally head to my cabin.

But when I find the door, I do a double take. I know I haven't had much sleep in the last seventy-two hours, but my photographic memory has its benefits, even through exhaustion.

But this time, I must be wrong.

I dig my ticket out of my pocket.

I look back up at the numbers and make sure I'm in the right car.

What the hell?

"Señor, may I help?"

I look up and find the same attendant who let the

woman into her room so she didn't pee herself in the hall.

He's studying me.

And I don't like it.

First, I don't like attention.

Second, the attention he is giving me is not good.

I hold up my ticket and tip my head to the door. I speak in English, even though I'm fluent in his native language and four others. "I've had a long day. Ready for some sleep."

He narrows his eyes. "Did you find the dining car?"

I shrug my bag up my shoulder and lie, because right now, I'd rather deal with the strange woman in my cabin than the nosy-as-fuck attendant who needs to get out of my face. "I did. If you'll excuse me."

I slip my card in the door and the light flashes green, confirming I have the right room and a strange fucking development to deal with. A strange woman on the other side of the door, who insisted on pushing her way into it. In the years I've been wandering the world, this has never happened.

And I don't like it.

The attendant doesn't give up and narrows his eyes. "Your wife didn't have her key."

"No?" I frown and shrug. "Swore I gave her one."

He shakes his head. "She was persistent. I let her in. She said she was ill."

"She'll be fine once she eats." I turn the handle but don't open the door, look to the attendant, and tip my head, because I need him to get the hell out of here so I can figure out what's going on. "Appreciate your help. I've got it from here."

With more dramatics than I'm comfortable with, he

bows slightly before moving away. "Señor. Have a good evening."

I don't answer as I watch him disappear down the hall and into the next car.

Then, I push the door open as I reach under my shirt.

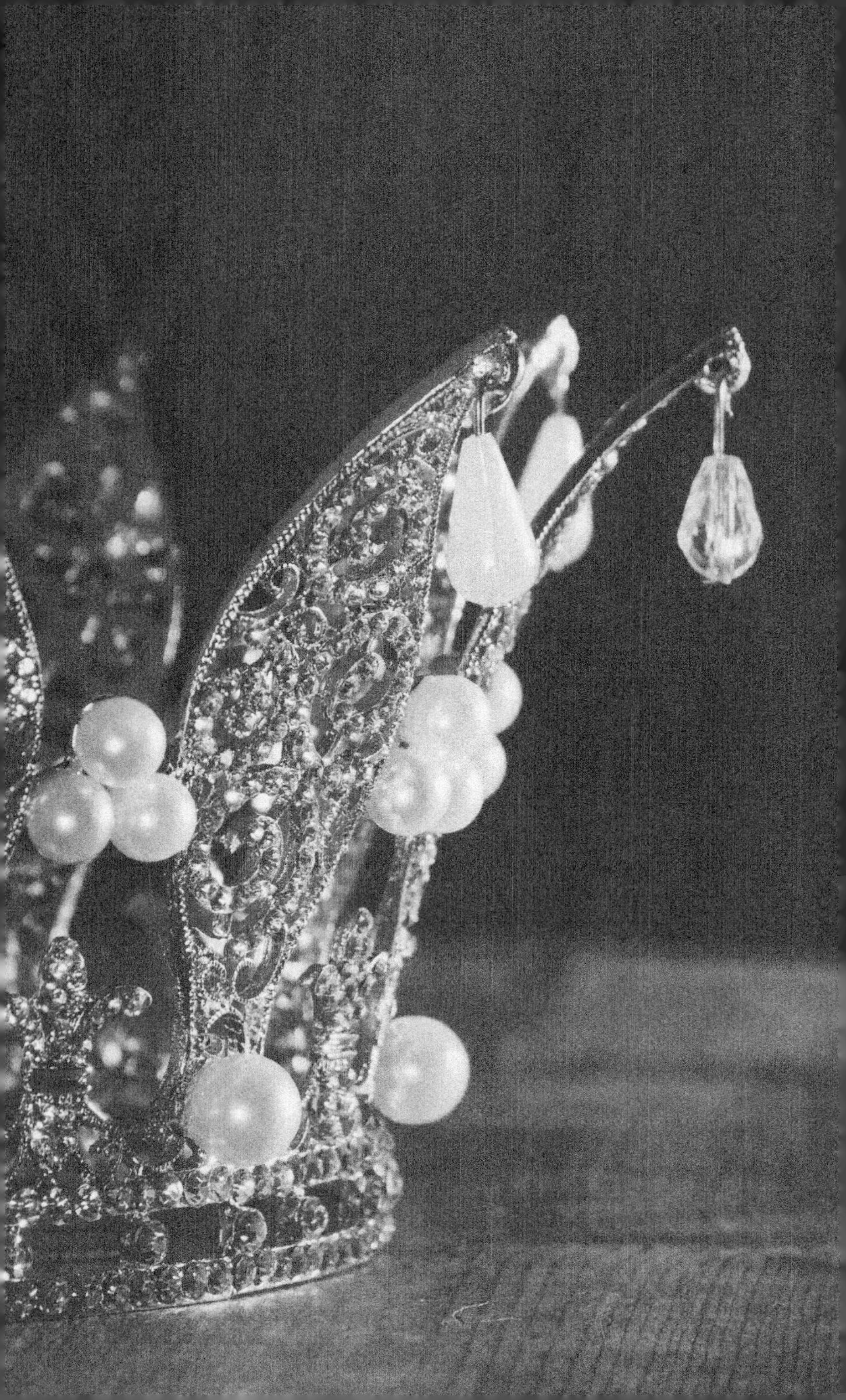

2

HOLLYWOOD ASSASSIN

Liyah

The train isn't at capacity. I checked before I boarded. In fact, it isn't even half-full.

I bought the cheapest ticket I could find on another train and snuck my way onto this one. There's no way I can show my face in this part of the world. I need to disappear. And aside from hiding in the public restroom all night, talking my way into a cabin was my best option, no matter how risky.

Sure, it was a gamble. But, at this point, I'm willing to bet everything I have to my name, and even more than I'm promised because of who I am.

I would give literally everything. Desperation does not begin to describe my current state of affairs.

I waited until we were moving to make sure I picked a vacant cabin. I've paced the narrow room ever since the door hit me on the ass. When we finally lurched forward, I thought my luck actually took a turn for the better, and I'd gambled on the right cabin.

Because nothing is more important than getting to Morocco, and if the last week has proven anything, I have no allies.

At least not ones who can offer the kind of help I need. The friends I do have can get me backstage at a concert or into the hottest parties in Malibu, but that's the last thing I need at the moment.

Those days are over.

The train picks up its pace as we pull out of Barcelona, and I catch a glimpse of myself in the mirror. I need a shower and sleep before the hardest part of my journey begins. I'm not sure when I'll have another opportunity. Maneuvering my way through Morocco will be the hardest thing I've ever done.

I exhale a deep breath and dump my backpack onto one of the narrow beds. It's not much—I couldn't pack as I normally would. I grab my things to shower when it happens.

Click.

No.

No, no, no, no!

The lock turning might as well be the trigger at my execution. The air in my lungs dissipates, and I lean onto the bed to brace.

Shit.

I wait.

But the door doesn't open.

Deep voices rumble from the other side and my gaze darts around the room, even though I know there's nowhere to escape. There's nowhere to hide but the bath that's barely larger than an airplane's.

And not even one in first class or a private jet.

I reach for the door of the bathroom when a

handgun appears first, followed by a veined hand, attached to a muscled forearm. With nothing but sheer instinct to survive, I yank at the bathroom door, even though my things are strewn all over the bed. My presence is no longer a secret.

One moment I'm about to take a step toward the bath, and the next, I'm flipped around. An impossibly big hand smothers my mouth and the floor disappears from under my feet.

But the most precarious of my current development ... the barrel of a gun is pressed firmly to my ribs.

"Who are you?" The words vibrate down my spine since my back is pressed to his front.

I kick and flail, but I don't dare make a peep. This is bad, and I don't need any more attention. I haven't even made it to Africa yet.

The gun jabbed in my side is a whole other situation I do not need.

I yank at the arm that has me suspended from the floor at the same time stifling any noise from me. I sink my nails into his skin, but it only makes his hold on me tighten to a point I fear for my rib cage.

"If you scream, it'll be the last thing you do. Understand?"

I freeze. The threat whispered through my messy hair is low and menacing. I knew this was risky, but I thought if I ended up in someone's room, I'd easily be able to talk my way out of it.

But a gun? On a train?

Gun regulations are strict in Spain and absolutely not allowed as a carryon.

"Nod if you understand."

I manage to answer, even with the strong hold he has on me.

He doesn't remove the hand covering my mouth, but the gun in my side disappears for a hot second. That same hand feels its way from under my breasts to below my waist. He shifts me enough to run it between us, over my ass, up the inside of my legs, and up my back.

His touch is efficient and all business, even though there's no point in searching me. Unlike him, I have no idea how to sneak a weapon on a train, let alone know how to use one.

My only weapon is my tongue. My mother would tell me I could skin a horse with words through sheer will alone.

I don't give up until I get what I want. I can't help it.

He lets go of me in one swift move, pushing me across the small space. I land on the mattress, next to the few possessions I brought with me, and work to catch my breath and settle my racing heart.

When I turn to get the first look at the man who threatened my life, catching my breath is impossible. No wonder he had me off my feet—he's a head taller, twice as wide, and as solid as the royal guard. He might have let me go, but now I'm staring into incensed blue eyes beyond the barrel of the gun he had jammed in my side.

"Who are you?" he demands through a square, stubbled jaw. He looks like he's been traveling longer than me, if the last time he picked up a razor is any indication. He's past due for a trim, too, as his curls are lapping his forehead. They hang in a way I'd bet they've been pushed from his face over and over and over, yet refuse to cooperate.

I straighten from where he threw me on the bed and

stand as tall as my five feet and four inches will allow. "Apparently, I have the wrong room. This nonsense," I wave my hand toward his gun, "is unnecessary."

He narrows his eyes before shaking his head once. "Bullshit."

I shoot back, "*Bullshit* it's not necessary?"

"No. *Bullshit* you have the wrong room. I heard you talk the guy into letting you in. You wanted in this room specifically. And since this is my room, I want to know who you are, why you're here, and who you work for."

My face falls in honest confusion, and I shake my head. My working, let alone for anyone else, is the most absurd thing I've ever heard. "I don't work for anyone."

"I don't believe you."

Damn. I decide the public restroom doesn't sound so bad right now. I turn to my things and stuff my backpack as quickly as I dumped it.

"You're not going anywhere until you tell me who you are and why you're here."

I don't give him the courtesy of looking at him as I speak, because what's he going to do? Shoot me on a moving train? "The gun was a shock, I'll give you that. But now that my adrenaline has settled and my brain has caught up, there's no way you can shoot me and get away with it. I'm hardly an expert, but I don't see a silencer on the damn thing. And really, who carries around silencers anyway?"

I glance over my shoulder to find a frown marring his thick brows.

"Exactly. Maybe if you were an assassin in Hollywood, but we're on a sleeper train moving south through Spain. No matter how menacing you're trying to be, it's time for me to move on and get out of your unruly hair." I turn back to the bed and stuff my last T-shirt into my pack, followed by the small bottle of shampoo, and try not to think about the hot shower that will not be a reality tonight. I can't talk my way into another cabin without raising all sorts of red flags.

"An assassin in Hollywood?"

I zip my pack, turn, and throw it over my shoulder. His brows are hiked, and he looks very much like a male model trying to get his start on reality television. Like he's been dropped into the wild, forced to live off the land, and travel through extreme conditions to survive.

If I were a betting woman—which I am—I'd put my inheritance on him.

American women live for that shit.

I might not be a true American, but I also lived for that shit up until a couple weeks ago. That's when life got real in the scariest way possible, and made reality television look like a children's cartoon.

I have no time for such ridiculousness now.

Regardless, he still has the damn gun pointed at me.

I've had quite enough.

"Move," I demand.

He shakes his head. "Nice try. Why are you holed up in my room?"

I cross my arms. "You are dense, aren't you? I didn't plan to hole up in *your* room—I thought the damn space was empty. I waited until we started moving and no one claimed the cabin. You must think you're special or something, but trust me, I want nothing to do with you. Now, step aside, and I'll be out of your way, once and for all."

He finally drops his arm, and the gun dangles at his side. "You're a stowaway?"

"I have a ticket." I don't elaborate that it's for another train going north into France, in case anyone makes the effort to track my whereabouts.

He opens his mouth to argue further as I push by him, but we're both interrupted by a rap on the door.

Shit.

I step back.

He doesn't move and continues to study me as if it's his favorite pastime, second only to target shooting.

Another rap turns into banging. "Señor Zimmerman. Open the door. We need to speak to you."

My expression falls right along with my stomach.

I shake my head at the angry man with eyes the color of a sunny day on the Mediterranean coast, silently pleading with him not to rat me out.

He tips his head, taking the time to contemplate me. Time I do not have.

"Señor—"

"Hang on." The man who just had me in a tight hold with the threat of death, looks away from me for the first time since he entered the cabin. He scans the room before settling his gaze back on me. Putting his finger up to his lips, he lifts his chin to the bathroom door.

I let out a breath and move, silently closing myself inside. The last thing I see is him lifting his shirt to stuff the gun into the back of his pants.

I hear the door open and the mysterious man who just threw me a lifeline speaks. "It's late. What do you want?"

"Señor, we're looking for a woman who was seen boarding this train with a similar description to the woman my attendant let in your room."

"I have no idea who you're looking for, but I can assure you the only other person in here is my wife."

I lean into the sink and thank the gods I picked this room.

"May we check your cabin?"

"No," he clips. "She's in the shower, not to mention she's not feeling well."

"Yes, that's what I've been told."

"She's pregnant and needs her rest."

I white knuckle the vanity I'm leaning against.

"Señor—"

"We'd appreciate some peace and quiet."

The door slams and the lock is turned with such force, I can hear it from here.

Not a moment passes, and the bathroom door swings open. Now he's got me trapped in an even smaller space than before.

His head looks like it's about to explode, which is odd, because when he speaks, his tone is weirdly controlled and steady. "I don't know who you are or why they're looking for you—"

"Thank you," I interrupt, my words rushing out in a whisper. "Thank you for that. That was very kind. I appreciate it more than you know."

"It had nothing to do with kindness and everything to do with curiosity. Even so, I'm not happy about having a spotlight on me, which is exactly what you've done."

My teeth sink into the delicate skin inside my mouth. I understand that more than he knows. It wasn't so long ago, I loved the spotlight, but now if I could roam the earth invisible, I would.

He sighs and scrapes a hand down his face before

settling a stare on me that's more irritated than angry, which is a step in the right direction.

I can deal with irritation.

"I'll be quiet," I offer. "I won't talk."

His brows pucker.

"I won't even look at you," I add. "You won't know I'm here. I promise."

His eyelids fall over his icy blues, and I swear, I hear a groan.

"Please?"

He looks down at me. "What the hell are you running from?"

If he only knew.

Because I'm not running from anything.

I'm running to it.

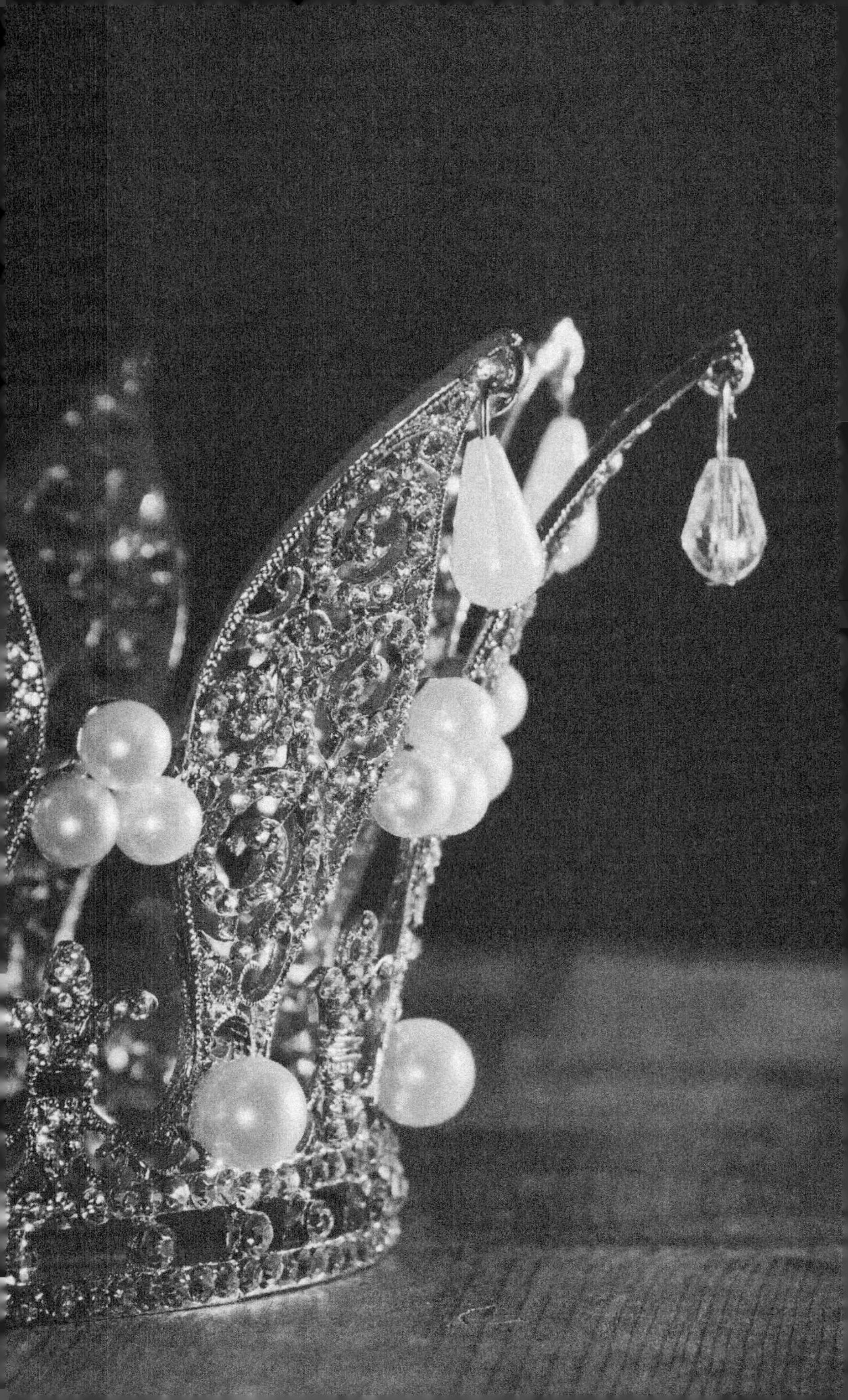

3

ROOMIE

Ozzy

"I'm the only one booked in this room," I state the obvious. She hasn't moved from where she stands in the bathroom that's barely big enough for her. Since I've had her in my arms, I can attest she's not a big person. "You can promise to leave me alone for a lifetime, but they'll be back. And soon. I'm surprised they didn't check the booking before now to find out there's a single ticket assigned to this cabin."

All hope that once bled from her dark eyes evaporates, and her face falls.

I put a forearm high on the doorjamb, lean in, and lower my voice. "Let's start with your name. From there, you can move on to why I shouldn't shove your ass out into the hall and be done with you so I can get a decent night's sleep."

I didn't know olive skin could turn a shade of crimson, but she just proved it's possible. And it's not a blush—it's pure, red-hot anger. Her dark eyes narrow. I swear they started out the color of freshly turned dirt, but are now darker than my blackened heart.

"That wouldn't be very nice to do to your *pregnant wife*, now would it?"

As much as I want to kick her out, doing that would make me a liar since I already claimed her because of my own curiosity.

Dammit.

"What's your name?"

She drops her bag to the bathroom floor and shakes her head. "If you're going to kick me out of your cabin, then you don't need to know anything about me."

"You're the one who barged into my life, and I'm the one dealing with the consequences. What's your name?" It's all I need. From there I can learn everything there is to know about her.

"Are you going to kick me out?"

"Depends on how persuasive you are."

"Well, Mr. Zimmerman, I'm not going to pretend I don't need your help right now. I need to get to the southern coast of Spain. For reasons you don't need to know, this is the safest and quickest way for me to get there. But if you're not going to help, let's be done with this so I can figure out my next move."

I shake my head and realize this could go on all night. "Let's say that guy believes me, and he isn't downloading the passenger manifest as we speak, proving I'm a single ticket. There is no wife … let alone a demanding, pregnant one. What's on the southern coast?"

She crosses her arms. "Why do you have a gun on a train? You're clearly an American and shouldn't be traveling internationally with a weapon."

"Do you always answer a question with a question?"

Her dark eyes, framed in more lashes than I've ever seen on one person, widen. "Touché."

I grit my teeth.

My gut tells me her picking my cabin was happenstance.

But my gut has been wrong one other time, and by the time I figured out where I went wrong, it was too late.

That was the last time I trusted my gut over cold, hard facts. Information is my world—I live by it.

I shake my head and mutter, "I have a feeling I'm going to regret this."

She grips the door with one hand. "Regrets are for those who live in the past, Mr. Zimmerman."

If she only knew.

Then, my nose is a half-inch from the door when she slams it in my face.

Who the fuck is this woman?

Liyah

I FLIP off the water after taking the quickest shower of my life. I decided to take advantage of the private facilities while I could. Who knows when I'll stumble upon a clean bathroom again.

Squeezing all the water from my hair I can manage, I wrap the towel around me and wipe down the mirror. Through my foggy reflection, I yank a comb through my hair, and pile it on top of my head with a band. If this Zimmerman man was right, I'm on borrowed time.

But the train is still humming. There's the faint

vibration under my feet and no commotion on the other side of the locked door. I know it's still early, but I may have lucked out.

I pull on wide-legged pants and a baggy sweater, rolling it at my wrists. I need to fit in and that won't happen wearing couture from the western hemisphere.

A dab of moisturizer and a quick brush of my teeth, and I'm ready for the next roadblock in my journey ... a journey I'm scared to death to take the next step in.

It's not the journey that scares me.

It's the destination.

What's waiting at the end of it. My worst fear is that I'm chasing what could be the darkest and blackest rainbow.

I pray there's a pot of gold at the end, like the ones my mother would paint with beautiful words in the fairy tales she'd create on the fly to fill the time during our travels. Ones with happy endings and things that dreams are made of.

Joy.

Love.

Life.

A pot of gold worth more than any bottomless bank account.

"Gather your wits, Liyah," I whisper to the woman I barely recognize through the streaked mirror.

Normally I'm put together, carefree, and—yes, even I'll admit—self-centered. I went to an all-girls boarding school in England starting in grade six. Then I did what every other woman from my country dreams of, and went to the States to attend Uni, experiencing the western world and living a dream.

My mother felt strongly about my leaving for school.

She wanted me away from the influence of my father's family. So much so, she wouldn't allow me to return from the States.

It's not like I went after a hard-hitting degree to support myself from here to ever after. I got the degree for the experience, and because I didn't have anything else to do.

Because of my mother's staunch feelings on the matter, I stayed in the States after graduation. My friends are from wealthy families. So much so, they might as well be American royalty. They certainly acted like it. I fit in. And fitting in allowed me to be normal.

It was amazing.

The best.

Good times.

As in, the *just-a-few-weeks-ago* sort of good times.

I never realized life could take a turn so drastically.

Guilt...

It's weighing on my soul heavier than I've ever envisioned, pushing me to take risks I never imagined.

You know, never—as in a few weeks ago.

I'm so out of my element, I don't know which way I'm going.

Other than home.

I try to swallow over the lump in my throat, and stuff the rest of the things into my bag.

I don't know whether to kiss the Zimmerman man for allowing me to force my way into his life, or kick him in the shin for threatening me with death.

I have enough threats on the table to deal with right now.

I slide the lock on the door and turn the knob as quietly as I can. The lights are dim as I peek around the corner. My roomie for the night is stretched out on one of the single beds. His feet, crossed at the ankles, dangle off the end. The rest of him comes into view as I quietly exit the bath.

His hands are behind his head, and his biceps are stretching his faded T-shirt that looks like it was once a darker shade of gray than it is now. Gray is the most boring hue. Not white and not black, it just exists in the odd land of varying shades of static.

Gray is horribly sad.

I tip-toe to the bed opposite his and set my backpack on the floor before I crawl onto the mattress.

"Finally done?"

I barely have a knee to the bed when I jerk and turn. He hasn't moved a muscle but his eyes are hooded, glaring at me through the small distance.

"I didn't mean to wake you." I fluff the pillow and turn toward the wall. "As promised, I won't look your way. Just a few short hours and I'll be nothing but a bad memory."

A few quiet moments pass. I try to forget about the man in the next bed, or what's to come on the next leg of my journey, or how I'm going to do what I need to do by myself.

"Name."

I sigh. "I'd like to point out that you're the one speaking."

"I never agreed to leave you alone. What's your name?"

I open my eyes to stare at the blank wall, and hug the pillow closer. "Liyah."

"Liyah." He tastes my name on his tongue. If I had to guess, it's sour. "I travel a lot and can't tell where you're from. You sound like a mix of European and plain-Jane American."

"Pretty much," I tell him the truth without elaborating. "I mean, sort of."

"I have a feeling you're wrapped in secrets. The sooner the sun rises and we can part ways, the better."

I agree on the first part, but not the second. I dread the sun rising.

I hear him climb to his feet and move to the bathroom without trying to be quiet. He bangs around for a few minutes before the water sounds.

I'm not an idiot. Sharing a room with a strange man, who's grumpy at best and dangerous enough to sneak a deadly weapon onto a train at most, is not a brilliant idea. But I've been awake for almost twenty-four hours.

I'm exhausted.

The last thing I hear is the water turn off. I can't keep my eyes open any longer. Tonight is out of my hands. I'm going to trust that Mr. Zimmerman would have killed me when he had the chance. And hope he doesn't have a silencer to put a bullet through my head while I sleep.

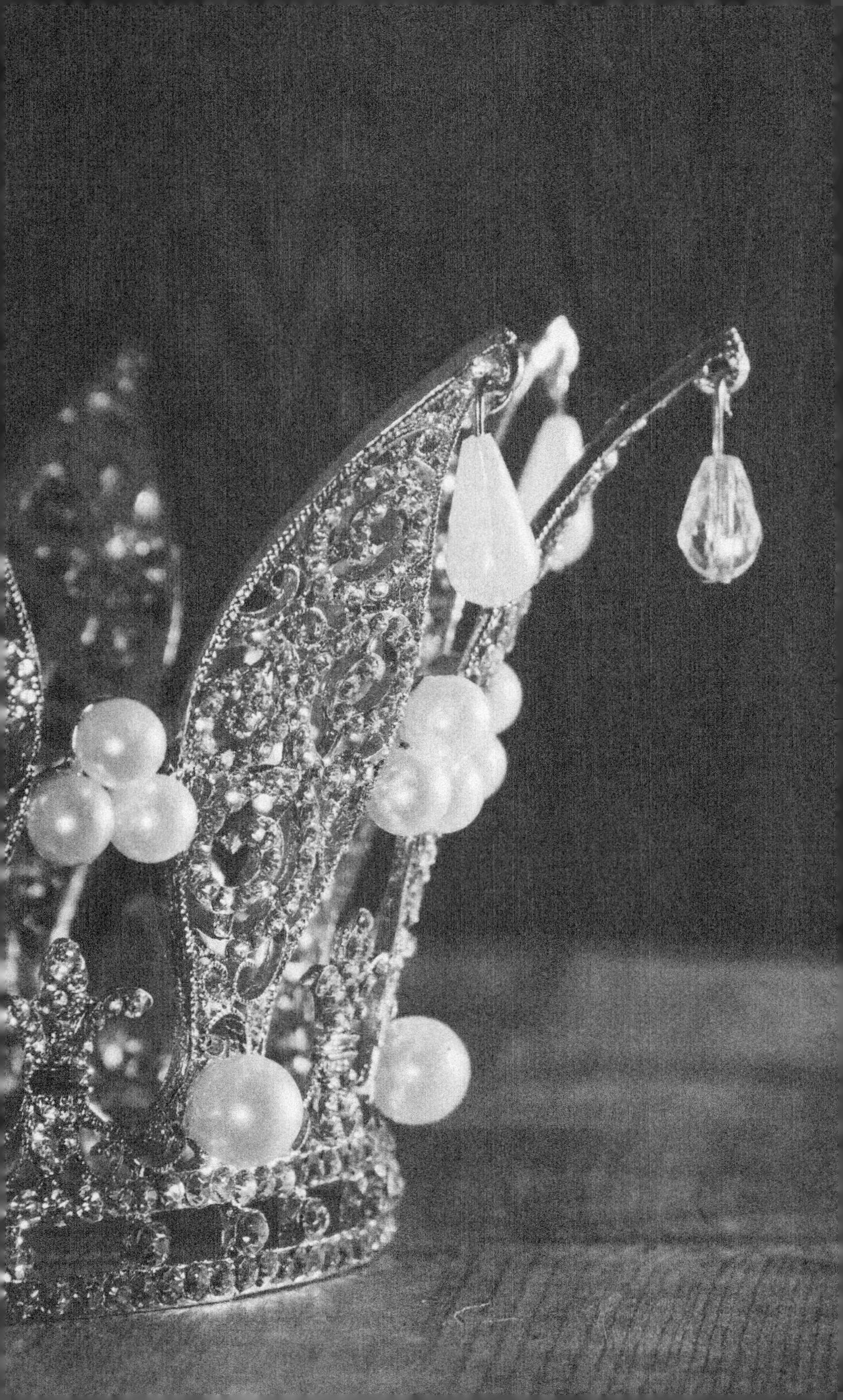

4

CURIOSITY

Ozzy

Aliyah Zahir.
   Huh.
      Liyah. I assumed it was Leah.
She has a Moroccan passport but carries dual citizenship in Spain. Twenty-two years old. An expired Pepperdine student ID is slipped behind her California driver's license. She's either a dropout or can't let go of old memories.

Besides a wad of cash and a Platinum AmEx, all she's got in her bag are a couple changes of clothes and toiletries. She doesn't even have a stitch of makeup.

But what's most surprising ... no cell. Unless she sleeps with it on her, which I can't really check without waking her, but most people charge their phones while they sleep.

What kind of idiot doesn't travel with a cell phone?

I stuff everything back in her bag and leave the bathroom. She's dead asleep as I place her bag on the floor next to her bed.

Curiosity is not a good thing.

I don't have time to be curious about anyone or anything besides my next mission.

Besides, curiosity killed the damn cat.

Been there.

Done that.

Didn't end well.

In fact, it ended in such shit proportions, I'm where I am because of it.

She's clearly in a situation and going it alone. A situation I should not give one shit about.

I ignore the smell of her soap and lie down. Hell, I don't even know what it smells like, other than a chick. Pushing the wet hair out of my face, I decide to ignore the woman and her smells, and go through the file Asa sent me before she became a pain in my ass.

I study the details of the operation that looms over me like a dark cloud. It's straightforward, not complicated, and on the surface, appears open and shut.

I log into Reskill, which is really just *killers* jumbled up, because isn't that what we really are? Fucked-up killers? I can't speak for the rest, but it's how I feel most days.

Does guilt rest heavy on my soul? Not really. But is this the life I saw for myself?

No. It's fucking not.

I set up Crew's very own satellite system a couple years ago before he let me loose on my own. Before I came along, Vega couldn't communicate with his people around the world when they were on a mission. Now, we chat safely until we're blue in the face. The communication is nice, but there are times, like today, I'd appreciate the ability to go dark. To not be ordered around, demanded to report back at camp, or watched like a hawk.

I'm basically alone in this world, but Reskill makes it impossible to be really alone.

Which is ironic, since I was the one who set up the satellite system that allows Crew and his entire team to keep tabs on me.

I crave aloneness.

Which makes the woman sleeping in my room more irritating than she should be.

Liyah.

Fuck it.

I close the file and open the secure site I created to break into any system I want to. I give the US of A the credit for my skills. Thanks to my training, I can breach the most secure and privileged IT systems in the world, including those of my own government.

Especially those of my own government. Even after traveling the world and seeing the shit I've seen, I trust Uncle Sam less than I do anyone on earth.

I almost have her last name typed in when a message pops up.

Asa – Change of plans. I booked you a charter out of Granada. You're going to have to find your way there. Pilot will be waiting tomorrow night at twenty-two hundred. Sending the address and details in a separate file.

That file appears in my inbox as I'm reading his message. A charter will make this job easier—clean and simple—the way I like it. And bonus, Asa doesn't try to boss me around like Crew does.

Me – I'll be there.

Asa – Stay safe. Crew tells me you'll be back next week. See you then.

I don't confirm, because it doesn't matter how much they want to demand my presence in Virginia, I don't plan on humoring them.

The bed rumbles beneath me.

The train rocks and the tracks complain.

Shit.

I drop my phone to the mattress and I'm on my feet in a flash.

Liyah rolls and pushes up to her elbows. Her eyes are hooded as she stares up at me through her unruly hair.

Brakes scream through the quiet cabin, and I lean over to hit the light.

"What is that?" she asks.

"We're slowing down." I pull up my GPS. We weren't scheduled to get to the station until five in the morning and it's barely after midnight.

Liyah moves to the window but there's nothing to see except complete darkness. "Where are we?"

I confirm what I thought I knew before I unlocked my phone. "In the middle of nowhere."

She swings around and panic etches her features. "Why are we stopping in the middle of nowhere?"

I grab my boots and talk as I lace them. "No idea. All I know is I travel the world and this shit has never happened until a strange woman wormed her way into my cabin." I get one boot laced and move to the second one. "I'm out of here. You've got about twenty seconds to tell me why they're looking for you and convince me you're worth the risk."

I stand and look down at her. Her hair is falling

around her face, still half-wet from her shower. She hugs herself in that big-ass sweater that swallows her, and since I've already had my hands on her, I know her frame is small.

She doesn't answer.

I bend to pick up my bag and swing it over my shoulder. "Ten seconds, Liyah, and you're on your own."

She says nothing.

Commotion and voices fill the hall outside our door.

I take one last look into her dark eyes and shake my head.

My fucking gut.

Something tells me this woman is nothing but a headache.

A headache is something I do not need.

I turn on my heel. "Pain in the ass. Good luck on your own."

I no sooner grip the doorknob when she blurts, "I'm looking for my mother. She's missing, and my father's family is trying to cover it up."

I turn.

She exhales and her dark eyes pool. "Please. I need to get to Morocco. I don't know who you are, Mr. Zimmerman, but they're looking for me. I know they are. I barely made it out of France."

"Fuck," I hiss.

Voices fill the hall as the train lurches one more time and we finally jerk to a stop no passenger car should experience in the middle of the night. I doubt it's because they're out of milk or toilet paper. I have a feeling it has everything to do with one of the people standing in this cabin.

Given what she just told me, in addition to my past

and what I do for a living, it's fifty-fifty on whether it's her or me.

She grabs her bag and slips on her shoes. "Whatever. I don't need your help, but I do need to get out of here. My father's family will stop at nothing, and their money can buy resources everywhere. And by resources, I mean people. Their reach is far and wide, and I need to avoid it. If this abrupt stop is about me, I cannot be a sitting duck."

She stands and wraps her hair up high on her head and pulls up the hood of her sweater. It's so big and baggy, I can barely see her face. When she starts to push past me to get to the door, I stand strong and don't let her through.

She looks up one last time and gone are the tears that had formed when she spoke of her mother. Fear might line her features, but her tone is as strong as steel. "Move, Mr. Zimmerman."

"Shit." I shake my head. "Don't make me regret this."

Hope washes over her. And fuck me, I forgot what hope looked like on anyone. She's a natural beauty, but the sight of hope filling her features is beyond that.

Especially when directed at me.

"And my name isn't Zimmerman."

Her eyes widen.

I turn to crack the door and peek out. There's a stir at the end of the car that's getting louder by the second. The old couple from across the hall are demanding to know what's going on.

I turn back to Liyah. "You can call me Ozzy."

"Ozzy?" She exhales my name, but I don't have time to think about how that sounds. And I wasn't kidding earlier, I don't need a spotlight on me.

We need to get the hell out of here.

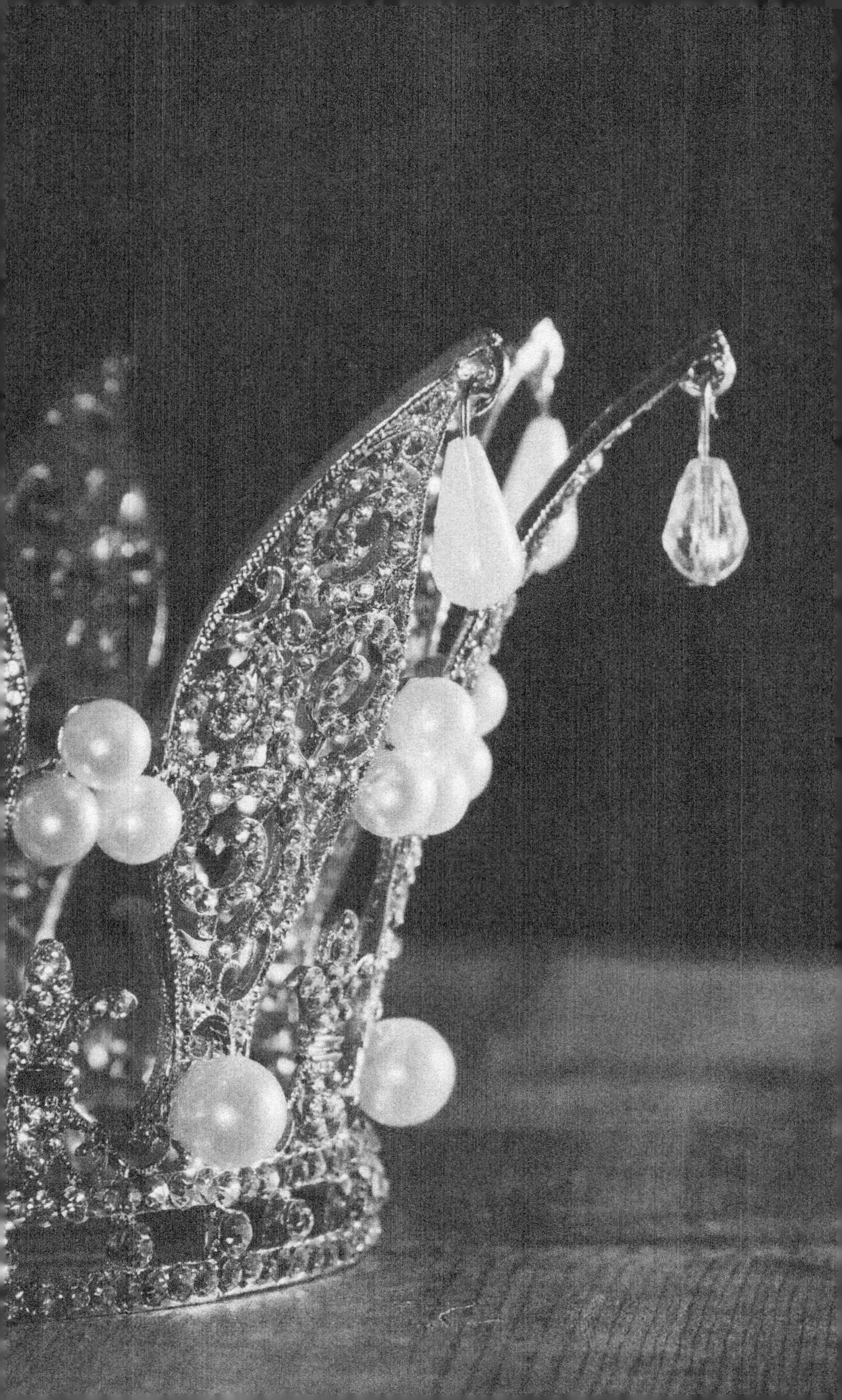

5
———

TURNING POINT

Liyah

Seems I'm not the only one with a secret.
    Mr. Zimmerman isn't who he said he was.
    It's an interesting development I could've done without.

This Ozzy fellow unearths a generic ball cap from his bag and pulls it low on his forehead. He grabs me by the bicep and moves me to the back of the train car. Then to the next one, and the one beyond that.

Traveling through Europe by rail is a new experience. I assume emergency stops in the middle of the night are not common given the upheaval. No one is paying attention to us—chaos is a good thing when one needs to disappear into thin air.

After telling me his real name—if Ozzy is, in fact, his real name, because I have no choice but to trust him at this point—he drags me through hordes of people who were not at all prepared for a quick getaway. He said he doesn't need the spotlight on him, and neither do I. With no time to make a decision and my only other choice is to run on my own, far be it from me to argue with a man and his gun.

With his forearm like a vise around my upper chest, he fuses our bodies as one, and uses his other arm to push through the crowd without apology.

His face presses into the side of my hood and his words are gruff and demanding through my sweater and messy hair. "Don't make eye contact."

That's not hard since the disorder is turning to bedlam. The crowds have multiplied since we've moved beyond private cabins to a passenger car. Everyone around us is arguing in Spanish and trying to move the opposite direction as we are.

I turn my head to him. "Where are we going? And why is everyone moving the opposite way?"

"Don't argue."

I trip over a bag that's fallen into the aisle and get the air knocked out of me. A forearm connects with my chest and a man with fewer manners than the one pushing me through the crowds yells in my face to get out of his way.

Holy hell. What have I gotten myself into?

But for the second time since I've boarded this train, I find my feet searching for solid ground. Ozzy lifts me and turns to the side. Using his free arm, the man who just barreled into me is now lying across two seats with his face smashed into the window.

I barely hear him groan as Ozzy wastes no time and keeps moving down the aisle with me in his arms. I'm still fighting for air as he moves faster.

"There!"

Oh, shit.

The man who I argued with until I was blue in the face to let me into Ozzy's cabin is at the end of the car pointing at us, fighting to get through the crowd.

Ozzy stops, and my feet hit the ground with a thud. I grip his arm that's still wrapped around me, because at this point, he's my best bet.

We turn in unison. More officials are entering the car behind us.

"Fuck," he hisses.

Fuck is right.

He holds me tight to his chest as his gaze swings from the front to the back of the car, assessing the impossible situation bearing down on us.

There's no escape.

He spins me to him and levels his intense blues on me. "Don't move."

For the first time since we left the privacy of our cabin, I lose the protection of his arms. He pushes me back as far as he can and climbs into a row of seats. With his hands pressed to the ceiling, he lifts a leg.

His boot connects with the window.

Shattering glass echoes from outside.

But inside, I'm engulfed in screams. All of a sudden I'm not in a crowd any longer.

Bodies scatter, but I don't look away from my man with the gun. He'll either turn out to be my savior, or I'll end up in some horrid, human-trafficking ring. At this point, whichever it is, I'm positive it will be one extreme or the other. I have a feeling there is no middle ground when it comes to this man.

A woosh of cool night air blankets us.

Ozzy doesn't get down from where he's standing in

the seat above everyone. He juts a demanding hand toward me.

I stare at it.

Then I take in the security officers fighting their way to get to me. Officers, who are no doubt, being paid by my father's family.

Their pockets are deep and their hands are dirtied with blood—not a good combination.

"Liyah," Ozzy growls.

My focus moves to him. He's towering over me—determined, formidable, and intimidating.

"Now," he demands.

I'm out of options. What was I thinking? There's no way I'll survive this on my own.

All I can think about is my mother.

Officers are closing in on both sides.

I have to make a decision.

I look up at Ozzy one more time. His blue eyes sear into me.

And right here, in the middle of pandemonium on a travel train, I make a choice.

I put my hand in his.

That's all it takes.

The moment our fingers touch, he takes over ... *everything*.

I remember my mother telling me about turning points. She said they hit you in life when you least expect them. Sometimes you have to trust your instincts.

Go with your gut.

Do what everyone else claims to be crazy.

She told me she had a turning point when she met my father. A young Spanish girl from a small, coastal, fishing village, falling in love with a Moroccan, whose family responsibilities were centuries old.

It was her turning point. She not only followed her gut, she followed her heart.

Ozzy yanks me up and I'm crushed to his chest.

His arms cage me and his hand comes to the back of my head, stuffing my face into his neck.

Then...

Then.

Ozzy puts a boot to the windowsill and pushes. The whisper of cool night air isn't a whisper any longer. The sound of chaos disintegrates behind us.

We jump.

No.

Ozzy jumps.

And takes me with him.

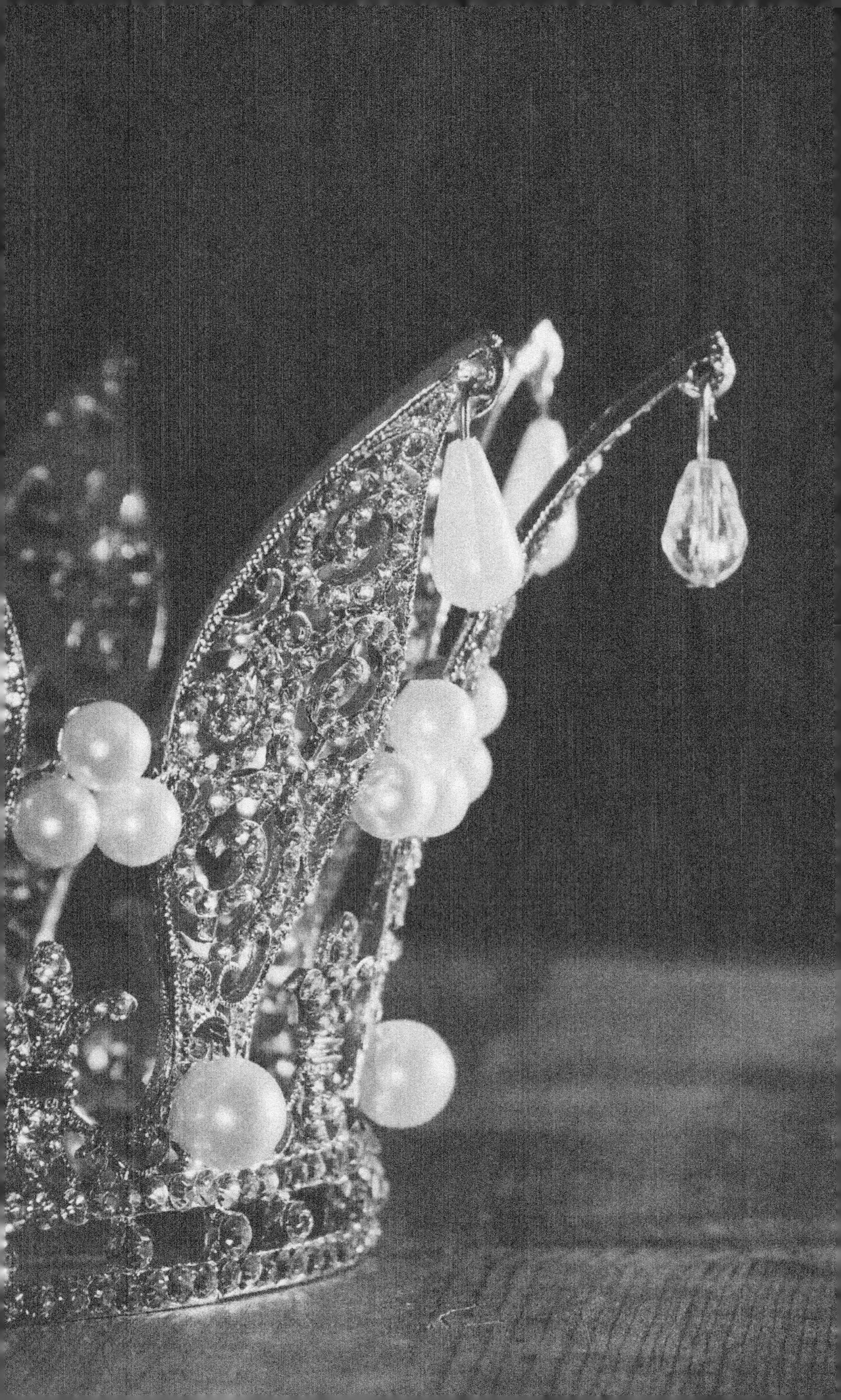

A GUN AND A MORAL COMPASS

Ozzy

Humph.

Fuck, that doesn't feel good.

Her scream is muffled when we hit the ground. I roll to take away the impact, holding her to my chest.

Of course we're on a hill, and it's pitch-black outside. We could've been jumping off a cliff for all I knew.

But I had no choice. We were sandwiched. And no matter who this chick is running from, I have too many ghosts in my past to take a chance. Though, my ghosts are alive, breathing, and causing havoc in the free world. I know this because I keep closer tabs on them than I do anyone. It fucks with my head, but I can't help it.

But if there's a minuscule chance I showed up on someone's radar, I'm not sitting around to let them get to me.

Leaving her behind would be an asshole move.

There was something in her eyes. I couldn't make myself leave her.

I force us to a stop on the rocky incline. When we finally still, she's flat on top of me, and my backpack is wedged between me and the ground. We must have rolled twenty yards, but given what's going on, it's not far enough.

I don't move, but she's trembling. Her breaths are shallow against my neck, and I realize I'm fisting her hair.

The commotion from the train waffles through the darkness. We need to get the hell out of here.

"You okay?"

She doesn't utter a word.

Her death grip on my shirt barely loosens. I let out a deep exhale and use the grip in her hair to raise her head. Fear laced with confusion and regret are etched in her features.

"Answer me," I demand. "You hurt?"

Her dark eyes stare down at me through the night. Then her breath catches, as if she just realized what happened. Then, she glances up the hill.

I tighten my hold on her to pull her back to reality. "Liyah. No shit, I need to know if you're okay. We can't hang out here all night. We need to move. Do I need to carry you?"

"No, I'm not. I mean, I'm not hurt." She looks around before her eyes jump back to me. "Where are we going?"

I'm about to tell her I have no fucking clue, that we're going to have to hoof it, when it happens.

"Shit!" I tuck her to me and roll one more time. I

barely have her body shielded and her face tucked to mine.

The darkness disappears and heat instantly fills the cool night.

Fire.

No, an explosion.

Debris rains down on us, and what I thought was madness on the train before we jumped, is nothing compared to now.

Liyah screams, and I press into her. She's small and my body covers hers easily. Even so, we can't get close enough to each other as the explosions light up the night.

I finally lift my head when the debris slows and look up the hill. "Fuck."

Her death grip returns, and I didn't know it was possible for two humans to be this close without actually fucking.

"W-was that our sleeper car?"

Fire becomes one with the starless sky from a hole in the train. If my sense of direction hasn't failed me—and it never has before—what was once our cabin, is now ground zero. I look back down at her. "Yeah, that was our car."

"All those people—" she chokes.

Her voice shakes, and I'm no expert, but I'm pretty sure I hear tears. I barely know how to deal with chicks, I really can't handle her emotional and crying right now. "Stop. Don't think about it. I'm stuck with you for now, so we need to get out of here fast. You up for that?"

She swallows hard, but nods.

"Good. We're going to move farther into the woods. Stay close."

She doesn't let go of my shirt, and it seems I've become one with the stowaway. "You don't have to worry about that."

Liyah

THE SUN IS BREAKING over the horizon.

The birth of a new day.

A day many won't wake up to because they happened to be on the same train as me.

My mind has spiraled. Watching the car we were in burn—listening to the soul-curdling screams—was too much. Knowing my father's family found me and would go to such an extent to stop me from looking for my mother, was too much.

I was too bold, too demanding, and too *me*. I pressed my uncle for information. I made emotional accusations that were really my worst fears.

I thought I was powerful. I thought who I was and where I came from actually meant something.

It was my worst mistake.

I tickled the beast.

My uncle doesn't like being pressed on anything or by anyone, but by a woman? And one as young as me? Morocco might be the most *western* country in that part of the world, but the ways of the West have not been adopted by my uncle. Since my father died, it's changed. Privately, within the confines of the family, women know their place and are expected to stay there. We have one face in public, but behind the curtain, we're to remain silent.

And if they were willing to do this to me, what have they done to my mother? I haven't spoken to her in weeks.

I shouldn't have waited this long.

We've been walking for a few hours. I've lost track of time, other than the day starting with the tragedy we left in our wake.

My stranger and I walk side by side. He's kept me close but insists on silence. He says it's because he needs to be able to hear if someone is around or following us.

Not that I feel talkative, but when he puts it that way, I'm all too happy not to utter a peep, which is completely out of character for me. It's all I can do not to fall into a pile of tears knowing people died because I chose to sneak onto that train. I'm an idiot for allowing my emotions to fuel my confidence. I'm no match for my father's family and the consequences rest solely on my shoulders.

I have no choice but to follow a man who radiates danger.

Ozzy leads, and I follow. If he's not directing me across the Spanish countryside, he's typing on his phone.

I've counted the ways I've gone wrong, no matter how few options I had. But I had to try. The last time I talked to my mother, she warned me. She told me not to come home. My uncle was putting pressure on her to carry out bullshit responsibilities for the family that would prevent her from leaving. I knew she was bearing the brunt of me not returning after graduation. My uncle requested it—no, he ordered it.

He told me if I didn't come home, there would be consequences. But my mother would follow up those conversations and insist I stay far, far away from Morocco.

This went on for too long. She did what she could to appease those around her who kept her on such a short rein, she could barely communicate with me privately.

Then it happened.

She called in the middle of the night. I was dead asleep and missed her call. Sleeping through that call might haunt me to my grave.

She said things at home were not good.

She told me, no matter what happened, to stay in the US.

No matter what—she stressed—*do not step foot in Europe or Africa.* She went on to explain she sent me away to school at such a young age after my father died to protect me. And when she insisted I attend Uni in the States, she knew she was setting up my future, so I could avoid her reality. By that time, I was so in love with western culture, I had no problem doing exactly as she wished.

At the time, she told me she had dreams for me—to spread my wings, find myself—and to become the strong woman she knew I could be.

By the end of her message, tears bled through her voice when she told me she was proud of me.

That I was the best thing she accomplished in life.

That I gave her joy after she lost the love of her life.

And that she loved me.

It was the last time I heard her voice.

I called her every hour the next day. Hours turned into days and days into weeks. I couldn't get hold of her staff who had been with her since I was young. Later, I got a call from a woman claiming she was her new assistant and that my mother was sent on a diplomatic mission, to fulfill her duties, and represent the family.

It was bullshit. She has refused to represent the family for years. It's not the same family it was when my father was alive.

I've listened to her last voicemail over and over and over.

I was out of options and had no one to turn to. I didn't know if I could trust anyone at the U.S. Embassy. When it comes to politics, everyone is self-serving. My father taught me that during his last year when he was battling cancer. As young as I was, I never forgot.

Now I'm forced to put my trust in a man who threatened to kill me.

He's already lied about his name once. Who knows who he really is?

"Yeah?"

It's the first word he's uttered since he told me to keep my mouth shut. I turn to find him on the phone. We're in the middle of the countryside. I have no idea how he has a signal out here.

He throws me a curious look before barreling ahead as he speaks, not at all worried about making noise. Maybe he just didn't want to talk to me.

Interesting.

"Yeah," he repeats, a statement this time. "That was my train. I'm on foot moving south. Not going to make that flight."

Seems I've screwed up everyone's travel plans.

"No clue, but it was bad," he adds, without mentioning the fact he has a travel companion or that we jumped from a window into the dark of night. "With the damage it did, who knows. What have you heard?"

The sun is quickly stealing the protection of darkness that has shrouded us since we started walking. I know Spain well. My mother is Spanish and we visited her family often when I was a young girl.

Ozzy stops in his tracks. "No shit?"

I continue for two steps before turning back to him. His expression is hard, and he stares at the ground in front of his feet.

Something about his tone tells me now is not the time to ask questions.

His eyes find mine, and he spears me with a glare as he listens. His full lips press into a thin line, and he shakes his head. "No. I got the hell out, but it wasn't without drama. They saw me take off, and that was before the explosion. Not that they can trace me, but I had their attention before. I had no choice."

I bite my lip and take a step backward. I wonder if I should make a run for it.

Ozzy narrows his eyes and takes a step toward me, as if he can read my mind.

I take another one back.

As the sun rises, his rugged features come into view. His strong jaw outlines his frown perfectly, and his creased brows act in supporting roles, exhibiting his irritation about our current situation.

His glare stabs me in the gut when he says, "I'll be there. Nothing's going to keep me from it. Don't worry."

I might not have to worry about making a run for it. Who am I kidding? This guy is going to ditch me at any moment.

Ozzy

"If you can't make the charter, you'll miss the window of opportunity, and it's the only opening we've had in months. If I need to send someone else, I will."

I stare at the woman who has become the biggest pain in my ass from the moment I stepped foot onto that train and wonder what the hell I'm doing. "I said I'll be there. I'll find a way."

Crew sighs, and Liyah takes two more steps back. "I know where you are. The pilot squeezed you in. I can push him off, but I don't know how long."

I reach out and grab her by the elbow to move us forward as I speak. She tries to pull away from me but doesn't utter a word. At least the woman has the good sense to keep her mouth shut while I'm on the phone. The last thing I need is for Crew to know I'm with a woman.

"Hold that plane. I'll make it—you know I will."

"You'd better double-time it," he warns.

"Have I ever failed to carry out an assignment?"

Crew answers immediately. "No, and this one can't wait. Get it done and get home."

I don't have time for his *get home* shit again, but I do double-time it and pull Liyah along with me. "Later."

I don't give him a chance to say any more and hang up.

"Let go of me," she demands.

I throw her a glance, but don't let go. "You looked like you were going to run."

She twists her arm again, and this time I let go. It's not like I can't catch her.

She mutters, "I was thinking about it."

I point ahead of us to the empty countryside, since there's nothing on the horizon other than wide open fields. "Can you find your way out of here?"

She says nothing and sighs, which confirms what we both know.

"I didn't think so. But I can. No matter how much of a wrench you've thrown into my plans, my conscience can't handle leaving you out here in the middle of nowhere."

"A man with a gun and a moral compass. Lucky me."

"I have a feeling you're the least lucky woman in the world by picking my cabin. And, no, I'm not going to explain why that is. But I not only have a moral compass, I have an actual compass. You have no choice but to stick with me until I can get you to civilization, where you can screw up someone else's schedule."

"Ozzy?"

She hasn't made a move to run and is keeping up with me just fine. "What?"

"Is that really your name?"

I pull a water bottle from my backpack and take a swig. "Pretty much."

"What does that mean? Or is it like Zimmerman all over again?"

I hand her the water. She's reluctant, but takes it. I've been with her for the last twelve hours and haven't seen her eat or drink anything. "Drink. The last thing I need is for you to pass out from dehydration. Carrying you will be the ultimate ball and chain I don't need."

She takes a long swig, proving I was right. I dig through my bag again and hand her a protein bar. She doesn't hesitate. She rips it open immediately. "We both know I'm between a rock and a hard place here. I need you, and it would be nice to know your real name."

I look over and take in her profile. Her hair is down, the waves reaching the middle of her back, swaying as we make our way over the rough terrain. Her hair is almost as dark as her eyes and shines in the morning sun. It's been a long time since I've spent time in the company of a woman that wasn't a one-off. Other than the army of irritating wives who relentlessly push their way into my business back in Virginia, it's been years.

When you're a vagrant, what's the point? I can't settle down with my job. Dealing with my life choices is bad enough. I feel dead in every sense of the word most days. I don't have the mind space to deal with anyone other than myself most of the time. Which is why going back to the States right now sounds like a worse sort of hell than I'm already living.

There's only so much my black soul can take.

I have no idea when I can get rid of my new ball and chain, so I pretend I don't already know by having invaded her privacy. Seems my moral compass doesn't point true north after all. "Everyone calls me Ozzy. Maybe I should ask if Liyah is your real name? Seems you're the one everyone is after."

She swallows before answering. "I've told you nothing but the truth. My name is Liyah."

I grab her arm and help her climb over a fallen tree. She doesn't pull away this time. I jump to the ground and she follows.

"Your name is Liyah, and you're looking for your mom." I look back, and she skips to catch up. "Where exactly do you think your mother is?"

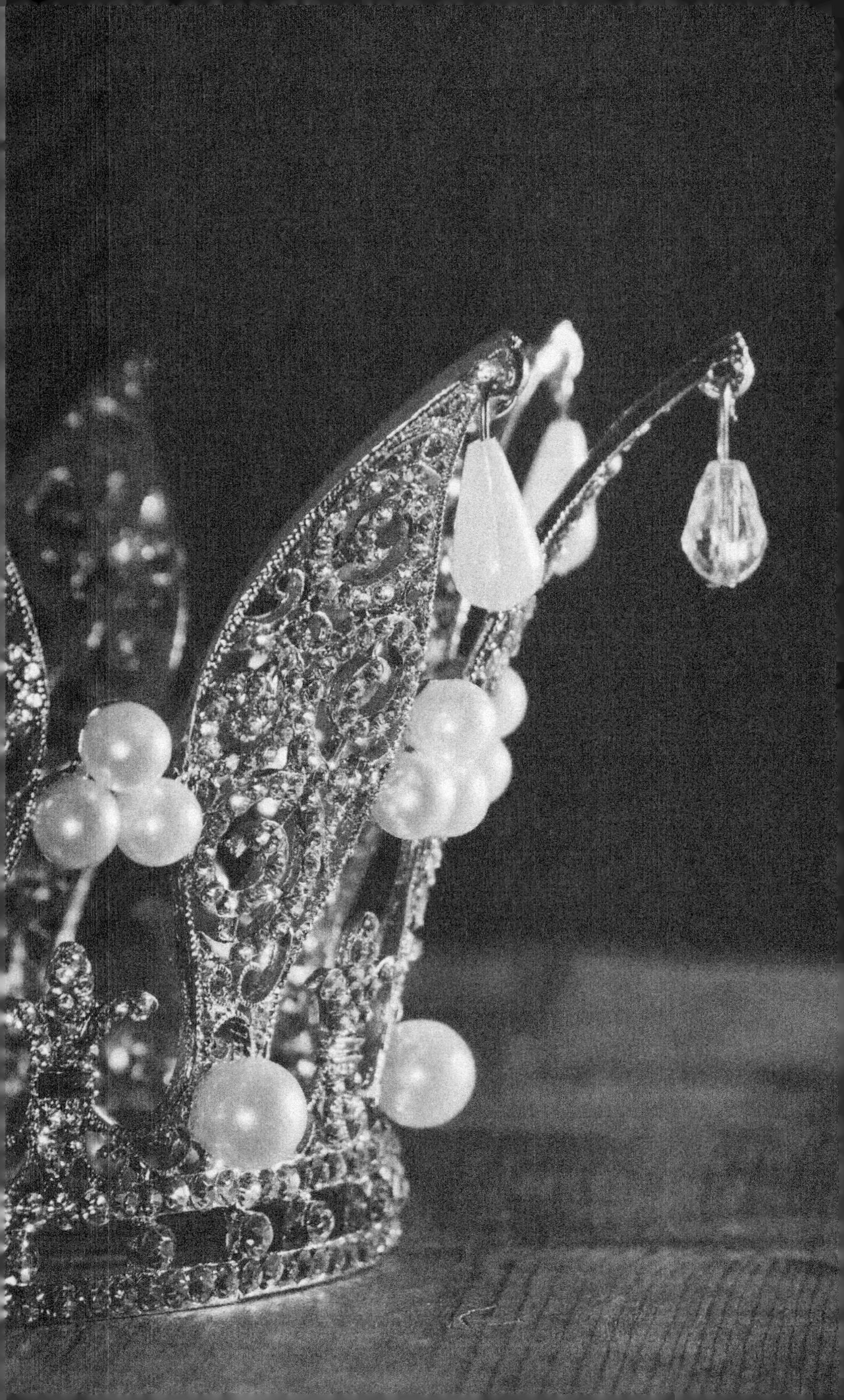

7

I WOULDN'T THANK ME YET

Liyah

Ask me if I have a plan.
The answer to that would be a big, fat hell no.

I thought I had a plan, but someone on the train caught sight of me. That plan, quite literally, blew up in my face.

Aside from following a man named Ozzy around my mother's home country, I have nothing.

This isn't good.

This is all sorts of bad.

I have no idea how I'm going to get to Tarifa from Granada, but I have to make it happen. If I have to steal a car to travel to the southernmost tip of Spain to get to them, I will.

I'm tired, starving, and fear I'm on my way to a point of dehydration like Ozzy spoke of. He's done more than any one stranger should have to for another, especially one who was stowed away in his cabin.

The sun is warm, despite the time of year. But no matter the temperature, I yank my hood closer to my face because I can't take the chance of being recognized. Ever since we got to this village, Ozzy has been eyeing me like I'm a crazy woman, but hasn't asked me anything else, for which I'm grateful. I've stuck as close to him as I can now that we're around others.

Quite honestly, I feel invisible by his side, which is fine by me.

Not being seen is a gift.

The man attracts attention no matter how low he pulls that ball cap on his head.

Everything about him screams *keep your distance*. It makes sense since he travels with a gun and isn't afraid to threaten anyone who gets in his way, even if his features are rugged and handsome with piercing blue eyes. I've lived in the States full time since I started college—American men are not a novelty to me—so I know when one stands out among the many.

Ozzy whatever-his-name-is, is not common or ordinary. He's exceptional as much as he is scary.

So, it could be that.

Exceptional and scary in a ball cap is a distinctive cocktail. Men, women, small children, and even farm animals have taken notice.

"We need a ride," he announces.

I'm usually the queen of complaining, but I've kept my grumbles to myself ever since Ozzy jumped out of a train window and took me with him. My travel companion does not seem like he'd care about my sore feet or that my back is aching from the weight of my bag.

"And I'd kill for a burger and fries," he adds.

"We won't find that here." I look up the street. "But there's a bakery."

Ozzy pulls a wad of euros from his pocket and shoves it toward me. "Here. Buy as much as we can fit in our bags. I'll search for a ride."

"No!" I grab his sleeve when he starts to move away from me. "How will I find you?"

He glances down at my grip and shakes his head. "I'll find you."

I take in my surroundings and panic brews low in my belly. All of a sudden, I've lost my appetite. "Please—"

"I don't have time for this. I've got to get to Granada by tonight."

My breath catches.

"I'll find you," he repeats, and this time there's something in his voice that makes me believe he might not ditch me. "Get some food, and meet me back at this spot."

Finger by finger, I unlatch myself from him. He doesn't wait for a response or for me to beg further—he's off. I watch him disappear down the next street.

I hurry to the bakery. The sooner I get this done, the sooner we can get out of here.

The moment I step inside, my mouth waters from the aroma of sweet and savory baked goods. I've decided carbs don't count when one is trekking Europe on foot while being hunted by royal assholes.

It's a small, modest establishment, and reminds me of the small town my mother is from, filled with lovely, hard-working people. A boy stands behind the farmhouse table that serves as a counter. I don't make eye contact when I speak in Spanish. I order what few meats and cheeses they have, along with too many cookies and small cakes. What we can't fit in our bags, we'll stuff in our faces.

When the young boy hands me a paper bag of homemade baked goods, I reach in and pop a polvorones de canele. The cinnamon melts on my tongue, and it's all I can do to suffocate the memories it brings back.

Summers in Spain with my mother were some of my best memories. That was a long time ago, when my father made sure my mother was free to do as she wished and could speak freely about what she was passionate about.

I pay the child and tip him generously—I'll pay Ozzy back. With one bag tucked under my arm and another in my hand, I reach up and tuck my hair into the hood of my sweater and turn to leave.

Ozzy is nowhere to be seen when I get to our corner. Everyone is carrying on with their day—going to work, busy with small children, or visiting with friends. Maybe this won't be as hard as I thought it would be. At least until I get to Morocco.

There's a commotion behind me, and I look over my shoulder. The boy from the bakery is running my way, holding the hand of a woman he's pulling behind her.

And they're coming straight for me.

"I told you, Abuela. It's her," he rattles off in Spanish.

The grandmother struggles to keep up.

"Ma'am! Ma'am!" the boy calls as his grandmother tries to hold him back.

I turn away and pull my sweater farther over my face.

"There's no way it's her, child," his grandmother works to catch her breath.

"It is!" he argues.

Shit.

"Lady!" the boy yells again and the word slithers across my skin like a snake as they get closer—too close. I feel a yank on my sleeve. I fight to pull away, but he's insistent. "Princess!"

Then, like a perfectly-timed hero from a fairy tale, Ozzy appears.

But he's no prince, and there's no chariot.

His baseball cap is turned backward and he's speeding toward me on a motorcycle that looks and sounds like it's seen not only better days, but better decades.

"Leave the woman be," the grandmother demands.

"No. You'll see, Abuela."

I pull my arm from the child as Ozzy's gaze on me is determined. He's at least ten meters away, but I can't afford to wait another moment, and move to the street.

The brakes on the bike complain when Ozzy screeches to a halt in front of me.

The boy yanks on my arm.

My stare pleads with the man I've all but tied myself to since I broke into his cabin.

Ozzy's gaze moves from me to the boy.

"No! Princess, wait!" the boy yells.

Ozzy tips his head and frowns. "Princess?"

My lips beseech him silently. "Please."

The boy tugs one more time but Ozzy proves to be stronger. He reaches for my other arm and yanks.

I find myself pulled across the motorcycle in front of him, practically sitting side-saddle. I grip his chest, so I don't topple backward. His mouth comes to the side of my face and his lips brush my ear. "Hold on, dammit."

I wrap myself around him as best I can. "Go!"

The rusty motorcycle complains beneath us, and my hood flies off behind me.

"See? It's her!" the boy screams as he and his grandmother fade into the landscape of the village. Ozzy revs the motor, and the back tire skids back and forth beneath us. The grandmother finally gets a good look at me over Ozzy's shoulder, and her expression falls where she stands on the cobblestone walk holding her grandson back. "Princess?"

"If you're a princess, then I'm Superman," Ozzy growls as we race away from the scene.

With the Spanish cookies and once beautiful mini cakes flattened between us, I hold tighter than I ever have, just like I did last night when I took a chance on the strange man who threw us from the train.

For the first time since last night, I realize picking Ozzy's cabin wasn't the poor luck I thought it was. It might have been the best thing that has happened to me since I received the life-changing voicemail from my mother. I dread having to part ways once we get to Granada.

Though, I'm sure he can't wait until I'm a piece of history he can put behind him once and for all.

Ozzy

DESPERATE TIMES CALL for desperate measures. The kid I bought the bike off of is now fifteen grand richer, and since I paid in American dollars, he'll be riding something ten times nicer in no time.

It's not the first time I've had to shell out that much to get out of a squeeze, and I doubt it will be the last. I'll never get used to the amounts of money we're given to travel with, let alone what we're paid.

It's not like I have time to spend what I make.

Liyah is fitted to me like a second skin. Her small frame wrapped around mine and holding on like her life depends on it. From the scene back in the village, I wonder if it does.

The brakes on this thing are shit, and we skid to a stop once I get outside of town. I put my hands to her hips and lift, setting her on the ground next to the bike and stand next to her.

She looks up at me with those impossibly dark eyes, and hugs the bag of food to her chest.

I'm sick of this shit.

"You know." I pull in a breath and grip what patience I have left. "It's been a day. So much so, I haven't had an extra two minutes to figure out who the fuck you are, and I think that's been my biggest mistake. Every time I turn around with you by my side, there's drama."

"I know," she whispers. "I feel bad about that."

"You feel bad about that?" I echo.

She bites her lip and nods. What the hell.

"The entire time we walked today, I told myself I was going to get rid of you. Hell, for about a half-second back there, I thought about ditching you after I bought the bike. I can get to Granada faster without you."

"I've got to be honest, I was afraid you were going to ditch me too."

I look at my watch. I was cutting this job close yesterday when I barely made the damn train. At this point, I might have to call Crew and have him hire someone from outside the group. That's never happened on my jobs before. Crew has only had to do that twice since he started building his empire.

I refuse to be on that list, which is why I almost dumped the drama queen.

"You've got one last chance to tell me who the fuck you are, because I do not have time to do the research on my own at the moment." I look at my watch. "And I want to know what the hell you're running from. Right now it feels like something is nipping at our heels."

She shakes her head, and her eyes glass over. That should make me feel like the worst kind of asshole, but I don't have the time to process it.

"If you want to leave me, leave. I was on my own to begin with, I'll make my way eventually."

I raise my voice and throw my arms out. "You don't have any idea where the fuck we are. You really expect me to dump you out here?"

Her voice raises, and her desperation bleeds into me. "You're dumping me eventually, so what's the difference?"

I shake my head, pull out my cell, and type her name into the system like I should have done last night. "Fuck me. What did I do to deserve this? I get my shit done and mind my own business."

She pulls on my arm, and tries to get a look at the screen. "What are you doing?"

I turn and hold it up higher so she can't reach it. "I'm doing what I should've done last night when I dug through your bag and looked at your passport."

"You what? I can't believe you!"

I get through five layers of security and type in *Aliyah Zahir*. She jumps for my cell, and I turn away and take five long strides, muttering, "I can't believe me either."

She panics. "I don't even know what you're doing, but stop!"

I've had enough. Holding my phone in my left hand, I wrap her up with my right arm, pinning her to my chest to keep her from clawing at me.

I skim the first screen that pops up.

"You've got to be shitting me," I bite.

I look down at her in my arms, and she freezes. Instead of fighting to get away, she grips my forearm and holds on tight. It's not lost on me that she's been in my arms more than anyone has in years, and she's practically a stranger.

"A princess? A *real* fucking princess?"

"Ozzy—"

"You have some explaining to do."

Liyah

He stares me down. I know he doesn't have time for this.

For me.

And now that he knows exactly how high maintenance I am, I'm sure he'll run off into the sunset as fast as he can. I'm not a runner, I can jog a couple miles at best. I'll never catch him.

"Yes. That's me. Not that it means anything—not anymore."

Ozzy looks back to his screen but doesn't let me go. Holding me captive to his hard chest, he scrolls and scrolls and scrolls. From what I can see, it doesn't look like he's learning about me through Wikipedia—which is oddly accurate.

It's strange to search for myself on the internet. I used to be obsessed with it. Obsessed how others saw me. Obsessed with what others *thought* of me.

Then I moved to America for college, and my newfound friends taught me how to not give a fuck. I listened and learned and adopted all the Americanisms, and not giving a fuck was at the top of the list.

Apparently being a foreign princess living in America makes one somewhat illustrious. I have millions of followers on my social sites combined. It has a great deal to do with the company I kept while living in California, but holding the title of Princess in modern times doesn't hurt either. Especially a princess who loved parties, yachts, and dabbled in modeling, for no other reason than I was bored.

One more reason for my father's family, the Palace, and the King—my uncle—to hate me and want me back in Morocco where they can keep me under their thumbs. So I can be controlled, like they do to the rest of the women behind the scenes.

Namely, my mother.

Which was why she told me under no circumstance to return home.

"Aliyah Zahir, Princess of Morocco." Ozzy continues to hold me captive as he reads aloud. "Daughter of late King Kamal and prior Princess Luciana," he mutters, and turns his scrutinizing blue-eyed stare on me. "Your mother is Spanish and was stripped of her title when your father died."

"Yes," I confirm. "It was ages ago."

He frowns deeper, which says something since he's been in a constant state of scowling since he jabbed his gun in my side. "You're only twenty-two. Define *ages*."

My heart pounds in my chest, and I shake my head.

He gives me a squeeze, and I didn't realize his hold could be tighter than it was. "I can keep reading, but it seems neither of us have time for that. Get on with it, Princess."

"I was ten when they stripped her of her title."

He nods curtly. "And now she's missing, and you're on your way to look for her."

His statement cuts like a knife. He's the only soul on earth who knows what I'm doing. I have no idea who he is, other than he lied about his name once. The only other one he gave me is beyond peculiar.

Instead of trying to push away from him, my desperation and fatigue take over, and I give him my weight, whispering, "Yes."

His eyes fall shut, and he lets out a breath so long, his exhaustion seems to match mine.

My fingers latch on to his shirt like a lifeline, which he very well might be. "Ozzy?"

He opens his eyes. They're so blue they match the clear, Spanish sky framing his masculine face when I look up at him. "What?"

"Are you going to leave me here in the middle of nowhere?"

His answer comes swiftly. "I should."

My insides turn, and it has nothing to do with my hunger turning into starvation.

"I don't know what I'm going to do with you. All I know is I have a plane waiting on me and missing it is not an option. I've got until we get there to make a decision."

I mean it with all my heart when I say, "Thank you."

He shakes his head. "If I were you, I wouldn't thank me yet. Let's go."

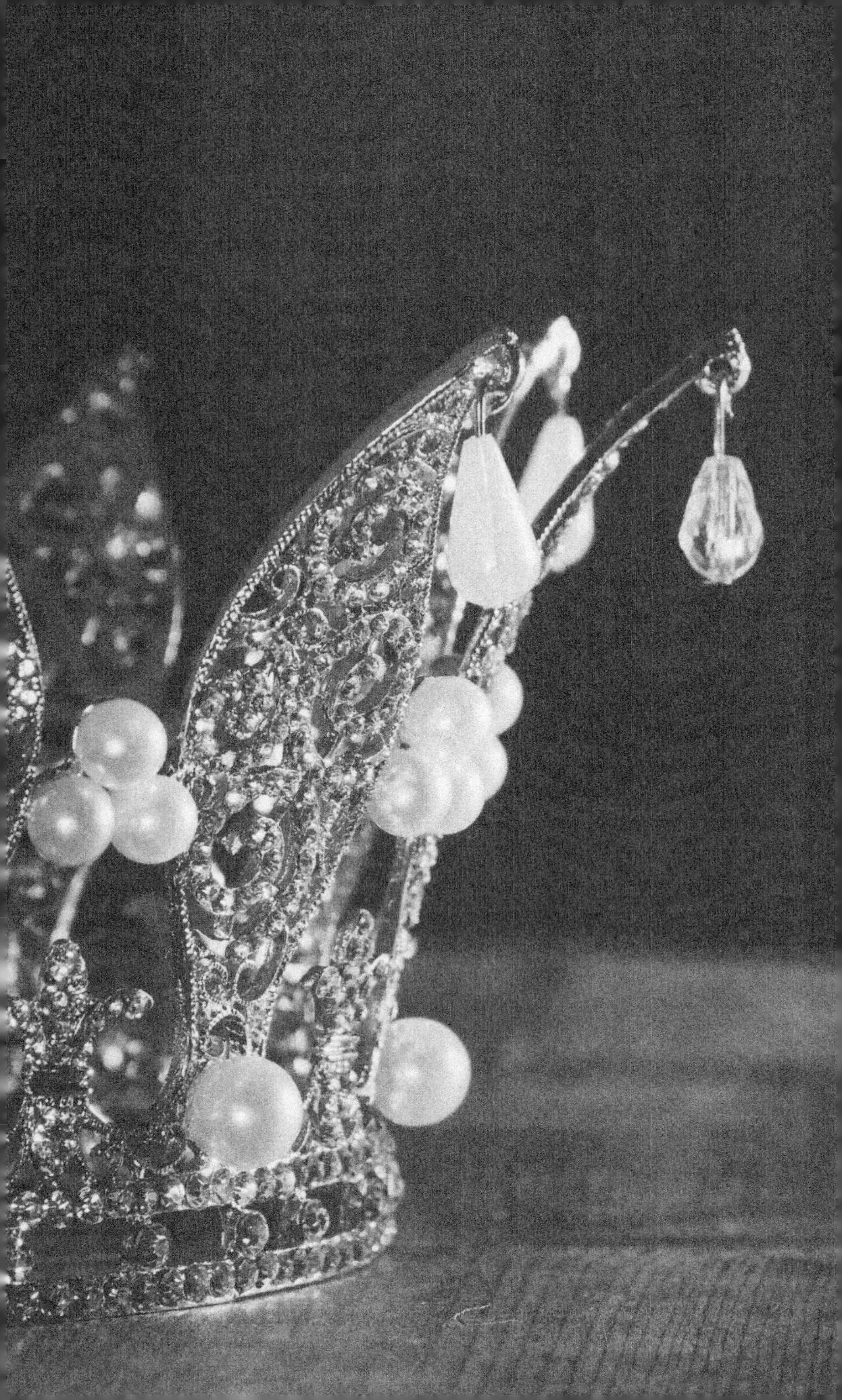

8

FUMES AND A PRAYER

Ozzy

If you told me two days ago I'd be racing through the country roads of Spain on a dilapidated motorcycle with an actual fucking princess glued to my back, I would've laughed in your face.

Who the hell am I kidding? I can't remember the last time I laughed.

And seeing as how this trip is going, laughing is definitely not in my immediate future. I've got more problems right now than any contract killer deserves.

We coasted into Granada on fumes and a prayer. The gas gauge has sat on empty for at least thirty minutes, but the last thing I have time for right now is to stop and fuel up.

I'd assume Liyah took a princess beauty nap if it weren't for her death grip. When I told her to get on the back of the bike, she didn't hesitate. She stuffed the bag of bakery items in her backpack and climbed on without thinking twice. Her arms rounded my waist, and she glued her small frame to mine from head to toe—her cheek to my shoulder blades, and her legs bracketed my thighs. Everything in between seared hot through our clothes. Even though I have no time for the long drive or the extra baggage she's turned out to be, I'm grateful for the time I had to get my dick under control.

It's been a long couple of hours, but he needed all the time he could get.

I follow my GPS to the small airstrip and spot my ride instantly. Asa does not fuck around when it comes to travel—it's the only jet on the tarmac.

I breathe a sigh of relief when I kill the engine, because who knows if this piece of shit will start again. But Liyah makes no move to untangle herself from me and I wonder if she really is asleep.

I wrap my hand around hers that grips my abs under my backpack that I had to wear on my chest. "Liyah."

Her entire body clenches mine. She isn't asleep—she's freaking the fuck out.

Confirming my thoughts, her tone is shaky. "I know, I know. This is it. I'll figure it out from here."

I peel her arms from me, and she slowly climbs off. I drag my backpack from my chest and swing my leg over, stretching my stiff muscles. I check my watch, only twenty minutes late. Not bad.

I look to the tarmac when I hear the jet engines rev. The stairs are lowered, and I recognize the pilot when he sticks his head out to give me a wave.

"Thank you, Ozzy." Liyah is wrapped up in her own arms. Her dark eyes well with unshed tears. I've seen that happen now more than any stranger should. "You've been accommodating and kind and, well," she shrugs and swallows hard, pushing back the tears. "You saved me more than once."

I say nothing and stare at her.

"Okay." She looks around and wipes a damn tear that escapes. "Um, bye."

Fuck.

"Where was your mom last seen?"

Her glassy eyes get big. "Morocco at the palace. But she sounded so desperate, I have no idea where she was when she left me that voicemail."

I shake my head. If Crew doesn't kick my ass for this, I might. "I'm on my way to Libya. I've got a meeting tomorrow that I can't miss. Come with me, and I'll look into your mom. I can't make any promises though."

She shakes her head. "I can't ask you to do that. You don't know what you're getting yourself into."

For the first time in who knows how long, my lips tip up on the sides. I wouldn't classify it as a smile, or even a sign of happiness. Call it karma, my own private gotcha moment, or straight-up sarcasm, but this chick has no fucking clue who she's dealing with. I close the distance between us and put my fingers to her chin to tip her face to mine. "Princess, it's you who doesn't know what you're getting yourself into. Remember the moment we met?"

She doesn't move out of my hold. "Yes."

"Well, I do carry a silencer. I'm not from Hollywood. And I'm dangerous as fuck."

She inhales a shocked breath through her full, parted lips.

And after our time together racing through Spain,

I've been in contact with almost every part of her body, but having her face in my hand?

I like it. Probably more than I should.

Still, I don't bullshit her when I go on. "What I can tell you is, if I wanted to hurt you, I would've done it by now. You might be a princess, but I'm the farthest thing from a prince. I do, however, have access to shit you never will—doesn't matter how far up the royalty chain you are."

She doesn't move from my touch. "What are you saying?"

"I'm saying, if you agree to do exactly as I say, I'll take you to Libya with me. I have shit to do there that can't wait. Then I'll work on finding your mom."

When she pulls that lip between her teeth, my gut churns. I realize it's nothing but red, hot envy, because I'd rather be the one biting it.

"My pilot is waiting. I need an answer."

Her gaze jumps to my jet then back to me.

"Now, Liyah. I'm already twenty minutes late."

She says nothing, but brings her hand to mine that still has a hold on her face. Her fingers are slight and thin, yet firm, when they wrap around my wrist. "Yes. Please, take me with you. I need you, Ozzy."

"Good choice." I let go of her face, but don't let go of her.

I turn her hand in mine and say nothing else as I lead her across the tarmac to the plane. When we get to the stairs, the pilot hikes a brow when I usher her up the steps where she hardly has to duck to get through the door.

"Oz," he greets me. "Does Vega know you brought a plus one?"

My royal shoots me a worried look over her shoulder. I put my hand to the small of her back and give her a nudge, glaring at him. "I'll make sure Crew knows, but it's none of your business. Stay in your lane and get us to Libya."

Liyah settles herself and immediately digs through her bag. I go to the mini bar and grab two bottles of water while the pilot secures the door and moves to the cockpit.

I crack open a bottle and hand it to her before settling next to her on the sofa.

She hands me the bag of food and takes a long pull of water. I take a bite of a broken cookie and talk while I chew. "This should be interesting."

"Yes," she agrees and wipes a drop of water off her full lip with the back of her hand. It doesn't seem very princess-like, and that makes me smile for the second time today. "Very interesting."

"I need to know one thing."

She's not at all shy and takes the bag from me to dig for food. "Hmm?"

"I saw you fight with the attendant on the train before he let you in my room. Are you really pregnant?"

Her thick dark brows pull together. "No! Hell, no."

I sit back and down half my water—relieved and impressed with her ability to bullshit.

And, also, not as irritated with life as I usually am.

Yeah, this should be interesting.

Liyah

My eyes fly open as my ears pop, but that's not what startles me awake.

I turn my head to find the man who has saved me more than once over the last who knows how many days, leaning over me.

His thumb brushes my cheek, and his other hand gives my thigh a squeeze, since my legs are draped over his lap. "We're landing. I let you sleep as long as I could."

The jet is nice, but it's small. I would know, my family has a fleet. I pull in a big breath and stretch on the small bench sofa. My butt is pressed to Ozzy's thigh. When I couldn't stop yawning, my new travel partner insisted I lie down. He had to prepare for whatever project we're headed to.

"Libya." I bite back a yawn and take Ozzy's hand that pulls me to a sitting position.

"Have you ever been?"

I shake my head. "Africa was my home for many, many years until I left for boarding school, but I've never been to Libya. The only time I traveled with my parents was for pleasure, and my mother preferred Europe and the States. They never took me on political or philanthropic trips, which were mostly in Africa."

I buckle in for landing, but Ozzy doesn't. He turns to me, stretching an arm behind me on the sofa, his other hand lands heavy on my thigh. "You're not going to see Libya this time, either. I'm going to explain something to you, and you can't ask any questions. Later you can, but not right now. Now, I need you to trust me."

"You're asking me to trust you now? I hardly know you, yet I'm here, blindly putting my life in your hands.

At this point, you're my best option. But you telling me to trust you now makes me wonder if I should've tried to go it alone."

His blue eyes narrow as he studies me.

"What is it that I need to trust you with more than I already have?"

He pulls a hand down his face and mutters, "I have no fucking clue how they do this."

"No clue how *who* does *what*?" I demand.

The plane descends, I feel it even though I can't see a thing outside in the black of night. Not even lights sprinkled here and there as we get closer to earth. Ozzy exhales dramatically and shakes his head. "The men I work with. Never mind. Listen, you being with me right now sounds like the worst idea ever, but given what we've already been through, this should look like child's play."

"Should?"

He shrugs like it's not a big deal that he's freaking me out more than I have been. "Yeah, but you never know."

I've already jumped from a train right before it exploded into a fiery ball from hell and was spotted in Spain. Taking a pitstop in Libya was not in my plan, but since my uncle's henchmen somehow knew where I was, I'm out of options. There's no way this can be worse.

I shake that thought away, because I know it could be so much worse. "Okay, whatever. Your job will be quick, right? I need to get to Morocco."

"*Okay, whatever*? Just like that? You're good to go?"

"As long as it means we can be on the search for my

mother, I'm good, Ozzy. No, I'm desperate." The landing gear cranks below us, and I sweep my hair into a quick bun on top of my head, not caring about what I look like for once in my life. "How long will it take?"

And just like he did earlier when he agreed not to dump me like a bad date, the smallest of smiles take over his features. Not his lips, but his eyes light a fraction. "Depends on how fast you can move."

I, on the other hand, cannot bring myself to mirror his reaction. "I've had a nap and I'm carbed up. I'll do anything if you'll help me."

He nods. "I'm already working on it, Princess."

I look out the window as the plane touches down in a nice, smooth landing. "I appreciate everything you've done for me, but if you call me *princess* one more time..." I hesitate, because there's nothing for me to do. But I can't listen to that title. I might own it by blood, but it was also given to my mother by marriage and then ripped away from her later. There's nothing beautiful or romantic about it, and it makes my stomach churn. "Just don't."

The man who hasn't shown a cautious bone in his body thus far, and never buckled for landing, sits back and looks down at me. "That's fucking interesting. Now I really can't wait to get my shit done so I can explore that further. I thought anyone born to royalty would gag for their title. You continue to surprise me, Liyah."

"I have one priority, and it doesn't include you exploring anything."

Ozzy stretches his arm behind me again to brace as the pilot hits the brakes. His thick body is pressed into mine, so he doesn't have to lean far for his words to tickle my ear when he lowers his voice. "If you expect me to help you, you'd better be prepared to dump your life story at my feet. There's no other way this will work."

Shit.

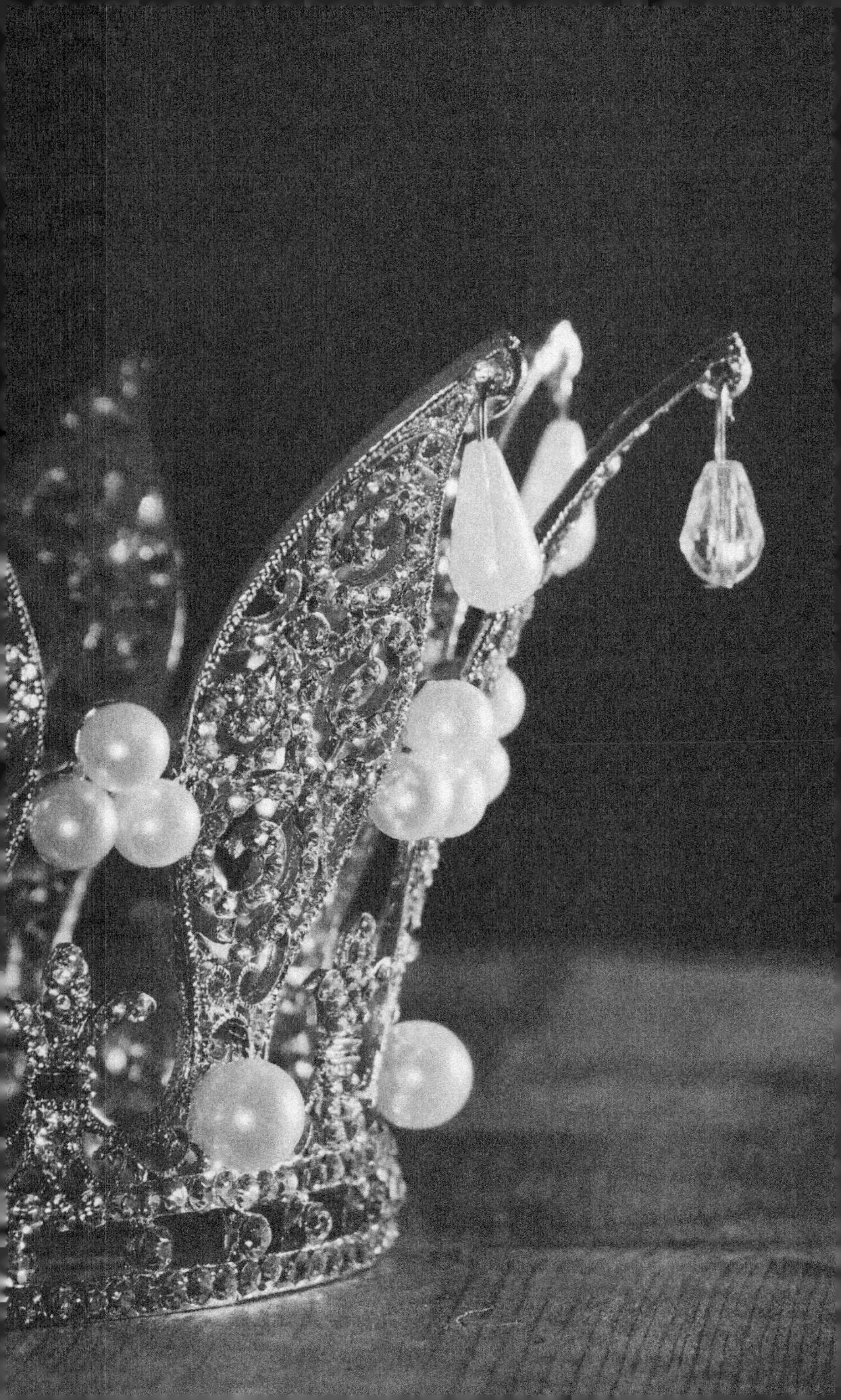

9

A KILLER AND A DEAD MAN

Liyah

"This is a first. Does Vega know you brought a guest to the party?"

Okay, that's the second person to ask him that question. I think it's safe to say Ozzy usually travels alone.

I shuffle a half-step closer to my hero as the wrinkled, crusty old man speaks without taking his eyes off me.

The last leg of our journey was an interesting one. It had nothing to do with Libya and everything to do with Ozzy. We arrived as unofficially as one could. There was no staff, no airport, and nothing official to record our presence.

I was shocked and grateful. One less paper trail for the King's guard.

When the pilot opened the door for us, Ozzy clasped my hand in his big one. No challenge could break his hold. Then he informed our pilot that *we'd be back* and *to not leave under any fucking circumstance.*

You would think *any circumstance* would ruffle one's feathers, but no. The pilot didn't seem concerned, but continued to glare at me the way he did before we left Spain.

Yes, Ozzy is a loner.

An unlocked car with keys on the floorboard was magically waiting for us when we got off the plane. I didn't ask any questions. We bumped along on backroads and ended up here—on the outskirts of Tripoli. The light of day is beginning to peek through the old buildings of the dirty alleyway we stand in.

The crotchety old man is as pleased to see me as the pilot was. He's a thoroughly irritated American, not bothering to turn his head when he exhales a lungful of cigarette exhaust into Ozzy's face.

"He knows," Ozzy clips. This Vega person must be important. Two people have mentioned him in a matter of hours. I'm pretty sure Vega knowing about me is a lie. "Give me my stuff so I can get this shit done."

The man lifts his smoke to his lips again for a long suck and turns his glare back to Ozzy. "I've seen a lot in my years doing this shit, but not this. You've got balls bringing a side piece to a job."

The need to step away from Ozzy to prove I'm no one's *piece* battles inside me. But I stay close because, right now, I'd rather be Ozzy's anything than separate myself from him.

Ozzy doesn't acknowledge me in the slightest. "Shut your fucking mouth, Brayner, and give me the coordinates. I don't want to lose my window, and my plane is waiting."

Brayner huffs a nicotine-filled laugh of disgust, flicking his cigarette to the side for it to die on its own. He stuffs his hand in his front pocket and produces a wrinkled scrap of paper.

Without a thank-you or goodbye, Ozzy grabs it and turns to claim my hand, once again.

We're halfway to the car when the man yells to our backs, "Don't let that pretty piece of ass get you killed, Graves."

Graves?

For the first time since he told me to find food in that quaint Spanish village, Ozzy leaves my side. His bulky, heavy pack is dropped at my feet and he has Brayner pinned against the cinderblock wall, fisting his shirt. "Watch it, old man. If you want to continue working for Crew, shut your mouth, and mind your own fucking business. I can knock the lights out on your pathetic life with one strike and it has nothing to do with the ticking time bomb of your decrepit heart. I also have Crew Vega's trust, and nothing you can do will change that. Fuck with me—I dare you."

My heart speeds as I remember the moment I met Ozzy with his gun stabbed in my ribs. Brayner's face flames, and a vein swells at his temple. Even though the old man has been nothing but ugly to me, I empathize. Being the brunt of Ozzy's anger isn't fun.

"Crazy fuck," Brayner spews and holds up his hands. Ozzy gives him a crushing thrust into the wall before letting go. Brayner pulls in a shallow breath, and steadies himself when he keeps talking. "You're your own ticking time bomb, Graves. Everyone knows it. Get the hell out of my face."

Ozzy puts an angry hand to his chest and shoves

one more time. "Don't push me, Brayner. And if you spew anything else about her or me, it'll be the last thing you ever do."

Even with Ozzy's back to me, the seriousness of his words fill the early morning air. If Brayner's expression is any indication, I'd say Ozzy's threat is not an empty one. "This better be clean, that's all I'm saying."

Ozzy stalks back to me, not offering the man a glance when he bites, "You know better than to threaten me. I don't do anything that isn't clean."

Ozzy shifts me in front of him as we make our way back to the car.

He doesn't say a word and I follow his lead, but only until we have privacy once again inside the car. He revs the engine and throws it in reverse when I turn to him. "Ozzy, I know you said to trust you, but —"

He interrupts. "Don't do that."

I pull the frayed seat belt across me, not sure it will do any good should I happen to need it, but it can't hurt. "Do what? I have no idea where we're going, what you're going to do when we get there, or how long it will take. And no one we meet seems to think it's a good idea that you brought me along."

He puts it in drive, and we are on the go again—to where, I have no clue because he refuses to tell me. "You agreed to trust me."

"Yes, but that encounter was strange at the very least. I think I have the right to ask."

He keeps his eyes on the road ahead of us as we maneuver farther into the city. His strong, square jaw tightens, yet he gives me nothing.

And I start to question everything.

My choice to travel to Morocco when my mother, in essence, forbade it.

Then putting my trust in a man I don't know.

The only thing I do know right now, is I've never felt more alone.

My voice cracks. "Ozzy, please. I just need to know I haven't made a mistake."

Finally, his gaze zips to me before landing back on the street when he throws his hand toward the sky. "I'm doing everything I can to get this shit done, instead of having to hunker down for another day. For what I need to do, I need to be set up before the sun rises. The sooner I do this, the sooner I can start looking for your mom."

"Oh." I lean back in my seat. "I'm sorry."

He exhales loudly, but stays quiet.

"So, are we going to make it in time?" I look back to him. "You know, for you to do your work today instead of tomorrow?"

He shakes his head, and looks as exasperated as he sounds. "It's looking good, but I'll keep you posted."

"Really?" My sarcasm has been in hibernation since the drama with my mother happened, but for the first time since I left L.A., I finally feel like I can breathe. "I'll believe that when it happens. I'm actually looking forward to it."

"I aim to please," he mutters, looking at his GPS.

He hits the brakes and whips a quick left, and I silently complain about his services as a travel guide. We're in an open parking space under a building—a relatively nice one. For this part of the world, I'd say it's quite posh, which is surprising. There's something about Ozzy that's made me assume he only operates in the dark and ugly crevices of the world. Having a gun and a silencer on a train being the first. I mean, there's nothing about him that screams official.

"This is it?" I ask.

"Let's go. I think we made it in time."

More than anything, I want to ask in time for what, but he's already out of the car. Clutching the only belongings I brought with me, I follow him to a door.

He stops, turns to me, and lowers his voice. "Stay behind me, and don't make a sound. Got it?"

"Are we breaking in?"

He turns to the door and pulls his gun from the back of his pants. "Not exactly, but you never know."

Holy shit.

The knob clicks when he twists it, and my breath catches. I think I put all my trust in a criminal.

Ozzy turns to look down at me, lifts his chin before pushing the door open, and peeks around the corner.

Like a crazy woman, I follow. I'm also back to wondering what I got myself into.

But I'm in too deep now, so here I am. And there's no way on earth I'm allowing Ozzy to leave my sight.

It's a residence—a small one, but a nice one. Ozzy moves silently through a kitchen and a family room. All the while, I stay glued to his back. We climb one flight of stairs where there are two more rooms, and yet another set to the third floor. Ozzy checks every room, every nook, and every cranny.

He comes to a stop in a bedroom, and stands in front of a window where the horizon meets nothing but a sea of concrete. The sun rises on the city that is now coming alive.

Ozzy nods once and turns to me. "Okay. Get comfortable. We could be here for a while."

What in the world?

Ozzy

THE WAY I SEE IT, Crew can't exactly fire me. I know everything there is to know about him. I also set up Reskill, his multi-million-dollar private satellite network that allows us to communicate from anywhere in the world and him to profit off information he sells to people he finds deserving. Good luck to him finding someone else who can break my codes to keep it up and running like I do. I can even manage it while on assignment.

But when he finds out I brought my stowaway with me on a job...

Well, he might not fire me, but he may just kill me. He certainly knows how and can bury my body somewhere on his vast acreage of land.

Yeah, when he finds out, he's going to be pissed.

I crack open an energy drink I grabbed from the mini bar on the plane. Dragging a stowaway around two continents proves to be exhausting. I should've had a full-night's sleep on the train and been here yesterday. I've been this long without sleep before, but it's been a while.

I'm set up and ready.

Now, I wait.

"What are we waiting on?"

I don't take my eyes off the house across the street and two doors down. "You ask a lot of questions."

"This is bloody nerve-wracking. What would you like me to do?"

I hear her get up from where she collapsed into a corner chair when I told her it was safe and to get comfortable. I sense her before she speaks when she stands close to my side.

"Well, you hardly ever answer my questions, and you look at me even less."

"You're demanding. And for the record, we've been a little busy running from whomever is chasing you. You haven't told me shit either, so I figure we're even."

She leans on the window trim, and I can't help my eyes from flitting to her for a nanosecond. When I told her it was safe, she used the bathroom. I heard the water going forever. Her hair is brushed, and a braid dangles down her back. Like it has been since the first moment I laid eyes on her, her hair has a mind of its own, small pieces falling around her face.

Fuck. I need to focus.

I look back to the house.

"Can you at least tell me why we're here?"

"Nice try. You first."

From my periphery, I see she tips her head to the wall and crosses her arms. "My father was the King of Morocco."

"We established that part. Tell me about your mom."

She sighs and there's a smile in her tone. "My mother is amazing. She cares about the poor, the hungry, and especially about the women of Morocco. She and my father met when he was on a diplomatic trip to Spain. She caught his eye. She was young and carefree, and my father was twelve years older. He refused to marry anyone the family tried to push on him. He always said once he met my mom, all bets were off. He married for love."

This is why bringing her with me was a bad idea. I can't help it, I tear my eyes from my target and look at her. "The King of Morocco married a Spanish woman. How did that go over?"

She looks up at me through dark lashes and shrugs. "Not well. But when you're the King, does it matter?"

I turn back to my target. "I wouldn't know. I'm the farthest thing from royalty."

"Well, it doesn't. Or it didn't. My mother always told me she was more loved by the Moroccan people than any princess born royal. She was real and caring and philanthropic. They adored her. Morocco is the most western society of the Arab world. Once my father went public with their relationship and proposed, his family could do nothing to stop it publicly."

A car drives by and slows in front of my target, but then takes off. "That's as Disney as ever."

"But privately it was a different story. Because my mother isn't Moroccan or Arab, the dynasty never accepted her, even when my father was alive. She's Catholic, a Christian living among sultans. My father protected her from that. But after his death?" She sighs. "Once I grew older, I understood why she sent me away. I'm half-Arab, half-Spanish. She knew I would never be treated as I should by the empire, especially when my uncle was crowned King."

I look at my watch. Shit. It's past prime time to get this done. If it doesn't happen soon, it probably won't happen today. "It's been a long time since your father passed away. Why the sudden drama with your mom?"

"My father was popular and well-liked during his reign. Men in Morocco can take up to two wives, but my father vowed long before he met my mother he would only ever have one. That alone made him different from others. But together, my parents were widely loved. Whether it's royalty or a simple president of a country, approval ratings are everything. When my father died, the country of Morocco mourned with my mother for their king. The dynasty couldn't exactly strike her down the next day. And she had me. I'm a princess by lineage, no matter if I'm only half-Moroccan."

She yawns, and I'm about to allow myself to steal another glance, when it happens.

Not just another car, but the car.

"Hold that thought, Princess. I want to know everything, but something is happening. I need to focus."

She stands straight from where she was leaning near the window. "Who is that?"

"A terrorist."

"What?!"

I put my hand to her stomach, and push her behind me. "Move away from the window, just in case."

"*Just in case* what? Ozzy, what's happening?"

"Liyah—" I start to argue with her, but they walk out the front door. His wife and two sons, followed by the target himself.

"Who are they?" she demands.

I don't answer and grab my laptop. Everything was arranged while we were in flight. He's here for two days to see his family. Apparently when you're the number two in the most hostile terror organization in the Middle East, you still get vacation time.

Either that, or he's got something else planned. Carson sent me the transcripts. This guy has fake passports and documents and is headed to the UK tomorrow. We've been after him for a year—this is the moment we've been waiting for. We knew the window would be small.

I wait for his wife and sons to climb in the car. My target shuts the car door and watches the driver pull away from the curb.

"Ozzy—"

"Hang on, Princess."

I pull up my satellite feed with infrared technology. When he walks back into the house, I follow on the screen.

"You can see him?" Shit, she won't stop.

He's alone. Finally.

I look down the street.

Two cars drive by.

Then another.

When the last one passes, I look both ways, and then back to my screen. He's in the kitchen, in the middle of the house.

Perfect.

Liyah places her hand on my bicep at the exact moment I do it. "Ozzy—"

One tap of my finger.

The house detonates.

Liyah screams and clings to me.

I look back to my screen that's nothing but red—it might as well be blood for all intents and purposes.

Then I look at the woman who had no fucking idea

what she was getting herself into when I demanded her trust.

Her stare is focused on what I just did—the life I took and the destruction I orchestrated, all with the click of a key on a laptop.

Then she looks up at me with eyes that are just as beautiful as before, but are now haunted.

And she knows who I really am.

A killer and a dead man.

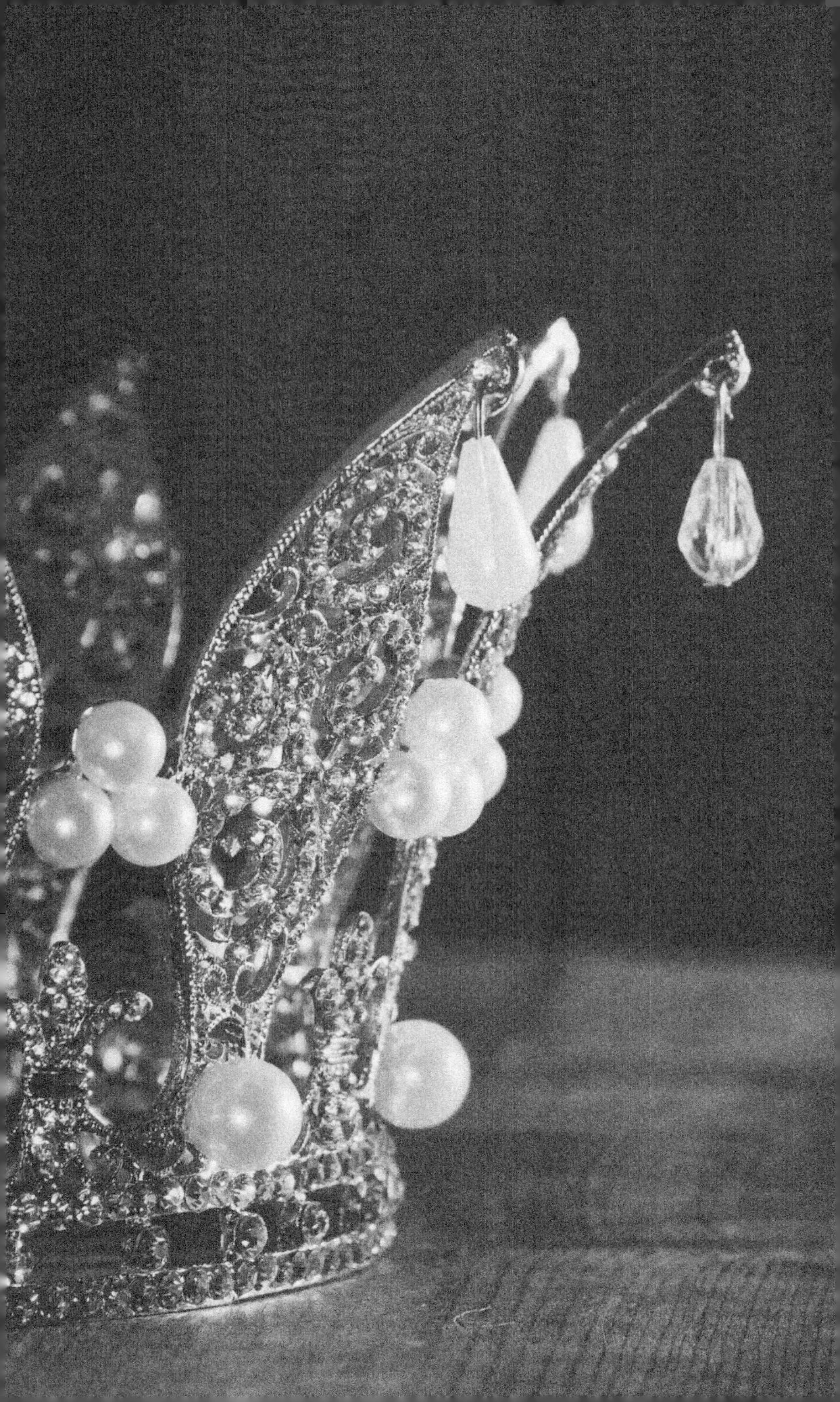

10

PLAYING GAMES WITH MY DICK

Liyah

My mother is the strongest person I know. She comforted me through the death of my father. She protected me from the oppressive dysfunction when my uncle was crowned King. She made sure I had freedoms I never would have if she kept me with her in Morocco. And I know without a shadow of a doubt, she missed me every moment I was away.

She married for love, gave up her life in Spain for love, and, for years, suffered the consequences of not bringing me home.

My greatest fear is that I'll never be as strong as her.

Today, my fear materialized. I was not prepared for what I saw.

Granted, I knew there was something dark about Ozzy, but I didn't expect that.

"What the hell's wrong with her?"

I can't catch my breath. I haven't been able to since I saw the house go up in flames—debris thrown for a city block. Ozzy had to carry me out of the house, along with both our packs. He shoved me in the front seat of the car as my lungs fought for oxygen.

Then he drove at a normal pace through the city streets as emergency vehicles sped past us to the carnage and death Ozzy left.

Besides that, I hardly remember the drive or bumpy roads.

Ozzy hoists me up into his arms like a virginal bride being carried over the threshold as he makes his way up the stairs and into the plane, and speaks to the pilot. "She'll be okay. Let's get out of here."

The door slams shut, followed by two thumps of our bags hitting the carpeted floor of the plane. Ozzy sits, never letting go of me, his thick strong arms holding me to his chest. I don't realize how badly I'm trembling or how cold I am until the heat of his body seeps into mine.

His hand is firm on the back of my head, my face is pressed to the bare skin of his neck when his lips land on my ear. His words are firm and not at all comforting. "That's what I do. Doesn't matter how much they deserve it, I'm still a killer."

A killer.

I fist his shirt until my fingers go numb.

"That guy was responsible for orchestrating more terror worldwide than anyone else in the last two years. Hundreds of people have died around the globe because of him. Probably more. All the intel points to it, even though the hard evidence isn't there to back it up."

I try to will my body to stop trembling, but I'm just so cold.

"Shit," he grits. The next thing I know, he wraps a blanket around my back as the jet engines rumble beneath us. He drags a hand down my hair over and over and over. "Breathe, Liyah. I might do shit like that, but I'll never hurt you. If I haven't proven that by now, I'm not sure what else I can do."

I give my head a shake as tears leak from my eyes. I'm not sure why I'm crying.

So, I've become travel partners with an assassin.

I mean, he just admitted the man he killed was a terrorist. If anyone deserves to die, it would be him, right?

I suppose it could be worse.

He groans. "Fuck me, you're crying."

"I'm sorry." I hiccup. "I'm exhausted. That was a shock. I don't even know what I'm doing."

"You've hardly slept in days, and I've slept even less." He sighs and slinks down on the sofa with me in his arms. "Shit, my phone is going crazy."

He shifts me, digs it out of his pocket, and puckers his lips into a silent *shh* to keep me quiet. "It's done. I'm in the air. I got out fine. Lots of chaos and traffic around the site, but I slipped out undetected. Brayner did his job—destruction was contained to the target, other than debris."

I'm sure what he would like to say is he got out fine, other than having to carry a woman out who was an emotional wreck from seeing him kill a man. Besides that, it seemed like a piece of cake.

But he doesn't admit to any of that.

I don't dare make a peep, not that I have much to say.

He's right. As my adrenaline falls from what I just experienced, exhaustion takes over.

"I've got some things to do while I'm here. I'll explain later. Yeah, I'll be back soon. I'll call you. I've been up for two days. I need some sleep."

Ozzy shifts the blanket and lies down. I don't argue when he sandwiches me on my side between his warm body and the back of the sofa.

I close my eyes and pull in a breath.

"Give me a few hours. I'll check." I hear his cell hit the floor of the plane.

Ozzy stuffs a throw pillow under his head, and I rest mine on his bicep.

During our time together, Ozzy has had his hands on me in many ways. The first, when he checked me for weapons, then when he shielded my body, and now, comforting me from what I just witnessed.

From seeing him kill a man.

Now, he's got one hand buried in my hair and the other so low on my back, the tips of his fingers are pressing into the top of my ass. I'm glued to Ozzy once again, but this time we're not jumping out of a train window into the dark night or running from someone who recognized me.

This is different.

And I'm too tired to think about it.

About how the man who was stuck with me by happenstance is comforting me after he took a life.

"I have no idea how any of this is going to shake out. I told you I'd help you find your mom, and I'm going to do that. But I'm sure as shit not waltzing into Morocco when everyone and their dog will recognize you if there's really the kind of threat you think there is. Let's get some sleep and regroup."

I nod, my face burrowed into his chest.

He sighs, and I feel it everywhere when he demands, "Sleep, Princess."

I squeeze my eyes and will myself to settle. I can't think straight anyway.

With no clue where he's taking me or what's next, I feel myself drift off, surprisingly faster than I should in such a situation.

Ozzy

THE PRINCESS from an Arab country was not kidding when she said she's been westernized.

I've scrolled through her entire life on social media, first during her years at boarding school in England, then at Pepperdine.

Liyah on campus, at parties, traveling with friends, hanging at the beach. What I'm looking at online is nothing like I've experienced since she's been with me. In the pictures, she's certainly not wearing clothes that are three sizes too big for her. No, she's showcasing everything I know from having my hands on her, but haven't seen. She's small with the right amount of curves, and the skin on the rest of her body is as beautiful as it is on her face.

I should know after stalking her entire life. She likes posting pictures of herself on yachts with friends while wearing bikinis so small, she's left very little to the imagination.

I slept for three hours, but Liyah is still out. I woke up on my back with the Princess draped over me—her head on my chest and legs tangled with mine. As I stare at the woman on the screen who's dead asleep on top of me, I've never fought so hard to keep my dick in check.

Since I can't shift or adjust myself, life is painful as fuck right now. But waking her doesn't seem like a good idea. I'm used to going without sleep for long periods, but I doubt she is. And since her using me as a bed is better than me explaining my hard-on against her thigh, which she will no doubt feel the moment she wakes, I opt to let her sleep.

And I've got to quit looking at her on the beach.

I should detonate all my fake social accounts so I won't ever be tempted to go back there again. Instead, I sign into the secure network for Reskill. I maneuver my way into the backdoor of the NSA. When I get back to Virginia, I need to create more paths. Keeping five to six available at all times is the best way to assure I can keep tabs on every-fucking-one.

But instead of obsessing over Demaree and Cannon, like I usually do, I enter in a search I've never considered before.

King Hasim Zahir.

Liyah's uncle, who she swears is behind her mother's disappearance.

The NSA keeps tabs on our foreign interests, as well as Americans they're not supposed to keep tabs on. They do shit they aren't supposed to all the time and file it away in case they need it in the future.

I should know, I used to do it for them. I had no qualms doing what I was told. I was too young, too blind, and too much of a patriot. I thought what we did was in the best interest of our country.

I was wrong.

I'm also the poster boy for those who stay in their lane and trust those around them, but then get struck down for always doing the right thing.

They say money makes the world go round.

They'd be wrong.

Sure, power can be bought, but you can gain a hell of a lot more with knowledge. With knowledge comes fear.

I've seen it.

I've even caused it.

I've been the brunt of it.

I pull up everything the NSA has on King Hasim.

The National Security Agency is nothing if not thorough. I'm not surprised to find private conversations and interactions between the King and his top brass. Those conversations have turned into orders. His main concern right now is the woman asleep on my chest, who's playing games with my dick.

I don't skim. I take in every single word, because each and every one is more and more fucked up.

Liyah stirs, and I put my hand on her head, running my fingers through her hair since I've already yanked out the band that held her braid. She makes a little noise, and I freeze when she turns her head to rest on her other cheek, and shifts so her legs fall on either side of my thigh.

I hitch my leg between hers, and she settles back into a deep sleep. We should be landing soon, and she should rest for as long as possible. When she wakes, I'll have some explaining to do, and I'm not anxious for that conversation.

Until then, I know three things for certain.

Liyah's mom is paying the price for standing in the way of bringing her daughter home.

The King has plans for the Princess.

And he's looking for her far and wide.

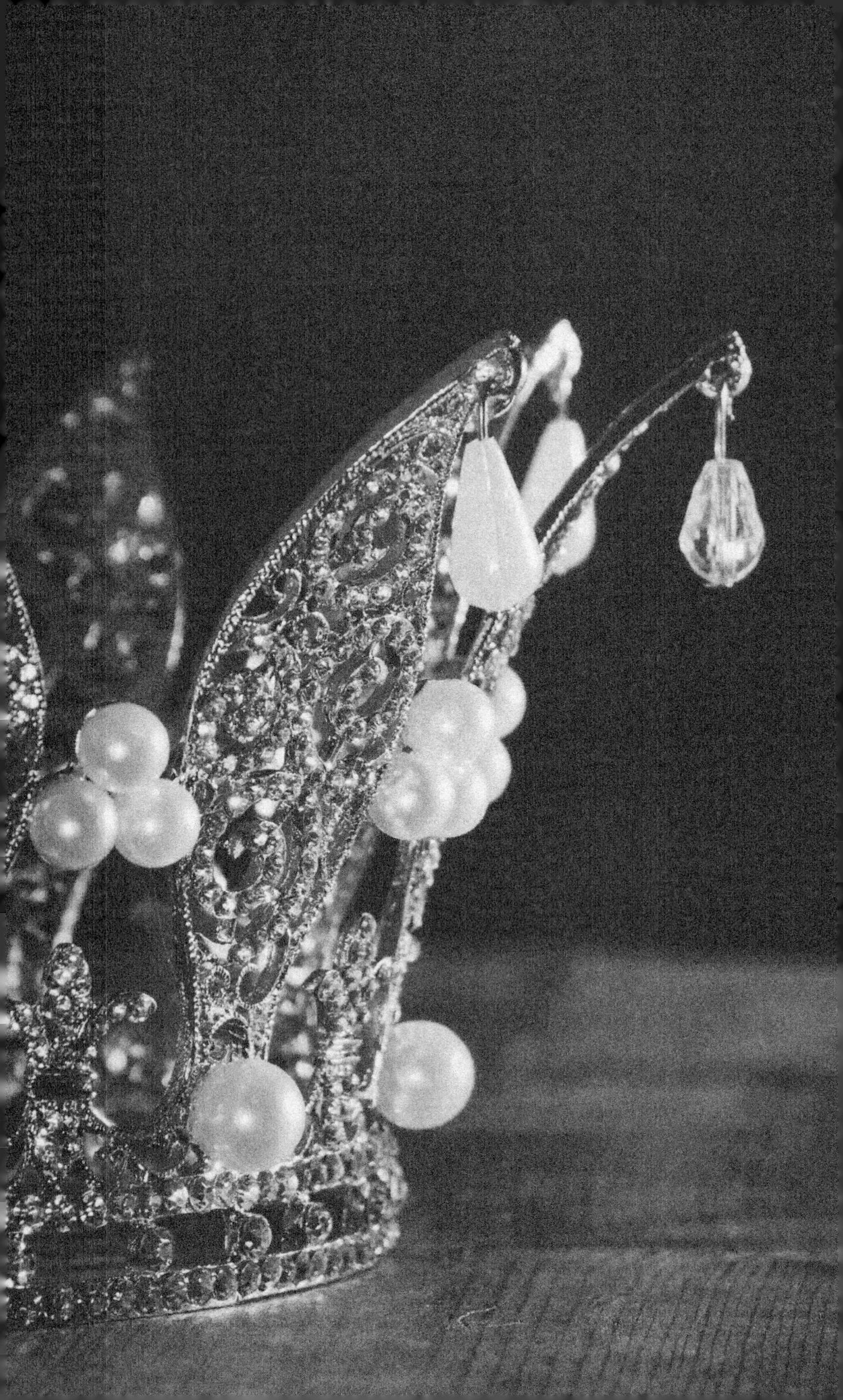

11

PROMISED

Liyah

"Where are we?"
I wake draped over Ozzy like a wet blanket. I'm warm and comfortable and groggy.

I've never gone without sleep for that long. Even in college during finals, I always had plenty of time to do everything. It's not like I had to juggle a job like some of my friends did.

But I do feel hungover in ways that remind me of spring break.

Ozzy practically picks me up and sets me back down on the sofa. "Paris."

That one word takes a moment to sink in, but when it does, I panic. "Paris? What are we doing in Paris? You said—"

"I said we'd regroup." He opens the mini fridge, pulls out two more bottles of water, and throws one to me. I barely catch it before it hits me in the chin. "Your mom is my second priority. My first is keeping us alive. And since our train car was blown up and you seem to have a face that's known around the globe, I need to figure out what the hell to do next. I can do that in Paris and know we're safe."

I don't realize how thirsty I am until the water hits my lips. I down half the bottle. "How are we going to do that in Paris?"

I hear the landing gear again, and wonder how long I slept if we flew all the way to France. He throws the bottle of water into what I hope is a recycling bin, and sits flush to me, with his thigh pressed to mine and arm stretched behind me again. He levels his gaze on me. "Trust me."

My eyes widen. "The last time you said that, I watched you blow up a house with a man inside. A living and breathing human, who is nothing but ash now."

He leans back as the jet descends. "I explained that. He was a terrorist."

"Then he should've been arrested," I claim. "Because that's how things are done in a world that's fair and just."

The wheels hit the runway. We're on the ground again, but not the continent I thought we'd be on.

"Ozzy—"

"Let me get you somewhere safe. Somewhere with food and a hot shower, and where I know, without a doubt, I can explain all these things to you and no one else is listening. I swear, you'll get all the answers you want."

"You keep telling me to trust you. How much longer do you expect me to do that blindly?"

The brakes engage, and we come to a stop on yet another tarmac. Ozzy stands, grabs both his bag and mine, slinging them over one shoulder, before extending his other hand to me. "Where would you be without me right now, Liyah?"

With that quick reminder, I see it all over again in my head—the explosion that lit up the night. The one meant for me...

I quickly take his hand, and I'm not embarrassed that my grip bleeds desperation. At this point, Ozzy knows.

And he knows I need him, despite what I saw back in Libya.

He gives my hand a squeeze. "You won't be sorry, Princess. I'll make sure of it."

Ozzy

I FLIP off the water and grab a towel. Three hours of sleep on the plane was barely a dent in what I need to function on the straight and narrow again. But I have an agenda before I can close my eyes.

Eat a real meal, dig deeper about the royal asshole King, and interrogate a princess.

I've kept my head down for years, done my job, and never wavered. How the hell have I ended up harboring a royal heir who's being searched for by her dickhead uncle? And she has no fucking clue what's in store for her if he finds her.

I throw on a pair of gym shorts with my mind on one thing—food.

That is until I open the double doors from the bedroom to the great room. Liyah is standing in front of the French doors that open to the balcony in nothing but my T-shirt. It hits her bare legs at mid-thigh. With her arms crossed, her hair wet and loose down her back, she stares at the Eiffel Tower. I let her shower first, but she was out of clean clothes. She took my last clean shirt.

I shouldn't wonder if she's wearing anything beneath it, but I can't help where my mind wanders.

"You hungry?"

She turns and takes me in from across the room, before forcing her gaze to my face. Her dark eyes go so deep, I want to know everything about her. "Honestly? I don't know what I am anymore."

She's fucked in more ways than one, but I need more information before I tell her that.

This penthouse is European central for Crew's organization. Most of the time, it makes more sense to stay here than travel all the way back to the States between assignments. Especially if we're in a holding pattern or awaiting orders. This place has become a second home to me. I prefer it here, where the language isn't my first, I'm an outsider, and, most importantly, I don't have to worry about anyone recognizing me.

I go to the fridge to see what's left from when I was here two weeks ago. Crew has had it stocked since then. There's one thing about working for Vega, we don't worry about anything but the end goal. He takes care of us as if we were his family—his blood. He might put that off on his wife, Addy, but we all know it's him. He did what we do before he retired, and Grady explained their past—the people they worked for didn't give two shits about them.

Crew changed that.

I pull steaks out of the refrigerator. "Sit down, Princess. You talk while I cook."

She approaches the island and pulls out a barstool. "I've told you everything. I think it's time I ask you some questions."

I hike a brow and nod once, digging back in the fridge for butter, garlic, and the ingredients for a salad.

I fire up the range and pull out a cast iron skillet. I'd prefer a pellet grill, but I'm sure that would ruin the aesthetic of the veranda overlooking the iconic tower.

Her voice hits me low and smooth from behind. Now that we're not playing defense at every turn, I've given myself a chance to let it sink in. I don't hate it. "What is it you do for work officially?"

I have no fucking idea what I'm going to tell her. I've never once in the years since I've been in training or working for Crew had to explain what I do to anyone. There's no one in my life anymore who'd want to know.

I avoid her question and throw back, "What do you do for work?"

"Nothing." Her answer comes quick and simple, as if she is accustomed to answering that inquiry daily.

I turn to her. "Nothing?"

She shakes her head. "My family has ruled over Morocco since the seventeen hundreds. When I say the monarchy is filthy rich, I mean dirty, grubby, messy rich, in every sense of the word. My father did what none before him did for a daughter—he dedicated a part of his wealth to me. I guess it would be what you Americans call a trust fund. So, no. I don't work."

I lean a hip into the counter and cross my arms. "Well, at least you own it, like any decent princess should."

"Funny," she deadpans. "It's money. I grew up with it, I've always had it available to me, and I use it when I need it. Would you rather me play the martyr, pretend it makes my life hard, and act like it's a burden?"

"Fuck no," I tell her the truth. "I didn't grow up hungry, but my family knew where every single dollar went. If I had buckets of royal gold and jewels, I wouldn't be shy about using them either."

"I'm not a theme-park princess, Ozzy. My money is in an off-shore bank account that's only accessible by me and my mother. I don't have caves full of gold and artifacts, guarded by dragons and knights."

The butter sizzles in the skillet behind me, and I unwrap the meat. "That's disappointing."

"Why are we talking about my bank account when I asked about what you do for a living?"

"Because I don't like to talk about me."

"Why?"

"Because it doesn't matter." It's the truth. I open the fridge again and pull out a beer and crack it open. "I've got beer, wine, and bourbon. And milk."

"Beer, please."

I reach for another beer and open it before sliding it across the island to her. "I took you for a wine drinker."

"I learned to appreciate beer in college. Maybe I'll have wine with dinner."

"Very American, yet so royal. You're a hard princess to crack."

She rolls her eyes and puts the bottle to her lips. Then she licks a drop of beer off her bottom lip and a pang of envy hits my chest like an arrow. "We're not talking about me anymore until you tell me what you do."

I throw minced garlic in the butter and keep my back to her as I speak. "I'm a contractor. I work hand in hand with the CIA, but not directly for them."

"Really?"

I turn back to her. "Did you think I'm some rogue who blows up buildings whenever the feeling strikes?"

She looks surprised. "I'm not sure I could have guessed that had I tried."

"There you go." I leave it at that. "That's what I do."

"Do you only blow things up? That's quite a specialty."

I take another gulp of beer. I don't tell her sometimes I shoot people. Other times I send in a drone. One time I took a life with my bare hands because technology decided to fuck me over. I was in a pinch.

I don't elaborate. "No. My skills are varied."

"I see." She takes another drink.

Garlic and butter permeate the air around us, and I sear one thick filet. "How do you take your steak?"

"Pink."

"Are you satisfied with my résumé?"

"You're more official than I thought you were. At least it explains how you had a gun on a train. I'm just glad you didn't use it on me."

"I'm going to tell you one more thing about myself."

She leans in and rests her chin on a hand. "I'm all ears."

"Part of my job is finding people. And I have access

to pretty much anything I want in order to do my job the best I can. Before I did this, my job was information. Foreign and domestic."

Her eyes widen.

"Yeah. And I was good at it, until someone took advantage of me. I don't do strangers and I really don't do friends. It's why you sneaking into my cabin that night set me off the way it did."

"Choosing your cabin had nothing to do with you. I thought it was vacant."

I throw lettuce, veggies, and cheese into a bowl. "I've figured that out. What I'm telling you, is that you need to be honest with me. If I ask you something, I need the truth—not part of it."

She doesn't hesitate. "I promise. As long as you'll help me find my mother, I'll do anything."

I turn to place the second filet in the skillet. Eating a steak done any further than rare should be illegal. I flip hers that's already halfway to pink. "Now that we've got that out of the way, we can talk about you again. Explain why your uncle wants you home, and why your mother went to such extremes to keep you away."

I don't need to know this. I already know. But I want to know what she knows.

She pulls that bottom lip between her perfect, white teeth, and hesitates.

"Liyah," I warn her.

She shakes her head and shrugs. "I assume he wants the money my father set aside for me. Like I said, actions like that are done for sons—future kings—not a mere princess who will never rule, make important decisions, or be anything more than filler for royal photo ops."

Interesting. She's halfway there. "What else?"

Her face falls. "That's it. My uncle is greedy, and my father knew it. When he was on his deathbed and knew there was no cure for his cancer, that's when he set up accounts for me and my mother. And our accounts are huge. My mother eventually turned hers over to my uncle. She shouldn't have, but she did. It was some sort of agreement for him to leave me alone. Or maybe allow me to go to college in the States. I don't know and she would never say. I had no idea then, but now I have a feeling she sheltered me from so much when it came to the hell he put her through."

The meat sizzles behind me, but I can't take my eyes off her.

She's twenty-two.

Young.

Really fucking young.

Too young for me, but definitely too young for what the damn King has planned for her.

Now that I know, there's no fucking way I'm going to allow him to do what he wants to do. He might be a king, but I'm a dead man with nothing to lose.

Literally.

I move to the stove, and flip the meat one more time before banging around in the cabinets for plates.

"Ozzy?"

Fuck it. I go to the pantry and grab a bottle of red from the wine rack and bourbon. I'm going to need it.

"Ozzy, what's wrong?" she demands.

I uncork the wine and pop the bourbon before placing the liquor and two glasses between us.

I pour one of each, plate the steaks, and push the

bowl of salad toward her. She doesn't lift a finger for any of it, never taking her heavy stare off me.

I walk around the island and claim a stool next to hers. "Eat, Princess. And drink. You're going to need it."

"What are you talking about?" Her eyes widen, and she whispers, "What do you know? Is it my mother? What happened to her?"

I shake my head and cut into my filet. "It's not about your mom. Though I'm all over that as soon as we finish eating."

"Ozzy, please—"

"Eat."

"No." Her tone is firm, and she pushes back both her plate and mine. She grabs my hand, demanding my full attention. I shift to face her, but she climbs off her stool and moves between my legs. After all we've been through, there's something familiar enough between us. It's not intimate, but definitely comfortable. She places her hands flat to my bare pecs and leans in. "Please, don't make me wait."

Granted, we were both completely dressed, and I've touched most of her in the last few days. So when I put my hands on her slim hips when she's wearing nothing but my shirt, I can't help but pull her in close.

I tell her what I found out while she was sleeping on the plane. "Don't ask me how, but I have access to systems that I shouldn't have access to, which means I know shit I shouldn't know."

"Fine. I don't care how you do what you do at this point. Just tell me what you know."

I give her a squeeze and lower my voice. "Do you know a man named Sahem Botros?"

A frown mars her beautiful face. "Sahem? He's the

President of the Congressional Court. His position is appointed by my uncle. What about him?"

My heart might pound out of my fucking chest having to utter the words aloud. I pull her closer, and slide my hand beneath my shirt she's wearing, over her panty-covered ass, her bare back, and press in between her bare shoulder blades.

"Ozzy, what about him?" she demands, her tone is sharp with a hint of desperation.

"You've been promised to him." I rip the bandage off quick. I go on. "For marriage."

Instead of pushing me away, she sinks farther into my body. She's confused. "That can't be. He's married."

I hold tight and bite out the words. "I know."

"Then you're wrong," she tries.

I shake my head and lower my tone. "No, baby. Your uncle promised you to him—as a second wife."

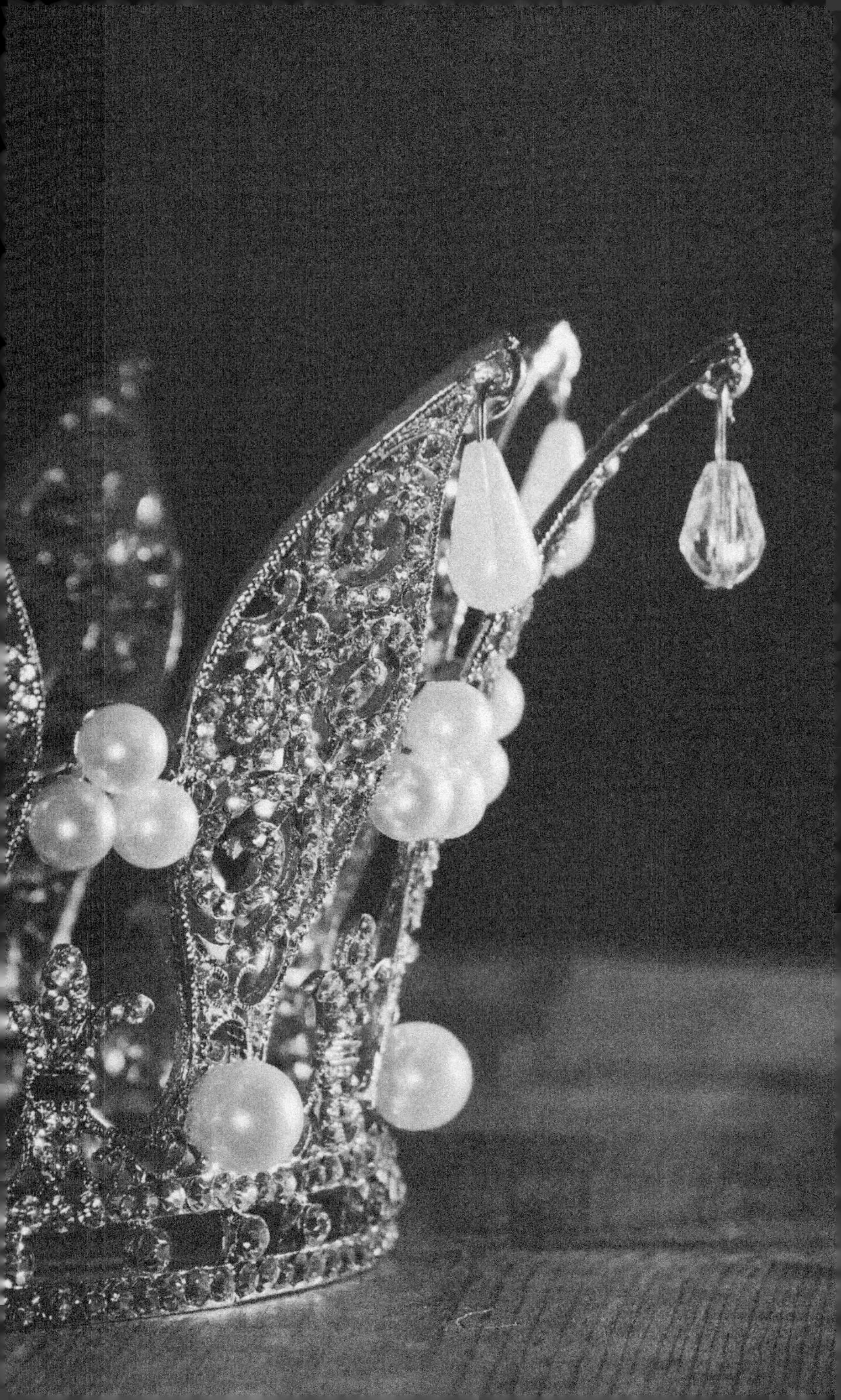

12

OUR LUCK IS SHIT

Ozzy

"It can't be." Liyah tries to digest what I just told her. "Botros is an old man. Older than my father would be today. Hell, his children are grown and older than me."

"Yes," I confirm.

"And ... he's married. Fucking married, Ozzy. There's no way I'm marrying anyone in Morocco, let alone him. You're sure?"

Her words come out on a hiss. She's as disgusted by the news as I was.

"I've seen the transcripts, Liyah. Transcripts of intercepted private phone calls and text messages. If I've learned anything working with intelligence, it's that private conversations are the most trustworthy. It's true."

"But..." What looks like panic that started to bubble low quickly starts to erupt. "It might be allowed by law, but taking two wives hardly ever happens anymore. Maybe out in the country or among the most wealthy, which I guess he is, but he's so old. And no man can take a second wife without the approval of the first, and it has to be approved by a judge."

I pull her tighter to me because there's more, and she needs to know it all. "He has permission. I told you I'm thorough. I've seen the court documents. Seems Botros is a very wealthy man, and he's willing to trade money and political favors, which is what your uncle is after."

"Because, by law, what's mine will be his," she whispers.

I look at her carefully, and have to keep the edge from my tone. "Among other things."

"For the love, what else is there?" she exclaims.

I grit my teeth, because to say this is uncharted territory for me is an understatement.

"Tell me."

I narrow my eyes. "It seems the King has not only promised you, your fortune, but he's also offering up your virginity on a golden platter ... the literal cherry to top off the deal."

Her face falls.

And I'm once again supporting her weight.

"Not quite sure how he knows that's available to promise, but you have a right to know, your virginity is part of their deal. Also not sure what's going to happen if that's not available to the disgusting old man."

"Oh my God," she whispers.

"The King ... he seems like an interesting guy."

Again, tears fill her eyes. The first was because of fear for her mom, but this is different. I'm not sure what this is.

Disgust?

Hesitancy?

Mortification?

Maybe I shouldn't have told her.

But this is even more of a reason why she can't just waltz into Morocco. If they find her, she's fair game. As fucked up as it is, they're royalty and have a lot of power. They'll find a way to keep her there against her will. They did the same to her mom.

"Liyah, if you don't want to marry some fat, hairy, old man, you're not going to." With her small frame tucked from my chest to my cock—one I'm currently in negotiations with to settle the fuck down—I do my best not to think about the status of her virginity. "I'll make sure of it, but you're not returning to Morocco. If you do, you're at the mercy of the King. I looked it up—when your father passed, you became your uncle's responsibility, which he considers property. That's fucked up."

Her eyes wander to the side, and she nods.

I tangle my hand in her damp hair, forcing her gaze back to me. "You okay?"

She shakes her head. "No. For so many reasons, no. This is what my mother was protecting me from. It all makes sense now."

"Why didn't she just tell you?"

"I don't know. To shield me?" She lifts a shoulder, and her expression is more lost than it's been since I met her. "I'm more worried about her than ever before. If you think the King selling me off to be the second wife of his oldest political friend is bad, that's the least of it. He's evil, Ozzy, and he'll stop at nothing until he gets what he wants."

I'm getting much too comfortable with her in my arms. I need to figure out her shit, make sure she's safe from kings and disgusting old men, and then I need to get myself in check.

She's ten years younger than me.

She's a fucking princess, and I'm nothing.

Well, I am a killer.

Who am I kidding? I brought her with me on assignment so she'd see firsthand what I do. That was supposed to disgust her—to make it easier to put space between us.

And look where we are. We're wearing one set of clothes between the two of us, and I'm left wondering if she's really a virgin.

I pull her face out of my neck and frame it with my hands. "We need to eat. Then I'm going to make some phone calls. Then we're sleeping in a real fucking bed. Tomorrow, I'll have a plan."

She swallows hard and nods. I start to drop my hands and turn back to our cold steaks, but I don't get the chance.

Her arms fly around my neck where she holds tight, and every swell and curve of her body is pressed to mine. "Thank you. Thank you for everything."

I stare over her head, and pull in a deep breath. "Don't thank me yet, Princess. Our luck is shit."

Liyah

"There's nothing more I want for you than to marry for love."

"Why wouldn't I marry for love?"

She takes my hand and gives me a squeeze. Warm,

Mediterranean saltwater licks at my feet, and the warmer sun kisses my skin. With my mother beside me, nothing could be more perfect on my eighteenth birthday.

"We've had this talk, darling. I've been vague in the past, but this is what I meant when I've explained you weren't born free. Not like I was. And without the protection of your father, I fear for your future in Morocco. There are so many reasons I don't want the royal life for you, but under Hasim's rule, it's even more imperative."

I squint through my Gucci sunnies. My mother is beautiful. She always was and always will be, but I don't get to see her often. Not nearly as much as I'd like because she can rarely get away from the palace. She's aged since the last time I saw her a year ago. She's thinner and fine lines frame her face. But what's most unsettling is the hopeless despair that fills her once vibrant eyes.

I'm the perfect mix of my parents. My skin color sits between that of my mother and father on the scale of medium to dark, and I might have my father's impossibly dark eyes, but the rest of me is a replica of her—petite and a mirror of her delicate features.

"Do you regret it?" I ask.

"Regret what, love?" She stares ahead of us, down the endless beach she was able to secure for us to meet on. She didn't want anyone to know I was here and risk being close to anyone in the dynasty. She managed to convince my asshole uncle to allow her a trip to Spain. There's no way he'll allow her anywhere near the States.

"Marrying Papá. Leaving your life in Spain. Marrying into the dynasty."

I'm almost the age she was when she met my father, which changed her life forever. I'm in my freshman year at Pepperdine. I can't imagine wanting to tie myself to anyone.

For the first time since we reunited, she gives me the look I'm most familiar with—genuine and full of love. "I would sit in a dungeon for the rest of my days and never once think of trading you or my time with your father. Love has a way of getting you through the darkest of times. I'd do it all over again knowing my destiny."

"You're basically sitting in a dungeon," I bite. "Hasim is a bitter asshole. If Papá would have died in any other way than by the poison of cancer, I would have assumed his own brother killed him. I don't even know how I share the same blood as Hasim. I worry about you."

She sighs, but doesn't verbally disagree. Instead, she looks at the bright side, though I have a feeling it's only to make me feel better. "Don't worry about me. Hasim hates me and the role I played while your father was alive. But he's also politically savvy. Morocco loves me, and he knows it. Aside from curtailing my philanthropic efforts and blaming it on losing your father, he knows there would be an outcry if anything happened to me. Or if he tried to force my hand in marriage. He doesn't want to deal with that."

I yank her arm and stop us in the sand at the edge of some of the bluest waters on Earth. "You need to find a way to come to California. They can't touch you there. The Guard might rear a heavy hand in this part of the world, but not in America. I have enough money for us to live forever. Please, you need to try."

She places a light hand to my cheek. "And ruin your chance at experiencing a true college education?" *She looks down at my swimsuit—one of the more modest ones I own but still leaving very little to the imagination—and spears me with a motherly glare.* "The Guard might watch me constantly, but I do have access to social media, and you, my darling daughter, haven't held back. I know how you've been *spending your time. Hasim knows, as well. You know his stance on women and modesty. Your new modeling hobby doesn't help."*

I look down at myself and give a little curtsy in my see-through sarong that hides nothing and has no use other than being sexy as hell. "Hasim can kiss my bare ass. If he thinks women need to be modest for the sake of men's lustful thoughts, he can go right back to the dark ages where he belongs."

She leans in and places a kiss on my cheek. "I love your spirit. And I agree. But he's a selfish bastard. He thinks the way you express yourself to the world reflects on him."

I start walking again and throw my arms out before turning in a circle. "Of course, he does. Because the world revolves around him."

She joins me and laughs. "My point being, live your life in America. You're beautiful and smart and free to do as you wish. I want you to stay that way. Which is why you can never come home to the palace. I fear what Hasim will do to you—the worst being you'll never be allowed to leave."

"Can we not talk about the damn King anymore?" My mom offers me a tight smile, but her heart isn't in it, so I try to cheer her up. "I want to plan our next getaway. Maybe New Year's?"

Her gaze wanders to the vast ocean that now acts as a barrier between her home country and what has become a prison for her. "If I can convince him to allow me."

I claim her hand once again. "Come with me to California. Please."

She shakes her head. "I can't do that to your father. And right now, I'm the barrier between you and Hasim."

I squeeze her hand in mine. "Thank you for sending me away when you did. I understand now."

"As long as you choose wisely in life and only marry for love, I will consider myself a good mother."

"You're the best," I correct her. "I want to be just like you."

"Well, this has been a downer. Tell me all about the modeling and your recent fame that has the King in knots. Nothing will make me happier."

I TRY to shift in the soft bed, but I'm stuck.

Last night was surreal. Learning my uncle has basically sold me in an arranged, polygamous marriage to a disgusting old man, who plans to make me a prisoner in the country I was born in, killed my appetite for dinner.

But Ozzy has been patient and sweet—well, sort of sweet—and kept me alive, even though he didn't extend the same refuge to a certain terrorist.

I have enough on my plate right now. I refuse to think about that.

I managed a few bites of steak, and Ozzy gobbled up my leftovers like a starved man, which I guess he was after only living on cookies and cakes for two days.

I did, however, drink almost the entire bottle of wine. It's not every day one is forced to come to terms with the fact she's been promised into an arranged marriage.

But, most importantly, getting back to the whole reason for my secret travels, there is the issue of my missing mother.

Ozzy paced the aged wood floors of the posh penthouse, curtly speaking to someone named Bella. He'd stop, look out at the Eiffel Tower, ask questions about my uncle, and start pacing again. He drank two pours of bourbon—more generous than the conventional two fingers—which made me feel better about my wine consumption.

Then he made two more phone calls—one to a Jarvis and another to someone named Grady.

He did speak of this Crew fellow, who's been mentioned multiple times in the last few days, but it was only to make Jarvis and Grady promise to keep my issues on the downlow.

I was too exhausted—mentally and physically—to ask him about any of it. And that's saying something given my curious nature.

That's when I set my wine glass down and curled up on the sofa. There's only one bed, and I've slept more than Ozzy in the last few days.

The wine, mingled with my exhaustion, made my body heavy. My eyes were closed, and I was almost asleep when Ozzy took my hand and pulled me to my feet. "The bed is big and you're half my size. No one's sleeping on the sofa. It's not like you haven't already used me as a mattress once."

He was right.

I barely remember my head hitting the pillow. I have no idea how long ago that was. The room is dark with the city lights barely peeking through the cracks of the curtains.

But now I can't move. A weight, heavy and hard, is pressing me into the soft mattress. And that weight would be the man I've bet all my cards on at the moment.

I try to shift, but his hold on me tightens when he mutters, "Be still."

I'm tangled in sheets and Ozzy—warm and comfortable—even though my head is pounding from the wine.

"Ozzy," I whisper. "What are you doing?"

His voice is low and rumbly, and I feel it everywhere since I'm glued to him from head to toe.

"Trying to sleep, Princess. If you wanted my side of the bed last night, all you had to do was say so."

And that's when I realize three-quarters of the bed is empty and rumpled in front of me—the very side of the bed I started on.

I try to move, but he's just that heavy. "I'm sorry. I don't have a side of the bed."

He sighs. "I'd disagree with that since you invaded my space in the middle of the night. I had to go on defense just to get some sleep."

I tell him the truth. "I'm a restless sleeper."

His body tenses around mine and he presses into me ... everywhere. "You don't say."

He's spooning me from behind with his thick thigh thrown over my legs, and his arm is bent, angled up the front of my body with his ape hand wrapped around both my wrists like handcuffs. If he hadn't already saved my life too many times to count, I might worry about the precarious situation I've gotten myself into.

But I don't.

All I can think about at the moment is another very hard member of Ozzy's body pressed into the small of my back. It's leaving nothing to my imagination since Ozzy's T-shirt has ridden up my midsection and I'm pretty sure the only thing separating me from his erection are his boxers.

I have no clue what to do. Every time I shift, I feel it, like a red-hot iron, fresh from the fire, branding me in a way that will leave a mark forever. Because of that, I don't move a muscle.

"Ozzy," I whisper. "I should move and let you sleep."

He holds tight. "For some reason I don't believe that. I pushed you back to your side three times before giving up. If you weren't so fucking beautiful, I'd think you were a leech."

Well, now. That's sweet and embarrassing. "I'm so sorry. I should have stayed on the sofa."

He pulls me into his chest ... and other things. "Go back to sleep."

"I can't," I tell him the truth. "Once I'm up, I'm up."

"Then be quiet, so I can sleep."

"I should move, and let you ... um..."

"Let me what?"

Shit.

"Look, my uncle might be auctioning me off as a virgin, but I'm no idiot." I arch and press into his groin. "If you need to take care of that, I can leave the room. That can't be comfortable."

He groans, and I feel that in his cock too. But then again, right now, his thick, long cock is all I can think about. "I don't know what you're talking about. Blue balls are pretty fucking comfortable."

My eyes widen. There's nothing I want to do more than roll and look into his to see if he's giving me shit or if blue balls really are a folklore used to ensnare women into having sex. "Are you serious?"

He buries his face in my hair, and mumbles, "No, Princess. I'm so far from serious, I might as well be swimming in a black ocean. And you talking about my dick doesn't make it any better."

I tell him the truth about something that's been

bothering me. "I really don't like it when you call me *princess*."

"Well, you talking about my morning wood when I can't do anything about it after you attached yourself to me like a spider monkey in the middle of the night isn't exactly my kind of party. I think we're even."

I bite my lip, but can't help myself. "Does it actually hurt? Like real pain?"

"You've got to be fucking kidding me," he mumbles.

"Well, they say it does, but I've never asked anyone."

"That's not something you ask. You Google that shit. And you really don't ask a man that after you slept in his arms and he's harder than fuck and can't do anything about it."

I turn my hands out of his grip, and he finally lets go of my wrists. I hold his forearm and pull it to my chest. "I'm really curious."

"So you turn my world on end, I agree to help you find your mom, and this is how you thank me? This is pure torture, Princess."

I arch and press into him harder this time. "Again with the *princess*."

He one ups me, and really presses his groin into me, his long, muscled leg getting in on the action, pulling me to him. "You're something."

"Tell me," I demand. But because I'm desperate, I add, "Please."

He hesitates, then shifts me to my back. I grasp just how far I traveled through the night, and I bet he's been hanging onto his edge of the bed for dear life. We might as well be sleeping in half of a twin bed instead of sharing a king.

Ozzy looks down at me with tight eyes, and I

wonder if they have anything to do with the color of his balls. "You really want to know?"

His lips are mere inches from mine, his chest bare, and the topic of conversation is now pressed against my hip. My panties are drenched, and the thought he's in his current state because of me is...

Exciting.

"Imagine you've traveled through the darkest and coldest storm. Through feet of snow, uphill, into frigid winds. But you know when you get to the end, there's a reward." He leans in as close as he can, shy of his full lips brushing mine, and I have a hard time finding oxygen. He's so close, his words don't just feather my skin, they sink into my soul. "And that reward is a bath. Magical and euphoric. Hot. Wet. Deep. Something you dive into, that heals the pains that the cold winds created, so that finally, after your long-ass fucking journey from hell, you feel nothing but relief in every cell of your body."

My head spins. "Really?"

"Yes," he bites, and goes on. "But when you get to that bath, it's not wet or hot. It's nothing but ice. And it hurts, Liyah. It fucking hurts after the long, cold journey."

My chest is rising and falling with short breaths. His words make me want to dip my finger between my legs, but given his expression, that's probably not a good idea.

Instead, I whisper, "I'm sorry."

"Do you always travel around the bed the same way you travel Europe?"

I tip my head and lift my shoulder a centimeter,

because I'm not in the habit of sleeping with anyone. "I don't know."

His nod is slow and laborious as his gaze travels down my body. I don't move to yank his shirt down farther. I might not be used to sleeping with anyone, but I am used to people looking at me. I've been modeling off and on for years now.

His pained blues travel back to my face. "I'm going to get up now and jump in that tub of ice."

"Um ... okay."

He exhales and doesn't move. Instead he stares at me as if he's trying to decide if he should throw me over the balcony to be done with me once and for all, or ravish me so he can avoid the ice.

"Yeah," he agrees, but it feels like he's mocking me. "*Okay.*"

When he gets up, I can't take my eyes off his very erect cock, and I wonder what he's going to do about it.

I roll to my stomach, pull a pillow over my head, and wonder if there's such a thing as pink balls for ladies.

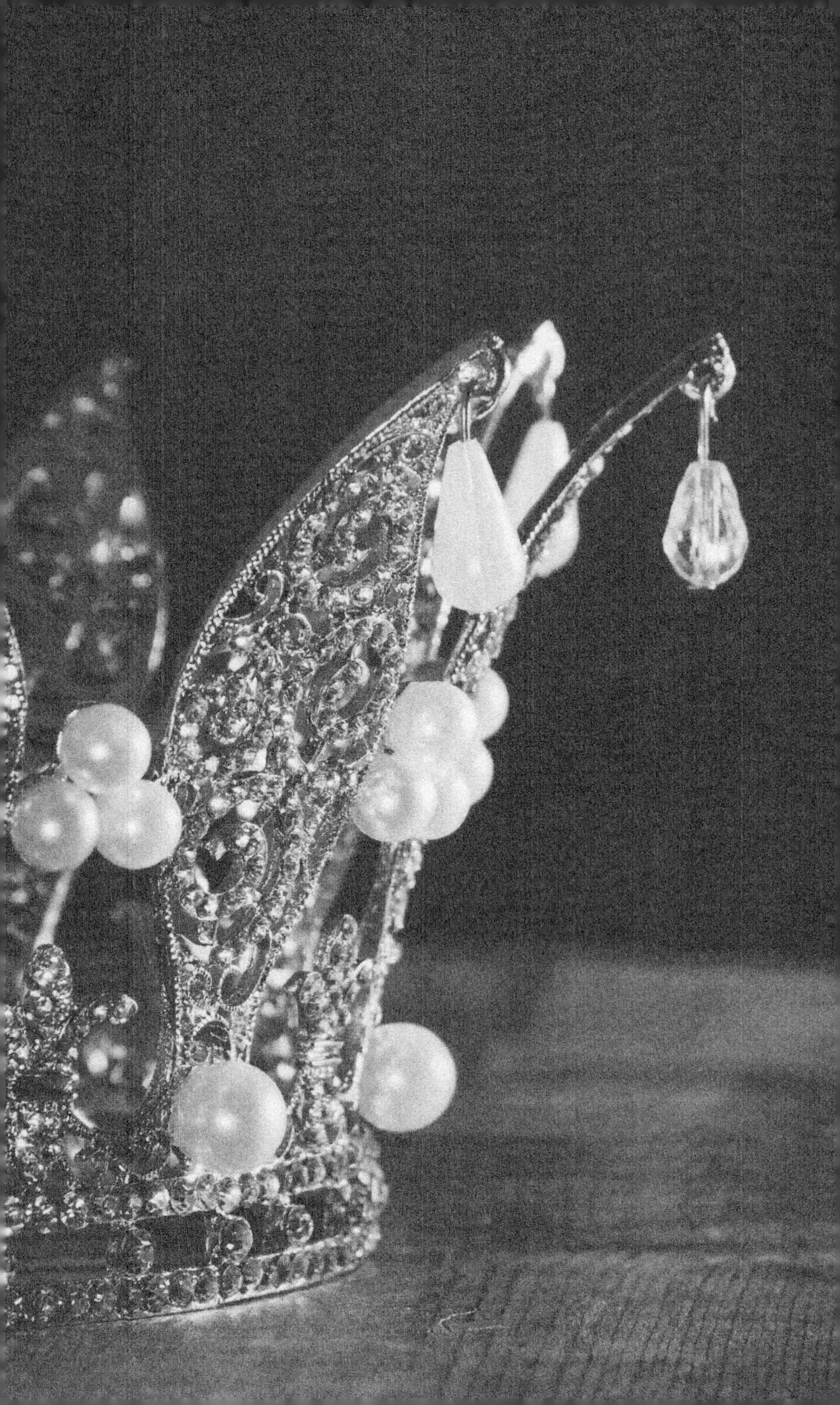

13

FUCK IT

Ozzy

Traveling with an internationally known princess with millions of followers on multiple social media outlets does not come without its struggles.

It's not like I don't have my own issues being recognized, but not in Europe, and especially not in Africa or Asia. My life might not have turned out like I thought it would, but at least I don't have to hide under a rock in most parts of the world.

I only have to do that in parts of the world that I'm actually from. Where I've lived and worked.

Just one more reason I don't have a home and avoid returning to Crew's base camp as much as possible.

Needing to get out of that damn penthouse has nothing to do with the fact I feed off fresh air, and I fucking hate being cooped up. No. Today it had everything to do with the way my blood churns for Princess Aliyah Zahir.

It's been a long fucking time.

Too long.

When I came in the shower with my hand wrapped around my dick harder and more desperate than I remember, I realized it's not about time or the solitary life I've lived since I started working for Crew Vega.

It's just fucking her.

Nothing has been more maddening, and if I'm honest with myself, soul-crushing.

And seeing as how my soul is all I've got left in this life I've been forced into living as a dead man walking, I'm not sure the situation could be more dire.

For me or my cock.

And if all that isn't bad enough, Liyah asking me in detail about my cock pushed me over an edge I was hanging on to with bleeding fingertips.

I needed to get out of the penthouse, and since there's no way I'm allowing my royal out of my sight, I brought her with me.

We need to kill time, at least a day or more. From the intel I gathered from the royal guard of Morocco when I woke this morning, they're pinging Liyah's phone. Seems the National Security Agency isn't the only entity illegally tapping into private information without a warrant.

Liyah's young and may be a virgin—which has not one damn thing to do with anything, other than it toys with my cock and carnal thoughts—but she's smart. She traveled all this way on her own without her cell. The Princess was in awe when I opened a program on my laptop and started moving her cell from tower to tower. Today she's traveling from LA to LaGuardia, and tomorrow she might go to Canada, when in reality, she'll be safe and sound—by my side.

Take that, you big, fat, old, hairy fuck who is getting antsy for the woman curious about my cock.

"Where are you from in America?"

"The country."

"That's a big area."

I look down when I hear a smile in her voice. She's peeking up at me from under the brim of my ball cap that I stuffed on her head. I don't need anyone to recognize her. She's back in her big, oversized clothes, thanks to the washer and dryer in the penthouse.

It shouldn't feel right to give her a part of me, but it does. She's not a threat.

I mean, she is. Just not that kind of threat.

I shift her bags from one hand to another so I can put my hand to her back to move her through a small group standing around a street vendor. "Pennsylvania."

She falls back to my side as we walk. When I told her we were going out to clear my head, she asked if she could pick up some things, since two outfits are not enough to travel the world. Once we were out, it wasn't that busy, so I followed her through three stores until I put a stop to that shit—not because it wasn't safe, but because it was miserable. She still made use of her time and bought a ton of shit. I have no clue how she's going to schlep it around with her if we start running around the globe again. "So, you're a country-boy, can manipulate cell phones from around the world, and kill terrorists in your spare time?"

"Not my spare time," I correct her. "I do it all the time. In my spare time, it seems I act as a bodyguard for royalty on the run."

"Royalty..." She lets that word hang in the air while she contemplates it. "I haven't felt like royalty in a long time. At least, not in the way I was born."

"I can't figure you out, Liyah."

"I can't figure myself out most days, either."

"You don't want a part of that life. The official part, but you don't seem to mind the princess part when you're torturing me in a mall spending your fortunes in cash." It's a guess based purely on her social-media history and the fact she doesn't seem excited to be in a polygamous marriage to a dirty old man.

"No. Not the way it is now. I was only a girl when my father died. I didn't realize how differently he ruled, especially compared to my uncle who followed him. As an adult, I see it. Hasim has moved the country back decades in many ways. He doesn't respect women, and his actions show it. He says one thing and does another."

We approach another group, so I use it as an excuse to grab her hand and pull her close, pushing the thought of her damn uncle and his plans for her out of my head. Imagining her at the hands of anyone right now, a grandpa or otherwise, makes my brain boil to the point my head might explode from feelings I do not fucking recognize.

Or even like.

But there they are, front and center. And they have me seeing red.

I change the subject. "Something is bothering me."

She doesn't move away or let go of my hand. "What?"

"Your uncle can't marry you off to anyone with that big dowry if you're dead."

"No."

"Then why would they try to kill you on the train?"

She follows my lead as I turn the corner to head back to the penthouse. We'll grab food on the way back. "At the time, I had no idea he was planning an arranged marriage for me. You're right, it doesn't make sense."

"It doesn't, and the more I think about it, the more it bothers me. And there's no chatter in the transcripts from the last few days about the train. I'm sure the King would be bragging about that shit to someone by now. Your uncle has a big head."

"That he does," she mutters.

I'm about to ask more, but my phone vibrates.

I put it to my ear and pull Liyah to a stop. "Bella. Did you find anything?"

Bella Donnelly Carson was MI6 before that went to hell in a heartbeat. She was in hiding for years and worked unofficially for Crew. When that hell blew up a few years ago, her now husband, CIA Officer Cole Carson, and Crew's entire team stepped up. Her shit tiptoed eerily close to my past—too close for comfort if you ask me. She had no desire to return to Vauxhall and works full time for Crew when he expanded his business into information, which was right up my alley. Finding information, turning that information into knowledge to work for you—or against you—is what I've always been best at.

I need Bella and her contacts in that part of the world to work for me right now.

"I haven't located the Princess's mum, but I have learned more about the current regime and their feelings toward her. Ozzy, it's not good, and with what you've shared with me already, the young woman has every right to be fearful."

I pull Liyah around with our connected hands until she's flush with my chest and hold her to me. I look down into her endless dark eyes. "I figured. What else?"

"Princess Luciana—though she was stripped of her title a few years back—was last seen at the border of Morocco and Algeria. My source has a cousin who works on the grounds crew. Apparently the palace has acted as a prison for Luciana the last two years, and she hasn't been allowed to leave. Hasim has slowly pushed her into the shadows. She hasn't been photographed with the royal family in at least a year. My gut tells me this is not an accident, but rather strategic and planned for some time. The King was not friendly with his brother before his death and hated that he elevated his wife to such a prominent role in the dynasty."

"I traced that call when she left a voicemail for Liyah. It came from the palace. She must have made that call before she escaped."

Liyah's head pops up, and she looks up at me in a gaze of shock. She tries to push away from me, but my arm around her back holds tight.

Shit. I haven't had to manage someone else's emotions in a long time. And when it comes to the seriousness of this, *long time* equates to never fucking ever.

I need to work on that.

"I've studied the transcripts you downloaded. There hasn't been any new chatter that's at all helpful. I know you've been busy and are probably catching up on sleep, and whatever else you do when you're gone, but step it up, Ozzy. Give them something to talk about."

I look down at the woman standing in my arms. A

young woman, but a woman all the same, and think of all the ways I'd like to give them something to chatter about.

I should hand it over to Bella. Let her husband, Carson, work on this shit. He's the CIA agent. Jarvis still works from time to time. I could feed him the information and let him find Liyah's mom.

What I should not be doing is putting myself out there. I can't afford to. Unlike the rest of Crew's team, I have the most to lose.

I should stay in my fucking invisible lane.

Maybe it's because it's been so long since I've been more than an associate to anyone. More than a coworker, a third wheel, fifth wheel ... hell, even an eleventh wheel at times. That the only people I have in my life are those I work for and with.

And because I haven't had balance in my life in years.

I'm not letting go of the Princess, and I'm sure as hell not going to allow anyone else to handle her shit. Because I know, without a doubt, no one is better suited for the job than me.

And I'm talking everything—technical and physical—not just acting as her bodyguard.

"Yeah," I agree, never letting her go and not looking away from her haunted dark eyes. "We'll give them something to talk about."

"Indeed." I hear a smile in her English accent. "However, a wee bit of a heads-up. I feel as if I owe it to you. Crew demanded to know why you're not home yet. Let's just say, there's nothing sacred in this organization. He knows you have a guest. You might want to give the boss a ring soon."

"Shit."

Liyah grips my shirt, and I don't hate it. I give her a quick shake of my head, and I feel her body exhale against my cock, which swells just enough to tell me how much he likes it.

"Not shit," Bella explains. "Crew worries, so his concern comes from the best place possible. The men have your back. Just ring him, yes?"

"I'll call when I have time. Right now, I've got a plan to put in motion."

"Let me know what I can do."

"Thanks, Bella."

"I do hope you bring her home. I've never met a real-life princess before."

"We'll see."

"Stay safe, Ozzy."

I don't say goodbye and disconnect.

"What was that about?" Liyah asks. "And what did they say about my mother?"

I wrap both arms around her as we stand here on a Paris sidewalk, off the main drag and away from tourists. We're in my favorite part of Paris, where local shops and restaurants rule and hidden gems are the norm. A place where I live out in the open and don't worry about anyone spotting me.

"Bella works with me. She was MI6 in her prior life and is now married to a CIA officer. She has sources far and wide. Your mom was spotted at the border of Algeria. She escaped. When she left you that message, she was still at the palace."

Her weight falls into my chest, and I enjoy it more than I should in her current state of worry. "I don't know whether that's a good thing or not."

I let my hand drag up her back and into her hair. "Do you trust me? With everything?"

Her teeth sink into the plump flesh of her bottom lip.

"You can trust me, Princess."

She exhales and hesitates a few beats.

Then, she nods.

I mirror her agreement, pushing away any and all reservations that have every right to settle in my gut. I have no business doing what I'm about to set in motion, but sometimes, you've just gotta say fuck it.

If anyone has earned the right to say that, it's me.

"All right then, baby. Let's get started."

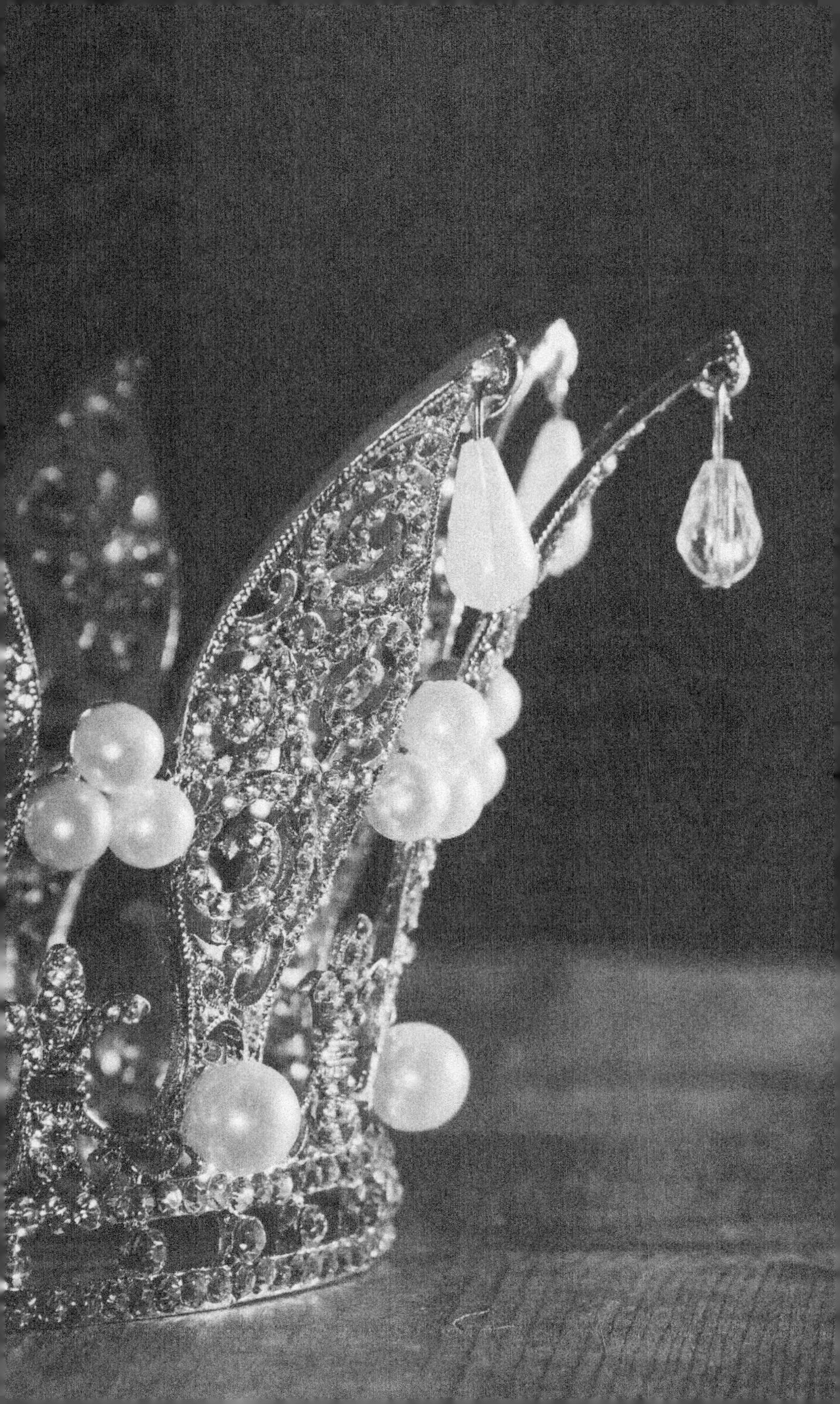

14

GOLDEN HOUR

Liyah

I look down at my hand. It's heavy with the burden that sits there staring up at me, no matter how beautiful and striking, and not at all what I ever thought I'd want, let alone like.

A single solitaire in an emerald cut. It's perched high on the most delicate band, embedded with tiny diamonds so bright, it will no doubt shine through the internet and gain the attention of everyone—those I don't care about and others whose attention I need more than anything at this moment.

Ozzy slides his cell to me on the island. "Do your thing. I'll upload the post. I can drop it to ping from where we need it to."

I look away from the impossibly simple, yet elegant diamond Ozzy slid on my finger in the small jewelry shop he whisked me to the moment I agreed to trust him with everything. "Do my thing?"

He shrugs like this sort of thing isn't well-planned

and thought out. As if one doesn't have to strategize around algorithms and prime posting time, or require perfectly edited photographs. The brute man actually thinks I can upload a snapshot to the internet of a diamond on my left ring finger, and expect it to go viral in a way that will reach even the King.

"What's wrong? We talked about this."

"You talked about this. I understand your philosophy, Ozzy. But it's not that easy. And I've never even tiptoed near a serious relationship, let alone been close enough to one for an engagement. You're mad in the head if you think this can be done in a matter of minutes."

"Fine. What do you need?"

"My followers are perceptive and keen. If this is going to do what's needed, it must be genuine and real. They need to feel the love." I pull in a breath. "Not just love, Ozzy. Lust. Passion." I look over at him again and he's lost the cocky smirk he's been sporting since he paid for this ridiculously expensive spur-of-the-moment purchase. His mouth parts, and I barely see his tongue wet the crease of his lips, as if he can taste the rambling words falling from my mouth. "I've built an image, and it's not a modest one, thanks to modeling. If we want this to work, it has to be done with a bang."

"A bang," he echoes.

"Yes," I tell him the truth, doing everything I can to bat away the butterflies tickling my insides. I ignore the diamond searing my left ring finger, as if Ozzy branded me himself rather than simply spending a fortune for a ruse I'm supposed to manufacture on social media. With my hands on my hips, I spin in a slow circle, contemplating where to start.

Going to the French doors that reach the ceiling that goes on forever, I open them as wide as they'll go.

"Princess, I told you you're supposed to make it look like you're anywhere but Paris. Unless you can make the real thing look like the shitty replica in Vegas, I suggest you shut the doors."

"If you want me to do this, then shut your mouth, Ozzy, and trust me for a change." I yank the white linen panels over the open doors. They flutter and move in the breeze with light filtering through, but it's opaque enough no one will know we're in the most romantic city in the world.

It's getting late in the day, and I'll lose the natural light. I should know, I've been through this too many times with irritable managers and skilled photographers in Southern California. Being bossed into perfection when the light is at its peak is when I've done my best work.

Letting the pressure take over, I hurry to the bathroom to dig through my backpack. I didn't bring much with me, but carrying a tube of mascara in every bag I own isn't unheard of. I do my best to ignore the man standing behind me in the mirror and coat my lashes with as much as they'll shoulder. I can get away with no makeup, but I might as well be naked without mascara.

My insides quake at the thought of being naked.

"You think this is all necessary to take a picture of you wearing a ring for the world to see?"

My irritated gaze shoots to him in the mirror. "Do you want the King's attention or not?"

Finally, he holds his hands up, palms to me, and gives in. I twist my mascara shut, throw it to the vanity, and rip the band out of my hair. Looking in the mirror, I shake out the layers with my fingers. The last thing I need is to look perfect. Rumpled is what I need.

And ... flushed.

After I flip my head up and down to give myself instant sexed hair, I pull in a big breath when I look at myself in the mirror.

Well.

Flushed will not be an issue.

I just hope I can pull this off without being a total and utter bumbling idiot.

I don't think twice when I push down the baggy pants I'm sick of, and reach for one of the shopping bags from today. I decide these will do, and yank the cutoff shorts over my ass. Denim. It's the most normal I've felt since I packed for my hellish journey.

I hurry back to the family room with Ozzy close on my heels. I grab his cellphone and toss it to him. "Unlock this, please."

He does as I ask and hands it back to me. I have the camera pulled up and flip through the settings until I find what I need. Then I prop it on about five teetering accessories so it's framing nothing but the billowy curtains.

"Shit." I look from the window to Ozzy. "We're almost out of time."

He looks confused. "Why?"

I jut my thumb over my shoulder. "The Golden Hour. Take your shirt off."

"What?" He cocks his head and his confusion hits its max. "Why?"

I say to him what he put on me earlier, but I'm not nearly as smooth or sexy. I'm flustered and bossy. "Just do it, dammit. Trust me."

"I can't be in any picture, Liyah. That's nonnegotiable."

I throw my diamond-leaded hand between us. "If you think I can take a picture of myself and expect almost two million people to believe me, you're crazier than I thought you were when you jumped out of that train window. I need a man in the picture and you're the only one available at the moment."

He sighs. "But not my face."

"Fine. Your rugged features will remain private for my eyes only."

He reaches over his head for his shoulder blades and yanks. This isn't the first time I've seen him without a shirt. His loose sweatpants sit casually on his hips, as if hugging such a beautiful being isn't the big deal it is. His underwear band winks at me, and I have to steel my spine when my eyes go to the V pointing to the cock I asked too many questions about earlier.

I exhale. "Okay, then."

I move to his cell and hit record on the video.

"I thought you were taking a picture?"

I turn to face him and I cross my arms, reaching for the hem of my tank. I rip it up and over my head.

Thankful for my darker skin, I heat from the inside out as Ozzy's eyes follow my movements like a hawk who hasn't eaten in days. I drop my tank on the back of the sofa that's framed in the edge of the video. I look up at the man who's done nothing but take charge since I met him on this crazy expedition I set out on, alone and scared.

I'm definitely not alone now.

Scared?

For my mother, yes.

But with Ozzy?

I don't know what I am.

My hand takes his, and I turn us so his back is to the camera.

"I'll make sure the ring is front and center, but I need you to do the rest."

His hand squeezes mine, causing his bicep to flex.

"What exactly would *the rest* be, Princess?"

Ozzy

I'VE NEVER SHELLED out that much money at one time for anything. It doesn't matter how fat my bank accounts are now that I work for Crew. I'm a simple man and always have been. It has everything to do with growing up on a farm in the middle of Pennsylvania. When I was hired by the NSA and moved to Maryland, I couldn't afford a down payment on an outhouse, let alone a home of my own.

Then my world went to shit.

I travel ninety percent of the time, and there's no reason to own anything when it's just me.

I've never even shelled out that much for a car, but I sure did on the ring I slid on her finger. I didn't even question it. Maybe, subconsciously, I did it just for the experience of doing it.

It won't happen any other time or any other way. Now I can say I did it, even if it means nothing.

"Just," she holds her arms up, wiggles her fingers—the ring I paid a mint for glinting in her *golden hour*—

and she pulls in a deep breath making her tits rise and fall in her lacy bra. "Come here."

She doesn't need to ask me twice.

I cut through the thick air as quick as I can, because my dick is halfway to hard, and put my hands low on her hips that are covered in the shortest shorts that barely cover her ass. She reaches for my shoulders, but gives her head a little shake. "I can't reach your hair."

I've had enough. "Tell me the end goal, Princess. I'll make it happen."

"An embrace," she spits quicker than I expected. "So I can focus on the ring. If you don't want your face to be seen then ... I don't know, tip your head down. I think I can make that work."

"This will get the attention you need?"

"For sure. If I know anything, I know that."

"And you want this?"

Her tits heave again, and the word comes out rushed. "Yes."

I lift my chin.

"We're running out of light," she whispers.

I don't let her say another word. My hands already on her hips tighten, and I lift. She lets out a surprised squeak, but I don't stop and her legs round my hips like they were meant to live there forever. She wraps her arms around my neck and we're as close as we were in bed this morning when she was asking how painful it was to be this close to her knowing I can't have her.

Now I'm going to experience that all over again.

Our noses brush, and I ask, "You good?"

She slides a hand up my neck and into the back of my hair, but says nothing. Instead, she shifts her legs and presses her pussy into my abs. I slide one hand down to her ass to hold her steady and the other disappears into her hair. I tip her head back and run my nose up the side of her neck.

"Is this what you want?"

She takes another breath, and I know it's deep, because her tits heave farther north, so close to my lips. My mouth waters, and I can't help it, I squeeze her ass.

She lets out a moan.

I'm going to assume that isn't an act since no one will hear it on a screenshot.

I've wanted to know what her beautiful skin tastes like since the moment she put her hand in mine to jump out the window of a fucking train. When I take my first lap across her collarbone, my roots singe. Her grip on my hair alone is enough to bring me to full mast, and for the second time today, my balls will be the color of the Mediterranean at high noon on a cloudless day.

I'm all out of fucks at the moment. When I put my lips to her neck and suck, her moan turns to a whimper, and she presses her pussy into me harder.

She's a ball of sexual tension—wound so tight I'm afraid she might burst into a million pieces and fall through my greedy fingers. My heart races from the taste of her sweet skin alone. But listening to her quick and shallow breaths?

I forget about everything.

About her mom.

The fucking King.

The disgusting, ancient fuckwad who thinks he's going to buy her, make her his second wife, and steal her virginity.

And, for just a second, I forget about the fact I have no life and nothing to offer her.

I tilt her head to mine and take her mouth. When I press my tongue between her lips, her body convulses around mine. I can't take it any longer.

All it takes is three steps and her back hits the wall. The evening breeze and white linen blow at our sides when I press my dick through our clothes and into her pussy.

Fucking clothes. I hate them more than I hate anything right now, and since there's a shit ton I hate in the world, that's saying a lot.

I can't get enough, and slide my hand under her ass, cupping her. When I press in, her lips go slack and she fights for a breath.

"Liyah—" I start but bite back my words when her head hits the wall and she presses into my hand.

Sweet. Beautiful. And still, I have to assume, as pure as the fresh driven snow.

She rocks her hips against my hold, and I lean to bite the edge of her bra and drag it down. Her tit pops out—full, but not big, with a nipple so hard and tight, it's begging me for attention.

I rub her pussy harder through her shorts and do everything I can to ignore my dick. Instead, I wrap my lips around her nipple and suck.

"Ozzy. Oh—"

I pull her between my lips harder, her nipple tight between my teeth, before letting her go with a pop. I don't want to stop. I'm also trying to decide which part of her tastes the best. But I'd bet what little life I have left that she's about to come, and I won't miss this for anything.

She draws her knees up and presses down onto my hand, her thighs tight on my sides. She's stronger than she looks. And when it comes right down to it, I bet her will is as strong as steel.

I look into her hooded, dark eyes, bleeding with lust and desperation.

My voice is low and demanding. "I want you to tell me something."

Her lips part, and her brows pucker.

"Are you a virgin?"

Her eyes close, and she stops moving, but I take over. Pressing, rubbing, even sliding a finger into her shorts to find her panties drenched.

She says nothing.

"You are," I answer for her. It's a guess, an educated one. If I'm wrong, color me stupid.

She drags her eyes open and bites her lip. There it is. I'm right.

I tell her what's going to happen, because right now, her body is begging for it and she's made no move to stop me. "I'm going to make you come, baby. Has anyone ever done that for you before?"

I dip my finger inside her panties this time. My index finger has no trouble sliding through her pussy and swiping her clit. It's enough to make her call out, but she doesn't tell me what I want to know.

"Answer me," I demand. "Has anyone ever touched you here?" I slide a finger inside her. Tight does not begin to explain what I find. I give her clit more pressure. Then a circle. Then I play with her pussy lips. "Has anyone ever done this?"

She fights it and wants it at the same time, which all but answers my question.

"Liyah—" I start to demand again, but she interrupts.

"No." That one word might as well be a gift worth more than her fortunes and a bucket of ice water.

For me that is.

Because, now I know.

"Look at me, baby."

Her heated gaze hits me. I press my lips to hers and pump a finger where no one's been but me. "You want more?"

Her teeth sink into her bottom lip, and she nods once.

I give her a second finger, stretching her, filling her, and keep at her clit. She exhales, and her lungs beg for a breath.

"There you go, baby. Breathe, but move. You can find it. Do what feels good."

She starts to move her hips. It's fucking amazing other than the feeling it stirs in my dick, which I don't need since he won't get any action. Her fingers thread my hair again, pulling me close.

If I could rip these damn shorts off her I would.

I tip my forehead to hers with our noses side by side, and breathe in everything she'll give me.

"Let go, Princess."

And she does. Her body sings as it squeezes mine. Her pussy convulses on my hand. And I might have two bald spots on the back of my head when this is all said and done.

I'll deal.

Because watching her come for the first time is nothing short of a religious experience.

She's a goddess.

My own personal, royal goddess.

And knowing what I know now, I'm not sure how I'll move on.

Because there's nowhere to go. Not for me anyway.

With her still impaled on my fingers, her pussy sopping wet for me, and her body wrapped around mine the way I'm beginning to be obsessed with, this pisses me off.

And I've got the whole thing on video to torment me forever, reminding me of my dead-end life.

This is going to be complicated.

"Fuck."

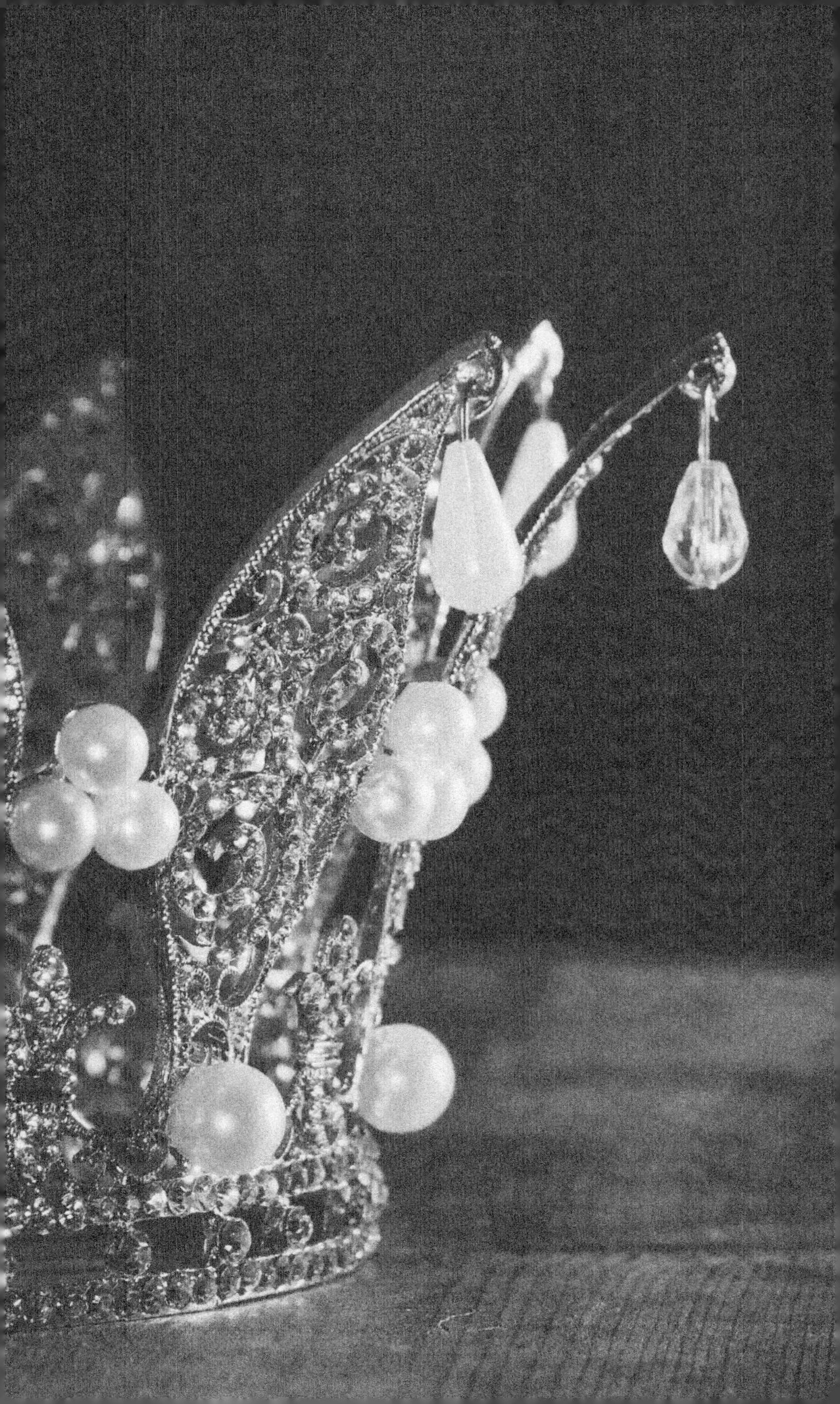

15

ANGRY

Liyah

I don't know why some people think social media is hard. I can gain the attention of my followers easily. Like a perfectly crafted cocktail tweaked for the current season, it's nothing but an equation with a splash of art to make it your own.

One doesn't have one point nine million followers without a few posts going viral.

I've had more than a few.

My mom would *tsk* me for some of the things I would post. Nudity will get you shadow-banned—or just sometimes thrown into the social media clink. Plus, nudity is boring. Everyone knows what the human body looks like.

But the hint of a naked body?

That stirs the masses like a second coming.

And, that's what happened.

Right after a simple photoshoot with Ozzy got out of hand.

Correction... After watching the video to create a simple screenshot to show the world I'm newly engaged, *out of hand* is the understatement of the century.

My social media footprint is not chaste or G-rated, and this post fits my brand to a T.

From here until the end of my days, I'll refer to it as *the post*. It's turning out to be that epic.

As far as the world knows, I'm naked besides the enormous ring on my finger

Ozzy's back muscles are defined in the perfect light—cut, chiseled, and a work of art.

My bare arms and legs are wrapped around him.

My head is thrown back and to the side.

My lips are parted.

My hair screams sex.

The white backdrop, shadows, and late-evening rays are blurred in the background.

And just as I instructed, Ozzy's face is tilted down, his identity hidden. The screenshot captures the moment he dragged his tongue along my skin for the first time. The sensation was so intoxicating, it was then that I lost myself. The moment I forgot about why I'm here, my end goal, and where I came from.

I wish I could go back to that moment and never leave.

Under the most epic picture I've ever posted, reads:

Forever with you can't come soon enough.

Then I hashtagged the shit out of that post.

It's perfect. My followers are eating it up. At least, I

think they are from the emojis I see. I haven't read my comments for years. They can be toxic, and I don't need toxicity in my life.

Hundreds of thousands of reactions and even more comments keep racking up.

All of this should matter. It's the end goal, after all. And if this doesn't get the attention of the damn King and his minions, nothing will.

The picture that was supposed to be fake, turned into so much more. Emotion bleeds from its perfection, because at the moment it happened, it was real.

Until it ended.

After Ozzy gave me my first earth-shattering orgasm that was not created by my own touch or the single toy I own, he set me on my feet and moved away as if I were hot lava.

Then he went to his phone, tapped on the screen about five million times, and handed it over without a glance. "Here. Let me know when you're ready to post so I can make sure your cell pings where we need it to."

And that was it.

Since then, he's had his head buried in his laptop.

If ghosting a person in the same room is a thing, then he's done it to me.

That was hours ago.

It's late, and I've had enough.

Enough of his silent treatment.

Enough of his regret.

I set his phone down on the marble, and since we're not speaking, I stalk silently through the bedroom to the bathroom. I wonder how many women Ozzy brings here, because the vanity is fully stocked with anything and everything a woman needs. And not travel-sized products or ones from a drugstore. They're the best French products money can buy. I should know, I've purchased many of them myself.

But the thought of who these might belong to creates a pit in my gut that sours the small dinner I scrounged up in the kitchen while Ozzy did a bang-up job of ignoring me.

After washing my face and moisturizing with another woman's things, I brush my teeth and crawl into the big bed, pushing back memories of how I woke up this morning.

I would curl up on the sofa and pretend nothing happened if he wasn't sitting in the middle of it tapping away.

Tap.

Tap.

Tappity-tap-tap.

They might as well be bombs dropping in the posh, Paris apartment. The silence is deafening, and I can't take it. I'd do anything for shit TV or music to lose myself in for hours.

But far be it for me to interrupt his busy work, which feels like it's for the sole purpose of ignoring me.

I move to my side of the bed and will myself to stay here all night. I can't make a fool of myself again. I might be inexperienced when it comes to sex, but I'm not stupid. I do have experience when it comes to men in general. The opposite sex might think they're cunning and smooth, but from my experience, they're transparent and shallow. At least the ones I gave half a chance to since I moved to America. The boys in college are no different than the men I worked with when I dabbled in modeling. They were interested in my body, my royal status, or the fortune they assumed my status came with, and not always in that order.

My mother taught me to be on guard. I took every word of her sage advice to heart. Friends would say I took it too seriously, but I've never had my heart broken by a frat boy like they have, so I always considered myself a winner.

Until tonight.

Ozzy's made it clear where I stand when the angry *fuck* fell from his lips while I was still impaled on his hand. It was dredged in regret and dipped in anger, proving my intuition is as sharp as a dull, rusty knife.

The tapping stops, and Ozzy bangs around in the kitchen before lights click off in the great room, one by one.

He follows my steps to the bathroom through the dark shadows. He's not worried about waking me, making more noise than he did in the kitchen. Water running, a flush, and more water running happen before the bed dips behind me.

When he sighs, I remember how his hot breath felt on my skin when he took over my body. I curl into my side tighter and hug the pillow.

"Liyah—" he bites, but I don't allow him to go on. I have no desire to hear what he has to say.

"It's fine." I sit up and reach for my pillow. "I'll sleep on the sofa. I should've done that last night."

One foot barely hits the floor when my T-shirt is pulled from behind. "No, you don't."

I fall back, and Ozzy's big hand—that I really don't

want to think about right now—splays on my stomach and yanks me back to the middle of the bed.

"Stop it," I bite.

"You're not sleeping on the couch."

"I damn well am." I pull at his arm, but he's too strong. My back is glued to his front, and we're both as tense as a virgin. Which I am, and he now knows the private fact about me because he demanded the information when he had me in a vulnerable state. A state I was peachy fucking keen to be in at the time, but now I'm pissed.

"Stop it, Liyah."

"Quit telling me to *stop it*. You stop it. I'm not sleeping here."

"I need you to be still for one fucking second so I can talk to you."

"Really? Now you want to talk to me? You just spent the last few hours acting as if I weren't here. I had no idea someone could ghost me and still be in the same damn room. But, congratulations, you did it."

I not only hear it, but feel the sigh that really sounds like a low growl.

Lord. Men can be so dramatic.

"I did not ghost you, Liyah."

"You really are dense. After what we did..." I swallow over the lump in my throat and force myself to steel my spine. "After what happened ... what you demanded to know about me ... you don't acknowledge my existence in the same small space for hours? If that's not ghosting, then I give up on life."

He pushes me to my back and throws a bare, heavy thigh over my legs. Holy hell, he's down to his boxers again. I ignore his almost-naked state and focus on his broody face. It pisses me off, because if anyone in this apartment has the right to be broody, it's not him, it's me.

He pulls in an angry breath. "Your post did what we wanted it to do."

The broody melts from my body. "What do you mean?"

"I mean the King is pissed. It took all of five minutes after you posted that for the chatter to begin. Botros is throwing a fit and threatening your uncle with political retaliation for his empty promises." Ozzy's face hardens further. "I'm not sure you understand how much he's looking forward to taking a second wife, but even more, that wife being you, Princess. He didn't like your naked body being wrapped around another man, and he really didn't like what it implied."

"They're talking. That's what we wanted to happen, right?"

My breath catches when he drags his hand up my body and between my breasts, landing on the side of my face. His stare bores into me when he lowers his voice. "I think you underestimate how much I really fucking hate your uncle. And just when I thought I couldn't hate anyone more, that disgusting fuck started talking about you. I might lose my shit. And Princess, I don't lose my shit. Ever."

I frown. "You don't?"

"No."

"What did he say?"

"You don't want to know."

My frown deepens. "I have a right to know."

His jaw goes hard and he hesitates.

"Ozzy," I demand. "Tell me."

He shakes his head once, but gives in. "He's still

willing to take you as a wife, despite the fact, and I quote, *your body has been used and he won't be the one to make you bleed*."

I gasp.

"Yeah," Ozzy agrees. "The asshole reduced his offer. The King threw a royal fit and is willing to do all kinds of shady shit to get you back. He thinks if he can get you to Morocco, he can make this happen."

My eyes fall shut.

"Princess," he calls.

I open my eyes and shake my head. "My father is the one who would have a royal fit if he knew this was happening. Not only because I'm his daughter, but because this is not modern-day Morocco. Sure, I've heard things like this happen in the shadows and behind closed doors. Bad things happen all over the world. But this is not what he wanted for his country."

"There's more," Ozzy adds. "About your mom."

My fingers grip his biceps and I don't let go.

"The King is sure he could've lured you back with the promise of seeing your mom. But the most important piece of information we gathered from the entire shitshow of a transcript, is how pissed your uncle is that your mom *escaped*."

My eyes sting, and my heart swells. "So she did escape?"

His thumb brushes my bottom lip, and he softens his tone. "He confirmed what we assumed. He thinks she had help. Do you know who that could be?"

I lift a shoulder. "I'd have to think. It could be so many people, yet I'm not sure how many would risk their lives to work against the dynasty. He gets what he wants and is neither fair nor just. That's an enormous risk."

"I get that. And to think you were going to waltz your ass back into Morocco by yourself to look for her. What were you thinking?"

"How was I supposed to know he was selling me off to a disgusting old man? That's basically sex trafficking."

"Not basically," he corrects. "It fucking is."

"Fine. I didn't know, but now I do. That would have literally been a nightmare." Ozzy plops down on the pillow next to me, and I roll to my side to face him. "I'm grateful. Really, I am. But this doesn't help me find my mother. At least I know she escaped, and my uncle didn't do anything to her. At least, not yet. As you can see, he'll stop at nothing to get what he wants."

"He's not going to get what he wants." All it takes is for Ozzy to wrap a hand around my hip, and my insides warm. His fingers slide down the back of my thigh and hitch it over his hip, wedging his firm thigh against my sex.

I tuck my hands between us while his hand strums the small of my back above my panties. My heart speeds as his fingers on my bare skin move slow and light, so different from how they moved on me earlier.

I force myself to think of something besides the orgasm I experienced earlier. "How am I going to find her? I have no idea what to do next."

His fingers don't stop when he speaks. "Bella is looking around. She has contacts all over Europe and Asia. I know you don't want to wait, but we need to give it time."

I close my eyes and try to allow his touch to relax me

instead of wind me into a fit of knots again. "Why did you ghost me?"

His fingers stop and I look into his handsome face with his messy hair.

"I told you. I was angry."

"At me?"

"No, Princess." He leans in and presses his lips to my forehead. "I'm angry with myself and other shit you don't know or understand. Then I read the transcripts and realized I had no idea what anger was."

I ignore most of that and ask, "What don't I know or understand?"

He shakes his head. "Nothing you need to worry about."

"But you know everything about me." I widen my eyes. "*Everything.*"

He almost looks satisfied. "Do I?"

I poke him in the chest. "You know the most personal things."

He smiles. It's rare and it's beautiful and it makes my heart skip a beat. "I do."

I narrow my eyes. "You don't have to look so smug."

His smile swells, and he transforms into someone new. He also doesn't argue.

"In exchange, tell me something about you. Something personal."

He pulls me closer, as close as two people can be without officially becoming one. He drags the tip of his nose up the side of mine and inhales. "I'm *not* a virgin."

I pull my head back as far as I can and roll my eyes.

He yanks me back. "What do you want to know?"

"How old are you?"

"That's easy. Almost thirty-two."

"Really? When is your birthday?"

"Soon. But I don't celebrate birthdays."

"That's strange."

"I'm a strange guy."

I shake my head. "Not strange. Mysterious, yes. Broody, definitely."

"Broody?"

I wind my finger around a perfect curl sitting on his forehead and give it a yank. "You ghosted me tonight after ... you know. If that's not broody, I don't know what is."

His blue eyes light. "You can say it, baby. It's okay."

I bite the inside of my lip.

"An orgasm." His smug smile returns, and he pushes me to my back with his wide chest, pressing me to the mattress with half of his large frame. "I made you come. Really fucking hard."

"Ozzy—"

"When no one has ever done that before. I'm the first."

I glare at him.

"And I'm looking forward to doing it again," he adds.

"I'll add presumptuousness to the list of your winning personality traits."

His head drops to mine, and once again, I'm consumed by the man who's quite right. He was the first, and if he wants to do it again, I'm one-hundred-percent sure I won't argue.

My lips mold to his. He tastes like mint and smells like soap—clean and crisp and masculine. My fingers play with the hair at his nape. I'm still wearing the ring he slid on my finger. As mad, and, yes, even hurt, as I was, I couldn't bring myself to take it off.

He presses his groin into my sex—into my clit—that learned what real pleasure was today.

It's greedy for more.

His cock is hard, thick, and ... intimidating.

But, even more so, intriguing.

I waited a long time. None of my friends in America gripped onto their virginity like I have. I had opportunities, but I held out for many reasons. In the end, it never felt right.

When he drags his lips from mine, we're both breathing hard. He shakes his head and flops next to me on the bed, but pulls me flush to his side. With his other hand, he reaches down and I watch him adjust what is certainly a set of angry blue balls again. He talks to the ceiling. "You're going to do me in, Princess."

I press into the side of him. He's warm and comfortable—no wonder he was like a magnet in my sleep last night.

He lets out a little groan that bleeds discomfort. Yes, definitely blue balls. "We should sleep."

I trace his abs with my index finger and look down his body at the very large bulge begging to be set free. "Okay."

"Yeah," he echoes his previous statement. "You might be the one to kill me before all this is said and done."

I smile against his pec where my cheek is resting.

His hand slides down to my bottom and squeezes. "I felt that."

I can't help it. My smile breaks into a goofy grin, and I'm grateful his gaze is focused on the ceiling.

"Go to sleep, Liyah. Tomorrow's a new day. We need

to be rested for all the shit that will no doubt be hurled at us."

I nod and don't take my eyes off his cock.
I think.
And wonder.
And dream.

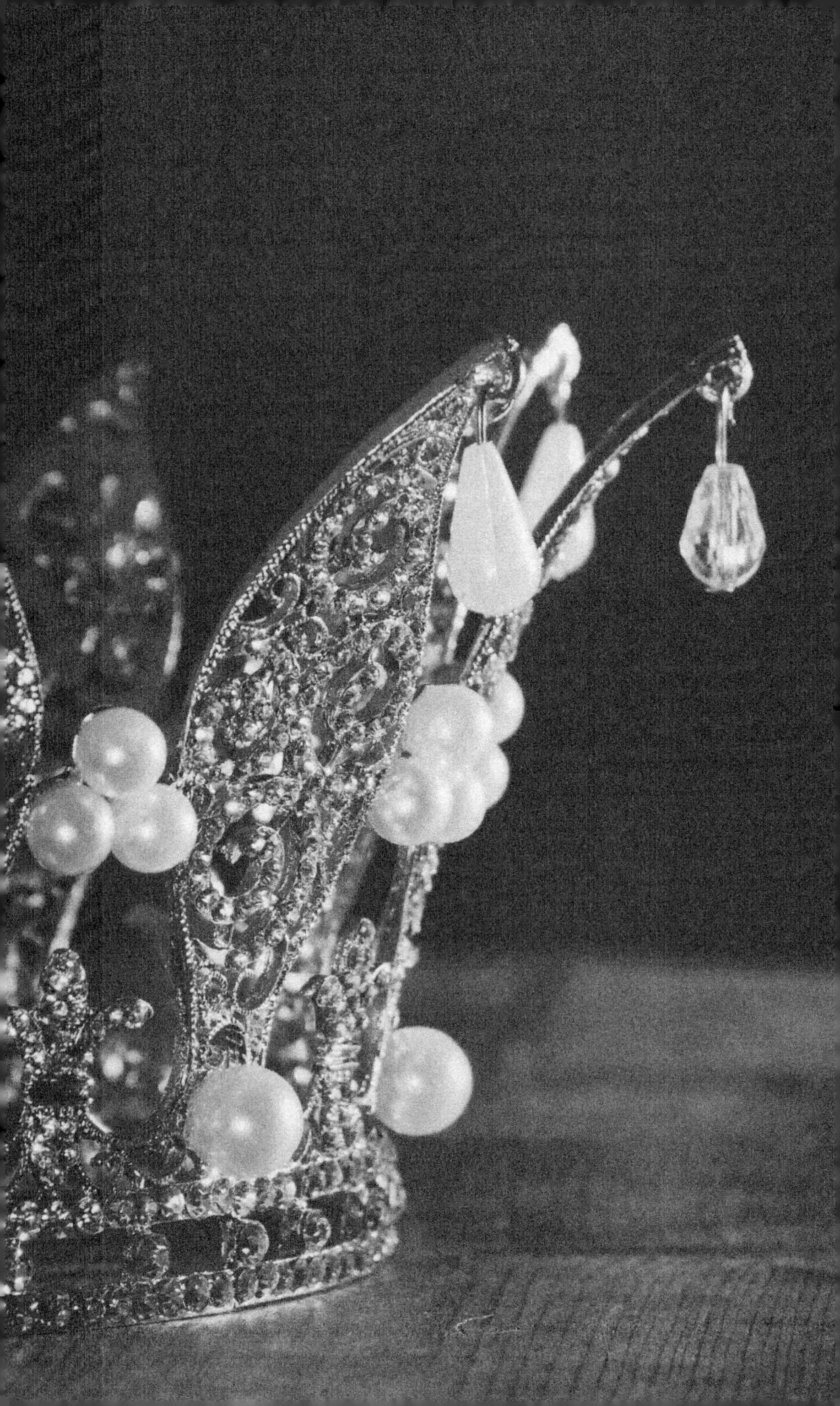

16

CRY INTO YOUR SELTZER

Ozzy

"I've never seen anything quite like it. I'm equally impressed and a bit sick to my stomach for you. You know how Cole and I like our privacy. I can't imagine how your Princess deals with such attention. But you two lovebirds are everywhere, Ozzy. Literally everywhere."

I ignore the lovebirds comment. The video of Liyah and me was on Reskill's private network for any of those nosy fuckers to watch for about two-point-five seconds. I buried that thing inside ten folders and password protected it for my eyes only.

Liyah's social post, on the other hand, announcing her engagement to her fake fiancé is everywhere for the whole fucking world to see. And apparently, it's her most viral post ever. When I woke up this morning, it was to a slew of texts from a certain British pain in my ass.

But then again, many things are proving to be a pain

in the ass lately, and that's not the only place I've experienced pain. So when my cell was about to vibrate off the nightstand, I didn't hesitate getting up to call Bella from the veranda, if for no other reason than to calm my cock the fuck down.

Bella keeps talking. "Gracie saw it first and called Maya, who called Addy. Addy started a group text, and even Bev is scrolling the internet. You're featured on E!, TMZ, and I do believe the Biebers have even shared her post offering their congrats and best wishes. Everyone wants to know if there will be a royal wedding that will rival that of her parents. I'm indeed anxious to know how you're going to handle that one."

I stare at the Eiffel Tower as the sun rises behind it. "Can we get back to her mom? If I can find her, this is done. There's no way Liyah is stepping foot anywhere near Morocco."

"The missing mum isn't your only problem. I think we can safely deduce at this point, King Hasim had nothing to do with trying to kill you two on that train. There's not been any mention of it. They didn't know Liyah was anywhere in the vicinity at that point. She might not be trained to sleuth around the world, but she's smart and handled herself well."

"They recognized her. I was there and saw it."

"Recognizing her and knowing she would be on that train traveling south in Spain instead of north on the train she bought the ticket for, are totally different things."

"It's been blamed on terrorist activity," I say and drag my hand through my hair. "A coincidence."

"Hmm," she hums her thoughts. "It still doesn't sit

right with me. I've asked Cole to dig deeper when he gets to work tomorrow, see what he can scrounge up."

"Luciana Zahir, Bella. Add that to Cole's list."

"Don't you worry that wavy-haired head of yours. That's at the top of his list. The other is purely because I'm nosy."

A call beeps in. I look down at my phone and sigh. "Crew's calling."

"Ah, yes. I meant to tell you he knows all. Enjoy!" And she hangs up before I can chew her ass for telling all.

I click over to my boss and think at least I won't have to explain what the hell's going on. I'm sure everyone there has already done it.

"Crew. What's up?"

"What's up?" Sarcasm bleeds through the phone from North America. "Let me count all the things that are up. One, you're not here. Two, you've hooked up with a royal from Morocco who's basically gone AWOL from her cushy life in SoCal. All her sorority friends are posting shit left and right while crying into their seltzers wanting her back. Three, that royal is ten years younger than you. Four, I know everything. By you hooking up with the Princess, you now have a target on your back from the two-faced King who, behind the scenes, is a class-A asshole and kills anyone who gets in his way. You know, not our kind of killer. Finally, five—and probably the biggest one yet—your picture is plastered worldwide. It might not be your mug, but it is a view of you I did not want to see. I could go on, but let's focus on those for now."

My jaw clenches, and I don't respond.

"And just to piggyback on that list, my wife is all over

my ass, and not in the way I like, demanding me to find out if you are really engaged to the Princess. If I don't come back with that piece of information, I might be sleeping with the cows tonight. Can you feel how happy I am?"

My ass drops to the chair on the veranda, and I tell him the truth. "It's complicated."

"I know for a fact if I go back to Addison with *it's complicated*, I'm going to smell like cow shit tomorrow, Oz. Tell me what the hell's going on."

"I bought the ring." The lights on the Tower click off, signaling a new day. All I want to do is take a shower, jack off, and crawl back in bed with Liyah to give her a new orgasmic experience. I have a feeling none of that is going to happen if I can't get my boss off the phone. "She posted the picture. It did what it needed to do. The King started talking again."

"That's what I heard. Tell me what you know about her mom."

I lean back and prop my feet up. "Should I assume you know everything? I don't want to bore you."

"Yeah. Assume I know everything. I meant tell me your plan. And your intent."

I let out a mocking laugh. "What are you, her dad?"

"No, asshole. I want to know what to expect. You've already got Bella on this, who's on my payroll. Bella has Carson nosing around at the CIA. And now the wives are on the rest of us to help you fix her shit so they can meet a real-life princess."

"I hope they're not disappointed. There aren't any dragons." I pause and decide I'd better not tempt the universe. "At least, not yet."

"Where are you starting to look for the mom?"

"Liyah said everyone on Luciana's staff has disappeared. My guess, they were paid off to slink into the Moroccan sunset with their mouths taped shut, or worse, silenced by the King for good. Liyah's mom is widely loved by the Moroccan people, but the fuckwad King has phased her out so slowly, her fanbase thinks she did this on her own because of grief. It's not like she was out lunching one day and gone the next."

"Not like her daughter," Crew counters, "whose disappearance has caused a stir."

I turn and glance through the glass doors to the bedroom where I left her sleeping in the middle of the bed. Pushing her away isn't an option anymore, and I gladly offered up my body for whatever she wanted to use it for while she slept.

I know there will be ramifications, but I'll deal with those later, since I have no fucking clue what to do about it.

"That stir worked to our advantage. She got the attention we needed and I'm pinging her phone from towers in New York and Canada to all over the eastern border."

"What's there?" Crew asks.

"Two countries for them to deal with. I've got her cell catching towers on both sides. Let them spin their wheels. From the transcripts, they have no fucking clue what they're doing beyond pinpointing her phone yesterday."

"They don't have an Ozzy," Crew mutters.

"I do what I can. But I know rudimentary when I see it. They might be royal, but they're about as basic as a white girl at a pumpkin patch."

"Hey," he snaps. "Addison planted pumpkins this year for the girls and customers."

I roll my eyes. "My bad."

"So, what? You're just planning on shacking up at my place in Paris until you get a lead on her mom?"

And there's the million-dollar question. Or the royal-fortune question. Looking for Liyah's mom in Africa and Europe is like looking for a flea on an elephant.

He calls for me, and it's not patient. "Oz."

For the first time since I answered the phone, my tone sounds like my soul. Lost, with nowhere to go. "I don't know."

"Will she come back here without her mom?"

"I don't know. Despite the fact she's wearing my ring, I'm not sure how far I can push her in that respect."

"I've got people in Africa. We can look for her from here. I'd feel better if you were here, and she'd be safe too."

Crew has a point. Aside from a few sources who provide me supplies when I get places, I don't have sources all over the world. Not like he does. He's also been at this a hell of a long time, as opposed to me.

"Is this important to you?"

I close my eyes. "It couldn't be more complicated. You get me?"

"I do," he confirms.

Crew knows everything. He knew everything about me before I ever knew he existed, before Asa made me the craziest offer I ever heard. An offer that was the only lifeline I had. I had no choice and took it. I've never looked back.

"Get home," he bosses when I don't offer any further

deep thoughts or feelings. "Let us do what we do. You can figure out the rest. Or, you'll help her find her mom and send her on her way. Up to you."

Send her on her way.

"Ozzy?"

Shit.

I never heard her get up, that's how deep I am in my thoughts, spinning scenarios. She's standing in my shirt that hits her bare legs at the top of her thighs. Her nipples, that I know are fucking delectable, are pebbled under the shirt, and her hair screams sex, even though it's as far from sex as it could be.

Ask my dick.

"Sorry, I didn't mean to wake you. I had to take this call."

She leans into the French door and it pulls at the T-shirt, showing me a hint of lace, which I know firsthand is really a thong. My hand found her bare ass many times in the middle of the night.

Yeah, I'm going to need time in the shower as soon as possible.

Just like every other time she's near, I don't take my eyes off her, but continue talking to Crew. "I'll see what I can do. No promises."

He sighs. "Fair enough. Look, man, one more time. Throw me a bone. Is the engagement real?"

I walk over to her and slide my hand up her side and around her back. I tuck my fingers into the back of her thong and pull her to me. Her dark eyes come alive from sleep when she feels her effect on me pressing into her stomach. "Not sure yet. That's the best I can do, Crew."

"Addison is going to kill me," he mutters.

A small smile settles on my lips, something that's foreign for me. If it ever happens, it's not genuine. It's fake and all show so those around me will leave me the fuck alone. "Enjoy bunking with the cows. I've gotta go."

I don't wait for him to beg for more information that I do not have. I shut it down and drop the phone on the chair I was just sitting in.

Then I lean down and bump her nose with the tip of mine. "You really know how to get attention. If you thought your post was successful before, you went viral overnight."

She tips her head but doesn't move away from me or complain about where my hand is sitting. "You mean, we went viral?"

I shrug. "Either way, you know what you're doing."

"It's not hard. Mystery and seduction get a lot of attention." She mirrors my shrug. "Sex sells."

My dick just got harder. If he only knew there was no reason to get excited. "That it does. Now we have to wait and see what your uncle does next. Until then, my boss and associates are doing everything they can to find your mom. And they have a lot of contacts around the world. You and I need to sit down and talk about all the places your mom might go to seek refuge. Nothing is too slim of a chance."

"Okay." She shifts against my dick, who proves he has a mind of his own. He thinks he's in paradise, when really he's in the worst kind of hell. And I know for a fact my royal goddess knows exactly what kind of torture I'm in. She licks her bottom lip and asks, "Should we do that now?"

"No." I couldn't fucking concentrate on walking across the street without getting hit by a bus right now.

"I'm going to shower. You..." I pull in a big breath. "Do whatever you want. Just don't leave."

"You don't have to worry about that."

I must be a masochist, because I lean down to take her mouth and dip my hand farther under her ass to cup her. I feel her moan on my tongue and the effect on my fingers.

She's wet.

This must be a special place in hell, and I have no idea what I did to get here. Or it's a special section of purgatory just for my dick. Either way, I love and hate it at the same time.

I groan into her mouth before pulling my lips and hand away, both from warm, wet places that kill me to let go of. I look down and don't try to hide my frustration or my basic, carnal craving for her.

"If I don't take a shower this very moment, I will literally die."

As opposed to my misery, the most beautiful damn smile lights up her face in pure fucking delight.

I squeeze her ass one more time, harder than I should, and move around her. I need to clear my head so I can fix her shit and then figure out what a dead man is going to do with a princess.

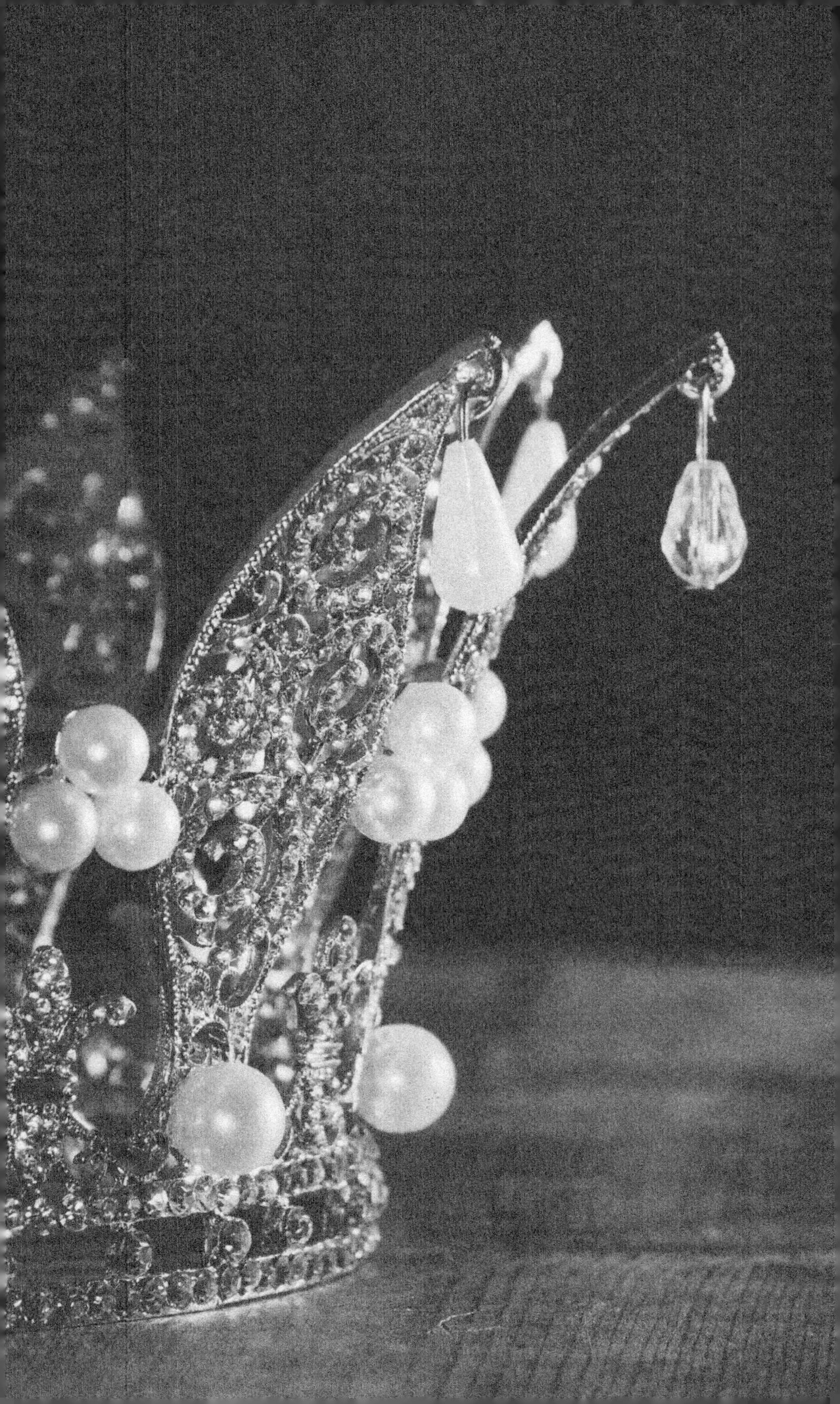

17

HUNGRY

Liyah

Should I be happy that I have such an effect on Ozzy?

This man stirs emotions in me I've never felt before and has me wanting to do things I've only read about in books, watched on TV, or heard my friends talk about.

Should it bring me this much joy that he's in such a knot of sexual frustration that he had to tear himself away from me?

The answer to that question should be no. I should not relish in the fact he might very well be taking a cold shower at this very moment. Isn't that what they do?

Because ... blue balls, right?

I should make a cup of tea. Nose around the kitchen to see what there is for breakfast. Or even fluff the pillows on the sofa and straighten up the beautiful space we're in.

But I don't do any of that.

The shower has been on for a few minutes. Ozzy must have been in such a state, he didn't shut the door all the way. A sliver of light from the bathroom mocks me where the door rests against the jamb.

I only need a couple centimeters. Maybe less.

My heart speeds, wanting this at the same time my brain screams at me to turn the other way. I have no idea what I'll do if he sees me. But my curiosity and need for ... something, wins.

I tiptoe through the bedroom and click off the light on my way. The spray of water continues to hit the glass in the oversized shower. Pumping blood echoes in my ears, but my will wins. My fingertips are light on the door when I give it a gentle nudge.

The shower is behind the entrance to the bathroom. But my breath catches when I take him in through the reflection in the massive mirror over the vanity.

Holy...

I've dabbled in the most shallow industry in the world long enough to understand beauty. Or, rather, the kind of beauty the first world pushes on us. The superficial kind. Contrived, Photoshopped, and airbrushed. The kind that takes ten hours of shooting just to find the perfect shot that's considered perfection by those who are so far from perfect in every way, it's not funny.

I know beauty.

Or, I thought I did.

Because what I see through the mirror is pure, raw magnificence.

Ozzy's profile is standing under a stream of water, naked, leaning on the marble wall with one hand and the other wrapped around his long, thick cock.

He's a work of art.

I think his eyes are closed, so I take a chance. Just another couple centimeters. Every muscle in his impressive body is taut, down to his beautiful ass and his clenched jaw.

Wetness pools between my legs and my nipples tingle.

I'm in awe of his entire body. Of him.

Violent isn't the right word, but there's a desperation in the way he's working himself. Fisting his shaft from its swollen head to its base. Like he's in pain, chasing and searching for relief, all at the same time.

The rugged features of his face I've become obsessed with over the last few days contort. Every muscle in his body tenses, from his biceps, his broad chest and back, down to his long, thick legs. I know firsthand how heavy and firm they are when he presses me to the bed. His big hand leaning against the wall even fists.

But I can't take my eyes off his cock. I didn't think it was possible for it to swell further, but it does. I remotely realize Ozzy throws his head back, but I don't shift my focus from the angry grip around his shaft when he comes.

And he comes and comes and comes.

I jump back from the door as if I've been scalded. That's how I feel. Flushed, hot, and my knees are wobbly as I stumble away from the bathroom. I move as fast as I can through the darkened bedroom to the family room, my eyes darting around.

I need to cool off. I need to collect myself.

How will I look him in the eyes and pretend I haven't seen that. That I haven't invaded his privacy for the sheer need to have more of him that I masked as sheer perversion of my curiosity.

Lord.

I move to the veranda where the most romantic city in the world is coming to life below us. I fall to the thick cushioned chair and wrap my legs up in Ozzy's big shirt.

I beg the crisp morning air to cool and calm me, forcing my heart to return to a normal, healthy rhythm and not that of a twenty-two-year-old woman who just ran miles on the beach.

Because that's how I feel.

Though, after a run, the need to dip my fingers between my legs isn't front and center in my mind. Who am I kidding? I really have no desire to touch myself. There's only one touch I want, and it's the man I watched jack off in the shower.

Liyah, who are you?

I close my eyes and try to search for anything else to focus on, but all I see are visions of him.

"Hey."

I jump and yelp at the same time the hand I crave so much lands hot and heavy on the back of my neck.

My eyes fly open, and I look up. Ozzy's hair is pushed back with the one hank that never cooperates curling down the right side of his forehead. His impossibly blue eyes are different than they were when he left me to shower so he wouldn't *literally die.*

Now, those same eyes have a sharpness about them —focused, alert, and ready to take on the world. So different than before, when he looked like he was ready to eat me alive, like the big, bad wolf from the nursery stories my mother would read to me as a young girl.

Those blue eyes bore into me as he wraps my hair

around his hand until it's in a tight fist, and tips my head back. Ozzy leering over me upside down is even more unsettling after what I just witnessed.

"You hungry?"

Yes. So hungry.

But I don't admit that.

"Maybe a little."

He lifts his chin before looking out at the Tower. "It's going to be a warm one for fall."

Warm. Lord, yes. "Is it?"

He nods and looks back down to me. "I need to work. Check in on the fucking King, and then start looking for a needle in the haystack."

I swallow hard, knowing he's speaking of my mother, but still can't string multiple words together. "Okay."

He lets my hair go and it tumbles down the back of the chair, but I don't look away from him. He slides a hand down the side of my face until his thumb comes into contact with my bottom lip.

My mouth parts at his touch and I'm back to fighting for a breath when he drags that thumb across my lips. All I can think about is his cock.

He doesn't show any reaction like the one stirring inside me, like a storm brewing offshore just waiting to create havoc.

He gives my chin a squeeze. "Let's eat and maybe later we can get out and go for a walk, if you think you can get away without being spotted. I'm not used to being on the lookout for paparazzi."

I fist the hem of his shirt where it's stretched at my ankles, and do my best not to act like I know what he looks like naked. "Well, you've officially gone viral, Ozzy.

They might be my followers, but trust me, you're the focus of that post. Almost two million people are wondering who the man is that I finally invited into my life."

He hikes a brow, and his grip on my chin tightens.

"You know," I add, "fictionally speaking."

"Right," he bites. "Fictionally."

I hold on to my resolve and pretend I'm brave like I did when I left California, stupid enough to think I could find my mother all on my own. Without breaking the visual embrace he's got me tied up in, I pry his grip from my face and entwine my fingers with his. "I'm hungry."

He purses his lips. "I bet you are."

Then he gives me a tug and pulls me to my feet. There's not another word spoken between us until he starts to rattle off my breakfast choices so he can return to the business of fixing all my problems.

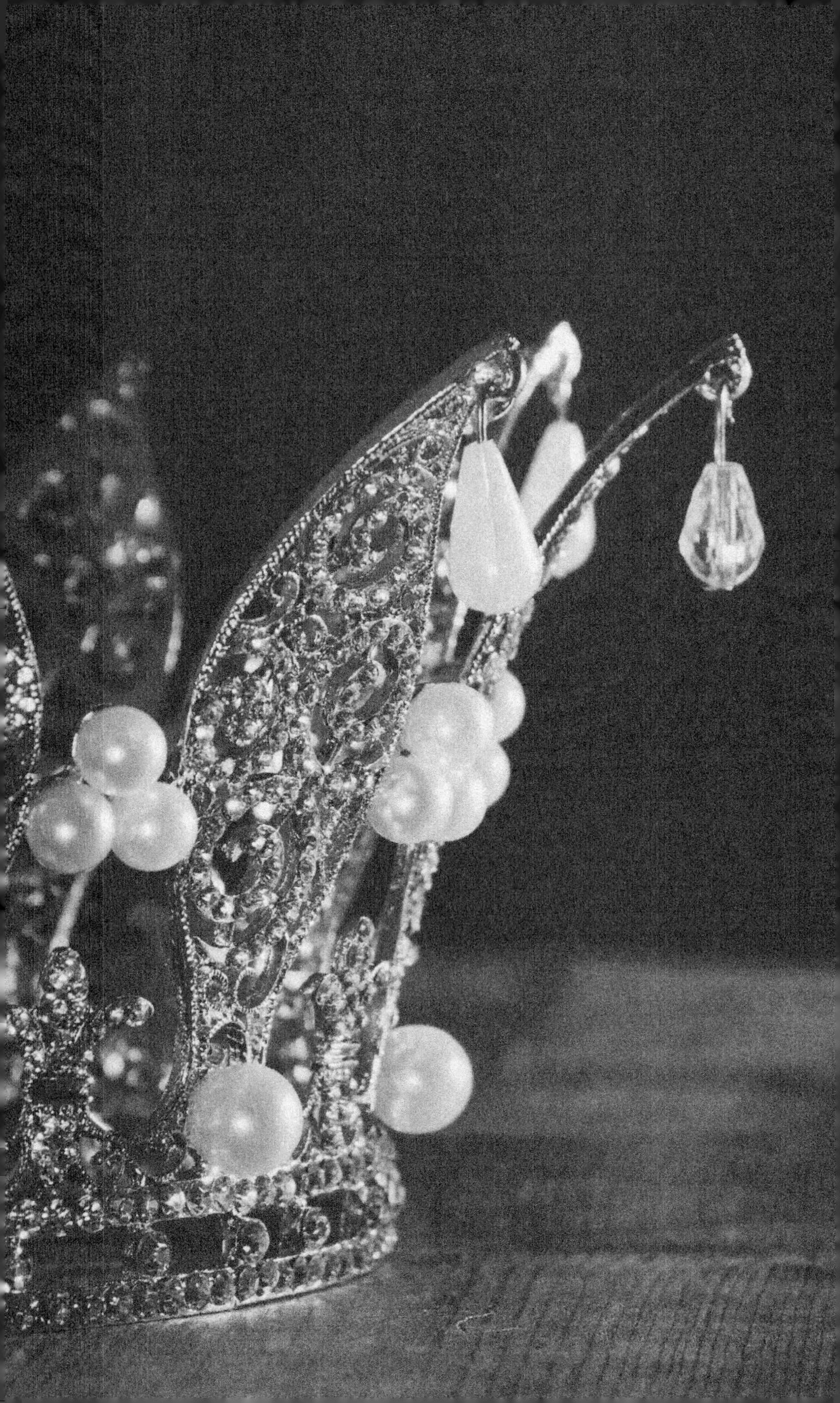

18

BOUNDARIES

Ozzy

"I'm on my way to the airport. Crew and I agreed. Tell your Princess to hold tight, I'll find out what I can."

My gaze shoots to Liyah before I stand and make my way to the veranda, closing the door behind me for privacy. "Where are you going?"

"Morocco," Bella answers. "Where else would I start?"

I wrap a hand around the back of my neck and groan internally. "Bella, I don't think this is a good idea—"

"Which is why we didn't tell you."

I sigh. "Your husband is going to have my head."

"That goes without saying," Carson snaps. Shit, I'm on speaker. "Though I'm not concerned. If Bella could do this in Pakistan for years, Morocco will be a piece of cake."

"I'm not starting cold," Bella explains. "My source is

meeting me at the airport. Luciana was rumored to be near the Algerian border, even though that border is closed. I have other business for Crew I can take care of while in the area. This is a two for one—you're welcome."

I turn when I hear the door open behind me. Liyah is standing at the threshold in a cropped grunge T-shirt expressing her love for NASA, of all fucking things, and the same cutoff shorts she wore last night when I touched her for the first time and watched her fall apart in my arms. She officially went from a woman I was trying to ignore, to an obsession in about two-point-five seconds.

I don't know what I'm going to do about that, but after this morning, I'm willing to get creative.

Because this is not something I ever saw happening. A commitment. A constant. Intimacy that goes beyond one act of sex before moving on, because there was never a choice.

A *relationship*.

These thoughts were never a possibility. They're still not. Not really. And I have no fucking idea how I'm going to spin this, but right now, I'm not looking past today.

Or maybe tomorrow.

Her dark eyes implore me for information, so I keep talking. "I appreciate it. Let me know what you find."

"Will do, loverboy," Carson pipes. Bella laughs, all of it at my expense, and since Liyah is standing in front of me looking like a mid-morning snack I didn't know I was hungry for, I don't give a shit. But Carson goes on because the cocky bastard is like that. "You know, I find this poetically ironic. Seems like just yesterday you were making us eat shit when you had to read our texts or listen to us on surveillance. And now look at you, posing in porn for the world to see."

I close my eyes and turn my back to Liyah. I'm about to argue, but Bella comes to my defense ... sort of. "It's not really porn, darling. Just back porn. It's a lovely picture of your lats, Ozzy. You've really been hitting the gym. Nicely done."

"Are you seriously talking about his back when your husband is sitting right here?" Carson argues.

"You know I prefer every part of your body, Cole. I'm just trying to make Ozzy feel better about his viral post. Oh, Ozzy. Did you know you're making your way around the morning talk shows? It just keeps getting more traction. Quite impressive for a first showing."

"Bella." I need to shut this shit down since I can't exactly argue in front of Liyah. "Let me know when you get to Morocco. And watch your back. I'm worried about you asking around about Luciana."

"What?" Liyah calls from behind me. "Do you know something?"

I turn and hold up a finger. "I've got to go. Let me know what you find."

"Wait, Oz," Carson yells to keep me from hanging up. "If you need any advice—"

"Goodbye," I interrupt and turn my phone off before they start talking about Liyah, or, fuck me, her virginity. Because at this point, I know they've read King Hasim's transcripts.

I slide my phone into my pocket and try to focus on her damp hair that blows in the breeze instead of her bare midriff. "One of my associates is on her way to Morocco. She's the one who had a contact inside the palace. If anyone can get a lead on your mom, Bella can."

She tucks her hair behind her ear. "I don't know any of these people. Why are they doing this for me?"

Because the woman drives me crazy in the best way possible, I close the distance between us and run my finger along her smooth skin between her shirt and shorts, before hooking my index finger in her waistband and hauling her to me. "They're doing it for me. It's what they do, because they're good people. And because they're now fully invested in what an asshole your uncle is. They know I can't leave you to look for your mom, so they're doing it." What I don't tell her is Crew wants me back in Virginia, and if it comes down to that, I'm taking her with me.

That little bit of news can wait. If she won't come with me on her own, I'm not sure what I'll do.

Princess-napping is an option. A little dramatic, but I haven't ruled it out.

"Let's get out of here." I slide my other hand around her and press in on her lower back. "I'm getting claustrophobic. Walk, get some food. I'll take you somewhere the tourists don't bother with because it's too far out of the way."

She tips her head. "I don't want to miss anything about my mom..."

"Baby, I have an entire private satellite system at my disposal. I don't even need cell service. I'm not going to miss a call."

Her eyes widen. "A satellite system?"

"Yeah. Don't be too impressed. It's not mine, I just run it."

"It's still impressive." Her lips tip, and I really want

to kiss them. But if I do, I'm worried we won't make it out of this apartment. Besides, pushing the boundaries too soon with the Princess is not a good idea, and I really need some fresh air.

"Do what you need to do to get ready. But this," I tug at her shirt, "isn't a good idea for where we're going."

She hikes a brow. "I don't have an evening gown."

I can't wait another second. I push her to the marble wall that makes up the exterior of the building. Before I know it, I've got one hand in her hair, the other palms her ass, and my lips are glued to hers. This is exactly why we need to get the hell out of this apartment. "You don't need a ball gown, but we're also not going to a frat party. You also don't need attention, which you'll get plenty of in these shorts alone. Change your clothes, baby. I know you have other things to wear. I watched you buy them, and I carried that shit all over Paris for hours."

Her lips are still parted as she catches her breath from my kiss. I also haven't let go of her ass—I really like it in my hand.

"Okay." She licks her lips, and it's all I can do not to pick her up, carry her to the bedroom, and spend the rest of the day pushing boundaries and driving myself mad. "I think I have something."

I give her one more squeeze and force myself to step back. "We'll leave in fifteen."

She turns for the door and I'm pretty sure the next fifteen minutes will feel like an eternity.

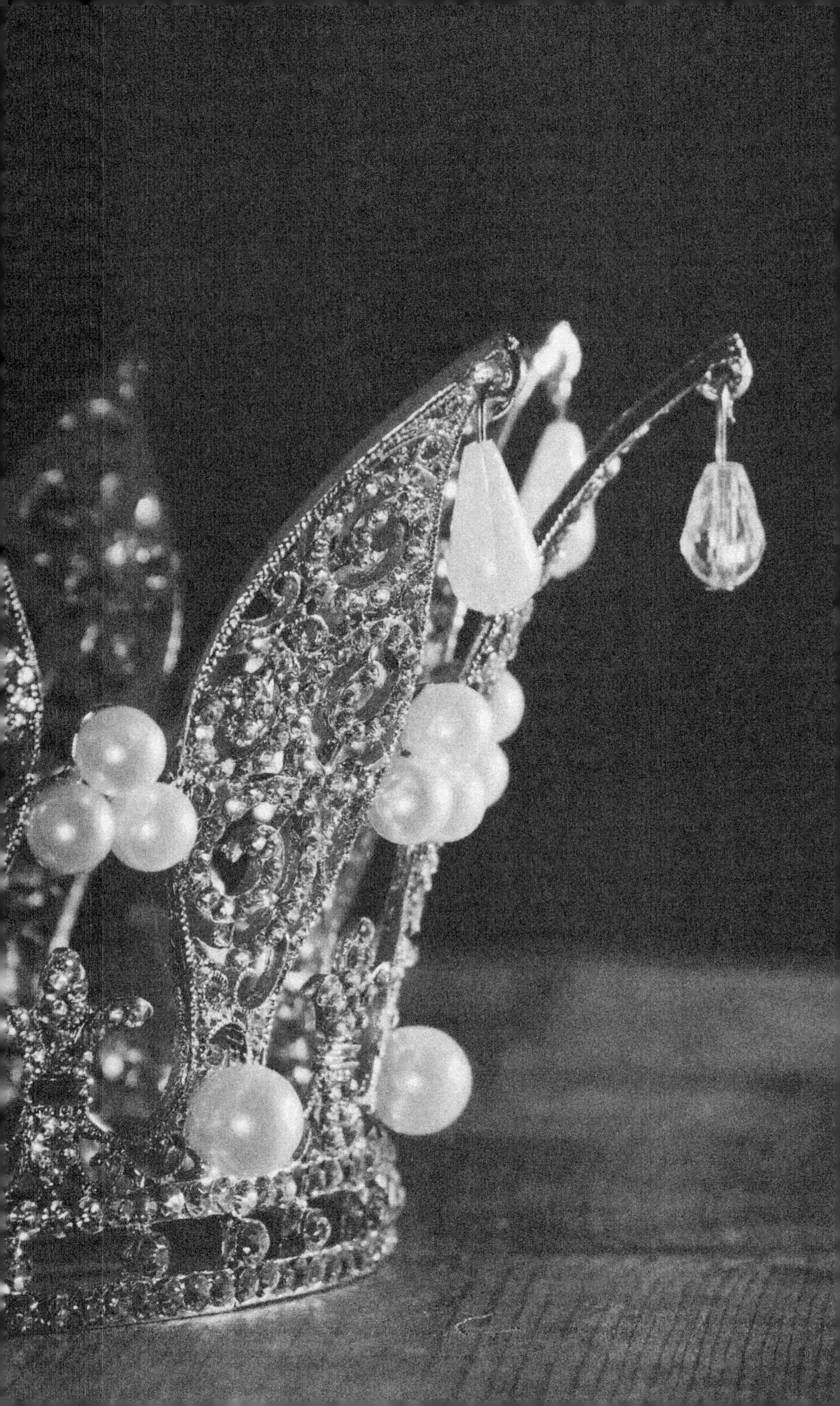

Liyah

I've been to Paris many times. My mother might've been a girl from a humble family who grew up in a Spanish fishing village, but she gave me her love for Europe.

History.

Art.

Love.

Heartache.

One doesn't have to look far to find any and all of these things that make Paris special. It's imperfect and old, and that's what makes it beautiful.

I lean over as I sit close to Ozzy, his thick thigh is pressed to mine where I'm tucked under his arm. "You brought me to a wedding?"

We're sitting in the back of Saint Sulpice, the second largest church in Paris, second only to Notre Dame. It took us almost an hour to walk here from the penthouse, and I remind myself to thank Ozzy later for having the forethought to tell me to change clothes. I'm happy I'm not in cutoffs and a crop top. Not that he dressed up for the occasion. He's still in the T-shirt and shorts he put on after his shower this morning.

A shower I gave him no privacy for.

I still have zero regrets.

The image of Ozzy pleasuring himself will forever be burned on my brain, and I'm happy for it. Not that I have many regrets in life. Not since I left the States. Even the close calls I've experienced since I forced my way into Ozzy's cabin brought me to this moment and have kept me alive.

I'm pressed to the side of Ozzy's chest, so he doesn't have to lean far when his lips hit my ear. "I brought you to a place that's quiet and off the beaten track. I had no idea there'd be a wedding."

The acoustics whisper around us like a ghost, and even though we aren't anywhere near the small wedding at the altar, we can hear every word the priest utters in French to tie these two together forever. We're surrounded by walls and arches and ceilings that go on forever. This place has seen so many centuries of history, it's eerie.

I turn my head to Ozzy, and he leans in to meet me halfway. "My mother had to reject her faith to marry my father. She said when you're in love, you do the craziest things. I guess that was one of them for her. She went through the motions for my father—to be with him—but in her soul, I don't think she ever did."

There are no pews in Saint Sulpice, just rows and rows of chairs so old, they creaked when Ozzy pulled me into the back row. Our spot is out of the way, and I'm not sure anyone has laid eyes on us.

His arm draped over the back of my seat curls around me, pulling me tighter—something I didn't think could happen. We're so close, we might as well be curled up in bed together. No one could hear us even if they were around, that's how hushed our conversation is. "All we have is what's in our souls. When you strip yourself bare, there's nothing left. Not what anyone thinks of you, not when they try to force your square peg into a round hole, and really not when they shatter your life into so many pieces you can never put it together again. Fuck them, and fuck the world, Princess. Sounds like your mom is a smart woman."

I lean back to look into his blue eyes. When we first met, they were cunning, guarded, and cold as ice. But not anymore. He might know my secrets and fears—I've been nothing but an open book—but it feels like he sees more. It feels like he's studying my hopes and dreams, things I've never uttered aloud.

"I'm scared for her. All she ever did was sacrifice herself for love. For my father. Then later, when she lost his protection, for me."

His gaze never leaves mine, and he nods once. "From what I've seen, you're worth it."

I swallow over the lump in my throat that forms out of nowhere. "I wish she hadn't. Right now, I'd give up everything to know she's safe. My royal status, money, education, and especially the shallow life I created in the States."

"I'm sure she did what she thought was best at the time. Regrets are nothing but a curse—don't do that, Princess."

"But I didn't see her sacrifices at first. And then I

didn't appreciate them. Not until now. Do you know what that feels like?"

I turn to the altar when the priest offers communion and settle into the protection of the man who hasn't left my side in days.

The wedding is small, only a few guests sit on each side. I think any young girl has grandiose dreams about their wedding. I know I did. In reality, every wedding I attended was royal, cost millions, and was all show.

I've never seen anything like this before. There's something beautiful about its simplicity in such a grand and sacred space. I'm reminded of the symbol that still sits at the base of my left ring finger. The very real diamond with a very fake meaning, even as I sit wrapped up in the man who put it there.

We don't say another word for the rest of the ceremony. The couple takes their vows, exchanges rings, and the priest announces them united as one.

Forever and ever, until death do they part.

I jump when the grand organ booms, filling the space like a monster. Ozzy's free hand wraps around my knee and slides up my bare thigh, under the short dress I threw on when I had no idea where we were going.

His touch is hot and firm as his thumb strokes the outside of my thigh rhythmically. And not at all to the notes of "Trumpet Voluntary," but rather to his own beat that does things to my insides I've never experienced before. My heart races and my pulse speeds, surely not at the normal level of a twenty-two-year-old who works out regularly. When I look into his eyes, they're as hot as his touch.

But he stops when he hits the top of my thigh, short

of other places he touched me last night. And places I wanted him to touch me this morning. I yearned for it.

For him.

A single photographer takes pictures of the couple walking down the impossibly long aisle. Their happiness is so great, it fills the enormous church. It's breathtaking, and to picture it any other way, would ruin their day. Crowds and pomp and circumstance at this moment seem wrong and invasive.

Beauty in simplicity.

We watch it play out until the grand organ plays the last note, and the few guests congratulate the couple. They're buried so deep in their happiness, I don't think they see us.

All of a sudden, I'm envious. I've never experienced that level of joy—so much that I was lost and oblivious to the rest of the world.

I want that.

I feel like an imposter to their lives. But, like this morning, I'm selfish and don't feel any guilt.

"Are you in Paris often?" The question falls from my lips before I even realize I asked it.

"Yeah. This is our European base. My associates and I can crash here between assignments."

I nod.

"What?" he asks.

I feel as if I have the right to ask, even though he owes me nothing. I mean, it's not his fault I barged into his life. I pull in a breath and just say it. My status might be the big V, but one thing I'm not is shy. "Do you do this often?"

He tips his head before looking around the church. "Do you mean this?" When he looks back to me, his hand slides an inch closer to my panties, close enough so the tip of his finger brushes my sex. I pull in a quick breath. "Or this?"

I shift my legs apart. "This."

His lips tip on one side as he takes full advantage of the space I've offered. It's not until his finger dips into my panties that I realize how wet I am for him. He slides a finger through me, and my heart skips a beat. "I've never done this in church."

I don't know why I ask, because right now I don't care. "You're Catholic?"

He nods once and gives me another swipe. "Apparently not a good one since this is all I can think about." He slides a finger up over my swollen clit. "You're all I can think about."

"That's not what I meant." I can't believe I have the wherewithal to keep up my end of the conversation. It takes an enormous amount of concentration, but I press on. "I meant, do you, you know, have women here with you in Paris?" His eyes narrow. My awkward words don't deter him. I win another swipe and a circle this time. "When you're between assignments."

That last question does have an effect, because I lose his touch and he looks around the now quiet church. No more weddings, no other tourists, and no priests. Ozzy jerks to his feet and grabs my hand pulling me with him. The next thing I know, he's pulling me into the shadows of the side aisle.

"Ozzy," I whisper. "No—"

But he doesn't listen. The door creaks when he jerks it open and he pulls me inside. It's dark, musty, and smells like centuries of secrets and sins.

"What are you do—" I start but can't finish when his mouth finds mine.

There's nothing gentle or slow or tender about his kiss. His grip on my scalp is desperate and his other hand reaches low and yanks the bottom of my dress up where he palms my ass—something he's done often since our first encounter last night.

I lose his lips, and the dark shadows of his masculine features fill my vision. He sits in the seat meant only for the ordained, the pure ... the celibate. He turns me, pulling my ass into his lap, on the same cock I saw for the first time this morning in the flesh. It's hard and imposing in the crack of my ass through our clothes.

"You drive me mad, Princess," he rumbles low in my ear.

"This is dangerous," I whisper.

I try to turn to look at him, but he reaches for my knees and splays my legs over his thighs. My feet dangle when he spreads his legs farther, spreading me. One arm acts as a vise, holding me hostage to his chest, his hand mauling my breast through my thin dress. Ozzy proves he's not afraid of anything, and yanks the hem of the dress up with his other hand and dips it into the front of my panties.

My head falls to his shoulder when he spears me with two fingers. He stretches me and his thumb doesn't waste any time. He was teasing me before, but not now. He smears my wetness all over my sex and I forget where I am or what could happen should anyone hear us or open the antique door.

He pinches my hardened nipple through the thin material, and I moan. I didn't bother wearing a bra. It's not like I traveled with a suitcase full of lingerie.

His breath is heavy on the side of my face as his words seep into me, as hot as it's becoming in this claustrophobic space. "No. I don't have women at my disposal here in Paris or anywhere else. Is that what you want to know?"

I exhale and whimper.

"Answer me," he demands. "Is that what you want to know? Because I take my dick seriously, baby. I'm not about a random fuck."

He dips two fingers into me again, but not deeply. Maybe only to the first knuckle. But it's enough to make me want more, especially after what he just said. I tuck my toes around the backs of his calves and spread my legs wider.

I want more.

He might not be able to read my thoughts, but he can read my body. "No way. If you want more, it'll be nothing but my cock."

"Oh, Lord," I whisper.

"No, it's just me." He might not fill me the way I want, but he doesn't ignore my clit. "I think it's time you come clean. There's no better place to do it than here."

I tense and try to shift, but he proves how strong he is and holds me in place.

His lips hit my ear, his words dripping in lust and desire. "Did you like what you saw this morning?"

I freeze, and all the air escapes my body. "What?"

"Shhh." He catches the lobe of my ear between his teeth. A warning. "You know what I'm talking about."

Shit. He knows?

When I don't answer or admit to anything, he spreads his legs more and I'm not sure I can be stretched farther in this small confessional. He takes full advantage, but I have trouble catching my breath again when he presses the pads of his fingers to my clit, my lips, the entire area, creating a storm between my legs that might do me in.

"Yeah, I saw you watching," he answers my thought, and I wonder if his superpowers extend beyond jumping from trains and the magic he's creating between my legs. "Something I should probably tell you, no one sneaks up on me. Since we're here and confessing sins, I make a living sleuthing in the dark recesses of the world. Like what you watched me do in Libya, I take lives and don't think twice about it, baby."

That should bother me. Is he trying to disgust me so I'll make him stop? Because right now, his words sound more like a dare, rather than a confession, telling me something I knew, or at least, assumed.

Because there's nothing more I want right now, so I arch my back and try to press my sex to his touch for more.

He gives it to me and there's a dare in his words when he asks, "You liked what you saw?"

I bring my hands up to his forearm to hang on, because my orgasm is building. My heart races and my breaths are coming so hard, there's no way I can answer, even though I want to scream *yes* so loud it would rival the organ that echoed off the centuries-old walls.

Instead, I turn my face to his and nod.

"Next time you can do it."

He presses his lips to mine and circles my clit harder. My body tenses, and I fall. When I come, he thrusts his tongue in my mouth, drinking my moans and silencing me. He holds tight, not allowing me to move or squeeze my legs together the way I want to—the way my body desperately needs.

Ozzy has proven he can control my body and knows my every move. He all but called me on it, forcing me to confess in a confessional and somehow made it a religious experience I didn't know I needed.

He doesn't slide his hand away from between my legs. He holds me possessively as my body calms and comes back down to earth.

Or, to church.

He brings a hand to the side of my head and strokes my hair as my heart returns to a normal beat. And it really sinks in that he saw me watch him this morning in the shower. Just when I thought I was brave, and in my own way, a tiny bit stealthily. Ozzy just proved I'm so very inexperienced, no matter how brave I might try to be.

"I've never come so hard ... knowing you were watching me."

He drags the tip of his nose up the side of my face, and despite the stagnant air created by our body heat in this centuries-old closet for priests and sins, a shiver runs over my skin.

"All I could think about were your hands." His fingers trail down my arm, entwining his fingers with mine. He continues to torture me with his words that are really just fantasies as he feels his way up my chest to give my sensitive nipple more attention with our joined hands. "Coming all over your beautiful body." His teeth catch my bottom lip. "Fucking your mouth."

"Ozzy."

"Since we're in confession mode," he presses in on my sex he's yet to let go of, "I'm not going to lie,

Princess. I've wanted a lot of things in life, especially the last few years. I've been desperate for them. At least, I thought I was, but I was wrong. Right now, there's nothing I want more than you. All of you. Every pure and sacred piece."

I bring my fingers to his jaw to tilt his face to mine.

He doesn't allow me to answer and keeps talking. "I want all of you, Princess. More than anything, you deserve someone who can give you everything, and I can't do that. I'll explain in time—there are things to know about me. But none of that makes me want you any less."

"Ozzy—" I'm about to demand to know what he's talking about. I want to know what could keep him from giving me all of him. Right now, that thought fills me with rage.

But I don't get a chance to demand anything from him. He shifts me to one leg when he reaches into his pocket for his phone. I start to stand, but he wraps a hand around my waist and holds tight.

He frowns when he looks at the screen before answering. "Graves."

His stare shoots from me to the door that has given us privacy in such a holy place. But unlike a few moments ago when his expression was nothing but depraved when he described all the ways he wanted to make me his, now he looks...

Haunted.

"There's no way," he bites. "You're sure?" He pauses. "I don't believe it. It has to be a mistake."

I can't make out the words on the other end, but they're rushed and anxious.

Ozzy stands, taking me to my feet with him. He

turns me to him, an angry frown is set in his handsome features. "Okay. Yeah, I'll figure it out. We'll be there."

"We'll be where?" I ask as he stuffs his cell into his pocket.

He wraps both arms around me. "I'm sorry, Princess. As much as I want to stay right here with you in Paris, something has happened. Or, might've happened. I hope to fuck it's a mistake, but I need to get back where I have everything at my disposal."

"Back where?" I demand.

"Virginia." His expression mirrors his words, not happy at all about whatever development has arisen. "And you're coming with me."

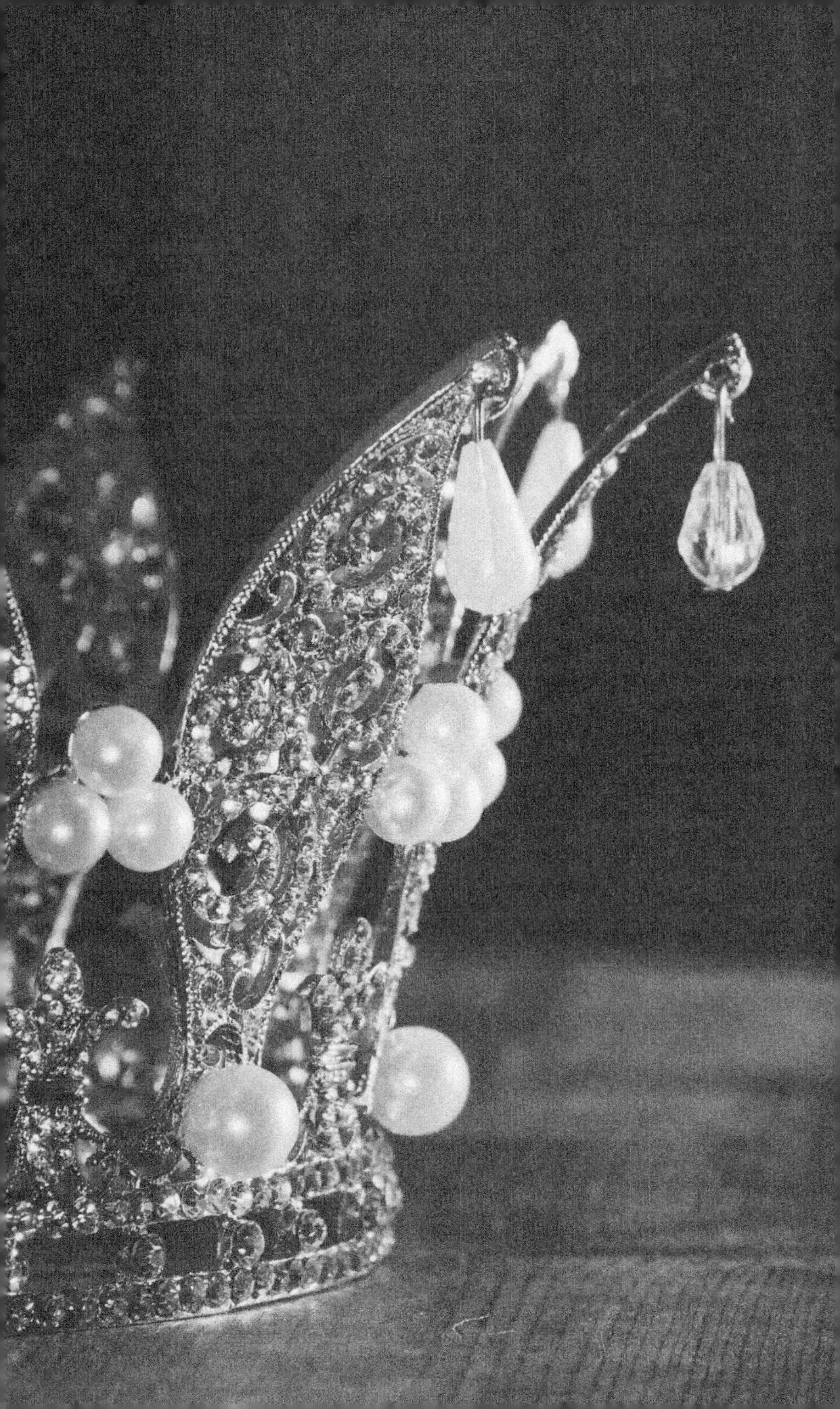

20

BLACK

Liyah

The last twelve hours have flown by.
  And not just because we've flown across the pond to America.

With my hand firmly encased in his, Ozzy rushed us back to the penthouse where he threw our things into an enormous duffle he produced from the closet in the bedroom. Apparently he packs heavier than I gave him credit for, because he had more things stored in the penthouse than any one man should need for a short stay.

I started to argue with him, because leaving Europe without my mother was the last thing on earth I wanted to do. It didn't matter how hard I was falling for Ozzy Graves. I know I don't have the resources or the skills to look for her myself, but if an ex-MI6 agent was on the search, the least I could do is be close when she's found.

Because she will be found. I refuse to believe there

will be any other scenario. Nothing is more important than my mother right now.

When I told Ozzy this, he stopped his haphazard packing and locked my face between his strong hands. "There's no way on earth I'm leaving you here. If anyone can find your mom, it's Bella Donnelly Carson. If you trust me, you'll follow and know that I'll fill you in later. Swear, Princess, if you come with me, I'll tell you everything."

The tease of everything from Ozzy was enough. That and the fact this Bella lady is on my side.

I had about three seconds to make up my mind before a car was calling from the lobby to drive us to a private airport. Even though I had a choice, I knew I really didn't.

Trusting Ozzy feels like my only option in life.

So, in the same dress I wore yesterday when he gave me an orgasm in a confessional of a Catholic church, we touch down in the Commonwealth of Virginia. This was my third private flight with Ozzy, and I'm grateful for it. Like last time, I slept on the sofa for most of it. But, unlike last time when Ozzy was utterly exhausted from my drama, he did not. I did use his thigh as a pillow while he worked silently on his phone.

Tires squeal on the tarmac as the private jet hits the brakes. I've been patient, and did what he asked—I've trusted him. And he owes me answers.

I pull my hair up and secure it on top of my head. "When are you going to tell me all the things you promised?"

Ozzy's gaze juts to the cockpit before focusing back on me. "When we can find a private moment. Not now, baby. But I do need to warn you, my boss is picking us up. I'm not sure how he's going to react to this." Ozzy motions between the two of us, as if we're one unit now. "But he's promised to do everything he can to find your mom. He'll be cool with you, just not sure about me. Don't worry. I'll handle it. Follow my lead, and when everyone else descends upon you like you're roadkill—but, you know, in the best way possible—just let it happen. The sooner they get it out of their systems, the better."

I look out the window and see a small airport where we're taxiing. I don't have a chance to ask how there's ever a good way to be picked apart like roadkill, because there are three cars parked at the end of the runway with even more people standing in the late afternoon sun.

I turn back to the man I've put all my cards on. "Are those the people who are going to pick me apart?"

He bends at the waist and doesn't miss a beat. "Yeah. Some of them. There are more back at camp."

"Camp?!"

He shakes his head. "Not really. That's what we call headquarters. But really, it's just a farmhouse and some barns."

My ass falls to the sofa. What have I gotten myself into?

When the plane comes to a complete stop, Ozzy pulls me back to my feet and straight into his arms. "When I get you alone, I'll explain everything."

"I think you should've done that before we left Paris."

"Probably," he agrees, but he doesn't look contrite. "But there was no time. In about forty-five minutes, we'll be at one of the safest places on the planet we can be. Trust me."

"And in forty-five minutes you'll tell me everything?" I narrow my eyes. "Promise me, Ozzy. Because I'm back in the States where I feel safe to move around on my own without the protection of my *fiancé*. I'll catch the first plane to Malibu."

The pilot opens the heavy plane door but neither of us move. Ozzy's face turns to stone at the mention of my leaving. "Everyone and their dog is looking for you, namely your asshole uncle and the fuckwad who wants to make you a sister-wife. You're not going anywhere on your own, Liyah."

I pull away from him and reach for my backpack. "Then I'll look forward to knowing everything in approximately forty-five minutes. I might even give you an hour because traffic around D.C. is hellish anytime of day. But that's it, Ozzy. I won't wait any longer."

He glares at me before picking up the enormous duffle that houses all of our things. I don't wait for his lead. I move off the plane, anxious to meet everyone who's a part of Ozzy's life. I might be timid when he has his hand down my panties, but in any other situation, I can handle my own shit.

If Ozzy knows what's good for him, he'll learn that sooner rather than later.

Ozzy

Liyah barely puts me on a one-hour timer before she's off the plane without me. I haven't slept since we left

Paris. I worked the entire time, but to find out what I really need to know, I need time on the main system. The triggers I have set were tripped. This happened one other time, and it was a false alarm.

My gut tells me this is too.

But I can't get to any of that until I introduce Liyah to everyone, and spill my guts about my life story. And I only have an hour to do it.

I pull the duffle over my shoulder and double-time it to catch up with her before the wives of Whitetail kidnap her out from under me.

I have no doubt they will. I've seen it happen. It'll get out of hand if I don't control it.

"Oh my goodness, she's more stunning in person, and that's never the case." Gracie Jarvis doesn't even try to mutter under her breath. I'm not sure who she's talking to because she reaches my Princess before I can catch up. Gracie takes Liyah's hand and a look of pure glee takes over her face. "I'm Gracie. Welcome to the shitshow."

Jarvis laughs.

I cringe.

I can't see Liyah's face, but what the hell did I ever do to Gracie that she'd lead with that?

"It's not always a shitshow," Maya butts in, wearing her own grin that tells me she's eating this shit up. Maya shoots me a glance before looking back to the woman who's proving to be ground zero. "Congratulations on your engagement."

I swallow back a groan.

"Yeah, man. Congrats." I'd wipe the shit-eating grin from Grady's face if it wouldn't cause the wrong kind of attention. "Engaged. Who would've thought?"

Asa slaps me on the shoulder. "Impressive engagement announcement."

I don't have a chance to say anything, because Liyah finally looks back at me and bites her lip. I hike a brow and shrug. Let's see how fast she runs away from me now. Instead of refuting that the very royal virgin standing beside me will one day, in fact, be my wife, I wrap my arm around her shoulders and pull her to my side. "Thanks. It's been a whirlwind."

She stiffens at my side. "Ozzy—"

"So it is real." Keelie looks like she's going to burst with excitement. She tucks her long hair behind her ear and steps up to us. "You're really a princess?"

Liyah sinks into my side.

Well then.

I'll hold back the *I told you so* for later.

"Yes. I mean, I was born a princess. Though I haven't had anything to do with the dynasty in many years. I'm just, you know, normal."

Gracie's gaze goes from the ring I slid on Liyah's finger with no proposal to go with it to Liyah. "I have a feeling you're far from normal. And I love it. I'm so happy for you both."

Jarvis steps up, their son, Eze, sitting on his shoulders. He offers me a hand, holding onto his son with the other. "Welcome back. I can't even remember the last time you were home."

"Thanks." I hold a fist up to Eze and he gives me a bump immediately. "Dude, you're huge. I think you grew a foot while I was away. What are you, fifteen?"

Eze cackles. "I'm four! And I'm getting a sister."

"You are?"

Eze nods as a grin breaks his face. I look to Jarvis and Gracie. "I have been away for a long time."

Gracie pokes me in the chest. "Right? Shame on you, Oz. We hope to bring Misha home from South Korea in about six months."

Gracie and Jarvis met Eze in an orphanage in Uganda. It took almost a year, but they fought through the red tape and made him theirs.

My gaze goes to the one who hasn't said a word yet. With crossed arms, he studies and scrutinizes us. I'm not worried. What's he going to do, fire me? I run his multi-million-dollar satellite system, and even though I've taught them to make their way around it, no one can do what I do. Now that he's in the business of information as well as killing for the greater good around the world, my job is secure.

Plus, it's not like I had Liyah with me because it was bring-your-Princess-to-work day. It wasn't safe for me to leave her behind. There was no way the woman was leaving my sight, especially in Africa.

As Crew approaches, I break the silence. "I'm back. Just like you wanted."

He lifts his chin. "You good?"

I know what he's talking about, and I don't want to get into it now. Not until I have a chance to see if it's true. "For now. I'll be better once I can get into the control room and see for myself. I still think it's a false alarm."

He never takes his intense stare off me and shakes his head. "I want to believe that, Oz. I do. But I think it's different this time. There have been new developments this morning. You'll see. We need you in there. The parameters have been scrambled. Our surveillance went black."

Black.

Shit.

I pull in a big breath and am about to demand what those developments are, but Crew turns his attention to Liyah. His expression switches from business to inquisitive. "Welcome to Virginia. My wife had an event at the vineyard and couldn't be here. Trust me, she was not happy about missing the welcome wagon. She can't wait to meet you. And don't worry, we're working on your drama too."

"Too?" Liyah fists my shirt.

I pull her tighter. "Yeah, too. This is what I need to tell you."

"She doesn't know?" Grady asks, which does not help my situation one fucking bit.

"Grady—" Maya starts, but I interrupt.

"We've been a little busy with kings and shit," I bite.

Grady widens his eyes. "That's no way to start a marriage."

For fuck's sake.

Crew keeps talking. "We should get going. It wasn't easy to spin, but no customs today. We need the King to think you're still in Europe where your passport was last scanned. They're scrambling and confused since your phone is pinging in Canada."

My timer is ticking, and even though I don't think there's any fire behind her threat, I have no desire to test it. The last thing I need right now is to add a missing princess to my list of problems.

"Let's get going." I swing the duffle back up my shoulder. "Who are we with?"

"You're with us." Grady flips his keys around his finger and hooks an arm around his wife's neck. "We'll give you marriage advice on the way home."

Liyah stiffens at my side, and I shake my head. "Ignore him."

Maya smiles and moves forward to pull my Princess from my hold. "Yes, ignore him. Come on, you've got to be tired and hungry. We've got everything ready for you at Whitetail. Please tell me you like wine."

"I've been drinking wine with dinner since I was twelve," Liyah answers as Maya pulls her to the Escalade parked in the middle of the convoy.

Maya looks over her shoulder and shoots me a cocky smile. "She's going to fit in just fine."

Everyone else moves to their rides but Crew.

Now that Liyah is out of earshot, I turn back to him. "My surveillance went black?"

He nods. "In the middle of the night."

"You're sure you guys didn't fuck up the feed? It's happened before."

"This is different, I can tell. It went black, Oz. Just ... black." Crew's intensity does not waver. Then again, it rarely does. But this time, it sends a chill down my spine. He lifts a chin toward Grady's SUV. "You haven't told her?"

I pull a hand down my face and want nothing more than for one thing in my life to be normal. "This isn't something I'm used to sharing. Not one person in the world knows besides those in this organization. This is ... different."

"By the look on her face, I can't tell what's real and what's not between you two. But you brought her all this way, which means it's more than casual. Are you going to tell her?"

"Yeah, I'm going to tell her. I just need a minute alone. Explaining this is…"

"Fucked up," Crew finishes.

"Exactly," I agree. "And not something I've ever had to do."

"Well, it's time, because if I'm right and we didn't fuck up the feed, your past is about to blow up in our faces. Which means there are people out there who know you're walking the earth, which, in turn, means they might know you're working for me. Not only do we have to worry about you, we have to worry about us. If that woman is what I think she is to you, then tell her so we can fix the rest of this shit."

I watch Liyah climb into the back of the Escalade.

Crew is right.

This isn't going to be fun.

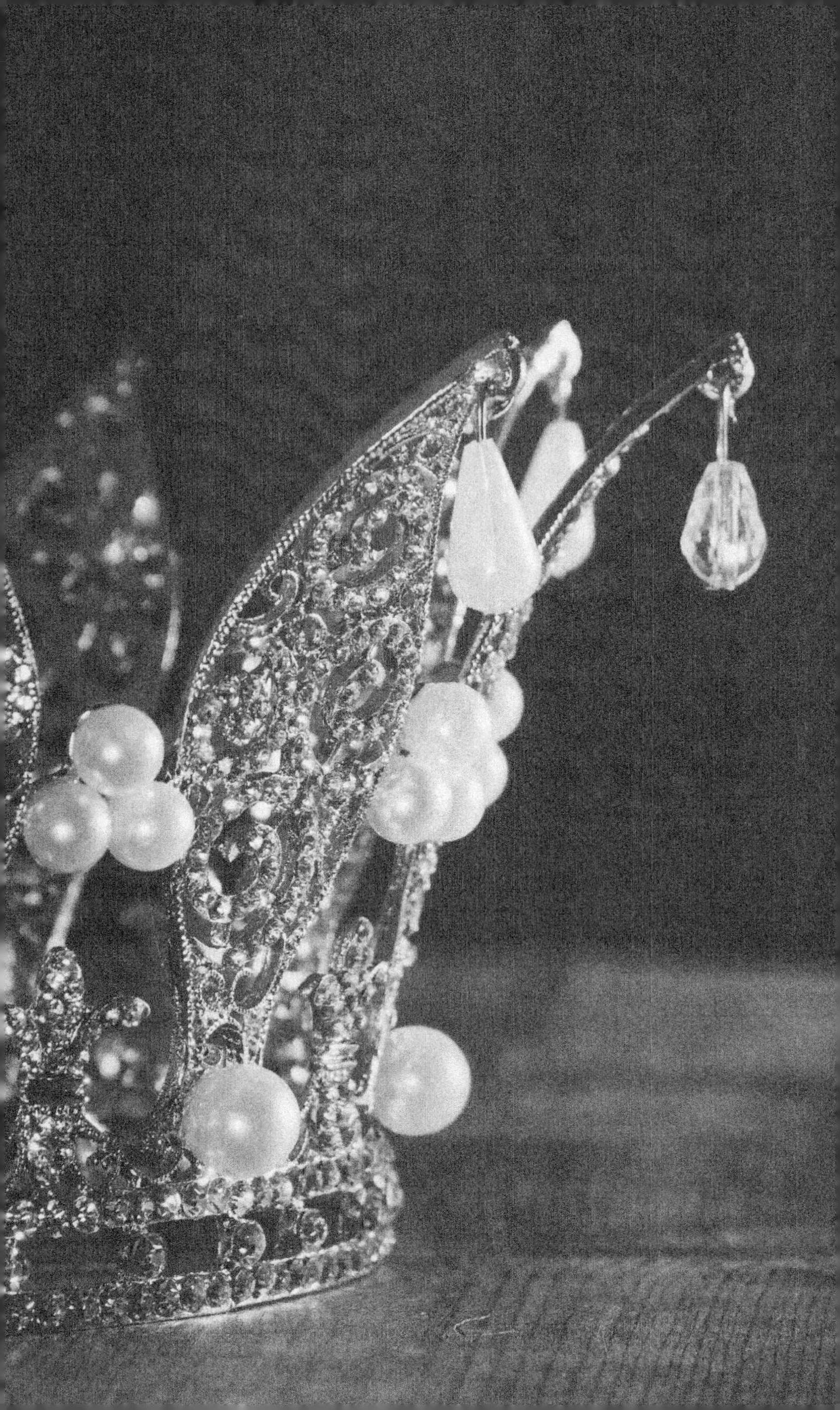

21

SECRETS

Ozzy

There was nothing more exciting than the first day I walked through the layers of safety measures of the National Security Agency. My background was cleaner than my mother's kitchen, and that's saying something. I slid through the hiring process without a hiccup, and they welcomed me with open arms.

I was perfect. My college days were that boring. My family was that honorable. I never even had so much as a parking ticket linked to my name, and it wasn't because I weaseled my way into the systems to change that shit. Because I could have, but I never would.

There are people who do the right thing when the world is looking, but those same people are willing to cheat, lie, and steal in the cover of darkness. Then there are others who do the right thing even when they can get away with crushing the world when they hold it in the palm of their sweaty hands.

And that's the difference between them and me. I was the latter of the two.

If there was a rule or a law—hell, even an unspoken code of ethics or moral hanging out there in the universe for decent humans—I followed it to a T. I gave new meaning to straight and narrow. If anyone was made to work with the most sensitive and secret information for the most powerful country in the universe, it was Austin Oswald Graves, III.

I attended MIT on a full ride. My stellar grades put me in the top of my class. Hell, I even had the volunteer hours to top my perfection off with a big, fat juicy cherry. All that meant I was recruited heavily in the public and private sectors. I was offered a hell of a lot more money than Uncle Sam could afford to pay me. But none of it was as exciting.

Because … *secrets*.

Secrets are exciting. Who doesn't want to know secrets?

The NSA didn't need to beg me to take their lower paying job. It was a no-brainer. I was made for that shit.

And I killed it for seven years.

Seven fucking years.

But when you're perfect and a rule follower and do all the right things when no one is looking, you tend to be an easy target.

That's what this Pennsylvania boy who grew up on a farm in the middle of nowhere didn't know. I was naïve. There's nothing I regret more in this entire fucking nightmare than that. Because, looking back, I might as well have walked into that shitstorm begging them to burn me alive at the stake.

And that's what they did. That fire was the hottest I've ever felt and drove me to where I am today.

A killer.

A sleuth on the dark web.

And a dead man.

Oh, and somewhat of a bodyguard, fake fiancé, and the only person on earth who's ever given the famous Princess of Morocco an orgasm.

Addy turns the key in the lock and pushes the door open with her free hand since she's holding Aimée on her hip with the other. When she turns back to us, she tosses the key to me, but doesn't look away from Liyah. "It's small, I'm sorry about that. You're more than welcome to stay in the main house with us, but I thought this might give you more privacy."

I stuff the key in my pocket and put a hand to Liyah's back to push her in. "We could've stayed at the farmhouse at camp. That's where my things are."

Addy looks horrified. "No! I'd never expect Liyah to stay there. I keep trying to get Crew to gut the whole thing but he doesn't want anyone on the property. I get that, but it's falling apart."

Liyah looks around the miniature house that's located on the vineyard property, tucked away in the woods for privacy. "It's lovely. We couldn't ask for anything nicer. Thank you, Addy."

I dump the duffle on the floor of the bedroom and Aimée attacks me the moment I turn around. "Up-up, Ossie!"

"Hey, squirt." I pick her up and throw her into the air before flipping her upside down to dangle her by her ankles. She screams and laughs and begs me to let her down, but she loves it.

I've been a part of this group for a few years. Long enough that I've seen some of these men get married, have babies, adopt from around the world, and basically go on with their lives, despite what they do for a living. And they've included me in all of it. They know all I have is them.

Crew and Addy's oldest daughter, Vivi, is quiet and reserved. I've seen her sit with a book for hours and she's only four. But their youngest? This one is going to be a hellraiser. It's a good thing Crew has a barn full of weapons. He'll need them to get her out of the trouble she'll surely dive into headfirst.

"You rile her up, Ozzy. She loves every bit of it and you." Addy leans into the arm of the couch and shakes her head. "Everything is clean. The bathroom and kitchen are stocked. Crew doesn't like strangers on the property anymore—Maya was actually my only paying tenant, but I always have the bungalow ready to go. You never know when we'll have overnight guests. Ozzy is right—the men who work for Crew that don't maintain a home of their own live at the property next door. But you're a princess."

Liyah crosses her arms and shakes her head. "Really, it's not what you think. I have nothing to do with that part of my family. It's not a big deal at all."

Addy collects Aimée from my hold where I was swinging her back and forth like a pendulum. "We've never had a princess here, Liyah. Don't steal our fun. It's a big deal."

"Thanks, Addy." I sit and slump low in the middle of the sofa. "I need a minute with Liyah. Then I'm going to camp to check the surveillance streams on Reskill, catch up on the King, call Bella about her progress in

Morocco, and maybe take a shower. After all that, I'll bring Liyah to Whitetail for a tasting. We'll probably be able to get to that next year."

Addy wrangles Aimée as she speaks to Liyah. "You don't need Ozzy to bring you. You can come to the tasting room or our house anytime. I left my number on the counter, as well as everyone else's. Call me. I'm always around."

"Thanks, but I don't have a phone. I left mine in California. I didn't want to risk my uncle tracking me."

"I'll get you a phone today," I tell her. "No one will be able to track you on it."

"Other than Ozzy," Addy amends with a smile.

Liyah's gaze shoots to me, and her dark eyes widen.

I shrug. "That goes without saying."

"I'll leave you guys be." She sets Aimée down and brushes the dark curls out of her face. "Let's go find Daddy and Vivi."

"Thank you," Liyah calls.

I thank no one and shut my eyes.

The minute the door clicks, Liyah speaks. "You've got approximately ten minutes to spare, Ozzy. As nice as everyone is—though I do believe their expectations for a royal princess are much higher than I can deliver—I want to know everything. Especially since you demand my trust at every turn. I've given it to you blindly, but you dragging me away from Europe where I could be close when someone finds my mother, is the last straw."

I open my eyes. She stands in front of me with her arms crossed, causing her dress to raise up a bit. It's cooling off in Virginia, and I wonder what she needs. Besides what she bought in Paris, all she had were the few things in her backpack.

"Ozzy," she presses.

I hold my hand out for her. "Can we do this sitting down? I'm wiped."

Her arms drop to her sides, and she sighs. Just when I think she might refuse, she takes my hand, and steps over the small coffee table. She's about to sit next to me, but I pull her into my lap. She comes without hesitation, which is good, since I have no idea how this will go.

She settles and proves she isn't fucking around with the time. "No more excuses, Ozzy. Tell me."

I tuck her hip tight to my groin with one hand and place the other on the side of her face. Her hair is falling out of the knot on top of her head, her dark eyes probe mine through her thick lashes, and she looks as if she's bracing.

She needs to.

"I never should have touched you."

She stiffens on my lap. "Why?"

I shake my head because it kills me to say the words aloud. "I'm selfish, but there's something about you. I did my best to fight it while I was doing everything I could to keep us alive—I swear. But we're here, and all I know is the thought of walking away from you—or hell, even worse, knowing you'll walk away from me to be someone else's someday?" I shake my head and force myself not to grip her so hard I'll leave bruises. "You'll do me in if that happens. Do you understand? I'll do anything to keep you from walking away. But I have no fucking idea how this is going to work. I could not be in a worse position right now."

Her expression is as telling as her words. "I have no idea what you're talking about. You're scaring me."

I slide my hand into her hair and hold tight. "I can't

offer you a normal life, Princess. It's not in the cards for me." I pause before stressing, "Ever."

Her beautiful face pinches in confusion.

"I'm a dead man, baby." I pull her hand to my chest to hold it over the organ that might beat out of my chest. "In every way but this."

Liyah

His heart pounds under my touch. Faster and harder than it should for any man in the shape he's in.

I should know. I've seen him naked.

"You're saying things, but they mean nothing." My words are frantic and desperate, mirroring my own heart at the moment.

His hand slides out of my hair and down my back. The look on his face is one of desolation and regret. I have no idea what he's talking about, and it puts a knot in my stomach.

"I worked for the National Security Agency right out of college. I fucking loved that job. It was a wet dream for a computer geek like me from the sticks. Do you know what their purpose is?"

I lift a shoulder. "I've only lived in America since I was seventeen, but I assume information ... spying. Things like that?"

He nods. "Yeah, all things like that. Their official responsibility is information assurance—breaking foreign intelligence codes through secure systems and encryptions. To land an interview, you've got to be good. To get hired, you've got to be the best. Which means there are a shit ton of smart people with access to highly sensitive information. And not just information, but systems. What I was too naïve to realize when I was younger, is when that many intelligent people are given access, there will be bad apples. I worked with two of them. And before I realized what was going on or what they were doing, it was too late. They framed me and put a target on my back bigger than a billboard. They were that good, and once I realized what they'd done, I had no way out. I was squeezed into a corner so tight, I couldn't prove my innocence. They made sure the evidence pointed at me was so tight it might as well have been the truth, even though it wasn't."

My sweaty fingers twist the material of his shirt into a knotted mess. "What did they do to you?"

"They were into some dark shit and profited from it. Hell, they still are. They use their clearance to gather information they have no right to, and turn around to sell that shit on the dark web."

"I don't understand. They've never been caught?"

"No. But they knew they were swimming in warm water when they decided to pin their shit on me. Our supervisors knew information was being gathered illegally, they just didn't know who was doing it. I wasn't the only whiz working there. We all were. They were good—as good as me—and they knew they were about to be lit up."

"But you didn't do it." I'm defensive of the man I've only just met. At this point, I trust him with my life.

And other things...

"No, baby, I didn't. But I told you, they're good. They created the evidence. Clear and concise, and there was nothing I could do to refute it, other than saying I'd been framed. Words are one thing—evidence is another, even if it was contrived. I gave years to the NSA. I know how they operate. They don't give a shit what you say if everything else is in black and white, wrapped in a fucking tidy package presented at their feet. The government does not do gray and they really wouldn't care about what I had to say when those two fuckwads made sure I'd go down for what they did."

This is new. It doesn't matter whether we're jumping from a train or he's remote detonating a bomb to kill a terrorist—Ozzy is calm and collected in everything he does. But not now. I can tell this has haunted him far too long and will continue to do so until the day he dies.

"Okay, but," I look around the small cottage where we landed on the outskirts of the Capitol, "how did you get here?"

His hand touches my face again, and this time he presses in. "I had no way out, baby. I might be good when it comes to tech, but they are too. I saw the writing on the wall. Had I stuck around to defend myself, I would've ended up in prison for a long fucking time. They were selling State secrets on the dark web to other countries." I suck in a breath. "And not our allies. Not only would I have been accused of stealing government property, but also treason and probably murder. I would've spent my life in prison."

"No," I whisper.

"Yes. And I have more to worry about than me. I have Crew and the team and their families. They took a chance on me. I can't allow anything to come back on them."

"Ozzy—"

But he doesn't let me finish. "I knew Jarvis as a kid.

He was a military brat, but we kept in touch. He left the Navy, and I knew he would be someone I could reach out to. I was right—he not only stepped up to help me, he offered me a job that I could do off the grid."

"You're on the run all the time? That's no way to live, Ozzy."

"No, Princess, it's not. They might be good and can get away with what they did, but I'm not shit at what I do, either. I knew I needed to disappear in a way no one would look for me ever again. I faked my death. There's literally a death certificate issued in my name. In the eyes of the government, the world, and even my own family—no, especially my own family—I'm dead. There's no way I could allow them to be put in harm's way because of me. That's probably the most painful part. They fought to clear my name even after I faked my death. They were torn apart—still are. And I have to live knowing I did that to them."

Tears well in my eyes. I have no words.

"So, yeah. I'm a dead man. And I have no idea what I'm going to do about this." He gives me a squeeze. "Because you deserve a life—one I'm not capable of giving you."

I shake my head, and a tear escapes, but then I remember. "What else happened? We rushed back here for a reason, and I know it wasn't my mother."

"I need to get in the control room. Crew has his own satellite system, and I run it. I've always kept tabs on the guys who did this to me, but when Crew bought Reskill, I was able to up that shit. I know where they are on a daily basis, who they meet outside of work, where they go to dinner, and the schools their kids attend. I want to see if they trip up. One of those lines was jumbled, or

Crew thinks so, which means they might know I'm not dead. If this is true, there's never been a time like now to clear my name."

I slide my hand from his beating heart to his stubbled jaw. "What are you going to do?"

His blue eyes narrow, and he takes my hand from his jaw, pressing the pads of my fingertips to his lips. Then his expression turns into something I've never seen before. "I've watched them, Liyah. Don Demaree and Bobby Cannon are the worst kind of cocksuckers who roam the planet. I've watched them live their lives—get married, have a couple kids each, buy as much luxury as they can without throwing any red flags on how they could afford that shit, because they're living too high and mighty for a couple of assholes with government jobs at the NSA. I watch every fucking move they make because that shit feeds something in me."

"Ozzy." His name comes out on a breath, and it's not lost on me it's similar to how I sound when he's got control of my body in a much different way.

"There's nothing more dangerous than a dead man out for revenge, Princess. I've got nothing to lose, and I'm going to get retribution."

My heart pounds, and I swear I feel it in every extremity. "What are you going to do?"

He tips his head, lowers his voice, and his words ... they're deep and passionate and full of every emotion that runs through his body. "I'm going to fuck them up. One way or another, they'll be done for good."

All the oxygen escapes my body.

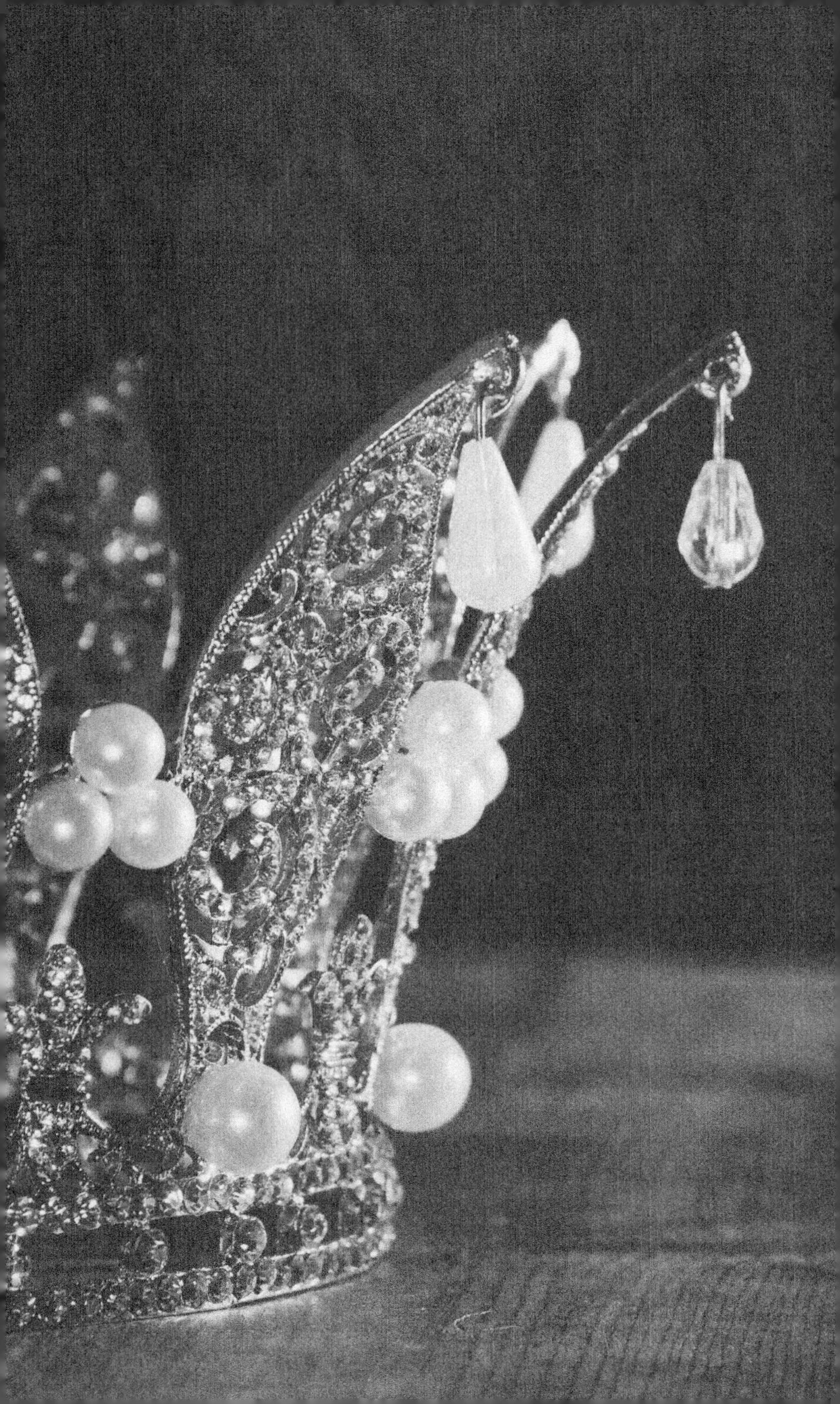

22

KINDNESS

Ozzy

I knew the moment I was fucked.
It was January. As my father would say, it was colder than a well-digger's ass in Klondike.

What Don and Bobby accomplished took more than brains. It took time, planning, and coordination. Their electronic trail went on for years. I knew those systems like the back of my hand. They can't be backdated. Those motherfuckers masterminded this for a long ass time.

I was their fall guy. If anyone ever caught on to their shit, I would go down. Never in my young, gullible naïveté did I think I'd have to watch my back because I might be targeted by my co-workers at the NS-fucking-A.

But that's just what happened.

The questions started coming from my managers. Questions that made me uncomfortable, to say the least. No one would tell me why I was being asked about highly sensitive information, about those in the Witness Security Program, informants for the CIA, and even about the programming I was in charge of when I was assigned to the Russian intelligence. No one told me shit before my security clearance was pulled out from under me.

Little did they know, I was skilled enough to not only use my skills for good, but I took advantage of an extra twenty minutes I found when no one was watching. I got on an unlocked computer and used my knowledge of the systems for purely defensive measures.

That's when I found it. I found all of it. And it made me look like a sloppy fuck who didn't know how to do my job. Even if I had decided to turn against my own country—which I damn well would never—I'd cover shit up better than they did.

That's the day I realized I was going down for treason. Not only treason, but potentially murder. And since spilling the blood of an entire family who were in the WITSEC program was not my doing, there was no way I was going to chance going away for something I had no guilt in.

That's when I risked reaching out to Jarvis. I didn't have long to make the decision. The Department of Justice was scrambling to draw up a warrant for my arrest. I knew because I busted into that system too.

I'll never forget the moment. I sat in the dining room at Crew Vega's compound surrounded by the men I now work with. The thing about this organization, they don't need a judge, a jury, and attorneys to fuck up a case or, in my situation, someone's life. I laid out what I had at the time, which wasn't a lot, but it was enough. It didn't hurt that Jarvis threw down for me, and apparently he'd never done that for anyone.

It was unanimous. Then it took all of two minutes to put the plans in motion. But before we hit the proverbial big red button that might as well be featured on a Roadrunner cartoon, I made one last call to my parents on a secure line.

That phone call lasted sixteen minutes.

My parents knew about the allegations at work. I told them I was being framed, swore to them I didn't do what I was being accused of.

I didn't have to beg them to believe me. They said they knew I'd never do anything so heinous. But I knew that was our last conversation. I did everything I could to make it normal. To give them one last memory that wasn't tainted.

We talked about my dad replacing the carburetor on one of the tractors.

We talked about the updates my mom was forcing my dad to make in her store over the winter.

We talked about my younger brothers, and how they thought Drew was going to propose to his girlfriend, and that Axel changed his major for the third time.

It was normal and basic and lacked any kind of emotion from me other than I had a few minutes to kill on my way to work.

My time was up—in so many fucking ways. I said goodbye like I always did. There was no way I was dragging them into this shit and couldn't let on that the call was anything more than normal.

Routine.
Habitual.
And also, the end.

Of everything as I knew it.

That was the day everything changed.

I'm grateful for it, and I fucking hate it at the same time.

That was the day I died.

"See what I mean?" Crew bites.

I've been sitting in the command room for an hour. I've combed through all the layers of surveillance I've put in place for Crew when Bella was running from the western world.

I pull a hand down my face. At first, I blamed it on my exhaustion. I'm going on a day without sleep. Again.

But a lack of REM has nothing to do with it. Adrenaline has a way of sharpening my focus, and right now, mine is honed in like a laser. Because Bobby and Don know someone is watching them, and I'm one hundred percent sure they know it's not Uncle Sam. If they found my taps, they know they're not official.

"Yeah. This is bad." I don't look away from the screen. I can't. The sun is setting on the East Coast, and Don and Bobby are scrambling in ways that give me way too much satisfaction. If they know, the stakes have been raised and the fire kindled on this fucked-up game that has become my life.

"Get the new surveillance up and running. Whatever hocus pocus you established was scrambled over twenty-four hours ago. I bet they've known longer. They might be good, but they don't have access to their own personal encrypted satellite system like you do."

My fingers hit the keyboard. I know what to do.

Before I officially died, there were three people in this world who knew without a shadow of a doubt I was innocent. Demaree, Cannon, and me. I'm the only ghost who can haunt them.

Don Demaree and Bobby Cannon know. Somehow, they know I didn't die in that explosion. I'd be willing to bet my freedom on it.

But what they don't know is they're dealing with a man who has nothing to lose.

I'm taking them down and will fuck with them in the process.

Liyah

I GUESS when you're so deep in your own hell, you're blind to everyone else's.

Ozzy brought me a shiny, new cellphone and assured me it wouldn't hook up to any tower anywhere, and I could call him, Addy, or surf the internet. But he told me if I decided to shock the world again with a post about my engagement, to let him do that so he could work his magic, so my uncle wouldn't know I was on some random vineyard in the middle of Virginia.

I told him he didn't need to worry about that. The best thing to do with a viral post is to let it simmer and feed on itself. Followers look for updates and sometimes, less is more. Letting them wonder and create their own outcomes was the way to go.

Then he wrapped me up in his strong arms and kissed me like he never has. It was different. There wasn't just lust or hunger in it. It was more. After Ozzy told me his story—no, his hell—it was like there was nothing between us. Like a thick, cement wall had tumbled.

Disintegrated into thin air, leaving nothing between us but truths and sorrows.

Ozzy stripped himself bare for me, figuratively speaking of course. Because he then left me with an ache for him I hadn't experienced to that point. And my desire for him already had me wanting things that were foreign. I'm stepping into uncharted territory.

"I'm sorry." I stare out to the vineyard from where I stand at the windows in Addy and Crew's family room. I look back at the woman who welcomed us to her property and gave us her cottage for as long as we need. Her dark, thick head of chestnut hair is pulled back into a low knot and her sweater drapes off one shoulder showing a lace halter wrapped around her neck. "I'm sure you're busy. I'm keeping you from your work and your family."

She shakes her head, and her smile is like a warm hug I didn't know I needed. The lump in my throat seizes me, and I realize my emotions are about to take over. I pull in a big breath and look back out to the rolling hills where her staff is busy.

"I'm glad you called." Addy throws her hand out, motioning to the scurry of work happening on her land. "It's busy, but I gave up running the day-to-day aspects of my business a few years ago. I have a great staff who manage this place as if it's their own. I've still got my hands in everything, but even if I had to step away for months, this place would still run like a well-oiled machine. The Harvest is our biggest event of the year. The private grape stomping happens tomorrow followed by a formal dinner in the vineyard. The dinner sold out the day the tickets went up for sale. I'll make sure you and Ozzy have a private spot."

I don't look away from an army erecting an enormous tent and tell her the truth. "You're very kind. Please don't go to any trouble."

"That's not the first time you said something like that. You're not used to kindness?"

She gets my attention, and I turn to her. Facing me with her arms crossed, she leans on the floor-to-ceiling window we're standing in front of. I shrug. "I'm used to my friends. Sure, they're kind, but their kindness is also self-serving. I haven't lived at the palace for a long time, but no, outside of my mother, I guess I haven't had a lot of selfless kindness."

"I'm sorry."

I look back out to the flurry of work happening. "I'm not used to the kindness of strangers. But then again, I've never really needed it."

"I understand that."

I turn back to her and frown.

She smiles. "I have a lot in common with Ozzy, you know."

After all that he just shared with me, that surprises me more than anything. "Really?"

She nods. "I lived most of my life pretending I was someone I'm not. It's complicated, and Ozzy knows it all. He can fill you in on the details. But you being here means he trusts you with everything. I know he's filled you in on his past." When my eyes widen, she bites back a smirk. "Yeah, sorry. We have a way of knowing everything about one another."

I bite my lip and hope my skin doesn't brighten, because my temperature sure rises a few degrees thinking of the things they probably know just because of my damn uncle.

"It's not a bad thing really," she assures. "What I'm saying is, Ozzy has been dealt a really bad hand, but he has a family here. I know him well. He's like the rest of the men, yet different. Despite what he's been through, there's something about him. He's become more and more intense over the years. I'm not sure there's any way to avoid that, doing what they do. But Ozzy has always had this underlying tenderness about him."

What she's saying shouldn't make sense, but it does. Ozzy bleeds intensity at times. Like just a couple hours ago when he explained how the men who set him up would either be dead or in prison as a result of him *fucking them up*.

But when it's only him and me, he's someone completely different.

"You get it. I can tell," Addy adds.

"Yes. He's all those things. And more."

A knowing smile settles on her pretty face. "I don't doubt it."

"Thank you, again. For everything."

She pulls her phone out of her back pocket and starts to type on the screen. "Don't thank me yet. I'm not sure how long you'll be here, but my guess is you need things. Give me your sizes. I'll get started on that."

"I'm really fine," I argue.

"We've had a warm fall, but next week we're expecting a cold snap. You walked off that plane with a backpack, and you might not be what I expected in a princess, but you're royalty all the same." Addy bites her lip, trying not to grin. "I also might've stalked you. You need some clothes and makeup. Seriously, if anything it will make you feel better. Plus, you're my guest, which makes it my job to make sure you have everything you need."

I relent quicker than I care to admit. "From the moment I left California weeks ago, I've hardly felt like myself. I won't turn down a good face mask."

Addy taps away at her screen. "That's at the top of the list. Don't worry, this isn't our first rodeo. We know what you need."

I'm not sure I want to know what that means.

"I'll pay you back," I promise.

Addy waves me off. "No way. This is what we do."

I decide to accept her kindness for the same reasons I've accepted everything Ozzy has done for me. Because I need it. And it feels good. But there was a reason I came here.

"Ozzy has done so much for me. Now that I know he's dealing with a crisis of his own..."

"He can do both," Addy assures me. "And he has help."

"Oh, I have no doubt he can do both. And I appreciate the help more than you know. Even this Bella person is now traveling Africa looking for my mother, and she doesn't even know me."

"When you meet Bella, you'll understand. She not only has a heart of gold, she's very good at what she does. Crew would say she's the best when it comes to sources in that part of the world. If there's a lead on your mother, she'll find it."

"And I'm truly grateful. But I'm talking about Ozzy. He's done everything for me. I don't know what I can do for him. I mean, I know there's nothing I can do. Not really." I pull in a big breath and drag my hands through my messy hair. I could really use a shower. "Do you know what I mean?"

Addy tips her head, and I thought her expression was gentle before. She lowers her voice, and when her words hit me, her advice is oddly sage, yet not at all what I was looking for. Her hand finds mine and she holds tight. "This is new. The two of you are new. I know this isn't what you want to hear, but you'll figure it out. The fact that you're asking says everything. That you care for him."

My answer comes swift. "I do."

She smiles. "Ozzy is like the younger brother who I can't get to come home often enough, so this makes me immensely happy. I thought it was the case, but I didn't want to assume."

My lips tip on one side. "You mean because I'm so young or because I've been labeled a princess?"

Addy shows me she's no bullshitter, because her smile grows into a grin when she answers honestly. "Both."

"I appreciate your sincerity."

Her response is immediate. "I appreciate your affection for Ozzy. There's only so much we can do, and there's really only so much he'll allow us to do. If this turns into something more between the two of you, you'll know. Trust your gut. These men will do anything for us, but they need us too. Don't forget that. And hold your ground. You'll know what he needs when he needs it. Especially when he thinks he doesn't need it."

"I hope I'll know," I admit.

"I have no doubt you will. You've shown your strength and bravery."

I look back out at the sun winking behind the horizon, calling it another day. A day that zipped by so fast, it seemed to blend into the others since I met Ozzy. It feels like a lifetime ago that I was in Malibu, living my life like I didn't have a care in the world.

How quickly things can change.

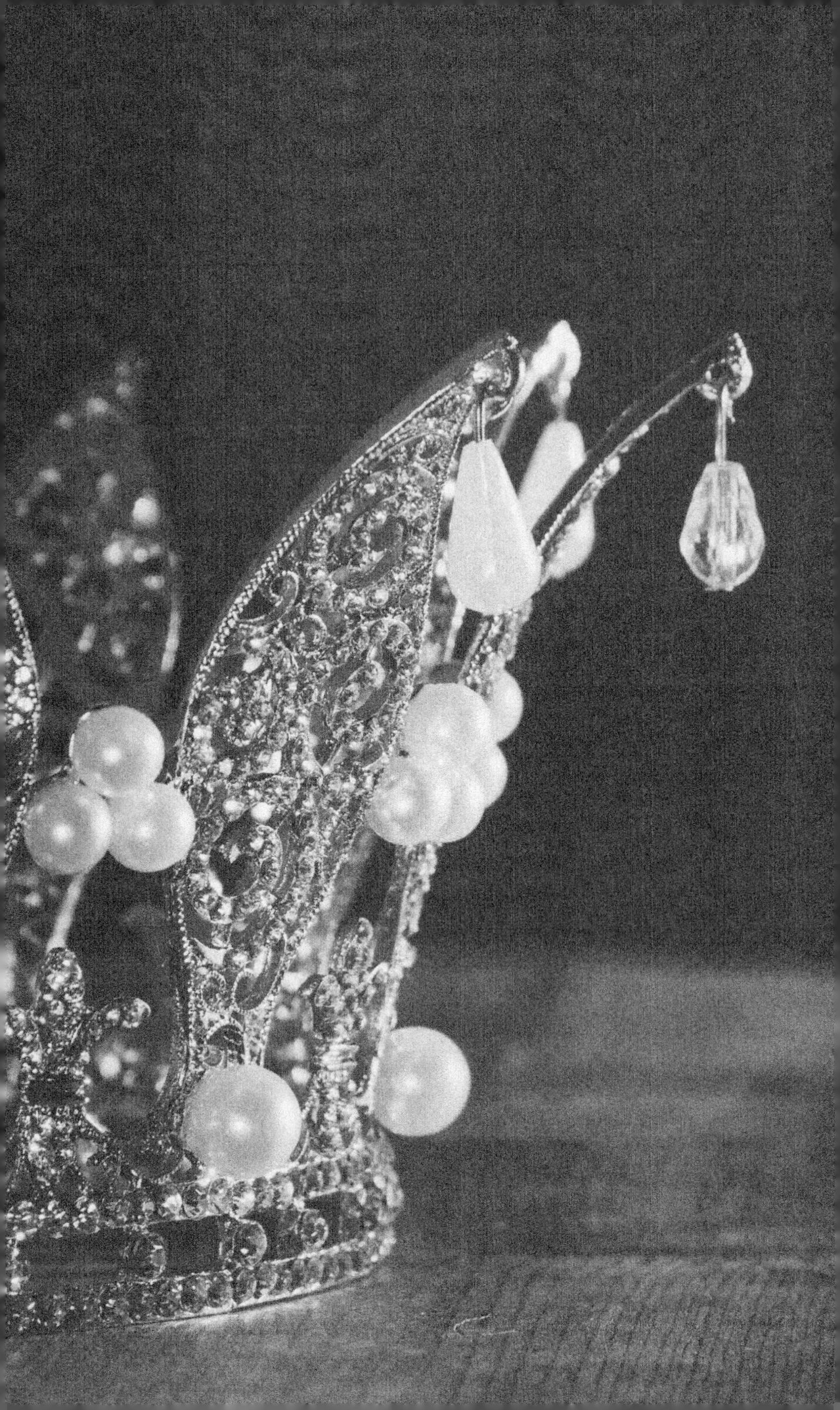

23

THE BEST PAIN

Ozzy

I open my eyes and filtered light fills the space. Between travel and lack of sleep, I have no idea what's up or down.

What I do know is that I'm getting really used to waking next to my mostly naked royal virgin.

My cock loves me and hates me for it.

Speaking of, I've never woken up as hard as I do with Liyah by my side.

I hated abandoning her right after we got here. But since Demaree and Cannon somehow found out I'm alive and breathing and didn't die in a fiery one-car accident on a dark night, that shit couldn't wait. When I got back to the cottage, she was asleep in the middle of the bed with her wet hair fanned on the pillow. I took the quickest shower I could, crawled in behind her, and passed out.

I have no idea how long ago that was, but I'm wide

awake now. Especially when she rolls in my arms, pressed against me from my neck to my rock-hard dick.

"What time did you come to bed?" she mumbles against my skin.

My hand lands on her ass that's barely covered by a tiny pair of panties. "I have no idea. I don't even know what time it is now."

The tips of her fingers dance up my side. I fight the urge to take her hand and wrap it around my cock. "Did you do what you needed to do last night?"

"Yeah. Now we wait. See what they say, what their next moves are at work." I drag my hand down the back of her leg and hitch it over my hip. That puts my needy cock directly where he wants to be. "Baby, you need to know that I'll tell you anything you want, but I have no desire to talk about them right here." My cock begs for more when I press it to her pussy. "Not when we're like this."

Her moan is soft. I almost don't hear it, but it vibrates against my chest and everywhere else. "Okay, I won't ask you about it here."

"Princess."

She tips her face to mine. Her eyes are sleepy and sexy as fuck. The longer I'm with her like this, the more I want. And I thought I wanted her before. I want to roll her over, slide inside, and watch those dark eyes come alive while I make her mine. I want to taste her. I want to travel the world with her, and not like we've already done where we're running from shit and hiding from kings and perverted old men.

I want to be normal.

With her.

And I want to do it over and over and over again. Forever.

I crave normalcy.

As if a princess and a dead man could have anything normal. I'm not sure there's a less likely pair than us when it comes to normal.

"What, Ozzy?"

I shake my head and hoist her up my body before rolling her to her back. Her legs part for me in invitation, and my hips fall between. I give her more of my weight and take her mouth. This is a spot I'm in no hurry to leave.

When I finally let up, her face is flushed, and she's never looked more beautiful than she does beneath me.

"About what happened in Paris," I start.

"A lot of things happened in Paris."

"True." I press my cock into her pussy one more time. "Specifically while I was in the shower."

She catches her bottom lip between her teeth.

"Yeah," I agree. "We had to rush off and didn't get a chance to talk about that."

Her brows pinch. "Are you upset?"

A slow smile takes over my face. "Fuck no, baby."

Her tits rise and fall beneath me, and instead of biting her lip this time, she's biting back a smile. "Well. Then I'm not sorry."

"Why did you do it?" I know why she did it, but I need to hear her say it.

I wonder if this is the difference between a really young virgin and one at the age of twenty-two. She's not shy. And she proves both when she says, "I was curious."

I lower my voice. "All you had to do was ask,

Princess. Think about how much more fun it would've been had you joined me."

If a gaze could deadpan, hers does.

I push her because I have to know. "What were you curious about?"

Two beats pass and she seems to steel herself. She's as serious as she's ever been when she answers. "Everything."

I'm surprised but not. The woman is strong and vulnerable. Sexy and innocent. And she's proving to have me more and more strung up as the moments tick by.

When I answer, I'm also as serious as my dead beating heart. "Ask me anything, and I'll tell you."

I've got her in the most vulnerable spot anyone could. She's half my size. But she trusts me. I've done a lot of shit in my life, but nothing has made me feel bigger and more powerful than her trust.

"When I was watching..." She slides a leg up my side and drags her heel over my ass. "Um, what does it feel like? You know, for you."

That was not what I was expecting. If all the blood wasn't already on its way to my cock, that topic of conversation certainly does it.

I feel like beating my fucking chest like a caveman as my brain tries to form the words, but more, because I'm the one who's got her right here. I'm the one she's asking.

If this doesn't do me in, I don't know what will.

Liyah

I can't help it.

Ever since watching him in the shower in Paris ... I've wanted to know.

I needed to know.

"What does it feel like? When I come?"

I give him a hesitant nod, because the topic of conversation is pressed into my sex—my clit. My heart is racing, and I want more.

I think I want everything.

Ozzy's voice dips, as if we weren't alone in the bungalow, in the middle of nowhere, surrounded only by the forest to listen to our secrets. He lowers his face and runs the tip of his nose alongside mine.

"It's like my first sip of coffee in the morning when, for just a second, I forget about the fucking day ahead of me. I know something is coming that's so good, I'll get to escape reality, and nothing else matters."

I exhale when he drags his tongue across my bottom lip.

"But that's only at the beginning when I know it's going to happen," he goes on, his words dripping like hot honey on my skin. I'm warm, but the tiny hairs on my arms stand at attention. "My brain shuts off, yet I'm acutely aware. My senses are sharpened, but there could be World War III going on around me, and I wouldn't give a shit."

There's nothing but him, his blue eyes, and his words searing me in a way I'll never forget. His lips hit mine, and he grinds his cock against my sex. Hard, rough. Thin silk and cotton boxers are the only thing keeping him from making me his. I can barely breathe as he presses me into the soft mattress.

I want more. I arch—my clit needs more. He lets go

of my mouth, and a moan escapes my lips. He brings a hand up to frame my face, his thumb drags across my bottom lip. He continues moving slowly, and I wish there was nothing between us. That he would rip my panties off and I'd feel him, his skin hot against mine.

"And then," he goes on, his own breath heavy and labored. "When I come, it's like the best pain. Like I could actually die, and I'd be okay."

I bring my hand up to his face, my knees to his sides. He rocks against me one more time, and I arch, feeling it start to inch over me.

"You gonna come for me like this?"

My eyes take a break, and I blink slowly, wanting it. Wanting nothing but to fall apart in his arms again. It might be selfish, but when he has me like this, I'm desperate for him to do anything.

I open my eyes to look up at him, moving over me. "Yes. Please, don't stop."

He gives me more of his weight, more of his strength. More of his cock right where I want it.

But he doesn't stop talking. "I can't wait for this. Because being right here, controlling your body like it's mine? Baby, you make me feel invincible and out of fucking control, both at the same time. You wring me in knots. I'm fucking gone for you."

I press my head into the pillow, doing all I can to get the friction I need. When I fall, I fall hard. It's good there's no one around but the forest, because this time I have no control when I let go.

Ozzy's body is relentless and demanding. More than he's been with me so far. Before, he was completely in control while controlling me. But not now. This is something different.

And I love it.

I'm barely coming down from my orgasm when my tank is ripped over my head. When I look up at the only man who's been my only sexual anything, he's breathing hard as he reaches for his boxers.

His cock springs free between us where he's pressed up on an arm. With his other hand, he grabs mine and wraps it around his cock.

Holy shit.

Hot, thick, soft, and still, hard as steel.

I'm mesmerized.

"Your turn." His words are heavy and curt, and the sensation between my legs continues. I barely have a chance to catch up when he starts moving again, but harder this time. I bring my other hand up and run it down his gorgeous abs. The need to touch him everywhere consumes me.

"Gonna come on you," he bites, looking down where I hold him in my hands. Even though he's orchestrating this, it feels as if the power has been transferred. I run my thumb over the swollen head of his cock—the beautiful color of red and purple, tinged with a shade of desperation.

I thought he was moving before, but it was nothing compared to now. His body rocks, every muscle above me on display and taut. I grip his cock and reach down to feel his balls that have been blue for me too many times to count. His strength is almost too much. When I grip harder, a groan escapes as his elbows drop beside my head.

His gaze is hot and heavy, searing my eyes. Yet, I feel more powerful than I ever have.

Him losing control by my touch.

Then he stills—his entire body tenses over mine ... in my hands. Veins bulge at his neck, his expression shows me the pain he described. And he was right.

This man is invincible.

Yet so out of control.

And I made him that way.

When he comes, it happens all over my chest. Hot, sticky, and I'm sure I've never witnessed anything so beautiful and uncomplicated and basic.

I'm in awe.

I let go when he finishes and he falls to my body in a way he's never done before. Warm, sweaty, and sticky. His bare cock is pressed to my tummy. Skin to skin. Heavy.

I love it.

No, I'm obsessed with it.

He brings his hand to the side of my face again, pressing his lips to my temple. His heart races against my breasts. I tip my face to his to kiss him.

"Does that answer your question, Princess?"

I hesitate, taking in his features, never wanting to forget this. "Yes. Thank you."

"No need to thank me, baby. I'll answer that question over and over again, every day if you want. The fact that you asked it to begin with does things to me I can't describe."

When I pull in a labored breath, he shifts his weight so we're on our sides, still glued together in so many ways. I tell him the truth. "I want to know everything, Ozzy."

His gaze lingers before he presses his lips to my forehead. "Don't know what I did to get here, but fucking thrilled to be the one, baby."

I'm about to agree to everything he just said, especially him being the one who's making me a sticky mess, but a phone vibrates on the nightstand behind me.

Ozzy reaches over me to grab it and puts it to his ear. "Yeah?"

His gaze moves to me.

I tense.

Shit.

"She's here with me. What did you find out?"

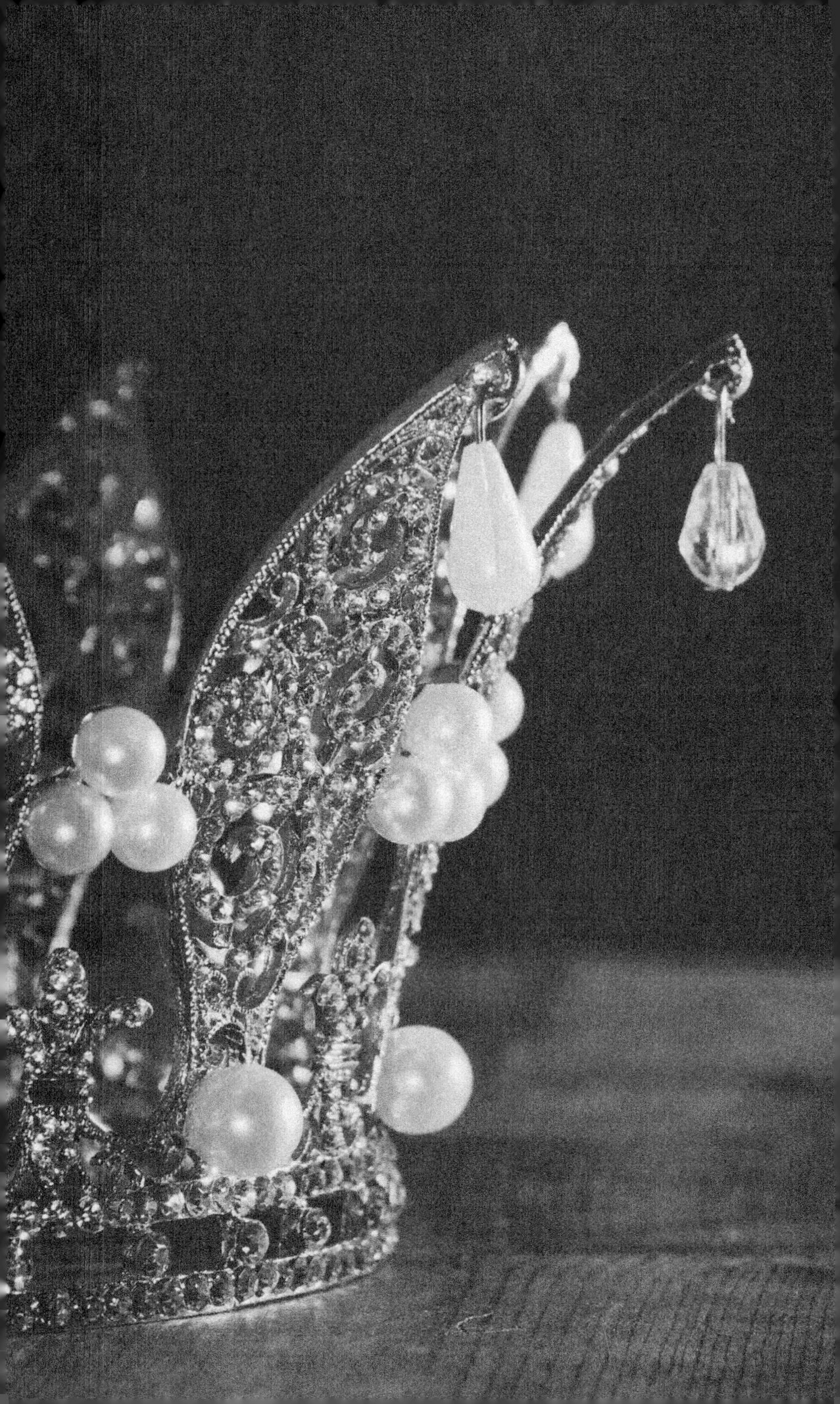

24

MAY YOUR COWS SMELL LIKE ROSES

Ozzy

"Your mom is no longer in Morocco."
This was not what I had in mind after what we just did. I planned on pulling Liyah out of bed, washing her from head to toe, and putting my mouth between her legs. My mental list of firsts I want to give her is long. But I've got too many balls in the air right now to ignore my phone.

Speaking of balls, mine are peachy-fucking-keen to not be cobalt blue right now.

"You're sure?" Liyah asks.

She's gripping my side, since we're still stuck together in the most disgusting yet sexy-as-fuck way possible. Her jacking me off as I came all over her bare tits was more than I expected when I opened my eyes this morning.

"As sure as Bella can be in this case. Nothing is one hundred percent, but her contact in Morocco insists she was headed to the Algerian coast. They're still following up that lead."

Liyah's eyes fall shut.

I put my fingers to her chin and tip her face to mine. "Who does she know in Algeria? Is there anywhere else she would go?"

"No, not in Algeria. Not that I know of. I know my mother, and I'd bet my life she's trying to get to Spain."

"Where in Spain?"

"Probably Tarifa. It's where she's from. But, then again, that's where Hasim would look for her first. So maybe not?"

I drop my phone. "This is good. Bella can work with this. Don't worry."

She nods, and I yank my boxers over my very happy cock. "If I put you in the shower, we'll be in there way too long, and I need to get to the control room. You go clean up, and I'll see what I can find for breakfast before I shower. I talked to Jarvis last night. Gracie will be over today to get you."

Her brows pinch. "Get me?"

I nod. "To hang out. Just a couple hours. I don't want to leave you here by yourself. Don't worry, Jarvis's property is safe."

"I don't need a babysitter, Ozzy. I'll be fine here."

I roll to my back and take her with me. Since I threw her tank across the room, she presses her bare tits tight to my chest. I run my hands up and down her back. "I know you'll be fine, I didn't mean that. I hate ditching you. Trust me, you don't want to sit in the control room with me. It'll be boring as hell for you. These people are like a family to me. No, they are family to me. The only one I have now, and I want you to know them."

"You have a family—your real family." She reaches up and tucks her hair behind her ear that falls around us. "It sounds like they loved you very much. Like my mother does me, and my father before he died."

"But this is the family that's available to me, baby." I reach up and thread my fingers into her dark hair and twist it around my hand before pulling her down to my lips. "Go take a shower. And take your phone with you today. All you have to do is send me one text and I'll be there within five minutes. But I think you'll like them."

"Okay." She sighs but doesn't move.

"Baby, as much as I want to lie here with you naked all day, I really need to check my new lines of surveillance."

"Ozzy?"

I can't help but smile. "Yeah, Princess?"

She pushes up my body and leans in to kiss me. "Thank you for this morning. And for not making me feel like a freak because I watched you in the shower."

That wipes the smile right off my face. I flip her to her back, fall between her legs again, and want nothing more than to stay right here all day. I kiss her, thrusting my tongue in her mouth like a hungry man, and she takes it, wrapping me up in her arms and legs.

When I come up for air, I'm half-hard again, regretting my shit life and the fucking royals and old creep who are fucking with hers. "I haven't allowed myself to want anything for years. Not one thing. I work and I work some more. I should've pushed you away. I have no business being right here, stealing your firsts. I have to live a non-life in the dark shadows—you deserve more." I give her a squeeze. "But I'm selfish. I want you, Liyah. I want you, all your firsts, and your future—even though I have no fucking idea what that's going to look like."

She should be alarmed. She should slap me and push me off her perfect, untouched body. She should run away to find some other man who doesn't make a living off killing people, even though those people don't deserve to walk the earth.

She doesn't do any of that. Instead she pulls me back to her mouth, proving she might be as crazy as me.

It's her turn to be breathless. "Like I said, I appreciate you for not making me feel like a freak. I've lived my life under a magnifying glass. The shadows don't sound so bad."

"Don't say that."

She shrugs a naked shoulder. There's nothing I want more than to steal her away and keep her in the shadows for the rest of time.

But she deserves more.

So much more.

"I might not mind that so much," she whispers.

I shake my head. I need to put a stop to this. "Go shower. I need coffee and food, and you need to quit tempting me. Plus, Gracie will be here soon to pick you up."

I roll off her and enjoy the view for the short amount of time she allows before pulling the sheet over her.

I pull on a pair of gym shorts and a T-shirt since I'm still sticky as shit before leaning down to kiss her one more time. "You've become an obsession, Princess. And I'm not going to stop until you're all mine."

Her eyes flare.

Yeah. I've got a shit ton of work to do before I can make that happen.

Liyah

"Make yourself at home. They'll be here any minute."

"They?"

Gracie doesn't look apologetic. "Yeah, everyone. But not the men, they're working. Though I wouldn't be surprised if they crash the party when they get hungry."

I look around Gracie's home as Eze pulls me through the family room. "I'll show you my room!"

Gracie grins before she unearths platters from the refrigerator. I don't have a chance to offer to help, because I'm being pulled upstairs by a four-year-old.

"That's going to be my sister's room." Eze points to a room filled with boxes, paint cans, and furniture piles in the middle of the room. I barely have a chance to peek inside when Eze yanks my arm, and we're down the hall and around the corner again. "This is my room!"

"I never would have guessed," I tease.

Eze's name hangs in big, stained wooden letters on a black painted wall. The rest of the walls are bright white and his furniture looks like it came from an old locker room, which fits with the theme since there's an antique basketball goal hanging on the wall opposite his bed. It's well-used if the scuff marks on the white wall around it are anything to go by. Those scuff marks say more about Gracie and Jarvis as parents than it does Eze's basketball skills. They're laid back, and let him be a child.

"Mommy told me you're a princess."

I catch a ball that flies through the air toward me. "I suppose I am."

"I don't like princesses." He catches the ball when I lob it back, and he shoots. "I like superheroes."

I smile big. "I do too."

He misses and runs after the ball. "But you're a girl and a princess."

I don't have a chance to explain that I'll take a superhero any day of the week over a stupid prince, because a herd of elephants barrel up the stairs. I'm not sure how they made so much noise, only one of them is bigger than Eze. But I guess when there are this many, they'd make a ruckus.

And that ruckus is loud.

Some greet me for a quick second before quickly getting on with life. They obviously visit often and know exactly where the toys are.

I haven't been around many children. I'm an only child and have no cousins my age. The palace was a much different place after my father died. I didn't have many friends because my uncle wouldn't allow them on the grounds, and I was educated privately until my mother sent me to Europe for boarding school.

The children quickly forget about me, and I slip out to return to the kitchen, where a whole other ruckus is stirring.

I stop at the mouth of the family room. The women are standing around the island, uncorking bottles of wine, and munching on cheese and fruit, surrounded by shopping bags.

Gracie holds up a glass. "Red or white? I think you've met everyone, right?"

It's after lunch. It seems Ozzy and I had a bit of jetlag and slept until almost noon. Instead of breakfast, he threw sandwiches together, showered and was out the door before I had a chance to dry my hair. But he did kiss me and told me to text him if I needed him to rescue me.

Again.

Such a superhero.

This is the sort of scene I do not need rescued from. If there's one thing my mother made sure of when I was growing up, I can handle my own in any social situation, but it was more than just representing the dynasty because of the title I was born with. She wanted that for me more than any royal family I might be representing. Boarding school helped too.

I recognize the women who greeted us at the airport, along with Addy from Whitetail. "White would be lovely."

Keelie picks up one of the bags from the island. "Addy said you didn't come with much, and The Harvest is tonight. We not only got you covered, but you have choices. Whatever you don't like, I'll return."

I accept my glass of white and take a sip. "We slept late, but you have been busy. Thank you."

Maya smiles. "Any excuse for a trip to the mall, and we're in. This should get you through until you have time to pick out some things for yourself."

"I imagine you can't go shopping yet, but order what you need and have it shipped to the house," Addy goes on. "The bungalow doesn't have an official address—Crew prefers it that way."

The wine is crisp and cold on my tongue and goes down easily. I pull out a barstool and sit in the middle of the women. "Ozzy hasn't said anything about The Harvest. I'm not sure if we're going or not."

"Oh, you're going." Addy pops a grape in her mouth and talks around it as she motions around the room. "This is the pre-party—we're just warming up. An army of babysitters will be here in an hour. The men will pick us up so we can get ready. This is the biggest event of the year for the vineyard."

"And you've got everything you need," Keelie adds. "Trust me. Aside from what this county likes to consider its very own Kentucky Derby, this is the event of the year."

Addy gives Keelie a friendly nudge. "Are you saying The Gold Cup is bigger than The Harvest?"

Keelie bites back a smirk and returns her gaze to me. "Sorry. The Harvest is definitely bigger than a horse race. My donkey might disagree, but cocktail dresses and wine stomping beat out big hats any day."

"Hell, yes, it does. But we need to focus on more important things." Maya spears an olive with her toothpick and points it at me. "Like you and Oz."

"We know the details," Gracie adds, and my glass freezes at my lips. Her eyes go big and she rushes, "I mean about how you met. The train, you having to trek across Spain, stuff like that. Sorry. Oh, and we know about your Uncle too. For real, what a royal asshole."

"Quite literally." Keelie pushes a plate of cheese to me, and I pick up a square. If I'm going to drink all day and night, I need to keep eating. "I mean, arranging a marriage for you? And to be a second wife? I googled him. Seriously—old and gross."

I'm about to agree. Especially after my last few days with Ozzy. More specifically, today, when we woke up.

But I don't have a chance to say anything because these women say everything I'm thinking.

Addy sits herself next to me on a barstool. "Well, that's not going to happen, so don't worry. Ozzy won't allow it, and neither will anyone else here. You've got an army at your back now like you never imagined. We might not be royal, but our husbands don't stop until things are taken care of for good."

I exhale and try to tamp back my envy. I wish I felt as certain about my future as these women do. To see what they have is ... eye-opening. "Thank you."

Keelie refills her glass. "Enough with the heavy. Tell us about Ozzy. He's the quiet one. I mean, we can barely get him to come home for Christmas. We want to know everything."

I run the tip of my finger up and down the stem of my glass. "Actually, I was going to ask you all about him."

The women glance at one another, but it's Gracie who speaks. "I probably know the most since he and Noah knew each other before. What do you want to know?"

I look into her pretty blues and tuck my hair behind my ear. "Ozzy explained everything to me. How he has you all. And don't get me wrong, he seemed grateful for it. But he really can't see his family? Ever?"

I'm not sure what the rest of them look like, but Gracie's expression turns melancholy, and her voice softens. "No. Not ever. The way Noah explains it, that's the way Ozzy wants it. He thinks it's safer for his family."

"I get that, but it's been years," Keelie counters. "And it's not like his parents didn't fight to clear his name.

They tried after he *died*. They refused to accept anything from the government. Not an insurance settlement, social security, nothing. They know their son—or knew—and insist to this day he was innocent. If you ask them, they think he was killed."

"It's heartbreaking," Addy says. "Can you imagine? Living through the death of a child, but that child is still alive and breathing? His poor parents ... and family. I've asked Crew multiple times if there's another way, and he shuts me down every time. He says it's Ozzy's choice, and Ozzy sees it as doing everything he can to make sure they're safe."

"I still say there's another way," Keelie adds. "With these men, there has to be."

"I agree," Addy reiterates. "No one will challenge Ozzy on this. Not even Crew. Trust me, I've pressed him, because, as a parent..."

Addy lets that hang in the air for a moment, until Gracie picks up where she left off. "True, but with the new developments, no one can blame him." Gracie looks at me. "That's what he's protecting his family from. If those bastards were willing to do what they did, they'll stop at nothing, including silencing anyone and everyone."

"I suppose." I take a sip and grab a cracker. "Maybe it won't always be this way. How long can they get away with what they're doing?"

"There's one thing to know something and another to know it legally. The good and the bad of this life," Addy says, and I frown. "My husband can and will do whatever the hell he wants. I love him for it, because, in the end, it's always for the good. He delivers justice his own way. Doing that officially through the system is next to impossible, especially when the evidence is collected without warrants."

"The system is broken," Maya states.

"The system fucking sucks," Keelie pipes.

Gracie grins. "That it does."

"But that won't stop Crew." Addy's hand lands on my forearm to gain my attention. "He hasn't come out and said it, but I think it's only a matter of time. Someone is going to slip up, and if what they think is right, that might happen sooner rather than later. Plus, we have a Cole Carson."

I frown. "What's a Cole Carson?"

Maya raises her glass. "Bella's husband. And our very own CIA officer. They're the power couple no one knows about."

"While Bella looks for your mom," Addy continues, "Officer Cole Carson is working on Ozzy."

Keelie looks offended. "Why didn't I know about this?"

"Because it's a new development, and you're too busy chasing goats," Addy says.

Keelie rolls her eyes. "Says the cow lady."

"Have you met the cows?" Gracie asks.

I do my best to keep up with the conversation. "Cows?"

"You've only been here a day. You'll run into them. Or, they'll find you. Don't worry, they're friendly," Addy assures me.

Gracie grimaces. "They might be friendly, but they stink."

"They're cows. I'm not sure what you want. They're going to smell like cows." Addy looks back to me. "They're pets. And sort of the unofficial mascot of

Whitetail. Customers like them." Addy spears Gracie with a glare. "Most people like them."

Gracie laughs and holds her glass up. "I love you, Addy. May your cows smell like roses, your harvest be plentiful, and your wine be fine."

Keelie lifts her glass in one hand and a bottle in the other. "To The Harvest."

The rest of us raise our glasses.

"And to Liyah and Oz," Addy adds. "May your lives be figured out sooner rather than later. I have a feeling there are good things on the horizon for you two."

I drink to that. We all do. I think about my mother. I think about Ozzy and all the things he's stirring in me. And I think about the heavy, very real diamond sitting at the base of my left ring finger with its very bogus meaning.

Because nothing else feels bogus.

Not one thing.

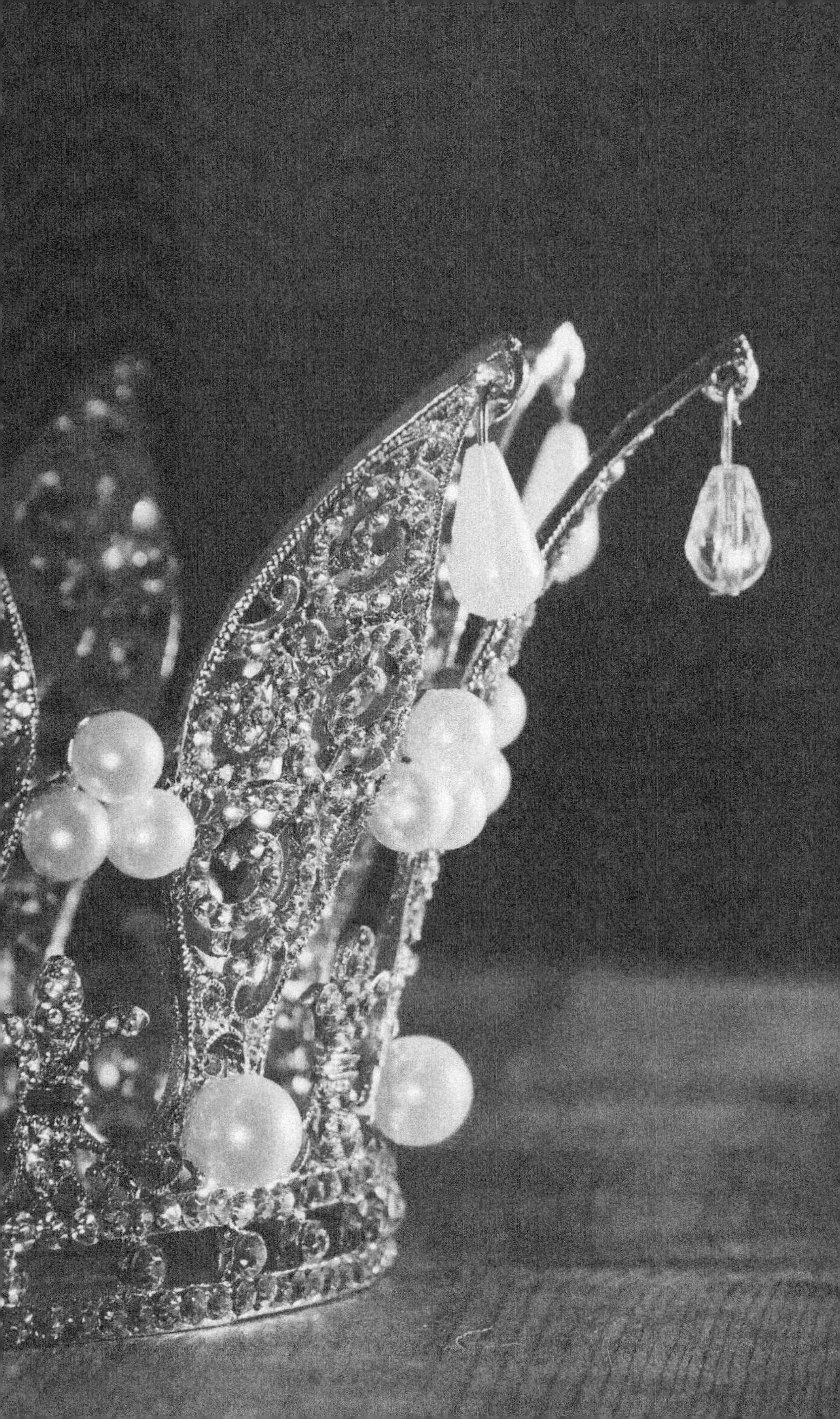

25

LESS THAN ROYAL

Ozzy

One thing I can honestly say, I never in my life thought I'd be going up against an actual fucking king because the woman he's trying to sell off to the highest bidder for political gain is wearing my engagement ring.

I must be making up for lost time. I've spent years alone, wandering the earth for Crew Vega, contemplating how my life went from pretty okay to being flushed down the shitter overnight.

The years have been long, slow, and depressing as hell. Not that I would have admitted that then. Then, I did my best, telling myself lie after lie, that I didn't need things. I didn't need people.

Was it self-preservation? I'm sure a shrink could figure that out, but I don't have time for a shrink. I don't even have time to get more than four hours of sleep in a row.

As the hours click by—that's right, hours, not days,

months, or even years since I'm apparently making up for lost time—there's nothing I want more than to scream for all the world to hear that Liyah is mine. My one and my only. That I'm not some sick fuck who wants to put her second in line. Because there's no fucking way Princess Aliyah Zahir could be second to anyone.

The woman has ruined humans for me in general.

And I haven't even had her yet. Not really. Not the way I want. And not the way I plan to.

Because I do have plans.

So many fucking plans.

It's also not lost on me that as the hours click on, my plans are being fueled purely by desperation and anger.

Desperation for her.

And, currently, anger at a motherfucking king.

The most recent development, a letter. Or a statement. Whatever the fuck it is, it's posted all over the fucking internet and international news, from the dynasty, signed by the grade-A asshole, himself.

To the Kingdom of Morocco,

I'm honored to announce the engagement of my beloved niece, Princess Aliyah Zahir. I am presenting her hand in marriage to Sahem Botros, the President of the Constitutional Court. We will welcome him to the Dynasty through marriage.
Please share in our joy and love for the future of Morocco and the legacy of the Dynasty that will live on through their heirs for generations to come.

Sincerely,

Hasim Zahir, King of Morocco

I roll away from the monitor in my office chair. If I don't, I'll throw the fucking thing through the ancient farmhouse window.

"You okay?" Crew asks.

I drop my elbows to my knees, stare at the floor, and take a breath. I need a breath. I probably need an entire tank of oxygen if I'm being real, but I'd probably throw it through the window too.

And I don't do drama.

If I'm nothing else in life and death, I'm in complete control of my emotions.

Always.

But I'm hanging on by a thread.

"What the fuck?" he bites when he reads the news on the screen that has me wanting to tear down walls in a rage.

I look up, and Crew is standing in front of the monitor. "Right?"

Crew turns to me and crosses his arms. "Has Liyah seen this?"

"I don't know. It was just released. I gave her a secure phone, but I doubt she has her notifications turned on from the King."

"This doesn't mean shit, you know."

I drag my hand down my face and glare at him. "I know that."

"He's goading her. It's in response to your ... ah, less-than-royal announcement of your engagement," Crew goes on.

"Do I look like a fucking idiot, Crew? I know all this shit."

He holds out a low hand. "Then calm the fuck down."

I hold my arms out. "Do you see me throwing shit out the window like I really want to do? I'm fucking calm."

"There are a lot of fucks being thrown around in here, just the way I like it."

I turn to find Cole Carson stalking through the door to the control room. "If you're here to give me more bad news, then turn your ass around and leave. I'm ready to tap out for the day."

He crosses his arms. "Don't be so dramatic, Oz, but brace. It's not bad, but it's not good. I'm here to give you an update from Bella."

I lean back in my chair, because Carson telling me to brace, is not a good thing. "Shit."

He shakes his head. "Bella's on her way home. Once she got to Algeria, that was it. She couldn't find any more on Luciana. Her contacts are doing what they can, but Bella was spinning her wheels. Sorry, man. The silver lining is Bella's sure she got out of Morocco and crossed into Algeria."

My head falls back, and I stare at the ceiling. "I need some good news."

"You going to tell her?" Crew asks.

"Oh, he'd better tell her," Carson spouts. "I'm pretty much the best husband in the world, and I say tell her. Tell her everything you know, otherwise that shit will come back and bite you."

"He's newly engaged." Crew grins. "He'll have to figure this stuff out on his own."

I shake my head and roll back to the monitors to email myself a copy of the damn royal engagement announcement that will never come to fruition so I can, in fact, tell Liyah everything. I didn't need Carson to tell me that shit, I already planned on it.

"What's up with Dumb and Dumber?" Carson asks.

I pull up the new feeds I set up last night on Demaree and Cannon. I've got fresh taps on their personal cells, their wives' cells, and their bank account activity. I was even able to tap into Cannon's car since the dumb fuck actually took the free one-year road-side service from Mercedes. If he speaks aloud in his car about the weather or his favorite bubble gum flavor, I'll have a transcript of it. "They've been quiet today. But their team is also on duty. They're being official, but probably doing who the fuck knows what while they're there."

"I'm doing what I can at work." Carson slaps me on the shoulder. "So far I can't connect them to the WITSEC murders. It's known far and wide those were Russian hits."

I swing my chair around and cross my arms. "Something I've never done is try to draw them out on the dark web. I've lurked there, but I'm leery to approach anyone. Those who are there range from stupid to as smart as me."

Carson and Crew glance at each other, but it's Crew who says, "You think it's time to take that step? That risk?"

It's selfish. Diving into the dark web isn't a big deal to me. I'm dead. What are they going to do, bring me back to life and charge me if I'm caught? I'm not on anyone's radar.

Or, I wasn't. Until a couple days ago when Demaree

and Cannon somehow found out I wasn't killed in a fiery explosion on the side of a highway.

It would put Crew and his organization at risk if I fucked up—if anything was traced back here or to Reskill.

Carson answers for me. "You want to."

I might be looking at a retired assassin and CIA officer, but I'm thinking of no one but a certain princess who I'm pushing the boundaries with in every way.

I don't have the chance to confirm or deny, because my phone vibrates on the desk. When I swing around to grab it, it's none other than the very topic of my every thought.

Princess – Ozzy!

Princess – Holy shit! Did you see? My fucking uncle! Did you see what he did??

Me – Yeah, baby. I saw. I was just going to call you. Don't worry about it.

Princess – Don't worry about it? Are you mad?

Me – I'm not crazy, but I am pissed.

Princess – I'm making another post. I need you back here to take another picture, and then you can do your thing.

"She knows, doesn't she?" I look up at Carson. "Sometimes there's a small window of time and you've got to act fast. You fucked up."

I roll my eyes and look back to my screen.

Me - I'll be there as soon as I can.

Princess – Hurry. The sooner I can put this out, the better.

I stand and stuff my phone in my pocket.

Carson rubs his chin and shakes his head. "You should've listened to me."

"She's not pissed at me. She's pissed at her uncle, dammit. I've got to go."

"Just make sure she knows Bella is still working her contacts when it comes to her mom," Carson bosses.

"See you in an hour," Crew adds.

"An hour?" I ask. "Unless Demaree and Cannon start making moves, I can monitor them from my phone. I don't plan on coming back today."

Crew shakes his head. "Not here. The Harvest."

"Sorry, there's no way I'm letting Liyah show her face there right now."

"You'll be fine. Addy made sure you'll have a private table. Jarvis dropped the women off about an hour ago to get ready. They've been wining it up all afternoon."

"A night out will make up for you not coming clean fast enough." Carson turns for the door and gives me one more piece of advice I don't need. "Just keep her glass full and you should be good."

Going to The Harvest was not what I had planned for the night. I honestly had no plans for the night. I'm too used to being on defense and reacting to every fucking thing that comes our way.

Actually, I did have plans for the night, and they had everything to do with replaying what happened this morning.

I have one suit to my name, the one I bought for Asa's wedding. I was still a recruit then and didn't have the excuse of hiding away on the other side of the planet.

Princess – Are you coming?

I sigh and head upstairs to the bedroom I've made mine in Crew's headquarters to grab clothes.

Me – Yes, baby. I'm on my way.

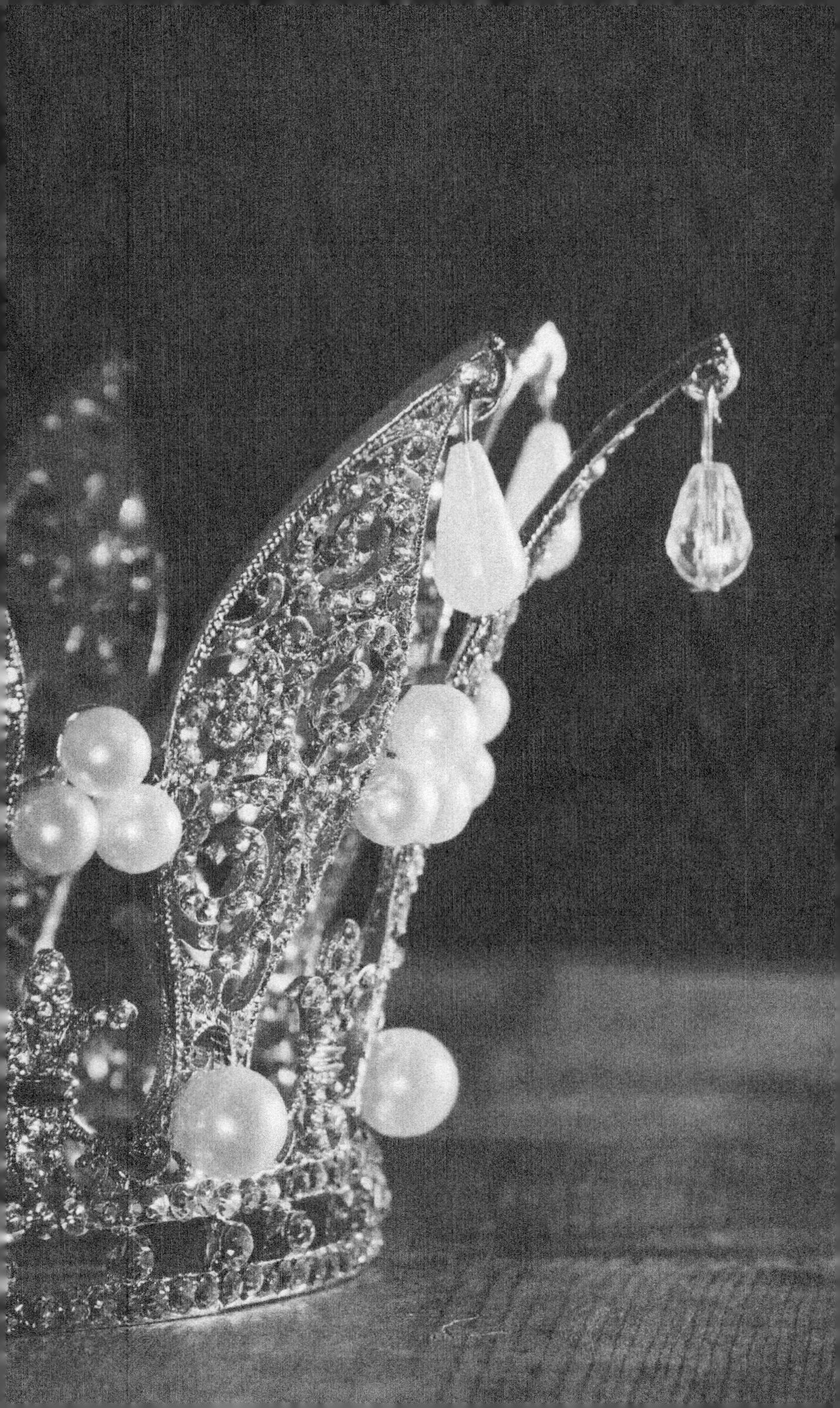

26

NO ONE IS KISSING YOUR ASS BUT ME

Ozzy

When I got back from the control room, the bungalow looked like a bomb went off. There were a shit ton of bags everywhere. Clothes, shoes, makeup, and everything else a chick would need or want to live her life in public covered almost every surface in the place. I didn't ask where it all came from. I knew. And I was grateful. One less thing for me to think about.

I interrupted Liyah from drying her hair and told her what I knew about the royal press release in which she was the topic, and then about Bella losing her mom's trail.

That last one didn't go over as well, but she was relieved to know her mom made it out of Morocco. I assured her we were doing everything we could, that I could do more to find her mom from here than I could in Paris.

I left her to get ready and took a shower.

We're already late, per Crew's timeline, so I pull my suit jacket off the hanger and drape the tie around my neck.

Living dead in a very much alive world has very few perks, but not having to wear a suit because I can't show my face most places is near the top of that list.

My hair is still damp when I walk to the family room and stop. My feet refuse to listen to my brain, but that might be because my brain has short-circuited straight to my dick at what's in front of me.

With her back to me, Liyah is swiping shit on her already perfect lashes in the mirror by the front door. She's in black. Or a little bit of black. The bit of material she's wearing isn't just short, but drapes so low, one of the dimples above her ass winks at me, daring me to slide my hand in there, because there is definitely enough room. Her hair hangs down her back in smooth waves. It hasn't been this perfect in the entire time I've known her.

My eyes go to hers though the reflection of the mirror. Her perfect lips that I've become obsessed with are painted red and her eyes are deeper and more defined. She looks older than her very innocent twenty-two years.

This is the person she's created for the rest of the world. The one she puts out on social media for millions to obsess over.

Since she's been with me, she's been makeup free. Aside from swiping her lips from time to time with a lip balm, she's been nothing but pure and real and all Liyah.

My Liyah.

I feel it in my dick, because I like this Liyah too.

I drape my jacket over the back of the sofa and move to her. How can I not? Like any other time she's in my general vicinity, the need to touch her is overwhelming.

When I get to her, I look at us in the mirror. She's inches taller than she normally is, still barely coming past my shoulder. The material drapes above her tits the way it does on her ass, and the straps holding this thing up are so thin, I wonder if they'll snap with a quick tug. Because right now, I can't think of anything other than ripping it off of her.

Her eyes find mine. "We match."

My suit is black, my shirt is black, my tie is black.

Like my soul. Or, like it used to be.

Unlike a few weeks ago, it's not the deep, dark hole of despair anymore. If it was black before a certain princess crashed into my life, it's definitely lighter now.

Gray.

My index finger finds the skin where her dress falls low on her back, and I was right. I only have to dip inside two inches to find the crack of her ass below the strap of her thong as thin as her dress straps.

A dress and a thong—the only things between me and all of her.

Talk about tempting the beast.

I look back up to her reflection. "This is the only suit I own. If you want me to put on jeans and a tee, we can stay right here. You, on the other hand," I slide my hand down the back of her dress and palm her ass easily, "aren't allowed to change."

One side of her perfect red lips tip north. "If we weren't meeting your gang of assassins and their wives, I would say this is all for nothing. But now that my uncle has reared his ugly head publicly, at least we're dressed for the occasion."

I slide my hand from her ass to her hip. "What occasion is that?"

"To shove it in his face that he's not getting his way. That he can kiss my ass in front of the world."

I shake my head and squeeze her perfect, smooth skin. "No one's kissing your ass but me, baby."

Her plump lips part, and her tongue sneaks out to wet them.

I really want to see if her other set of lips are wet too.

I look back up, and our eyes crash into one another, not unlike other ways I want to crash into her.

"We're going to be late," she whispers.

"I'm okay with that."

"It's rude."

"They're used to me being rude."

She gives her head a shake, pulls in a breath, and my hand is forced away from its new favorite place—inside her dress—when she turns in my arms. She puts a finger to my collarbone and slides it down my skin until it catches on the first button. She unhooks it and slides my tie from my neck.

"You're undressing me. I'm definitely okay with this change in plans."

She might as well break my heart, because she moves away from me to grab her phone. "Nice try. Roll your cuffs. I need you casual."

I'm about to argue that I want no part of casual when it comes to her, but rolling my cuffs doesn't sound half-bad, so I do as she says. I slip my cufflinks into my pocket while she does the thing with her phone again.

She comes back to me, and this time turns me to

face the camera. "Don't worry. I won't introduce the world to your handsome face."

"Another video to add to my collection," I mutter. "Are you trying to kill me?"

She spears me with a look so sexy that I decide she will, in fact, be my official demise. "I have a feeling you'll survive."

"If you knew what blue balls really felt like, you'd think twice about that."

She fits her small frame to my front, and if she thinks I'm kidding about the color of my balls, then she's not royal, and I'm not legally dead.

She places her hands on my biceps and looks up at me. "Slip your hand into my dress like you just did."

"Gladly." I wrap one arm around her and reach across to do just as she said. Her opposite cheek fits into the palm of my hand perfectly. If she wasn't created just for me, then I'm not a basic farm boy from Pennsylvania. I squeeze her ass and bring my hand to mess up her smooth hair, tipping her face to me. "How pissed will you be if I mess up your lipstick?"

"You can't kiss me without being in the picture."

I tip her head farther and lean in to put my lips to her jaw under her ear. "I don't give a shit about the picture. I want to mess up your lipstick."

She shakes her head. "You messing up my lipstick will mess up all my makeup. So, yeah, I'll be pissed."

"Pissed like you're pissed at your uncle, or pissed like I can make it up to you by yanking your dress up and putting my mouth between your legs for the first time?" I work my way to her ear and catch her lobe between my teeth that now holds a diamond stud, and I wonder where it came from.

We'll discuss that later. From now on, she won't wear diamonds unless they're mine.

Her exhale hits my face in a rush. "Ozzy."

I fist her hair and pull her back an inch to look into her dark eyes. "Because I can't wait to do that."

Her face warms and her lips part, begging me to take her mouth and rip off the dress that would look way better in shreds on the floor.

"I want everything you'll give me, and I'm willing to do shit I've never been willing to do to clear the road for a future."

Her breaths quicken, and her chest moves against mine in desperate pants.

"I've been a patient man, baby. I accepted my life sentence, but not anymore. I'm going to fix my shit, and then I'm going to fix yours. I'm done fucking around."

She nods and her eyes fall shut. She might be affected by my words, but she's also a woman with a mission. Her left hand showcases the promise I put there and it isn't as empty as it was the day I bought it. She grips my bicep and she looks over her shoulder at the camera. I grip her ass in a way I've never done before, and she melts into me.

Not fake.

Not for show.

And definitely not only for her damn uncle.

This is real.

The Princess is mine.

The King and his fucked-up friend can go fuck themselves.

Liyah

EVEN THOUGH WE'RE only going next door, Ozzy said there was no way he was going to make me traipse through the forest in heels to get to the main building of Whitetail. I'm grateful he thought that through.

Ozzy is done fucking around, apparently.

I think I know what that means, but we didn't have time to fully flesh that out. Honestly, it could mean so many things right now, and I can't think of one that I wouldn't like.

Yes, I think I'm very okay with Ozzy not fucking around anymore.

After I finished interrogating the women about Ozzy and his family today, wine time with the ladies ended up being fun and even relaxing. I learned that The Harvest is the event of the year at Whitetail. Tickets are sold out months in advance and it has turned into one of the most sought-after social scenes in the area.

Addy wasn't kidding when she said her staff is the best and her vineyard is now a well-oiled machine. Apparently it wasn't always that way. It was a flailing business when she purchased it all by herself years ago. But as we descend the stairs to the basement cellar of the main building, Addy looks relaxed and confident the night will go off without a hitch.

Keelie bought me three dresses to choose from. The short cocktail dress was a no brainer once I saw the maddening engagement announcement from the Palace. It's so short, sitting will be an issue. It shows a ton of skin, leaving little to the imagination. It's everything my uncle is against when it comes to women.

By the look on Ozzy's face when he walked out of

the bathroom, I knew I chose wisely for more than one reason. His hand hasn't left my skin since our second photoshoot for the world to see, and it's still glued to the small of my back.

He leans into my ear. "What do you want to drink?"

I had two glasses at Gracie's house, but I'm pretty sure my anger toward my uncle burned through whatever buzz I had. "Sauvignon blanc, please."

The women and the men are segregated—the men casually linger on one side of the room, but the women are not casual or lingering. They're huddled. The moment we catch their eyes, the huddle breaks open and every single one of them grins like my childhood friends would when we were talking about sex at my all-girls school in England.

"I'll get your drink, but I'm going to leave you to this," Ozzy mutters, giving my hip one more squeeze.

Keelie reaches for my hand. "You look amazing. This was my favorite of the bunch. It was made for you."

"She's a model and a princess. She could wear a gunny sack and look perfect," Maya says before she holds her phone for me to see. "We want to talk about *this*."

All of a sudden, I'm swallowed in their huddle and see the topic of their focus.

The post.

Ozzy spun his magic so it would connect with my old phone in Malibu. This picture is different than the first, but no less erotic. I might be poking the dragon, but I don't care. The world needs to know.

It reads:

His Majesty is correct, I'll soon be married, though he has the wrong fiancé. My life will not be arranged, nor will I be sold for political gain. No one controls my happily ever after but me. If my parents taught me anything, it's that love will prevail.

With love,

Aliyah Zahir
Princess of Morocco
Heir of King Kamal and Princess Luciana

I thought my first post with Ozzy was a success. It has nothing on this one out of the gate. But as always, I don't read the comments. I never read the comments.

"Please tell me this isn't an act," Addy begs. "Even though there's no way I can take credit for you two getting together, I want this to be real more than anything. I'll give up my chance at a blue ribbon for my Meritage blend this year. And it's so good, I really think we have a chance at winning."

"This is real." Gracie reaches around me and double taps the picture, giving my post another like, adding to the hundreds of thousands that are stacking up before our eyes. "Oz practically had his hand down her dress when they walked in here. There's no reason to put on a show for us. This is a private party."

I still haven't said a word as I look around. If I didn't know I was in Virginia, I'd think I were in Europe visiting the catacombs. But there are no skulls or bones, just walls and walls of bottled wine. The beamed ceilings are low, there's a tiny chill in the air, and we're surrounded by stacked stone. There's also a table for two set in the corner.

I jump when a warm touch hits my lower back again and a glass of white wine appears in front of me. "Cheers."

I look up at Ozzy who says nothing else, but he is glaring at the women around me. His fingers linger on my skin before he escapes to his designated side of the low-lit room.

My body heats from his touch, and mixed with the cool room, goosebumps run up my arms.

"Okay, yeah. It's real." Keelie rips the cellphone from Maya and takes a sip of her red as she stares at the screen. "Just look at his hand fisting your ass through the dress. I mean, his forearm is even flexed. Did you use a filter? How did you get your engagement ring to shine that bright in the picture. There's so much sex oozing from this picture, my poor eyes don't know what to focus on."

I hold my hand up and look at the ring that I've been referring to privately as "the ring" and not "my engagement ring". "I'm not sure. I think it's just that bright."

Gracie points at the phone again. "Your expression says it all. You're telling the world this is real, this is what you want, and for your uncle and his nasty friend to fuck off. I'm sorry, Noah showed me the picture of the old man your uncle is trying to sell you to. Disgusting."

The group agrees. But really, who wouldn't?

"Give her a chance to talk," Addy butts in and turns her focus on me. "Honestly, if you two aren't a real thing, I might die."

I peek over my shoulder. Ozzy is standing with the men, sipping bronze liquid from a lowball, but his eyes are on me. It's either butterflies or the wine, but my stomach does a somersault. I look back at the women and the picture they're still ogling. "We're something. There's just a lot going on."

"Some of us have known Ozzy since he arrived here to work for Crew," Maya says. "None of us have ever seen him like this. Ozzy goes through the motions. Does his work, socializes with us as little as possible, and works some more."

"She's right," Keelie agrees. "The only thing that has ever stirred any emotion in him is when Crew bought Reskill. He loves that stuff."

"Because he has a way to watch those assholes who framed him," Addy adds.

"Here's the thing." Gracie moves to the center of our huddle. "It doesn't matter that Ozzy is older than a couple of us. He's everyone's little brother who's refused to do anything for his own happiness, until now. And those men over there—" when she points to the group across the room, her husband frowns back, "—need a life outside of work. Without us, they would be miserable. I've seen it with my brother and my husband."

"To be fair," Maya interjects, "I'd be miserable without him too."

"Fuck, yes, I'd be miserable." Keelie raises her glass before spearing me with a smirk. "Still, they're lucky as hell to have us. And our little brother of the group over there needs that too."

I'm not sure I'll tell Ozzy he's being referred to as the little brother. But I do like knowing he might need me as much as I need him.

Addy puts her arm around me and pulls me to her side. "I'm going to say it here and now: I predict by next year's harvest, this will look completely different. The two of you will be able to celebrate out in the open with the rest of us. I refuse for there to be any other ending. You're the only princess I've ever known—you're staying right here in Virginia. You can live happily ever after in horse and wine country. You don't need a palace and you certainly don't need a damn king. Your prince charming is over there dressed in black, looking hungrier for you than for the five-course meal I'm about to serve. That's all any woman needs."

Wow. The idea of being Ozzy's meal is enough to make my knees weak.

I take another sip and think I could use some food too. The real kind, that will soak up the alcohol and take my mind off all the things I want Ozzy to do to me.

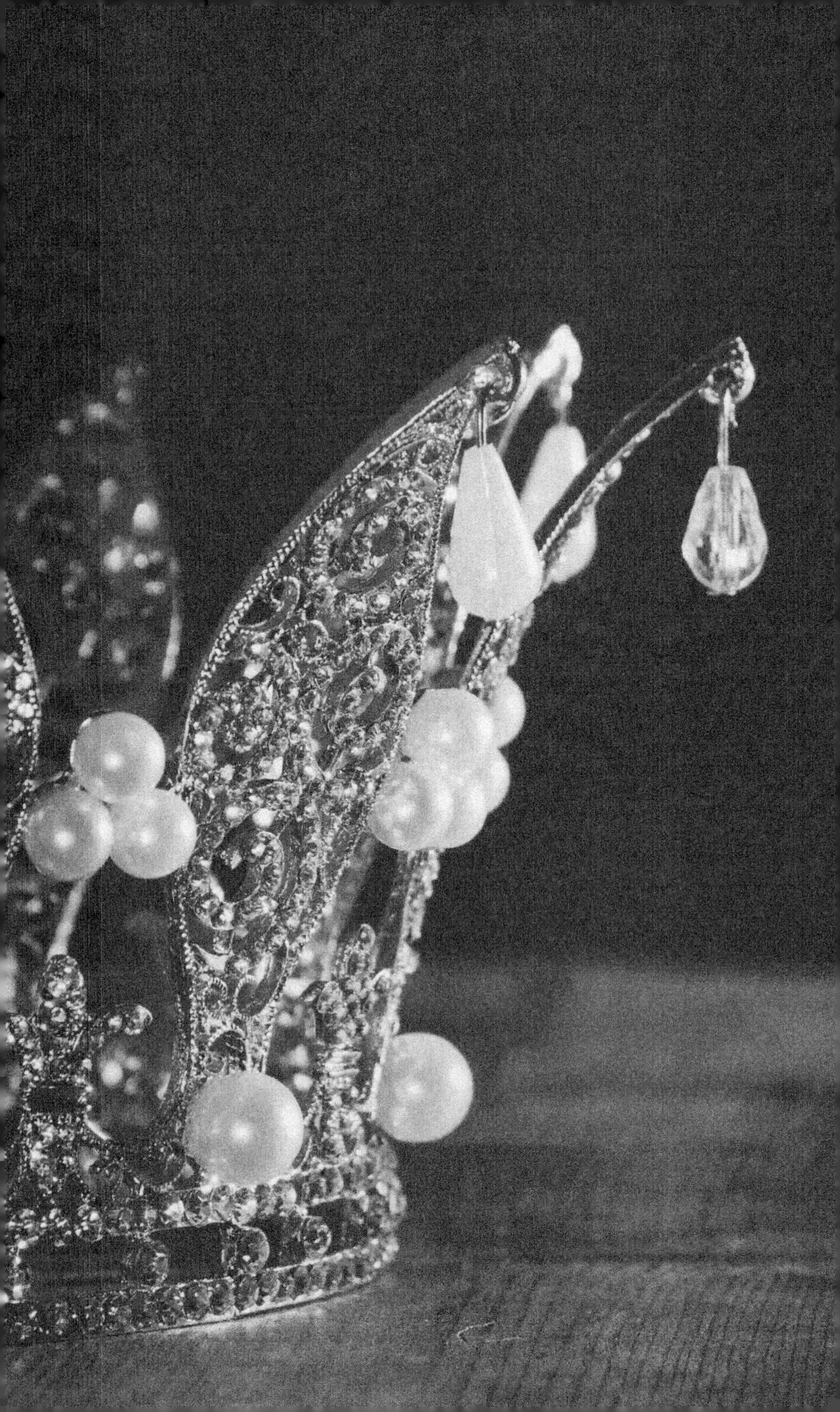

27

RAW

Ozzy

Oysters Rockefeller. Caesar salad. Butternut squash bisque. Prime rib. Cheesecake.

But no words.

The group left us. Addy needed to be present at her own event. And since Crew rarely lets Addy out of his sight, he followed, and so did the rest of them. But since there was a table for two set up to begin with, this was the plan.

My Princess is chatty, so when she turns it off, it's eerie. From the moment I walked into my train cabin, and she promised not to talk to me, silence hasn't existed.

And since she feels perfectly at ease asking me how it feels when I do or don't come, I know for a fact the woman isn't shy.

She devoured everything until she got to the prime rib, then picked at the rest of her meal. She also moved from wine to water, so I don't think she's tipsy.

I throw back the last of my whiskey and let my glass hit the table with a thud. "Do you want to stomp grapes?"

She sets her fork down after only eating two bites of her dessert. Bringing her napkin from her lap to her lips, she finally speaks. "Is that really a thing?"

"It is. Messy as hell, but it's a thing."

"I don't mind getting messy, but not really. Not tonight."

"Okay. Then what's wrong?"

She looks around at the thousands of bottles of wine and stone surrounding us, and motions to the table between us. "This is strange."

I narrow my eyes but don't say a word, because I agree.

"From the moment I met you, we've been on the move. Or at least waiting for our next move. This is like a date. Don't get me wrong, I like it. I like it a lot. But it feels weird. Good weird, but weird."

My lips tip on one side. "Do you want me to throw you over my shoulder and run laps through the forest? Would that make you feel better?"

She rolls her eyes, but that wins me a smirk of her lips that aren't as red as they were when we got here. "Maybe."

"Because I can make that happen." I lean in, rest my forearms on the table, and lower my voice. "I can make all your dreams come true."

Her smirk disintegrates into the stale, basement air. "I don't know what my dreams are anymore—or if I ever had any. I've always lived in the moment."

I lean back in my chair. "We have that in common. But mine is out of necessity. Or sheer self-preservation."

A sad smile appears. "I think mine is from shallow immaturity. I have enough money that I'll never worry about how to support myself, and I didn't know what it was like to want anything that mattered. You know? That mattered so much, that if it didn't happen, I'd experience soul-wrenching heartache."

"Your mom?" I guess.

She nods. "Among other things."

I get that, but don't admit it. Not when her mom is unaccounted for and the dynasty, which has powers far and wide, is looking for her too. Because Liyah's right. That heartache would leave a mark on her soul so deep, it would never look the same—never feel the same. I experienced it when I watched my family bury who they thought was their oldest son.

I gave them that pain.

"You're not shallow or immature, Princess. You're brave."

She pulls in a big breath and shakes her head. "I don't feel brave. I feel helpless."

"Bravery has a lot of faces, baby. Don't doubt yourself."

She's about to say something else, but a notification pops up on my phone sitting on the table next to my empty dessert plate.

Reskill.

The new lines of surveillance.

My blood warms, and it has nothing to do with the woman who's been warming me in other ways since the moment I laid eyes on her.

"What is it?"

I read the transcript coming in. And it's coming in fast.

"Ozzy?"

I stand, grab my jacket from the back of my chair, and hold my hand out to her. "Sorry, but normal doesn't last long when it comes to us. I need to get to the control room. We've got to go, baby."

She proves she's brave. She has been since the moment she decided to step out on her own and look for her mom by herself with no resources or help. Not the kind she needed.

Her taking my hand now isn't unlike how she did on the train when I jumped into the dark night with her in my arms. She put her trust in me wholly then, and she's doing the same now.

Blind, unreasoned trust.

But, fuck. This is not good.

Liyah

I GUESS I see why they call camp *camp*. Ozzy drove me through the woods in his old truck to the property next to Whitetail. The headquarters for whatever these men are a part of is no more than an old farmhouse.

Addy wasn't kidding. It's seen better days.

Ozzy lost his tie, and his cuffs are once again rolled. He sat me in an office chair in a back room that buzzes with electricity. The house might be old, but the technology is not. Screens line one wall, and there are almost as many keyboards. Ozzy is focused on the biggest one in the middle.

I don't understand what's happening on the screen. Coordinates on maps that are black from the darkness of night fill screens within screens. Little red blips are the only things that set themselves apart from the rest of nothingness.

But what fills the air of the old farmhouse is not nothing. The conversation we're listening to is clear as day, and so important, I don't dare make a peep to ask how this is being done or who these men are. I can assume the latter. I know when to keep my mouth shut, and this is one of those times.

"I told you, and this confirms it. He's not only alive, he's been watching us. Again. It's got to be him. There's no one else it could be. This isn't the way the NSA works. We both know it." The man speaking is angry. Each word is spit with more rage than the one before.

The other goes on. "I don't get it. If he faked his death—which is really fucking hard to do, even for someone like us—why, after all this time, is he just now fucking with us? Why wait?"

Ozzy runs a hand through his hair, gripping the back of his neck so hard, the veins on his hands and forearms bulge. This is exactly what he feared. The men who framed him are as good as he said and know he's alive when he should be dead.

They keep talking. "It's not like he was worth anything. How the fuck does he have access to what he needs? I don't know how he managed to tap us. He can't be on his own. No way. Which means he has help, and other people know about us."

The oxygen in the room goes stale as their confessions bounce off the walls, confirming everything Ozzy assumed. Information he was desperate for, but also afraid of. His fear of exposing his associates.

His friends.

I jump when a door slams and multiple feet stomp across the old hardwoods of the farmhouse. Before I know it, every man Ozzy works with surrounds us, looking just like him. They've lost jackets, ties, and their shirts are unbuttoned at the necks. Their intense stares dart from me and land on the screens, but no one utters a word.

They listen to what's going on in the car where the two men who stole Ozzy's life are somehow being surveilled.

One of them says, "I get that before, but not now. We're good. I killed the satellite lines. How the hell he had access to a whole fucking system to do what he did is beyond me. But they're scrambled. We're good at home. I put an extra barrier on our networks. But for a while, we need to lay low at work."

"You know that's not an option. Marat Kruglov is not going to wait. It's taken longer than planned to get the location he wants, and he's already paid for it. Graves is the least of our worries with Kruglov on our backs," the other answers.

"If you think Graves isn't a threat, then I might off you myself. He faked his own fucking death, Bobby. He has nothing to lose."

Hmm. The other is Bobby.

"How the fuck did they find you in the first place?" Asa bites.

Ozzy makes no move to speak, but he does shake his head as he stares at the screen.

"I still say he didn't make it. There's been no change or new interception since Spain. We got him, Don," Bobby says

I freeze. Not that I was moving before, but now I struggle to find a breath.

"The fuck?" Ozzy whispers.

Bobby goes on. "There's no way he made it off that train. The blast was bigger than we expected. It hit the whole car and part of the ones on each side. We know he was on the list and made that connection. He could not have survived that."

The train car.

I'll never forget that night.

The explosion.

The fire.

The screams in the dark ... in the middle of nowhere.

The blast I thought was meant for me. Guilt still gnaws at me.

Ozzy's hands come to his face, and I watch his entire body go taut. So different than when I saw him naked in the shower. He's different.

"Shit," Crew hisses from behind me.

And no sooner does that word permeate the air, something happens I've never seen since I've met Ozzy.

His carefully managed control cracks.

No. Not just cracks.

Ozzy loses it.

He reaches forward and the first thing he touches is hurled across the room. A keyboard flies through the air and connects with the wall beside us with a menacing crash. "Fuck!"

The men move.

But I'm already on my feet and get to him before anyone else does.

The moment I place my hand flat on his back, he freezes. I feel his every labored breath, shallow and incensed. When he stills, I take the chance and slide my hand around to his abs, fitting my front to his back and press my cheek to his lats.

He radiates heat and ire and ... pain.

I thought people died that night because of me. But no.

It was because of him.

And now that I know him, the real him—not the one who pressed a gun into my side the moment we met—my heart hurts. I wish like nothing else I could erase what we just learned.

I'd gladly carry the burden of those lives again. He doesn't deserve it. He's had enough darkness thrust on his soul.

By these horrid men.

Ozzy wraps a hand around mine and holds me tight to his body. He's been my lifeline, time after time.

I don't know how to be someone's lifeline. I'm not powerful or strong or courageous.

But I hold tight, because I have no idea what else to do.

Don keeps talking. "We can't assume he died on that train. Just because nothing changed in the lines we found doesn't mean anything. If he's still breathing and walking this earth, thinking he can fuck with us, he's gonna lose. We've got too much on the line."

Ozzy's grip on my hand tightens to the point of painful, but I don't move.

"We stumbled onto his feed to begin with. If he survived the train, how the fuck are we going to find him again? He could be anywhere," Bobby says.

The sigh over surveillance fills the room and proves the quality of the technology. It's clear—not one blip of static. Their frustration is palpable.

But it's only quiet for a few moments.

"We've gotta find a way." Bobby keeps talking. "That fucker couldn't prove what we did then, but he might now. There's no option—we have to find him and do it fast. We'll regroup at work tomorrow. Oz was good, but we need to find a way to trace that tap. Cat and mouse. He's the mouse, and we're the fucking lions. Let's find a way to play with him. He'll come up for air eventually."

If I thought Ozzy was tense before, I was an idiot. I fist his shirt and turn my face to press my forehead into his back, and hold tight.

"Fuck," Don hisses. "I don't like this. Between Graves and Kruglov, it's too hot."

"We have no choice at this point. We've got Kruglov waiting on us, and he isn't a patient man—not when he's already put a payment down on his order. We need Graves gone," Bobby growls.

A click of a car door sounds. Oh, they're in a car. Wow. Ozzy really is good at what he does.

"Get this done," Bobby demands. "We'll finish Graves off once and for all—the real way, where he's not going to claw his way from the ground again."

The car door slams, and an engine revs. Everyone in the room stays silent, waiting for something, someone to give another clue or piece of information.

Finally, the engine is turned off, and the feed dies.

"Oz." Jarvis calls for the man who hasn't moved a muscle under my touch. "You okay?"

Ozzy stays silent.

"They don't know where you are. They would have

said," Crew says. "I'll call Carson and update him. He should be on his way to the airport to pick up Bella as we speak. He can start working the angle from Marat Kruglov. That's official, and we can get to Cannon and Demaree that way."

"We need to figure out how they managed to arrange that bomb in Spain," Asa goes on. "It's not the Middle East. That shit couldn't have been easy."

"Remote-detonated." Ozzy pulls in a breath, and I feel every word he utters course through my body. He hasn't moved and is still staring at the dark, empty screen. "I'd bet my life on it."

I squeeze my eyes shut. The thought of anyone betting their life on anything at the moment makes me physically ill.

"We can't do anything tonight," Jarvis says and moves in beside us. "I'll stay here and make sure nothing else happens. Go. Take a walk. Hit the gym. Do what you need to do to process this shit, but get it under control."

Ozzy peels my grip from his abs and turns. He doesn't look down at me when he pulls my front to his side and speaks to the room. "They're going to try to trace the tap to Reskill. I made sure they couldn't do that. Even so, nothing pisses me off more than the fact that this operation might be a target because of me. They're going to be watching to see what I do next. I can't risk setting up new taps."

"If you make a move now, they'll know you tapped his car, and you'll lose that feed too. Nothing can be done tonight," Asa points out. "Go. Calm down. We'll figure this shit out, Oz."

When Ozzy exhales, I feel it in every cell of my body. At this point, I'm so connected to him after all we've been through, it's hard not to feel his every emotion.

The man in my arms is raw.

And I hate that more than anything.

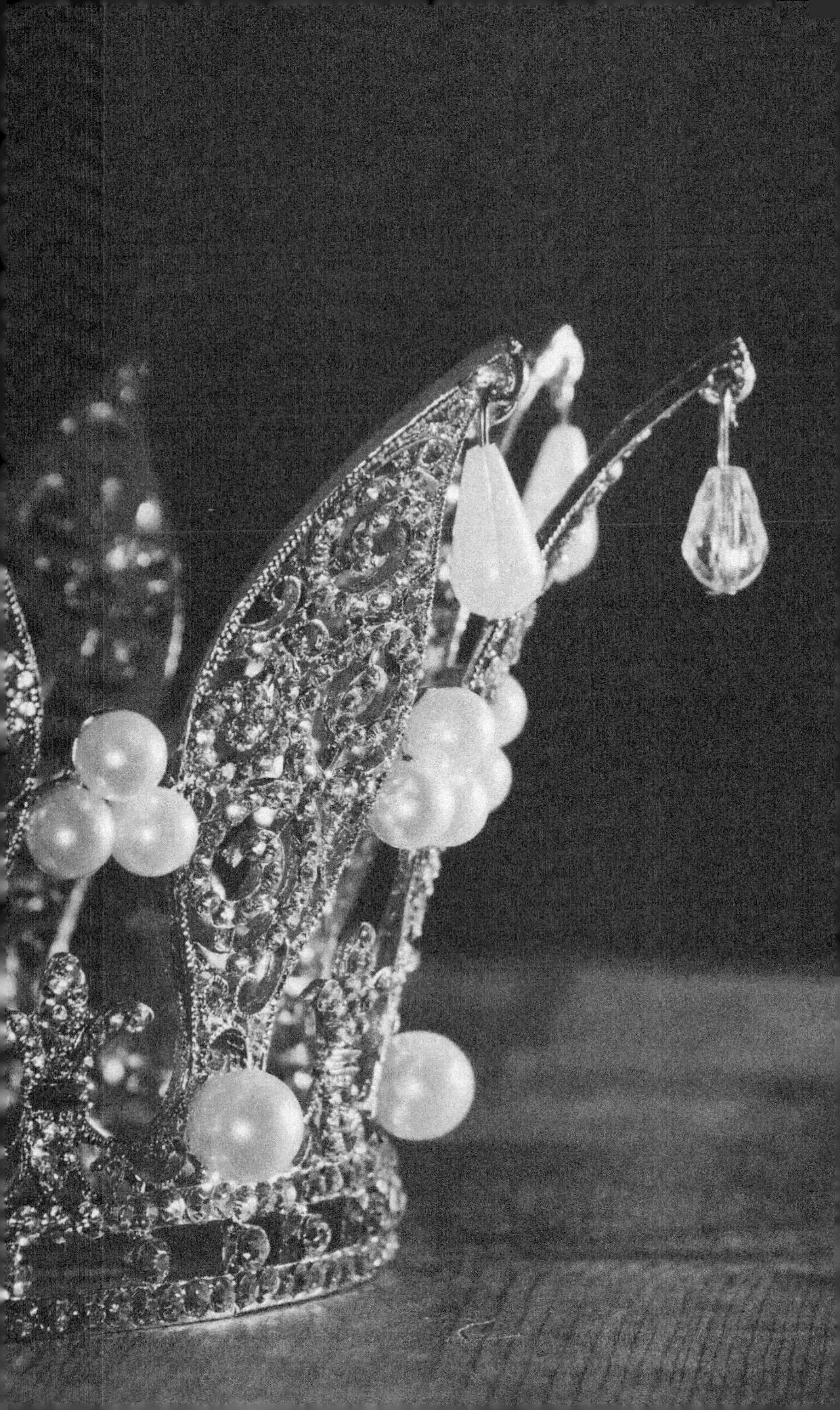

28

HEARTBEATS

Ozzy

I might have avoided prison by faking my death, but I'm no idiot. I know the life I've lived since I joined Crew's organization has been, in some form or another, a penitentiary of a different kind.

Learning that bomb on the train was meant for me... Fuck.

People died that night. A lot of them. All of them innocent, living their lives, going from point A to B. They just happened to be on the same train as me.

Knowing this shouldn't change anything. When Liyah thought it was her, I told her to snap out of it because we needed to move on. Then I dragged her to Libya, kept her in Paris, and now she's here.

I told her to fucking *snap out of it*.

The men all but kicked me out of the control room. I lost it, and I never lose it.

And since there's no way I was in the mood to stomp grapes, we came straight back to the bungalow.

I stare at the ceiling from where I fell to my ass in the middle of the sofa, contemplating my next move in life. The sofa dips next to me, and I feel her delicate fingers wrap around the top of my thigh and squeeze. "Are you okay?"

I close my eyes and inhale. "No, Princess. But what's new."

Her hand slides up my chest and lands on my jaw. "I'm so sorry. I don't know what to say."

I open my eyes and turn to her. "When I told you I can't offer you a life, this is what I meant."

She shifts closer and lowers her voice. "Don't say that."

"I'm saying it because you deserve more. It doesn't matter if I want to give you everything. I'd give you the world if I could. But I can't."

She pauses for a second before bending at the waist, unhooking one shoe clasp around her ankle, and then the other.

She plants a knee next to me on the sofa before gripping the material at her hips. Before I know it, her dress, that left little to the imagination, is hiked around her waist. She swings her other leg over and straddles me.

My hands go to her ass and hers go to my jaw. Her makeup is heavy, but all I see is my Liyah.

Beautiful, sweet, strong.

She leans in to kiss me. She's never done this, so I let her control it. Her tongue slips between my lips and laps mine. It's slow and methodical and addictive. She presses into me, and I squeeze each globe of her ass and try not to think about all the reasons I should push her away.

My dick swells and she rubs up and down my shaft.

It's all I can do not to flip her over on her back and take control.

"Ozzy," she whispers against my lips between kisses.

I try not to groan. "Yeah, baby?"

"Do you want me?" I tense but she doesn't move away from my lips when she keeps murmuring, "All of me? And I don't just mean this." Her pussy presses into my hungry cock. "Forget your life. What you should want. What the future might throw at us. I mean do you want *me*?"

My hands run up her sides, over her tits, and I cage her face in my grasp. Looking into her eyes, I hope she feels just how serious I am. "Baby. I've never wanted anything more. Ever."

She speaks to my soul when she says, "I've never wanted anything until you. But now, I know what it's like to want something. Someone."

My Princess reaches to her waist and grabs the thin material. She pulls it up and over her head, leaving her straddling me in nothing but a pair of panties that are so small, they shouldn't be considered more than a scrap of material.

My hands land on the bare skin of her hips. "Baby."

Her thumb drags over my bottom lip. "Ozzy."

I catch it between my teeth before asking, "What are you saying, Princess?"

She licks her lips, and my eyes roam her body. When I look back up to catch her gaze, she pulls in a big breath. "Don't make me say it."

I shake my head. "No way. I want you, more than anything right now, and that's saying a lot, because there's shit I'm fucking desperate for at the moment. But I'd throw all that out the window for this." My hands return to her ass and pull her to me. "I take this seriously. But what I want right now doesn't mean shit. This is all you."

She leans forward, pressing her bare chest to my dress shirt and wraps her arms around my neck. "I want this. I want you."

I'm up and off the sofa with her in my arms in a heartbeat. There were days in the last few years I thought there were only heartbeats in my future. Lonely, depressing heartbeats.

I lay her back to the bed and she squeezes her thighs together, drawing her feet to her ass. I look down at her as I rip the buttons open on my shirt and drop it to the floor. My finger traces her legs where they're pressed together and all the tension in her body dissolves on an exhale.

She relaxes.

My gaze trails down her body and I think about what she's doing.

What she's giving me.

My hands land on either side of her head, and she parts her knees to make room for my hips to fall between her legs. When I look into her eyes, a new resolve builds inside me, one I didn't know I needed.

"I'll fix everything," I promise, running my hand down her left arm until I find hers, never breaking our connection. I bring our hands between us and kiss her palm where the thin band sits that I put there in one of my recent *fuck it* moments.

Now is not one of those moments.

I thought I needed a lot to move forward. Turns out, the only thing I need is her.

I feel my name as she breathes it across my lips. "Ozzy."

I lift her hand above her head on the bed, not letting go of it and the ring I put there. "I'll find a way, but there's one thing for certain, this," I finger the diamond I put there in Paris, "is real. You get me?"

Tears pool in her dark eyes. "I get you."

Liyah

IT'S REAL.

I want it to be. More than anything. The only thing I've been scared of besides finding my mom is Ozzy walking away from me. There was no other option than for me to accept his non-proposal at the time, but there's a reason I haven't taken off his ring.

Every muscle in his body goes taut as soon as the words fall from my lips. His mouth crashes to mine, and he does what he always does when we're like this. He consumes me, but this time it's different. He's not holding back.

Desire courses through him. I feel it from my head to my toes. When he breaks his kiss and I'm left breathless, his gaze travels down my body, like he doesn't know where to start. He brings my right hand up with my left and grips them in one hand. "Don't move."

I lose his weight and his heat. He stands over me in the dim room, lit only by the lamp shining from the corner. His fingers catch at the thin straps of my panties and he tugs. A chill that has nothing to do with the crisp fall night travels over my skin when he tosses my panties to the floor, leaving me bare.

For him.

Only for him.

"Fuck," he bites, looking down at me before his gaze catches mine. "I have no idea what I did to deserve you. As crazy as it sounds, I'm thanking God right now for every inch of hell I've crawled through to get right here. That's something I never thought I'd say."

He rips his trousers open and adjusts himself before his hands land on my knees and push.

My breath shallows, and my heart speeds.

His fingers trail down the insides of my thighs and my hands, still over my head, grip the sheets with all my might to not move. His finger swipes easily through my sex and barely dips inside me.

"There's no going back."

My eyes fly open when he speaks. His intent stare is on his fingers and what they're doing to create a storm inside me that's brewing so deep, I wonder how I'll survive.

His finger circles my clit and drops down, spreading me and circling my opening. "I don't mean this, I mean me." I look up to him and frown. "Once I make you mine, that's it, Princess. I need you to understand that. I haven't even had you yet, but I know once I take you, there won't be anyone else for me. And there sure as hell won't be anyone else for you. I've never been more serious about anything. I need you to understand that."

My words are shaky for so many reasons. His fingers, me spread before him bare, and the threats he's making, which are really promises. I want to wrap them around my soul to keep forever. I lift my left hand and finger his ring to accentuate my point. "You could break me, Ozzy. If you're not serious, I'm in trouble."

His blue eyes sear me and I lose his finger. His big hands grip the insides of each of my thighs possessively, and I have no idea what he's doing until I lose his intense blues.

That's when he rocks my world.

His mouth lands on my sex.

I moan.

His lips, his tongue. He starts out slow, but slow doesn't last long.

From my clit to my sex, he's everywhere. Sucking, spearing, nipping. I lose all timidity I had a few moments ago and arch my back. His groan vibrates against my clit as his tongue swirls.

I never knew it could be like this. This is like nothing I ever imagined.

I want more.

I need more.

His hands come to my ass and I feel his thumbs part me farther.

"Ozzy—"

He lifts my ass and wraps his lips around my clit.

"Oh, please." This is unlike any other orgasm Ozzy has given me.

My hearing tunnels and I see nothing but fireworks behind my eyelids.

I gasp. Moan. Call for him, but he doesn't stop. He holds me hostage in a way I never want to be let go.

When he finally does, I gasp with relief, but he doesn't leave my sex. He licks and kisses. His tongue circles my opening as I lie limp, recovering from the out of body experience he just gave me. His thumbs follow his tongue. In all the times I've thought about this moment, I didn't expect this ... this kind of attention.

He laps me one more time from my sex to my clit before pushing to stand. He drags a hand over his mouth and reaches to the nightstand where his overnight bag has exploded. I hear him rustle around before he drops a condom on the bed next to my ass.

"I wish you knew the storm brewing inside me, baby. The need to take you and make you mine is warring with the part of me that's afraid to hurt you."

"You'd never hurt me." I lift my left hand and place it over my bare chest where my heart speeds. "Not here anyway. Not where it matters."

He shakes his head once, but I can't focus on his expression because he pushes his pants down, pulling his boxers with them.

Just like when I watched him in the shower and again when I touched him for the first time, he takes my breath away. But now, in a whole other way, knowing it will be all mine.

And, also, wondering how it's going to fit. I mean, I know it will. But wow.

"Relax." As if he could read my mind, he fists his cock and works his length.

I lick my lips. "If you say so."

"Birth control?"

I shake my head.

He picks up the condom and bites it before ripping it open. "We'll work on that soon."

Ozzy slides the condom down his cock, and a pang of envy hits me. I think I'd like to do that.

I swallow hard and think about all the things I'd like to do with Ozzy. Things I've seen, read about, or heard my girlfriends talk about. They'd go on and on about how the boys at school didn't know what they were doing. Now, more than ever, I'm grateful to be here.

Ozzy's hands follow his lips, working their way up my body. I let him, lying here, ready for whatever he'll give me. I dip my hands in his wavy hair and hang on as he pulls my nipple between his lips. Those lips have been all over me, tasted me in so many places it makes me warm thinking about it.

His cock teases my sex, as he rubs its underside against my clit. I'm still sensitive, and my breaths come quicker. Ozzy reaches between us and slides his fingers through my sex again. "You're so fucking perfect. So wet. You don't know how bad I want to slam into you. This gives the blue balls you like to talk about so much new meaning."

My eyes fall shut when he circles my clit again, and I press my face into his neck. "I'm sorry."

"Never be sorry." He replaces his fingers with his cock again and my eyes fly open. "Pull your knees up for me, baby."

I do as he says and feel myself open.

"Higher," he demands.

I give myself props for all the yoga classes I've attended back in Malibu, and pull my knees easily up his sides.

He leans down to kiss me, and I feel him. His tip, it's right where I want it. "Look at me, Princess."

My gaze angles to his.

"Never letting you go." Determination bleeds from him. "You're mine."

Then, it happens.

Ozzy, the man who held me at gunpoint the moment we met, makes me his.

And he doesn't do it slowly or gently.

He takes me in one thrust.

I gasp.

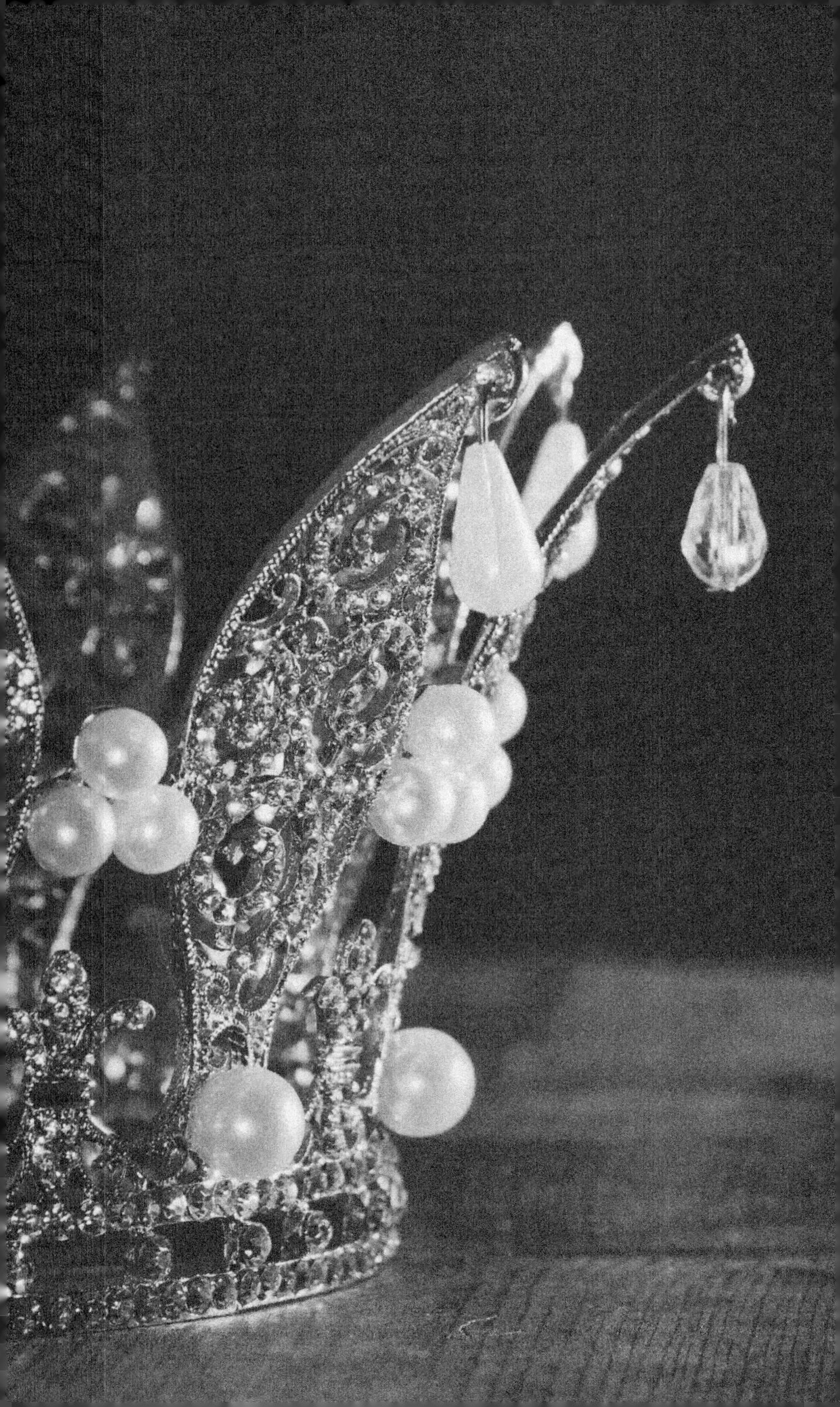

29

NEW OBSESSION

Liyah

Ozzy answers my gasp with a groan. Then, he stills.

I feel ... full. Stretched to fit him. Every inch, swell, and bulge.

For only him.

There was no reason to wonder how he'd fit. He just does.

It's not lost on me we're the most unlikely pair. A princess and a dead man. Two souls, lost and wandering. Though neither of us truly has one, I finally feel home.

I was made for him. For this.

My arms circle his broad shoulders, my fingers grip him. His entire body is tense and it reminds me of when he was in the shower.

His voice is strained, and he turns his head so his lips hit my ear. "You okay?"

I nod. "You're so big."

He exhales. "I'm already here, baby. No need to stroke my ego now."

He pulls out a bit and presses back in. He does it again. The next time he pulls out farther. Every thrust gets bigger and carries more strength.

It also hits my clit exactly where it needs to.

"Tell me you're okay, Princess. I want to give you more."

He slides in and out of me, hitting every delicate spot inside and out. My pulse races, and I allow my head to fall back. I'm able to lift my knees farther.

"Fuck, yes," Ozzy growls and slides a hand under the small of my back.

I'm not chilled now. Together, we're hotter than we are separately. I understand people's obsession with sex.

But, really, it's my obsession with him.

He splays a hand on my ass and lifts, causing him to sink deeper within me. My body grows accustomed to him as his movements quicken, become erratic. With every thrust, he hits my clit just enough.

"Oz—" I start, but he takes my mouth. I'm surrounded, inside and out, by Ozzy Graves. Every muscle and emotion that hangs in the balance between us is electric.

"You gonna come again?" His breathing is as labored as mine.

"I don't know. I think..."

He rocks his pelvis into my clit, and my fingertips bite into his biceps. It doesn't matter that this is new or that my body isn't used to the invasion of his. Right now, everything falls into place.

This is amazing.

Sex is amazing.

Ozzy, though, is my new passion. Orgasms with him inside me at the same time?

Life-altering.

He must have been holding back before, because once I come, he really moves. And I want it.

I want it all.

He thrusts two more times before he groans, hot and heavy, in my hair. He gives me all his weight and tries to catch his breath before he rolls, taking me with him.

My legs fall on either side of his hips where we're connected. He's still hard inside me. As much as I love what we just did, I can tell I'm going to feel it.

He gives me a squeeze where he holds me at my ass and head. "Did I hurt you?"

I press up on my forearms and look down at him. "No. I mean, I feel it, but no. It was everything. And since it was you, it was even more."

He brings his hands to my face and pulls my mouth to his for a long, hot kiss. When he lets me go, his expression has never been more steadfast. "You know how to light a fire under a dead man. I'm going to give you everything, Liyah. Fuck anyone and anything who gets in my way. I'll take them out myself. Kings and traitors had better watch their backs—I'm coming for them. And once we find your mom, we can live a normal life."

A smile settles on my lips. "I'm quite obsessed with you, Ozzy Graves."

He shakes his head. "I'd like to see someone take you away from me. Fuck them."

"Yes," I agree. "Fuck them all."

Ozzy

I'VE LOST track of time, which is something I do a lot of when I'm not on assignment. I have no commitments, no priorities, and certainly no one to answer to.

But I've also never had a life-changing Royal tear through my life.

I wake up to a new day with new problems.

Don Demaree and Bobby Cannon know I'm alive.

Luciana is still missing.

And I deflowered a princess and explained to her that the ring on her finger is very, very real. The need to scream that from the rooftops, or have Liyah post that shit all over for the world to see as a fuck you to the King, courses through my blood.

All this has me wondering about the logistics of a dead man acquiring a marriage license.

That particular problem fuels me. And what seemed like the end of the world last night has given me new energy this morning. I'm awake, energized, and ready to play offense in the game that is my life.

My fiancée is also wound around me naked and there's nothing I want more at this moment than to roll her to her back and take her again. I've only had her once and I know for a fact, I'll never have my fill. But I'm afraid she's sore, so losing myself in her this morning isn't an option.

She stirs.

Her hand trails up my side.

We're glued to each other again, but naked this time. It seems when we have each other, there's no need for blankets. We only need our own heat to survive, which is pretty damn fitting since that's the only way we've endured since we met.

I brush the hair from her face when she lifts her heavy lids to look up at me.

She smiles.

I've never seen anything like it. I must be turning into a sap who just attached his own ball and chain to the naked woman in my arms, because this smile on her face is different. It's private, just for me, and screams that the memories from last night are the only thing she's thinking of.

I lean in and press my lips to her forehead. "Morning."

She stretches before curling back into me. "Good morning."

I run my hand down her back until it lands on the swell of her ass. "You okay?"

I lose her face when she tucks it in my neck and nods against my skin. "I'm more than okay."

Winding my fingers through her hair, I ask the thing I can't stop thinking about since I opened my eyes. "You sore?"

She rubs her legs together and hitches a shoulder. "Not bad."

I bring my fingers to her chin and lift her face so I can see her when she's talking. "You sure? Do you need anything?"

She shakes her head. "I'm good. Like, really good, Ozzy."

Even more fuel for me to get all this shit taken care of as soon as possible. My number one goal in life right now is normalcy.

"I wish today could be different—that we could hide

out here all day, ignore the world, and all the shit coming at us. But I have a lot to do and that means I'm in the control room all day. But I do have some news. Well, not really news. But an update on your mom."

Gone is the relaxed and sated woman in my arms. I have to hold her to me to keep her from sitting up. "What happened?"

I place my hand on the side of her face. "Bella got home late last night to a message from her contact in Algeria. He has some pretty reliable intel that says she was seen getting on a boat."

Liyah's body goes limp in my arms. "Thank goodness."

"You need to realize this is only intel, baby. Temper your expectations. But Bella's contacts are good, so this is a step in the right direction. Now we can focus on the areas of Spain you think she might go for refuge."

She nods and that smile returns, proving she's an optimist. "What if she already made it to Spain? I wish I had my phone, what if she tries to reach out to me? Although, no one is more aware of Hasim's wickedness than her, so she probably knows not to. How will she find me?"

I need to be careful and not crush her glass-is-half-full outlook on everything. It's who she is, the complete opposite of what I am. If anything, I need some of that to rub off on me.

"If she made it to Spain and she's as savvy as you say, she won't contact you. It will give up her position and put you in harm's way. We'll find her. It'll be easier in Spain than Algeria."

She pushes up my body and presses her lips to mine. I roll to my back and pull her on top of me. Her hair is a mess, and her makeup from last night is smudged since we stayed right where we were after I trashed the condom.

"Thank you." She beams.

I silently make it my mission to make her look like this every single day. "Don't thank me yet, Princess. We've got a long way to go."

"I have a good feeling. Things are going to change. How could they not after last night?"

I change the subject to something I'd rather talk about and roll us so I'm on top. "I'd like to give you another good feeling."

My dick stiffens when she pulls her leg up and drags her foot over my bare ass. "I thought you had to get to the control room?"

"I do. And you probably need a minute after last night. But I'm just putting it out there, the only thing on my mind is you." What I don't say aloud is we have a lot to figure out. Like what life will look like if going on the offense backfires on me. I can't exactly hide in the shadows while living the rest of my life with a princess. "You want me to bore you to death all day in the control room or do you want me to see who you can hang out with?"

"I want to see what you do, and I really want to see what you plan on doing to the men who framed you."

"Love your curiosity, Princess, but I have a feeling you might be disappointed. Today, I'm laying the groundwork. No bombs will be detonated." She widens her eyes, so I amend, "At least, it's not on the agenda, but if I've learned one thing since we've been together, it's to never say never."

She bites her lip at the talk of bombs, but her curiosity gets to her. "I still want to come with you."

"Done." I lean down and kiss her, wondering where the day will take us.

All I know is, I'm ready to put my plan into action. It's time to dangle a carrot in front of the big, bad wolves.

Seems all I needed was something to live for besides myself.

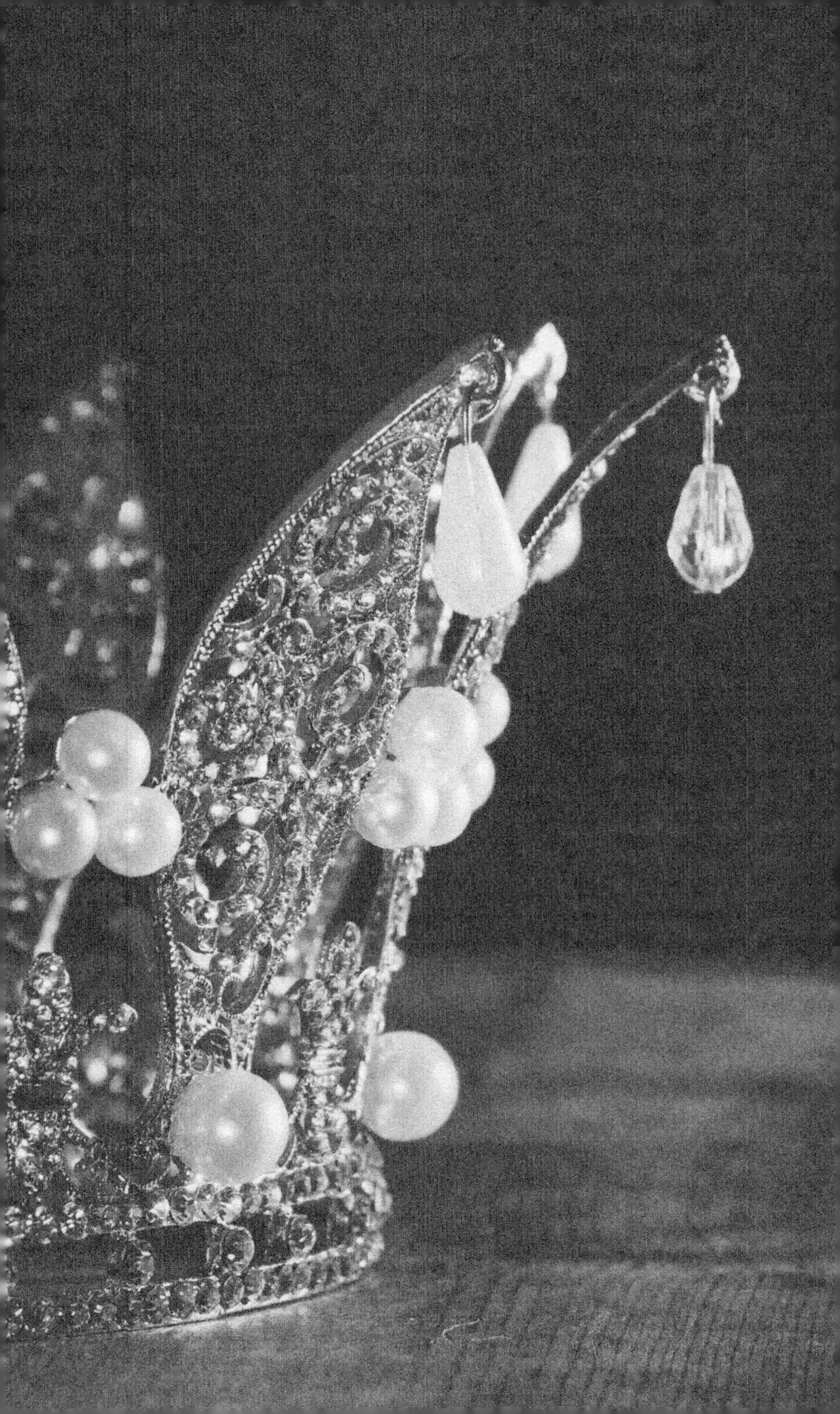

30

HEIFERS

Liyah

I should've listened to Ozzy.

As interesting as the morning started, it quickly became slow and tedious.

After we made quick work of getting ready for the day, Ozzy and I trudged through the forest to the next property where his associates were waiting in the old dining room for him.

Ozzy pulled me to his side and made no bones that they could speak freely in front of me. After a few side-eyed stares and a smirk from Jarvis, they got on with business.

This is how it went…

"Do it," Crew demanded. "It's a risk, but we can manage it. They want to play a deadly game, we're diving into that shit headfirst. No more defense, Oz. This isn't a suggestion or me giving you a nudge. This is a fucking order."

I cringed.

I had no idea what he's talking about, but diving headfirst into a deadly game didn't sound appealing. Everyone else in the room, however, wasn't fazed.

"You sure?" Ozzy asked.

"I don't give an order I'm not sure about. End this. It's time," Crew said.

Jarvis lost his smirk. "This is your *get out of jail free* card, man. Do it."

Ozzy was not incensed like he was last night when the keyboard met the wall. His expression was electric and laser-focused. "Fuck, yeah, it is. Let's get this shit done."

That was hours ago. I'm doing everything I can not to ask him a million questions, because getting shit done does not seem like a quick process, no matter how much I want to know the details.

I've tried to busy myself with things I used to be happy doing for hours—scrolling my phone. My friends might have made a few posts about me when I first left California, but have since moved on with their lives. This might have bothered me before, but I really don't care anymore. My life has turned on its end and I'm shockingly happy with where I've landed.

Happy might be an understatement.

I can't stop watching the man I gave everything to last night. He continues to fascinate me. Especially now, doing what he's good at, even if it does involve deadly games.

Ozzy's hand comes to my foot that's perched on the edge of his chair. He looks over at me for the first time in what feels like an eternity. "You hungry?"

"Did my growling stomach give me away?"

"Who's hungry?" I spin in my chair and see Gracie

walking in with a heavy paper bag and a smile. "Noah called and explained that Ozzy is holding you hostage, but don't you worry. I'm here to save you from the tedious business of computers."

She plops the bag on the desk in front of Ozzy, and he spins to face her. "You brought us lunch?"

"No." She grabs my hand and pulls me to my feet. "I brought you lunch. I'm taking Liyah with me." Gracie turns to me. "Sorry I wasn't here sooner. It was a late night, and we're all moving slowly."

Ozzy leans back in his chair and looks up at me. "You want to go?"

I raise a brow. "Do you mind?"

"Of course he doesn't mind," Gracie butts in. "Making you sit here and watch him work is cruel and unusual. Addy ordered a spread from the tasting room. Since you all had a private party last night, this is our chance to hang out with Liyah. Bella is home and you'll get to meet her. She's the shit."

I'm afraid I accept too quickly. "I'd love to go."

Ozzy's lips tip up on the side. "Ouch."

"Right. Boring as hell." Gracie laughs. "She'll be with us for the rest of the day and you can create havoc on the dark web. Good luck and watch your back."

I turn back to Ozzy and reach for his hand. "You're sure?"

He gives me a tug and a peck on the lips. "I was kidding. I'll be at this for hours. Go do something not boring."

I slip my shoes on and follow Gracie out of the control room. My stomach looks forward to food, and I look forward to meeting the woman who is helping find my mother. And to pick the brains of the people who know Ozzy best.

"Princess Aliyah. I'm sorry I'm late. I was getting caught up at home with the kiddies after being gone. It's wonderful to finally meet you."

Bella Carson's English accent hits me like a warm hug. I spent many, many years in England in boarding school. Other than living away from my mother for most of that time, the United Kingdom feels more like home than Morocco.

"I can't thank you enough for helping to look for my mother. It means the world to me."

She starts to spoon various salads onto her plate before joining the rest of us around the table that acts as an island in Addy's old kitchen. It's Sunday. Children are once again running amuck. This group is a tight bunch, that's for sure.

Bella flips a napkin on her lap. "Anything for Ozzy, and now that you're engaged, anything for you, as well. That goes without saying, Liyah."

This is real.

Ozzy's words echo in my head as they've done all morning. Last night plays in my thoughts like a favorite film that I've memorized every word, lyric, and scene.

I'm engaged. I'm actually engaged.

And no longer a virgin.

"About the engagement." Addy breaks into my thoughts with a sly smile. "We like to throw parties. It doesn't take much for us to find a reason to celebrate life."

"We do like a party," Keelie affirms.

"And Ozzy is like a brother to everyone," Addy adds.

"Not just to the men. To us too," Gracie says. "But he and Noah are especially close. They've known each other forever. Since they were little."

"What we're getting at." Maya looks around the table before directing her kind but nosy gaze on me. "We're fascinated, basically. By the social media posts. The ring on your finger. Your royal status, Ozzy's status, which is ... dead. We're dying to know. Are you two really getting married?"

I shift in my seat, wipe my lips, and fold my napkin to the left of my plate on the table. I'm not sore, but I do feel the effects of my first time. It's not uncomfortable, and I wonder if I'm a freak because I like it. Liking the constant reminder, of not just my first time, but our first time.

I look around the table at the curious women waiting for an answer.

"I think." *This is real.* "No. I mean, yes. Yes, I guess it's real. But we haven't made any plans or anything. I think what I'm trying to say is, we've agreed that it's real, but it doesn't feel real. I'm prattling on, but do you know what I mean?"

They all nod as they try to bite back wolfish grins, but it's Maya who reaches out and grabs my hand. "I know exactly what you mean."

I ignore the rest of them. "You do?"

"I do." Maya holds her left hand up between us. "Grady slid this ring on my finger as a big, fat fuck you to my ex—and my mother. I freaked. He told me to wear it for a while and see how it felt, but he wouldn't let me take it off. And I never did."

"There was no way my brother would have let you take that ring off," Gracie concurs. How did I not know Grady was Gracie's brother?

"I was engaged on a dare," Bella shares between bites. "There's always something with these men."

Addy ignores them all and declares, "I knew it! I told you all it was real."

"It's not like we disagreed with you," Keelie throws out. "We were just tempering our excitement because it's Ozzy." Keelie turns to me. "This is so not like Ozzy, because of ... everything."

I pick up my glass of water and take a drink before leaning forward on the distressed wood table. "About Ozzy's predicament—"

"We're going to get that fixed," Bella interrupts. "Cole went into work today to see what he can find on his end. It's tricky with the CIA since they don't *officially* work in the States, but a little wiggle niggle here and there doesn't bother my husband."

"Wiggle niggle?" I ask.

Keelie lowers her voice. "Carson pushes the boundaries."

"Carson doesn't know what boundaries are," Addy says. "Carson can start digging. You know, unofficially, because it's not an assigned case, but also officially because the Russian guy is actually in Russia. So, it's all good."

This is all making my head spin, so I get to what I really want to know. "Tell me about Ozzy's family. I refuse to believe it's necessary for them to believe he's dead."

My question acts as a cold, wet blanket thrown on

the party. The women around me sit back in their chairs, and wince, sigh, or shake their heads.

It's Gracie who answers. "That's on Ozzy. This tribe that you're now a part of? We keep secrets like the best of them. I think it's what makes us as close as we are. This wouldn't work if we weren't all in, in every way. But Ozzy feels if his parents knew, it would put them at risk. Noah has tried to convince him it would be okay, but Ozzy isn't willing to chance it."

"It just..." I sigh and put my hand over my chest. "It hurts my heart, you know? For Ozzy. And his family. The way he described them—his love for them is deep. They don't deserve this. And selfishly, I want to know them."

Addy looks from me to the women sitting around the table. "Yeah, she's in love. This engagement is the real deal. And you know what that means."

My breath catches at the word *love*. I know it's stupid and crazy and outrageous, because Ozzy told me this ring was real, and I agreed, yet neither of us have so much as tiptoed around that word.

"That means we're having a party!" Keelie exclaims.

"An engagement party," Maya says. "It's a good thing we have an entire vineyard at our disposal."

I shake my head. "I don't know. Ozzy seems really busy."

"There are enough badasses to go around. And then there's me." Bella smiles and picks up her glass. "We will get you both sorted, I promise. There is plenty of time to celebrate your engagement."

"He works for Crew." Addy's smile reminds me of the Cheshire Cat I had as a child who always got his way. "And Crew will do anything for me, so don't you worry. Crew will make sure he's there."

"There's really no hurry," I insist. "I'm sure it will be a long engagement."

"Really?" Gracie frowns. "I thought with the King and all, it would be sooner rather than later."

My mouth goes dry at the thought. "We haven't had the chance to talk that through."

"There's no hurry," Keelie counters. "Not while you're here. You're safe, don't worry about anyone's schedule but your own."

"I had to live years without any contact with my family."

I turn to Bella. "Really?"

"Yes, love. It was brutal, as we are a close lot. My situation was not nearly as final as Ozzy's. I can't pretend to understand how it would feel as a child or as a parent. But I do know once your family is standing with you, as they should, life has a way of falling into place. Once we find your mum, life will settle for you, as well."

"Thank you, Bella."

Her smile lights up her face, until her eyes dart to her cell that's sitting next to her plate on the table. She slides her finger across the screen and hikes a brow. "Well, then. Cole just turned onto Crew's property. I wonder what he was able to dig up through Uncle Sam."

Ozzy

"Marat Kruglov owns corporations across southeast Russia and into Ukraine, which isn't good for business right now because of tension between the two countries. Not all of his shit is on the up and up, but that really has nothing to do with your shit, other than it proves he's willing to stick his neck out and be an asshole to make a buck. Business is suffering, even his illegitimate revenue streams have taken a dip. Also, it must be known, he's got a shit ton of kids by more baby mamas than any one man can juggle. The guy must be more desperate than a sinner on Sunday morning."

I can weasel my way into a lot of systems, but there is something to be said about good, old-fashioned intel. That is when it's nice to have Cole Carson around.

"Are these baby mamas going to help clear my name?" I ask.

Cole's expression twists. "Hell no. I just thought it was interesting. Who needs that kind of drama in their life?"

"Then get to the point," I bite.

Asa laughs.

Crew rolls his eyes.

Carson looks offended. "I'm trying to lay the groundwork that the guy is desperate and started dabbling in the business of information. That's how he met your resident cocksuckers on the dark web."

Those cocksuckers have been quiet today.

The only conversation I heard in Bobby's car this morning was when his wife called him on his way home from the gym to put in her order for a pumpkin-fucking-latte and donuts. I wonder if she knows that her more-than-cushy life is being supplemented by stolen state secrets.

I drag my hand down my face. "Still waiting…"

Carson looks to Asa. "Some people don't appreciate the history that supports motivations."

Asa deadpans, "I appreciate you, Carson. But I think we'd all appreciate the twist in your romance novel sooner rather than later."

Carson points at me. "This is where it gets good. I looked into Kruglov's family. He's a second cousin to the Assistant to the President of the Federation."

I pause. "No shit?"

"And I have transactions that go back and forth for years, far past your drama." Carson holds his arms out. "Who's your hero now?"

"The WITSEC murders?" I barely hear my own voice. If this is true, it could be my ticket to proving Demaree and Cannon sold the information that was pinned on me, which has me sitting right where I am today.

Before my shit went down, an entire family was murdered who'd been in witness protection. The parents were immigrants who made their way to America. They were Russian, and the wife was a nuclear physicist. The Russian government forced her to work on weapons that violated treaties. Russia isn't what it used to be, but when someone works on shit like that, the government has eyes on them all the time. She managed to get across the border and bring her family with her. In exchange for information about what her government was developing, Uncle Sam put her whole family into protective custody.

They were good until Demaree and Cannon sold their location. Then they weren't good anymore because they were dead.

And not my kind of dead.

Carson goes on. "I haven't connected the murders yet, not with the hard evidence you need. But that woman who was put into WITSEC created nuclear technology that went against the United Nations' agreements. The story blew up around the world when she came forward. Not that the Russian President gives two shits what most of the world thinks about him, but his closest allies cockblocked his ass. You know, politically speaking."

"We need that connection, Carson," Crew demands.

"I have no doubt I'll get the connection, but your boy here needs to find a way to prove that information came from Dumb and Dumber, and that it wasn't him."

"I laid the groundwork for that today. All I need is for them to bite."

"They'll bite." Asa's confidence in Demaree and Cannon bleeds through his words. "The request you put out there is lucrative enough, no greedy traitor would turn it down."

"Ozzy Graves, playing on the dark web." Carson nods with approval. "I like it."

I spin in my chair to pick up my phone when I get a text notification.

Princess – I guess I'm going to take a walk with some cows.

I bite back my smirk.

Me – Enjoy. I'm still working. Making progress.

Princess – Lots of progress? I hope so. Also, I need to warn you. An engagement party is in our near future. I don't even know how you feel about parties. I tried to tell them it wasn't necessary.

Concentration is never an issue for me, but today it's

been a struggle. Especially when it's my own shit—I should be laser focused.

But it seems like my cock isn't the only part of me that's obsessed. My mind ... this knot in my chest. Consumed is not a strong enough word to describe my preoccupation with my royal princess.

Me – They like to party. Don't worry. I'm good.

Princess – Okay. Well, I guess if you need me, I'll be with cows. I've never taken a walk with a cow before. So many firsts for me lately.

With that, my blood rushes to my dick.

Me – Envious. I like having your firsts. I'll look for you soon.

Princess – Don't make me blush around cows, Ozzy.

Me – Now I'll find you very soon. BTW, if you keep molasses in your pockets, they'll crowd you.

Princess – I'm not sure if that's a good thing or not...

Me – Depends on how you feel about cows.

Princess – Walking with cows shouldn't be stressful.

Me – If you need me to rescue you from the heifers, give me a call.

Princess – That's not nice lol

"I'm not sure anything can make my romantic, sappy heart happier than this." I look up and Cole Carson has a hand over his chest. I roll my eyes. "Man down—that's all I'm going to say. Man fucking down."

I really doubt that's all he's going to say because the man likes to hear himself talk.

Me – See you soon, baby.

Princess - xx

Asa stuffs his hands in his pockets and grins. "Yeah, he's a goner."

I guess I'm lucky the whole team isn't here.

"Any updates on the King?" Crew asks.

I recline in my chair and find that today the royal asshole doesn't bother me as much as he did before, and I'm sure that has to do with making Liyah mine last night. But I'm not about to share that with this bunch. "More of the same. I'm not worried about him, not with Liyah here. But, I need him to talk about Luciana."

"Bella put out feelers in Spain. Now we wait," Carson says.

"Waiting is the story of my life," I mutter and look at the screens when a tone sounds. I feel the men close in behind me to look over my shoulder.

"Looks like you won't have to wait. Your bait must have been nice and ripe. That didn't take long," Crew says.

My lips tip on one side.

"Motherfuckers," I mutter. "I knew you assholes wouldn't be able to resist."

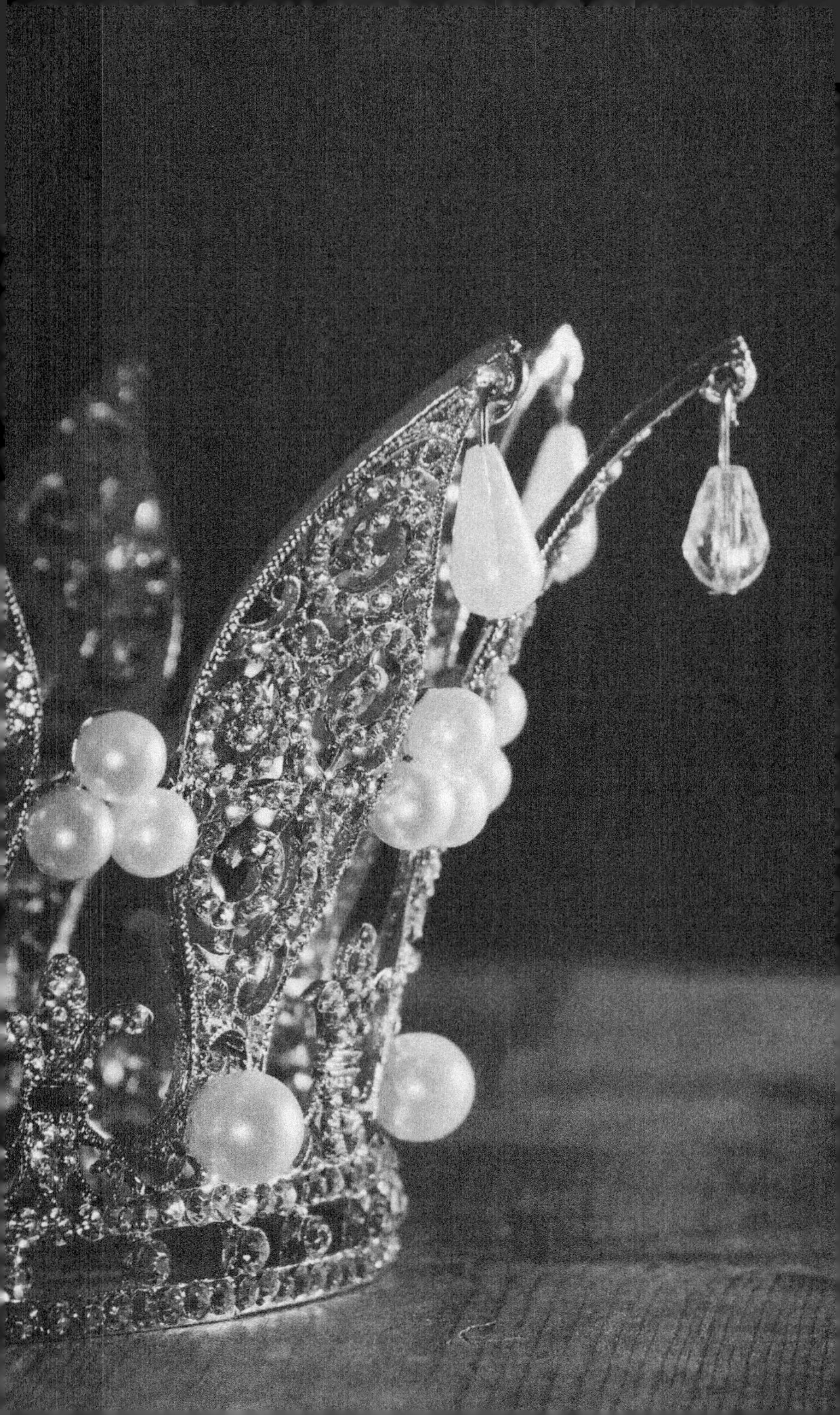

31

SILK

Liyah

"**O**zzy."

My fiancé swirls his magical tongue around my clit, and I have to press my weight into the tile wall to keep from toppling over.

Lord, he's everywhere.

Ozzy's advice about cows did not go unheard. I mean, he did grow up on a dairy farm. If anyone knows cows, it's him.

And the owner of Whitetail, I guess, since she keeps them as pets.

Addy insisted I feed her beloved cows handfuls of molasses. She said it was a sure-fire way to make them love me.

I never knew I needed the love of a cow. I'm still on the fence about it.

It was a beautiful day. I enjoyed getting out and seeing more of Addy and Crew's property. But when cows crowd you, you end up smelling like a cow.

Ozzy didn't seem to mind. The moment we stepped over the threshold to the bungalow, he stripped me naked and led me to the shower.

It seems I'm not the only one who couldn't stop thinking about last night.

I run my fingers through his wet hair since he's on his knees in front of me. He throws one of my legs over his shoulder when my knees go weak to support my weight.

This.

Just when I think he's given me the end all be all of orgasms, he goes and ups his game. I'm not sure I'll survive. Standing, slippery, wet ... and Ozzy's tongue.

My fingers grip his hair and I hold tight. "Yes. Oh, my."

His tongue presses in before my clit is wrapped in his full lips. One hand lands on my breast, and the other on my ass, because my knee gives out when I come.

I'm completely at his mercy.

And I love it.

My moans fill in the shower around us, echoing in the bathroom as my blood churns.

For him.

The next thing I know, I'm up, in his arms, and I wrap my weak legs around his waist. He sits on the small bench and holds me tight to his chest with his rock-hard cock pressed between us.

His lips land on my temple. "Doubt I'll ever get used to this."

I press my face into his neck. I'm limp and sated. I should do something for him, but I don't know what. He's led me, in every way since we met—especially when we're like this.

He doesn't make me wait long to wonder what's happening next. With one hand under my ass cupping my sex, he turns my face to his. "No sex. Maybe tomorrow. You were so tight, I'm afraid to take you too soon."

I press my lips to his and tell him the truth. "I'm fine."

A slow smile tips his lips on one side. "We can do other things, baby."

"Like what?"

The hot water blankets us and steam swirls. "You can do whatever you want."

I push away from him but stay seated on his lap. He spreads his thighs to support me, but when his eyes drop to my body, he takes me in splayed before him. My intense stare, on the other hand, goes directly to his cock standing at attention between us.

Ozzy rests his shoulders against the tile and grabs my ass to pull me tight to him.

The tips of my fingers feel their way down his chest, over every sculpted muscle and rippled ab, until I reach far enough south, I wrap one hand around him. My other index finger lightly traces his swollen head in a circle.

I'm fascinated by Ozzy's body, especially this. Because this is for me. He's this way because of me.

I don't even know if that's normal or selfish, but I love it. I'm becoming obsessed with everything about this man, and, deep in my soul, I want nothing more than to be the same for him.

Isn't that what every woman wants? To have the man her heart beats for be consumed only with her?

I haven't looked away from his cock and jump when his hand cups my face. His icy blues are hot and searing as he drags a heavy thumb over my bottom lip and presses in.

Oh, Lord.

I instantly fist his cock as my tongue swirls the tip of his thumb.

Ozzy's lips part. His tongue catches a droplet of water hanging on for dear life on his top lip.

I squeeze his cock and part my lips farther to suck his thumb into my mouth.

Ozzy's broad chest rises with a labored breath. I'm tempted to reach out and place a hand over his heart. There's nothing more I want right now than to feel his pulse race.

Call it desperation, I don't care. I've never been desperate for anything in my life except when I listened to that voicemail from my mom.

That was the moment that led me here. I'm no less desperate, but it's in a whole other way.

Ozzy presses his thumb farther into my mouth. I fist him with both hands—up and down, up and down, all the while, I suck.

"Don't stop, Princess. You don't know what this is doing to me. You might do me in for good just watching you."

His words empower me, and my grip on his cock tightens and quickens.

Ozzy begins to slide his thumb in and out of my mouth. My eyes fall shut, lost in the moment he's giving me. I suck harder and imagine it's another part of him.

Longer.

Thicker.

Harder.

His fingers bite into my ass. "Look at me."

I do as he says, and immediately chastise myself, because I'm in awe of the scene in front of me. How dare I close my eyes and miss this.

My pulse races, and I wonder how he does this to me. I'm not the one about to orgasm, but watching him and wondering...

"So good," he breathes, never looking away from my face. Never once glancing at what I'm doing to his cock. I wonder if he's dreaming about his cock in my mouth too.

Full.

Hard.

Like silk on my tongue.

"Don't stop, Liyah. You're so fucking beautiful right now," he pants.

That spurs me on. If I thought I was emboldened before, it's nothing compared to now.

I jerk harder and suck deep.

Ozzy groans.

"Fuck, I'm close."

His eyes narrow, but we never break visual contact. I could get lost in his soulful blues forever. They've changed since the night we met on that train.

They changed for me.

His chest rises and falls, and his brows pinch. Every beautiful muscle in front of me flexes, and I feel him in my hold. He never looks away when he comes, and I pull his thumb into my mouth as hard as I can.

He groans and I force myself to break our connection when he comes so I can watch. It's hot and sticky, running down the sides of my hands where I'm milking him for every last drop.

His hand falls from my face, and I suck in a breath

when I lose his thumb. I feel his muscles relax beneath me, but I don't look away from his cock between us. From what we just did.

No, from what I just did.

I swirl his tip like I did earlier. Curiosity gets the best of me, and I bring my finger up and touch it to my tongue.

"You really are trying to kill me."

I look up and smile around my finger as I lick it clean.

Salty.

I'm not sure what I was expecting, but I don't hate it.

Ozzy shakes his head, and his hands return to my ass. His breaths start to even, and he gives me a yank. I'm tucked to his chest, and he wraps one arm around me and his hand returns to a spot I'm getting used to, between my legs.

"I feel like one lucky fucker that you picked my train cabin, Princess. Everything with you is an experience I didn't know I needed."

I press my lips to his pec. "I could say the same."

The water starts to cool on my back. Ozzy feels it too and stands, setting me on my feet before reaching for the body wash. "I need to feed you before the women try to use mealtime as an excuse to nab you again. We're not leaving this tiny house until the sun rises, Princess."

Ozzy

As royal as my fiancée might be, she certainly doesn't act like it. She sat on the marble island with her legs crossed in the same cutoff shorts and NASA shirt she wore in Paris. I stood next to her as we ate spaghetti smothered in jar sauce.

Growing up, it didn't matter how busy my mom was chasing three boys and running her shop in town, there was always dinner, and it was always made from scratch. Even if we were too busy to sit down and eat it together. If we were hungry, there was something home-cooked sitting in the fridge waiting on us.

Jar sauce is jar sauce, but Liyah didn't bat an eye and ate her entire plate. Apparently walking cows and shower sexcapades creates an appetite. Something for me to remember.

We ate, and she talked.

Or, more specifically, she interrogated me.

I'm not used to answering questions for anyone. Everyone in my life knows my story, and there's nothing more for them to know.

It didn't matter how curt or vague I tried to be, Liyah wasn't having it. And I'm pretty sure this says something about my future that I'll end up giving her everything she wants.

Dairy farm, small-town Pennsylvania, Friday night lights, and boutiques. Brothers, basketball, my favorite foods, and my first car.

I had no idea there was that much to know about myself.

Apparently my cock isn't that special, because the Princess of Morocco is curious about everything, not just what it feels like when I come.

Or don't come.

I hope those days are over. The last twenty-four hours have been pretty fucking fantastic. And knowing she's mine and mine alone is something I've never felt before. This need to dominate, protect, and give everything in the world I possibly can to her courses through me.

She didn't bleed last night, but I still need to give her time. The thought of hurting Liyah in any way—especially that way—rips me to shreds.

She's the reason I'm finally dabbling in the dark web. It's a risk, but every risk is worth it if it means having a normal life with her.

The fucking King and his disgusting old friend have been droning on and on about how my fiancée *looks and acts like a whore to the world,* and the fact that once Luciana stepped foot on that boat off the coast of Algeria, her trail went as cold as the deepest, darkest sea.

But, other than all that, I don't remember when life has been this good.

Even before my fictional death.

Liyah is curled up next to me in bed. We turned on a movie thirty minutes ago, but she's out.

I turn down the volume and open my laptop. Bobby Cannon is on the move at eleven-thirty on a Sunday night. There's no way I can tap their phones again. Not when they know I'm able to listen in. Our game of cat and mouse has been upped to expert levels. They're on high alert and are good enough to know when they're being surveilled.

As long as Bobby doesn't realize his one-year free roadside service and full internet package is giving me access in his car, I'm good.

I listen through my ear buds as the car door slams.

"This couldn't wait 'til tomorrow?" Don asks. "I had

to pour the milk out so I'd have a reason to leave the house."

"Do you think my ass would be out this late on a Sunday if it could wait until tomorrow?" Bobby has always been the bigger of the two assholes. "Here. I picked up a couple of burners so we don't have to sneak out of our own damn houses until we can find Graves."

Interesting.

I click over to another screen to take over the cell tower they're closest to. If I can triangulate their location, I can tap into their burners since they feel so safe with prepaid phones.

"This makes me nervous," Don says. "I say we cool our shit for a while. Wait for him to make the next move, then we can find him."

"All I can tell is the tap was coming from a satellite. Nothing official through the cell companies and definitely no warrant. He could be any-fucking-where in the world."

Little do you know, I'm right next door in Virginia, assholes.

Twelve devices ping off my tower. I narrow my triangle and hope they keep talking and this meeting wasn't just a drop. My gut tells me the burner phones are just icing on my cake.

"We have a new prospect," Bobby announces.

I smile.

"No," Don rebukes. "No fucking way. Not right now. Let's work with Kruglov for now. We know who he is. There's no need to vet anyone new. We'll flesh out Graves and go from there."

"We can't turn this down. This offer makes Kruglov

look like a value meal at a drive-thru. This is big," Bobby argues.

Why, yes, motherfucker, my fake-ass offer is not only generous, it requires information you don't usually work with. He'll have to break into a new system, and that's where Carson will jump in.

"What do they want?" Don asks.

"I traced the contact back to Algeria. I guess there are rumors about the President of Morocco. They want proof and only the kind that can be found privately. They want to buy a scandal," Bobby explains.

Two birds, one stone. When I was contemplating what the hell to corner them with, I figured why not?

"I don't know." I assume it's Don who sighs. "I really think we need to give it a rest for a while. Make sure things aren't too hot."

"I already accepted," Bobby clips.

"What the fuck? Without conferring with me? No way. You can do this shit yourself. I'm sitting this one out."

"That's hardly an option, and you know it. Take your burner. I'll send you the details of the order. We'll get this done, and then I promise I won't accept anything else for a while. But this is too easy, and the money is that good. There's no way we're turning this down."

"Fuck," Don hisses.

"Don't be a pussy—you'll be fine. Get out. I've got to get home."

It looks like there's trouble in traitor paradise, because they don't say goodbye. Instead, Don gets out of the car and slams his door.

"Fucker better not think of walking on me," Bobby mutters to himself. "He'll fucking regret it."

The radio turns up, and I watch him on GPS. He doesn't give me any further information other than he's really into eighties hair bands and goes straight home where he parks in the garage despite the fact his wife's car sits in the driveway.

I look over at my Princess and run my fingers through her hair.

I might've dragged my feet making a move into the dark web, but I couldn't be more excited now. I did what I had to do. There was no way I was going to prove my innocence while sitting in federal prison, but I can do it from here.

Who knows if I'll actually get my life back. What I do know, is these two assholes won't be living free much longer.

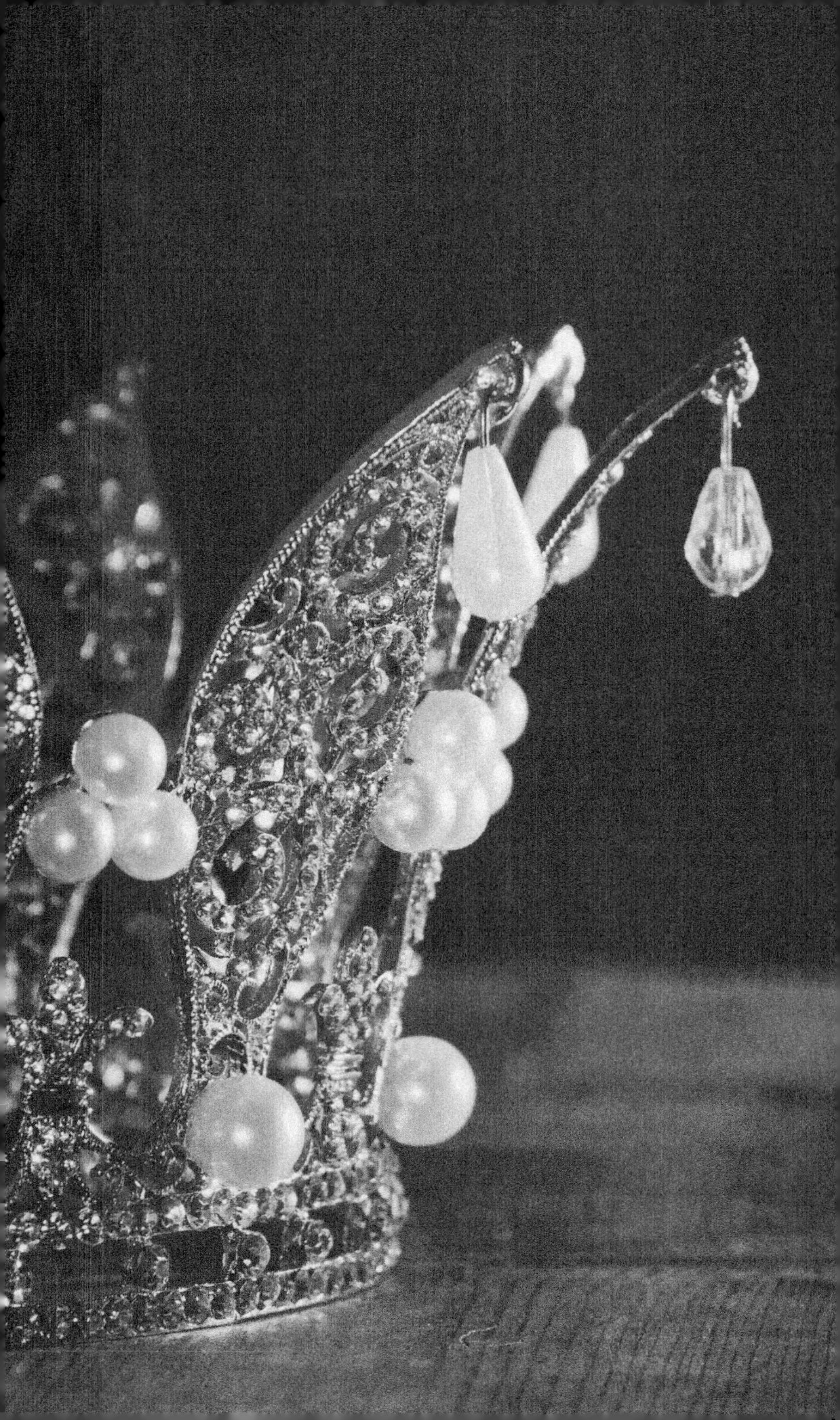

32

EMOTIONALLY HIJACKED

Liyah

A dream and a nightmare.
This is my life at the moment.
And I keep asking myself, how is this even possible?

It's been three days. Three days at a vineyard in Virginia, with my fiancé—my protector.

My everything.

Ozzy.

The days have flown and dragged. I guess this is what happens when one finds themselves newly engaged —even if it is by accident—and worried senseless because there has been no word about one's mother.

Nothing from Morocco, Algeria, or Spain. Bella feels horrible that her contacts in the region haven't been able to dig anything up. She keeps apologizing; her guilt and emotions are profound. And now I feel the burden of it.

I've spent my days with the women of Whitetail.

Even the caretaker's wife, Bev, has taken to me. She and I babysat Crew and Addy's girls yesterday while Addy had to go to town to meet with a supplier. I've tasted all the wine, stomped on grapes, and walked miles and miles and miles with Addy and her cows.

Ozzy spends his days in his control room managing both our life crises.

And we spend our nights wrapped up in one another.

The pure and utter obsession with my husband-to-be is getting out of control and courses through me hot and heavy, to a point I'm anxious about my future. The *what-ifs* drive me mad. I'm desperate to find something else to fixate on besides finding my mother and Ozzy clearing his name.

Our very public engagement and my very private fiancé continue to create buzz around the world. My uncle hasn't made any further public declarations about his plans for me, but, privately, he and the President of the Constitutional Court are about to lose their self-righteous and disgusting minds.

"You're a million miles away, Liyah."

I turn to Bella who stands at the sink in her enormous kitchen that's open to the first floor of their home. Their son, Isaac, is playing in the sunroom off the back of the house. Fall has blanketed Virginia. The once green and lush landscape is painted the colors of gold, citrus, and burning flames.

"I'm sorry. Just thinking." It's early. Ozzy was up hours before the sunrise to go to the gym before the control room.

The wives have not explained a schedule to me, but I'm not an idiot. I know they're taking turns entertaining me. Or, more specifically, distracting me from the shit swirling around us.

Bella texted me last night and informed me she was picking me up right after she dropped Abbott at school, and we would find something *fun to do*. I'm not a control freak by nature, but being handed off from one kind soul to another, day-in and day-out, is niggling at my need to do something *I* want to do.

Even though that something might not be a popular idea among some.

The water at the sink flips off, and Bella sets a skillet on a kitchen towel to dry. "What are you thinking about, love?"

I shrug. "How much I really want something that isn't possible."

She dries her hands and leans into the island across from me. "What do you want that isn't possible?"

I clamp my mouth shut because saying it aloud isn't only ridiculous, it's a bit reckless. Even I can't deny it, but it doesn't make me want it any less.

"Nothing is impossible, Liyah. It might seem like it right now with the weight of the world on your shoulders. But, I promise, there will be a light at the end of your tunnel. And it will be beautiful. Tell me what you think isn't possible. I might be able to help."

I exhale and decide to just throw it out there. "Is it crazy that I want to meet Ozzy's family? I mean, I know they believe he's dead. I get why he thinks he's protecting them. It's his nature—look what he's doing for me. But I lost my father when I was young. My mother is missing. I have no siblings. I know this is selfish, but I want to meet the people who made Ozzy the way he is. Because, Bella, he's everything."

Her expression softens. "Yes. I can tell he is."

I slide onto a barstool. "It's cracked. I'm sure I'm fixating on it because I'm worried sick about my mother."

"I suppose so." Bella crosses her arms and contemplates me.

I bite on my thumb nail before adding, "His mother owns a little boutique in the small town where he grew up."

My English friend narrows her eyes. "You don't say?"

I nod. "I looked it up online. It's darling. It has a little bit of everything, you know? Home stuff, clothes, jewelry. The store is close to Lancaster. I bet she gets a lot of tourists who want to see the horse and buggies."

"I'm sure it's as cute as a button."

"And this time of year, the fall foliage…"

"Yes," she deadpans. "It's spectacular right now."

"It's only three hours from here," I note.

"You, my young friend, do not do subtle well."

I lean forward on the island and lower my voice as if I'm worried little Isaac will give away my secrets. "Will you take me? If we leave now, we can pop into her shop for a few minutes. I can buy a couple things and make small talk. We can be back before dinner."

She exhales. "Ozzy will have my head."

"No," I argue. "I'll tell him it was my idea, but that's only if he finds out."

"Oh, he'll find out."

"He's so busy and he thinks I'm here. Bella, I'll be fine with you. You took on the entire British and US governments a few years back. Gracie told me all about it. It's not like I'm asking Maya or Addy. I'm asking you, the female James Bond. You have no qualms waltzing into Morocco to look for my mother. I'm only asking you to drive me three hours north to Pennsylvania."

"Liyah—"

"Please, Bella. I need this right now."

She pulls in a big breath.

I hold mine.

She narrows her eyes. "He'll be so angry."

"I can handle Ozzy." I'm pretty sure that's a lie. I think back to when he threw the keyboard across the room. I'm not sure Ozzy can be handled when he loses his temper. Who am I kidding? We're too new for me to know.

Bella glances at her watch. "I suppose I could ask Maya or Addy to take Isaac. Keelie could pick up Abbott from school."

"Yes! I'm sure they won't mind." My smile breaks my face, but I widen my eyes at the same time. "Just don't tell them. I don't want it to get back to Ozzy."

"I have conditions." Bella holds up her index finger. "You're not to leave my side."

I shake my head. "I'd never."

She adds another finger to the first. "When Ozzy finds out about this—and I have no doubt he will—you'll confess to emotionally hijacking my better judgment."

"Of course. I'll claim full responsibility."

"And lastly." A third joins the first two. "You will do exactly as I teach you on the drive. You have zero chill, Princess Aliyah Zahir. If you so much as begin to give up the fact that their son is not cold as ice and six feet under, I will tackle your petite frame to the ground and drag you out of there myself. Understood?"

"Chill. I can do chill. You can teach me, and I'll do exactly as you say. I swear."

Bella tags her cell sitting on the marble and mutters, "Why do I feel like a teenager sneaking out the window in the middle of the night?"

I can't bite back my smile. I'm too happy.

"Addy." Bella spears me with a stare as she speaks into the phone. "Liyah has been cooped up for days. I thought I'd get her out and see the colors. Do you think Isaac could hang out with Aimée today? He's such a little monster when he misses his nap." She pauses for a moment before smiling. "You're a gem. We'll drop him soon."

I beam. "Thank you, Bella. You won't regret this."

"You know, I have a feeling I'm very much going to regret this. But Ozzy's story has always sat heavy on my heart. I'm more than curious about his family, so this is also selfish. We need to get going if we're going to make it back by dinner. I'm sure we'll hit traffic in the District on the way home."

She's already on her way out of the kitchen, and I call to her, "Where are you going?"

"Millions of people know who you are," she yells. "There's no way I'm chancing that. I'm getting you a wig and a hat."

I smile to myself. I knew I asked the right person. Bella might just be my new best friend.

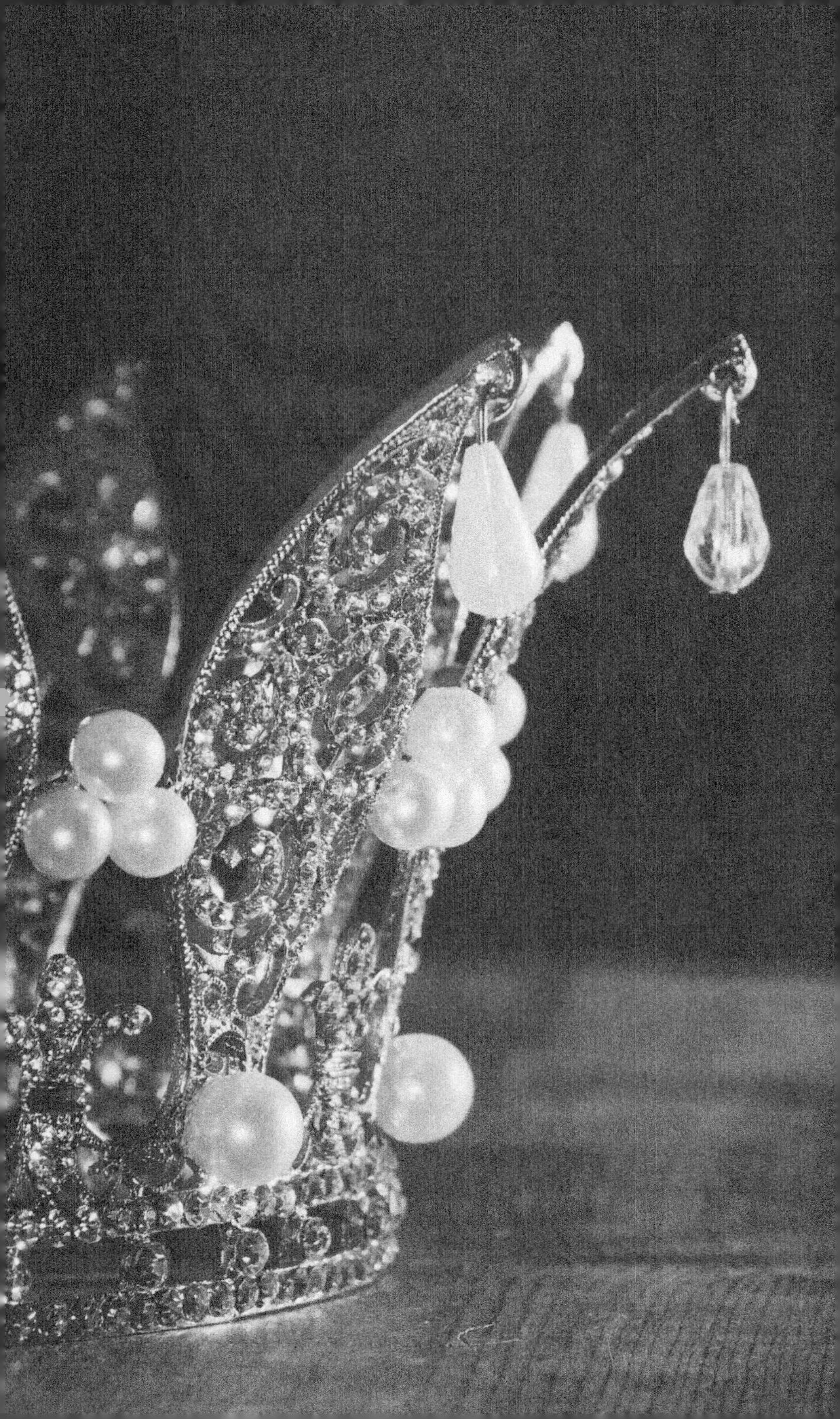

33

WTF

Liyah

Bella throws it in park and turns to me as I adjust the hat over my streaked, dark-blond hair in the mirror. Stuffing a wig over my real hair is no joke—it's taken me thirty minutes to get it right. When I pull on the Yankees ball cap she gave me, I make it a messy low pony with wispies falling around my face. The blond couldn't look more fake against my dark skin, but it does the job. I hardly recognize myself.

Bella warned me over and over on the way here, she's giving me fifteen minutes. That's it.

I knew this would all be for naught if Ozzy's mother wasn't working today. I called the moment the store opened to ask about their hours. I'm not sure why Hollywood makes this covert stuff look so difficult. With Bella at my side and Ozzy's mother announcing her name as soon as she greeted me, it's been a piece of cake.

I've also done my research. Austin and Nettie Graves

prove to be hardworking pillars of their small community. I'm not surprised Nettie answered the phone to her business. From what little Ozzy has told me about his parents, I expected nothing less.

"You understand my directions? You cannot act like you know anything about her. Small talk about her business, the area, that's it. Nothing personal that might tip her off that you're digging for information about her family."

I stuff a finger under the hat to scratch my scalp. "I get it. I promise I'd never do anything to hurt Ozzy. I only want to see his mother."

I look up at the sign that hangs over the door to Charming Nettie. If there were a commercial for small-town America, this street would be its star. Colorful leaves decorate the brick sidewalks. Every storefront lining Main Street is unique. Banners hang from the streetlights showcasing local heroes for Veterans Day. I have a feeling everyone knows everyone, and I'd bet my royal status there's an apple pie within a one-block radius.

"Are you going to be able to do this?" Bella eyes me critically. "If you think you can't handle it, we'll turn around and leave. As curious as I am, it's not worth the risk if you don't think you can carry this out smoothly."

I don't have a chance to answer, because the cell that Ozzy gave me vibrates in my clammy hand.

I don't have a chance to answer Bella, because the snapshot I took of Ozzy when we were alone at the bungalow eating pizza the other night pops up. It's a text from my fiancé.

"Shit."

Ozzy – WTF?

"He knows," I whisper.

"Yes, he does." Bella doesn't whisper and holds up her cell. Crew is calling her. "If we're doing this, we need to do it now. These men might be powerful, but they can't magically teleport to Amish country. Do you still want to go in?"

I look up as three women exit the store laughing, talking, and carrying bags for days. My heart races.

We came all this way. This isn't unlike me taking off across the world thinking I can find my mother on my own, with no clue as to what I'm doing.

Fifteen minutes. I can do fifteen minutes.

Don't be stupid and chicken out, Liyah.

I look at my cell and decide my husband-to-be is more powerful than I gave him credit for. I feel his anger through the silent vibration.

"Now Cole is calling. I do believe we've stirred the hornet's nest," Bella states with zero emotion. She's calm and cool, exactly the opposite of my racing heart.

I'm here. And I have a feeling this will be my only opportunity. Now that Ozzy knows what I'm doing, he'll never allow it again. I just hope he doesn't take his diamond ring back and dump me in the middle of the forest.

My teeth sink into my lip, but I toss the cell, and it lands in Isaac's car seat. If I'm going to do this, I can't have that piece of technology buzzing my ass the whole time. I need to concentrate. I turn to my partner in crime. "Let's go."

Bella smiles. "Well done, Liyah. Let's go shopping. Just don't fuck this up."

I'm pretty sure my expression falls as I reach for my door handle.

Bella's right.

I cannot fuck this up.

Ozzy

"I'm going to kill Bella with my bare hands," I growl. What I don't say aloud is something that has never crossed my mind, but I'm also going to tan the ass of a certain princess—right after I kill Bella. "What the fuck are they thinking?"

I zero in on the satellite of my mom's shop. Bella's BMW crossover is parked, front and center, on Main Street, a place I grew up running up and down with my brothers after we hauled boxes of shit from the back alley into her store.

I don't know what it's like to not work. Her store, our farm, my part-time jobs—my every memory includes working.

Crew sets his cell on the desk and gives up, too, as we watch the two women get out of Bella's car. "Is Liyah wearing a wig?"

I zoom in closer. My Princess looks smaller than normal on screen. Crew's right. Blond hair trails out from under a ball cap. But I know it's her without a doubt. It's the same hoodie and ripped jeans she was wearing when I groped her before I kissed her goodbye.

"At least there's that," Crew mutters and crosses his arms. "Bella won't allow anything to go bad. Still, this shit is ballsy."

Ballsy my ass. This is reckless. I watch the woman I stripped naked this morning, the same one who dropped to her knees in front of me and tasted my cock for the first time after I made her come in the shower. There was no way I was going to come in her mouth the first time she did that, but I did let her jerk me off again. We made such a mess, we had to take another shower.

"Well." Crew pulls in a big breath and shakes his head. "There's nothing we can do from here. This will make tomorrow's team meeting interesting."

I yank a hand through my hair and brace. I need to do something about my fiancée's fucking curiosity. Especially when it strays from my dick.

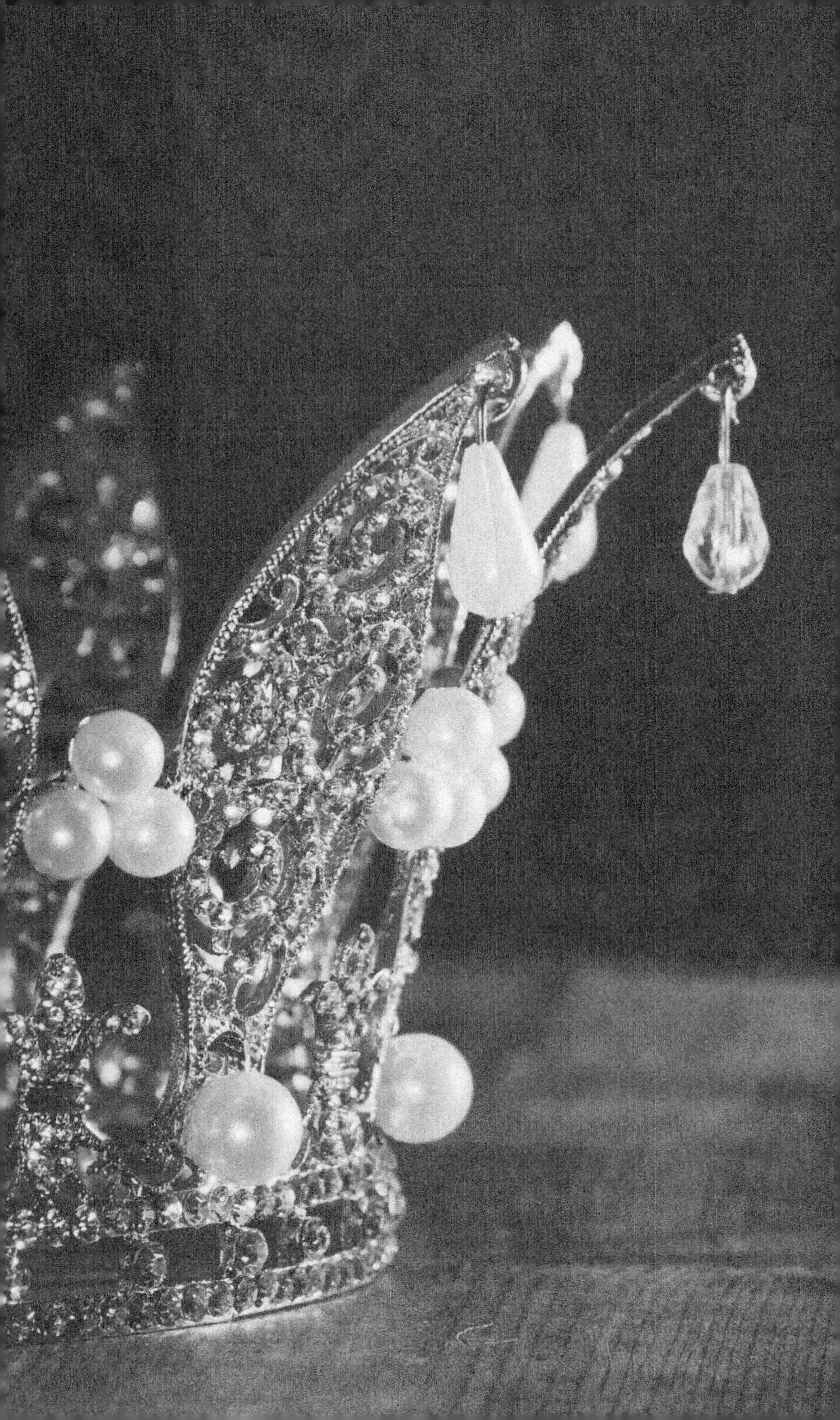

34

CHARMING

Liyah

"Let me know if we can help you find anything."

I smile, but don't get a word in, because Bella answers for both of us. My English friend turns off her accent like a light switch. "Thank you. We saw your shop on our way through town and couldn't help ourselves."

We've been here for ten minutes. The boutique proves to be a popular spot. There has been a steady flow of shoppers in and out during our short time here. Ozzy's mother has been busy behind the counter for the most part, checking people out or clicking away at a computer.

Shopping is my thing. I love it. I can shop anywhere. I'll even poke through racks of trinkets at gas stations. American gas stations are the best.

But not today. I can't focus on a thing at Charming Nettie.

Nettie Graves is beautiful. Mid-fifties with blond

hair that perfectly matches her light complexion. She's taller than me, but most people are, and her style matches that of her store ... sophisticated yet casual. A sweater dress hits her above the knees showing a hint of leg on this cool day. Her tall suede boots boost her a few inches taller than she already is.

I return her smile for the first time, but mine is timid. Her eyes are the same as the ones I've become possessed by since I met her oldest son.

I turn to a table full of bracelets and accessories, while Bella flips through a rack of maxi dresses for fall. She holds one up in front of her. "What do you think? I'm forcing cruel and unusual punishment upon the fam to take holiday pictures next week. This might be just the thing."

I swallow hard as I try for my best American accent, no matter how badly it sucks. "You're so tall, that will be perfect."

Nettie leaves the register and multitasks, refolding sweaters. "That's been a popular one this year. I can't keep it in stock."

I'm not sure how Bella does this. It's hard to focus on anything when all I want to do is stare into the woman's blue eyes to see what's hidden beneath them. I want to hug her pain away. I want to tell her Ozzy did what he had to do. That he did it because he loves her. He loves his family.

And I want to tell her the man she raised is wonderful and perfect, and even though I barreled into his life like a storm, I want to give him everything.

But I can't say any of that.

The faintest bells break me from my trance.

A little boy runs his fingers through chimes that are so gentle and lyrical, it calms my frayed nerves.

"Don't touch those." The boy's mother grabs his hand and pulls him from the display.

Nettie moves to the register and takes the woman's things. "He's fine. He can't hurt those. They're made to be outside."

"Still, he shouldn't play with display items." The woman side-eyes her son.

"I've carried those chimes since I opened and always have one hanging on my porch. Most wind chimes are obnoxious, but not these. They're like a little angel whispering in your ear while you sit in the quiet."

I move to the chimes and do what the boy did. I can't blame him, they're so beautiful and delicate, it's like an invitation to touch them.

"They're gorgeous," I murmur, and listen to the soft bells, wondering what Nettie's front porch is like.

Nettie's smile is small when I look up, but I don't concentrate on her long, because something else catches my attention. Sitting on the counter against the wall is a picture.

"You ready?" My English friend with the perfect American accent materializes at my side with her arms full. When the mother and her son finish paying, Bella drops her goods on the counter.

My allotted time has zipped by, and if we weren't standing right in front of Ozzy's mother, I'd beg Bella for just a few more minutes.

Nettie smiles at Bella, and envy stabs at me. "A great choice. This will be beautiful in family pictures."

I can't help myself. I nod at the spot behind the counter I can't stop staring at. "That's a great picture."

Nettie turns, as if she doesn't know what I'm talking about, even though it's the only one behind her. When she turns back, she doesn't look at me and continues through the motions of scanning tags. "My boys."

I already knew that.

Three little stairsteps—I'd recognize the oldest in my sleep. The picture is in black and white, taken in the country with an old truck as a backdrop. Ozzy and his brothers are barefoot and shirtless, wearing only jeans that hang low on their little frames. They're flexing and laughing. The memory was caught while the youngest was jumping in midair.

"Talk about family pictures. They were so ornery that day." Nettie shakes her head and exhales a sad sigh. "Thought I was going to wring their necks before we were done. Finally, I had enough. I told them if they were going to act like a pack of wild monkeys, to just do it. My oldest ripped his shirt off, and that's all it took. Once I let them be, everyone was happy. It's my favorite picture."

My throat thickens with emotion, and I croak, "You have a beautiful family."

Bella hands over a stack of bills, paying in cash, and turns to me. "You ready?"

"No." I shake my head. It came out too strong, but I'm desperate. I used my precious time to ogle the woman who raised the man I plan to marry and spend the rest of my time with. My eyes flit to the chimes. "I'll take one of those. Perfect for my porch."

Nettie turns to open a cabinet behind her and pulls out a box. "Here, all packaged for your trip. Where are you two from?"

"California." Bella answers before I can, probably to

shut me up. "We're in the Capitol for work and had a free day, so we thought we'd see New England in the fall."

My fingers tremble as I pull out enough bills to pay in cash. "You have a great store. I'd love to come back when we have more time."

Nettie gives me one last smile—one I'm sure she gives anyone who enters her store on any random day, and not someone who knows secrets that could change her life. "Please do. Enjoy your day, and safe travels."

I take the bag and feel a yank on my hoodie. I look one last time at the picture of Ozzy and his brothers, and think about how lucky he was to have such a wonderful mother who allowed her children to thrive in who they were, instead of stuffing them into a mold they didn't fit in.

Not too different from the gift my mother gave me when she sent me away, so I wasn't raised under the strict scrutiny of my uncle, and the dynasty he perpetuated.

"Get in, Liyah." We're back outside and at Bella's car before I know it. Her words are firm yet gentle as she pushes me toward the passenger door. I flip out my sunnies and push them up my nose because my eyes sting.

As Bella looks for traffic, she tags my phone and hands it to me, and we slowly drive through town square.

"Are you okay?"

My phone blew up during the fifteen minutes I was allowed to ogle Nettie Graves. Phone calls and texts coming in from my new friends who are only friends through association. But most importantly, I have a slew of messages from my fiancé.

"Liyah, are you okay?" Bella presses. She's driven through the only two stop lights in town, so I reach up and rip the hat and wig off my head.

I swipe away a tear. "I'm being ridiculous. I don't know why I'm so emotional."

"It's okay." She reaches over and gives my knee a squeeze. "You did very well for your first undercover op. I'm very proud of you."

I read through my messages. "Ozzy is angry."

"We knew he would be. I'm honestly surprised it took him as long as it did to stalk you. Though, I'm sure he had no reason to believe we'd take a trip to Pennsylvania today."

I'm about to text Ozzy back when Bella's phone rings over the Bluetooth. My fiancé's name pops up on the screen. My gaze slides to Bella, who's side-eyeing me in return. She presses a button on the steering wheel and hits the gas as we enter the highway. "Hello?"

"Hello?" My breath catches when his low, tense voice rumbles through the car. "That's all you have to say to me?"

"Would you like to speak to your bride-to-be?"

My hand reaches out, and I grip her bicep.

Bella smiles.

She bloody smiles.

"I'll talk to Liyah when we're alone." My eyes fall shut. "I don't know what you think you're doing, Bella, but if you have any other field trips on the agenda today, consider them canceled. You'd better not make another stop. Get her the fuck back to me. Do you understand?"

"For your information," Bella starts, not at all flustered by Ozzy like my insides are at the moment. "I have dinner in the crockpot that I need to tend to. I don't have time for any other sightseeing today. I'll deliver Liyah in no time."

It's all I can do not to groan.

"Straight home, Bella."

"How about you two come over for a bowl of chili?" If I didn't know better, I'd think Bella was demented and not at all worried about the catastrophe I orchestrated today.

"Dammit, Bella. I don't want anything besides Liyah. I'm watching your every fucking move. Don't make me come and get her."

The line goes dead.

Shit.

"Well, then." Bella reaches forward to flip on the music. "We'll have you two over for dinner another night."

I lean back, close my eyes, and clutch the wind chimes in a death grip. A little bit of the confidence I had when I pitched this idea this morning would be nice right now.

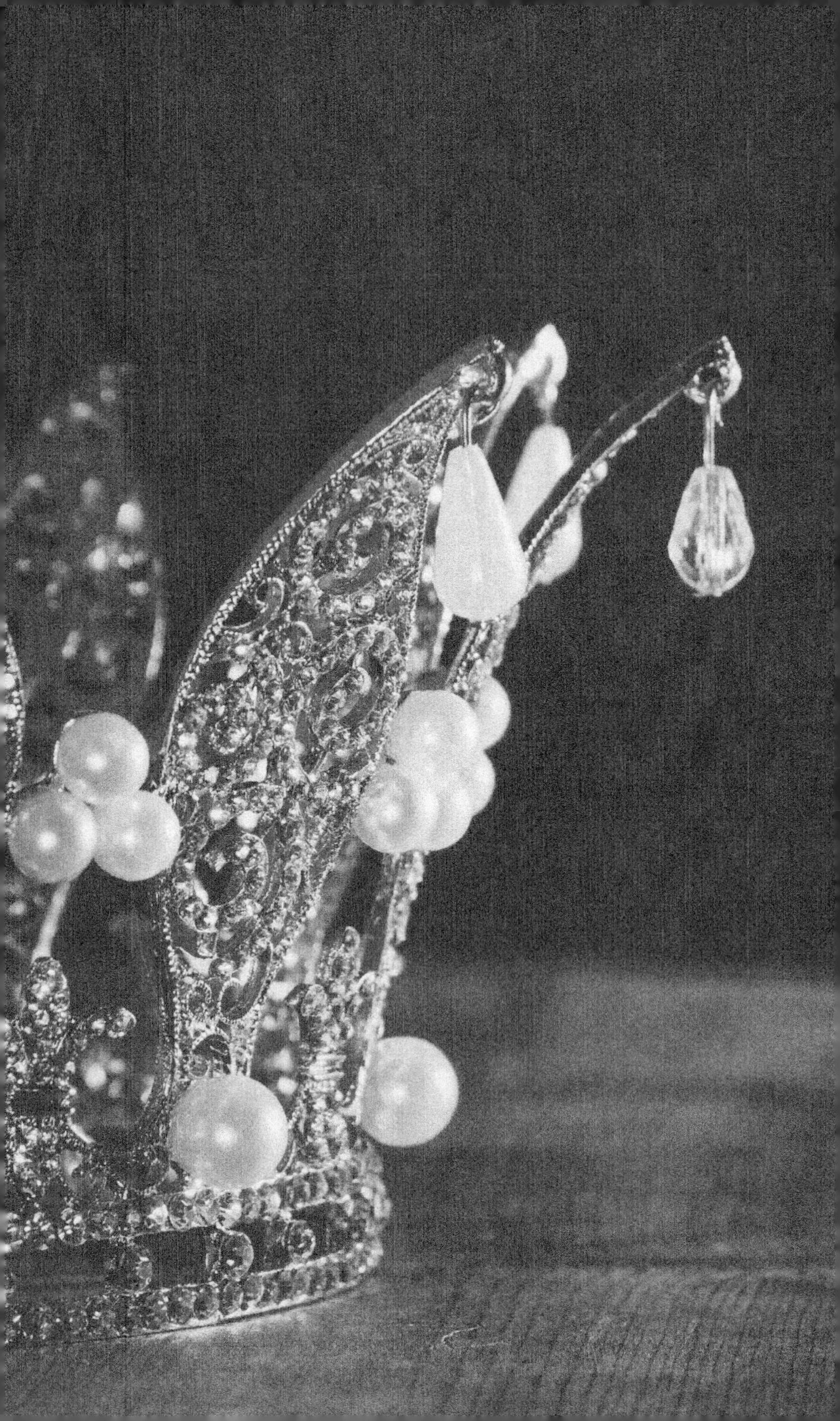

35

MIGHT

Liyah

Gravel crunches under the tires, and my chest tightens.

Bella puts her SUV in park next to Ozzy's truck and turns to me. "You had your reasons for wanting to go. Explain it to him. He'll be fine. And if he's not, he will be in time."

My gaze turns to the bungalow. A dim light burns through the window, and I curse my damn inquisitiveness and impulsive behavior. The same behavior that landed me right here.

The sun has almost set, bringing another day with Ozzy Graves to a close. So much has happened, I could almost forget what life was like before that dreaded voicemail from my mother. How my shallow and happy-go-lucky life in Malibu seemed so perfect.

I had no idea what perfect was.

Bella grabs my hand and my attention. Her blue eyes are sage and serious, even a bit motherly, when she tips her head to the bungalow. "He'll be fine. Whatever reasons you had for wanting to go today didn't come from malice. They came from your heart. Make him see that. I would never have taken you if I thought it would bring harm to anyone."

I nod and start to reach for the door, but she stops me.

When I look back, there's a satisfied smile on her face. "I like your spirit. Don't ever let anyone crush it."

I huff a breath. Easy for her to say. I'm not a ninja or secret agent. I have a useless college degree, I was born with an even more useless title, and beyond posing in front of a camera and understanding social media algorithms, I have zero life skills.

"Thank you for today. I might need you to come and get me if he kicks me out."

She rolls her eyes. "That man is not going to kick you out. If I know anything, it's that."

I'm not so sure. "Keep your phone close, just in case."

Her smile swells. "Go on. Be brave. I know you are."

I pull in a breath and climb out of the car. I barely shut the door, and she rolls off into the forest.

I walk through her dust, up the steps, and don't stop until I turn the knob.

It's unlocked.

When I push the door open, all I see is him.

Facing me, he's slouched low in a club chair with his legs splayed wide. He doesn't blink when I step over the threshold to my demise, his stare cutting through the thick, stale air of the small home. I shut out the hum of the forest and the door clicks at my back. It's so quiet, I hear my blood churning.

I don't move any farther inside, but drop my cross-body and souvenir to the sofa.

My fiancé is stock-still aside from the slow, methodical way he's swirling the amber liquid in a highball. My eyes flit to the small coffee table where a lid sits next to an open bottle.

Now doesn't seem like the time to ask for a shot of my own, even though I don't drink hard liquor cut with anything, let alone straight.

Well, now might be a good time to start.

I pull in a breath and hold my head high at the same time I cross my arms over my chest. Two very conflicting actions. "How was your day?"

His eyes narrow.

Shit.

My arms tighten, and I decide to go for it. Or fill the air, because silence drives me mad.

"I'm sorry," I start on an exhale. "Wait, no. You know what? I'm not sorry. But I am sorry you're upset. That was not my intention."

"Your intention." His voice is rough, and I wonder how long he's been sitting here counting the reasons he should've kicked me out of his cabin on that deadly, fated train. "Let's talk about that, Princess. What the fuck was your intention?"

My body temperature spikes because he's never talked to me like this. Desperation simmers inside me, and my words come out in a rush. "I would never do anything to hurt you. Never. Or your family."

He pulls in a breath and looks like he's doing everything he can not to yell or scream or tear down the bungalow. "I explained this to you. Have you forgotten the very literal heat from the fire that killed innocent people right before your eyes? Did you forget it was meant for me?"

My face falls farther, and my voice comes out on a breath, because I'll never forget that moment. I thought that blast was for me—that those people died because of me. "Of course not."

He finally moves, but it's slow and methodical. Throwing back the last of his whiskey, his glass lands next to the bottle with a thud. I feel smaller. Or he feels bigger. Either way, my back hits the door as I retreat.

"Ozzy—"

"Why did you do it?"

He rounds the coffee table and is almost on top of me when I put my hand up. "Because."

He stops. "Because? That's all you've got?"

"Because." I shake my head and swallow my nerves. "Because I feel helpless and powerless. I'm desperate. And desperation makes me do things I shouldn't do, okay?"

His face is set like stone. I'm tortured by his silence.

My arms fall to my sides, and my rambles continue to pollute the space between us. "My mother is still missing. I'm not an idiot, Ozzy. Every day that passes, I know the chances of hearing her voice again are more slim than the day before. I'm here with you, with people who are kind, but they're really nothing but strangers to me. And then there's this." I throw my left hand between us that's heavy with a commitment that scares me and excites me equally. "There's us—there's *you*."

He bites back immediately. "What about me?'"

I pull in a breath and hold it.

He cuts the space between us in half, and I swear I feel his heat.

His words are so cutting, they have teeth to them. Angry, sharp, biting. "What about me, Liyah?"

We prove to be exactly as we have been since the beginning, exact opposites. My feelings are frenzied and rush out of me in a messy flood as he stands there in total control. "I'm desperate for ... something. A piece of you. More of you. I wanted to know how you are the way you are. I wanted to see where you came from, because..."

"Because why? Why would you do the exact thing I told you could not happen? What the hell could be so important that you'd risk that?"

My heart pounds in my chest, and I throw the words at him because I have no other answer. "Because I think I love you. Okay?"

I didn't mean to yell it, but I did. It's been bubbling inside me for days. I didn't recognize it at first, because nothing about Ozzy and me makes sense.

His expression doesn't change a bit, and he says nothing as he processes my words.

But I don't regret them. It feels oddly like a relief to put them out there.

"Nothing has happened in the right order. I've followed you around the world when you were nothing but a stranger. You slide an enormous ring on my finger for no reason other than to take a picture. I gave you *me*, because nothing feels more right than being yours." I hold my hand up between us one more time. "And then you tell me this is real without discussing it. But the crazy thing is, I want it to be real more than anything. And this," I thrust his ring closer to him, "is fueling my desperation. So I'm not sorry about today. Your mother is beautiful and kind. I'm sure she'll never give me a second thought, but I'll never forget her. Now I have another piece of you. I'm sorry you're angry, but I'm not sorry I did it. Are you happy?"

His biceps flex when he fists his hands. "You think you love me."

Not a question.

A statement.

"Yes," I confirm, holding my shaky ground as best I can against the force that is him. "I mean, I might."

My precarious profession of love dangles between us as I cling to the bravery Bella told me I'd need. Bravery isn't something I've needed in life until recently. No one needs to be brave when you're sporting couture with a royal fortune in the bank to support your shallow habits.

"You *might* love me," he growls.

My arms fall to my sides. "Stop repeating me."

Ozzy's chest rises and falls. I'm not sure if he's going to kick me out or ravish me.

If it's the former, I don't know what I'll do.

"Liyah." He shakes his head once. It looks like he's making a decision.

Lucky for me, he chooses the latter.

My face is in his hands.

His lips land on mine.

Every ounce of anger that was raging through his body zips through me. Our teeth scrape. When he slides a hand into my hair, my roots sting under his grip.

He pulls away from me just long enough to lift me under the arms, and my legs round his waist. "You made me fucking crazy today, Princess. No one has control over me like that. No one."

I wrap my arms around his neck. "I don't know what

you want me to say, but I'm not sorry I went. I did it because of you. I'd probably do it again if I had the chance."

His grip on my ass tightens as we move to the bedroom. "I know you would, which means I have a feeling I'm fucked."

I yelp when I bounce once as my back hits the bed. Ozzy rips his shirt over his head, every muscle tense and agitated. He reaches for my jeans and yanks at the button. "Ozzy—"

He shakes his head and rips them down my legs, grabbing my sneakers on the way. I'm left in my panties and hoodie when he unbuttons his pants. My eyes drift to his cock when it springs free, and he's standing over me, wired, agitated, and beautiful. "Clothes off."

"I don't know if I want to do this while you're angry." I frown. We've done a lot, but we've only actually had sex once—the only time I've *ever* had sex. "This doesn't seem like a good idea."

He reaches down and yanks off his boots. "I'm angry, Liyah. I'm fucking angry at the world and have been for years." He leans in and puts his hands on the bed on either side of my head, caging me in. "You haven't been out of my sight or off one of our properties since I sent you for food in Spain and had no fucking idea who you were. When you're on one of our properties, I've got eyes on you all the time. Every fucking minute I can check on you."

That's creepy. I put a hand to his chest and push, but he doesn't budge. "I was with Bella."

His blue eyes ice over, and he growls, "You could be with the entire damned Joint Armed Forces for all I care. My point is, you left the safety of this organization and you weren't with me."

I keep a firm hand on his bare skin. "See? You're angry."

He shakes his head. "No, baby. I'm crazy. I'm fucking crazy for you. You're making me feel things. Do shit I don't ever do. And I don't know how to deal with it right now. But what's making me the most crazy is that you only *might* love me. And that's a surprise, even to me. Not that you might love me, but that it's making me crazy that it's only *might*."

I freeze, but he doesn't. My hoodie and bra are no more, and his hands land on my hips, ripping my panties down my legs.

He moves over me at the same time his fingers find my sex. I shouldn't be surprised I'm already wet. I think my body has been in tune with his since we met. "Not sure what you dreamed of when you thought about the rest of your life, but I'm sure it wasn't explosions, running from your king, or wearing the ring of a dead man. In my wildest dreams—those dreams I never allowed myself to contemplate—I sure as hell didn't think I could have anyone like you."

He spears me with two fingers at the same time his thumb circles my clit, and this time he isn't gentle the way he's been so far. He's demanding and hungry, desperation rolling off him in waves.

I recognize it. It's what I feel more and more every day that I'm with him.

"Yes." I pull his face to mine and spread my legs.

I lose his hand when he gives me his weight, but I gain something else.

His cock.

Bare.

I'm filled with his bare cock for the first time.

His kiss is bruising as he moves in and out of me. I feel him everywhere, inside and out, and this time it isn't new or foreign. My body stretches exactly to his length. I've never wanted him more.

Our connection is as deep as it can be when he stops and reaches between us. His thumb finds my clit and circles. "Want to feel you come when I'm inside you—want you to feel that too. When you come around my cock, I want you to remember whose ring you're wearing. Who'll go to the ends of the earth for you. Who'll protect you from any-fucking-thing. Who is that, Liyah?"

Between his thumb and his words, my heart races. "You. Only you."

"Damn right, it's only me." His thumb moves faster and he thrusts into me once to enunciate his words. "From now on, you will not go rogue on me. Do you understand?"

I nod. My breathing shallows, and I can't form words.

"Answer me," he demands.

My fingers dig into his wide shoulders. It's breathy, but I manage one word. "Yes."

His control is the complete opposite of my vulnerability. I'll do anything he wants, anything he asks. But who am I kidding? I've done that since the moment he jammed a gun in my side.

Other than today. Today doesn't count. And I'll never be sorry for that.

"And we're going to drop *might* from your vocabulary." I drag my eyes open at his words, but it's hard. I'm so close. His words and angry tone continue to hit me like a ton of bricks. "This *might love me* shit will be no more. I'll do everything I can to make you love me, Princess."

I huff an exhale.

"Find it baby. Come on my cock and show me you're mine. Because I don't want anything but you, no matter if I'm dead or alive. Forever won't be enough time."

His words. I can't. They're too much and everything all at the same time. And they're burned on my brain when I pinch my eyes shut and press my head into the mattress.

Ozzy was right. Coming with him inside me is ...

Everything.

I moan, call out for him, and fight for a breath.

"Fuck, your pussy's milking my dick," he growls and doesn't let up on my clit. "Just when I didn't think I could be obsessed with you more. You give me this."

I lose his hand, but my sensitive clit gets a new experience. Ozzy starts to move. Really move. And I realize he was holding back my first time. He leans in to take my mouth—taking me in every way he can.

I'll give him everything he wants and more. It's my new goal in life.

He drags his lips away from mine, and his heated blue eyes sear me as he slams into me. "Need a condom, baby. This is no time to be careless."

I nod, but pull my knees farther up his sides. "This feels ... so good."

"Taking you bare..." He shakes his head once. "Never had that. You're so fucking perfect."

He's right, this is no time to tempt the gods. But,

there's never been anything more perfect than this. "Pull out. Just don't stop."

His eyes fall shut and he moves. Faster, harder. Taking me with all his power and strength. I never imagined it could be like this.

He groans into my messy hair and tenses. I've only experienced it once but I recognize it. Just when I think he's not going to pull out, he does. Just in time.

His cock, hard and wet, presses into my lower tummy. Ozzy comes hard—harder than I've seen him so far—all over me, marking me as his in a whole new way. Giving me something new.

But everything with Ozzy is new, and nothing could make me happier. He was right. Forever won't be enough time.

He's spent, giving me his weight, making another delicious mess between us. I hope that means a shared shower is in my future.

His breaths are heavy on my forehead where he holds me tight to him. "Did I hurt you?"

My fingers dance up his back. "No. That was amazing."

He tips his face to mine. "You make me crazy in every way, you know that?"

I smile.

He kisses me. This time it's softer, but no less possessive. "Let me know when I've convinced you to drop the *might*, Princess."

I bite my lip, and my only answer is a silent nod. I'm afraid if I speak now, I'll say all kinds of things that it's too soon for. Things that don't make sense, that are warring between my heart and my sense of responsibility.

He leans in and kisses me one more time. "I've worked hard all my life, but I'll stop at nothing until you love me completely."

I say nothing and press my face to his neck.

He forces me to look at him and kisses me one more time. "Let's shower, and then I'll feed you."

A smile creeps over my face. A shower with Ozzy. "Please."

"Baby, you saying please is going to make me hard again."

"Then it's a good thing we're taking a shower."

He kisses me one more time before pulling me from the bed in a naked, sticky mess. The thought of him making me messy for the rest of my life warms me in a whole new way.

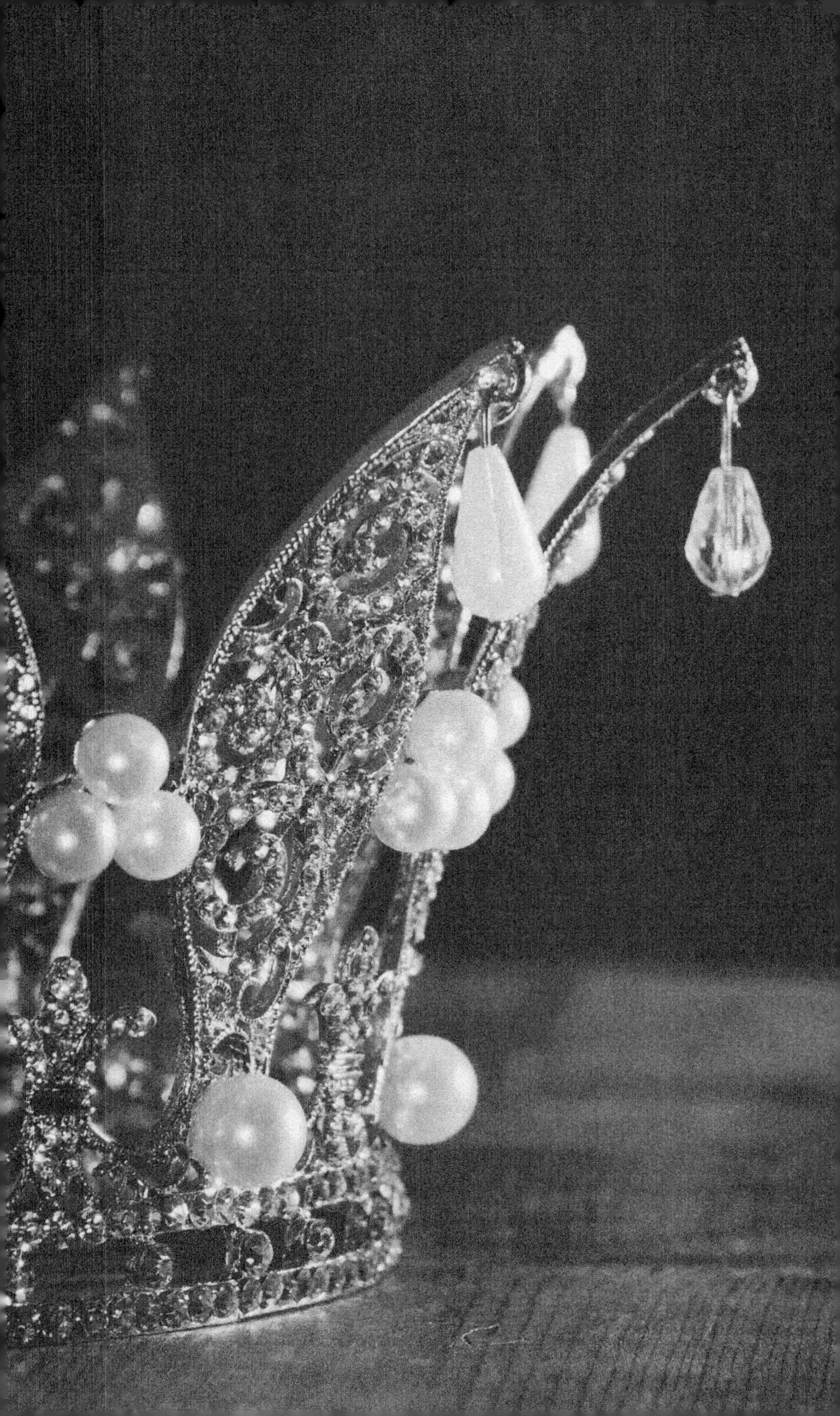

36
GRAVITY, MAGNETISM, OR JUST BASIC FIXATION

Ozzy

"I just got off the phone with my source," Bella says. "The priest knows nothing. At least he says he knows nothing. Maybe it's because he's older than dirt and there's a language barrier, but my source isn't convinced. Then again, I doubt many people come looking for the Princess of Morocco who don't mean her harm."

I move out of the bedroom. Liyah's dead to the world. After we ate dinner and I made her promise me in about ten million different ways that she'd never do what she did today ever again, we went to bed. Looking back on my day from hell, I realize there wasn't any real risk to my parents, but I was fucking angry that my fiancée was out from under my protection.

That's a new emotion for me.

When all this is said and done, I'm going to need to get a handle on that.

"It's been too long since she was seen at the border,

Bella. I'm not feeling good about it. Throw in the shaky relations between Morocco and Algeria, Luciana's future is looking bleaker with every day that passes."

"Agreed. I'm running out of options on my end. I don't want to quit for Liyah's sake, but without a warm lead, I can't do much."

"Speaking of Liyah." I unlock the door to step outside so I don't wake the literal sleeping Princess. But the moment I open the door, I freeze. All I can do is stand in the doorway and stare.

And listen.

The world melts away.

"I hope you went easy on her. For such a young woman and all she's going through, I think she's incredibly strong and handling everything as best she can."

I step onto the porch, but leave the door open behind me.

Bella keeps talking. "She cares for you deeply. I could see it today. Don't break her spirit, Ozzy."

I grip the cell in my hand and ignore everything Bella's saying, because I know she's right. I know all that about Liyah and more. "For anyone to infer that I'd break anything in Liyah pisses me off. I don't want her any other way than she is right now. But if you so much as take her anywhere again without my knowledge, we're going to have more problems than we do right now. I don't give a shit that you can lay waste to ninety percent of the population. Don't think about doing what you did today again."

She sounds as chipper as the fucking Queen, and that pisses me off more. "Ninety-nine percent, but I'll let that slide and heed your warning. I'll also add, watching the two of you fall in love is a beautiful thing to witness.

I wish you could have seen her today. She was determined and nervous and brave. For what it's worth, I'm honored to be a part of it."

"Don't fucking do it again. And call me if you hear anything."

I don't wait for her to wax on about the state of my life or the woman I want to get back to. I hang up and focus on the faint bells that take me back to my childhood.

I don't know when Liyah did it, or more importantly, how she knew to do it. But chimes dance in the breeze.

Soft.

Faint.

Like a whisper from my past, singing to my soul.

I don't remember a time these exact chimes weren't hanging on the porch of my childhood home. When something is that much of a constant, they tend to blend into the background of life as if they were never there.

Until they're gone.

And then reappear, after the woman wearing my ring goes undercover because of some crazy notion that seeing my mom in the flesh will give her a piece of me.

I have no clue how Liyah knew about the chimes. I didn't ask her about her undercover op in Pennsylvania. I was wound so tight, I didn't want to know anything.

I turn, lock the door behind me, and am dropping my shorts to climb back in bed in no time. Call it gravity, magnetism, or just basic fixation on the woman who makes me crazy, no matter what she does.

I fit my front to her bare back on my side of the bed that's become ours. The Princess does not understand personal space. Not that I'd change that. Not now and not ever.

She fidgets in her sleep as I settle and press my lips to the crown of her head. She sighs, makes a little noise, and when I know she's asleep, I whisper into her hair, "No might about it. Love you, Princess."

Her breathing is deep and even.

With all the shit swirling around us, I've never felt so right.

Liyah

"Let's do black tie," Addy suggests. "We never get the excuse to dress up."

"Are you forgetting your own harvest event?" Maya asks. "If I tell Grady he has to wear a suit two Saturdays in a row, he'll explode."

"But he'll do it," Gracie argues. "You know he will."

"I vote for formal." Everyone looks at Bella. "What? I wasn't here for The Harvest and missed out. Cole is dashing in a tux."

"It can't be casual. If we do casual it won't be special." Keelie's gaze shifts to me. "Cocktail? I think you have a few dresses to pick from my shopping trip. Or if I have to hit the mall again, you won't hear me complain."

"I like cocktail." Gracie beams. "If the men complain, we'll remind them they don't have to wear a tie."

"This isn't necessary." I look around at my new group of friends who are planning my engagement party. If you asked me yesterday how comfortable I was with the notion of celebrating anything, the answer would have been not at all. But with Ozzy's declaration of making it his main goal to wipe the word *might* from my vocabulary, I feel better about it. "I don't want the men to have to do anything they don't want to do."

"Our husbands like to complain, but if you think we're a tight bunch, it's nothing compared to them. They consider themselves badasses who have each other's backs, but they're really nothing more than a bunch of grown-ass-men BFFs." Addy waves me off with a smirk. "But we don't point that out to them."

The longer I'm here and thrust into the mix with these women, the less I feel like an imposter. From the outside, their friendship looks much different than the ones I had in college. Deeper, meaningful, and definitely deliberate.

"Ozzy has so much to worry about right now. I'm sure he doesn't have the time to deal with the distraction of a party."

"About that." All eyes turn to Bella. "I have an update on Demaree and Cannon. Cole called when I was on my way here. Things have taken a turn."

My eyes widen. "Something bad? What happened?"

She shakes her head. "No. For once, the universe is handing your future husband a gift wrapped in glitter. Cole has traced the funds from Kruglov to an offshore account that takes regular draws. Those draws are proving to be hard to follow—Demaree and Cannon are no slouches in the tech department."

"Tell your husband to get a move on," Gracie jibes with a smile.

"Right?" Bella agrees. "I'll relay the message. But what's more interesting, is the little delectable carrot Ozzy dangled on the dark web. It's been nibbled on by those same tech geniuses." Bella levels her blue eyes on me. "It's only a matter of time, love. Everything is coming together. And as long as you stay far, far away from the evil King, there's no need to worry. Plus, you're taken. Soon, you'll be officially off the market."

I pull in a big breath and try my best to be grateful and happy about all the good news, but I can't. "If my mother would come knocking at the door, life would be perfect."

Addy's hand finds mine. "I know. Stay positive, Liyah. That's all you can do right now."

"I know. And I'm trying. It's just getting harder and harder as the days go by." I look at the women around me. "I can't thank you enough. For everything—the distractions, the friendship." I look to Bella and smile. "The road trips. I'd go mad if I didn't have you."

"It will all work out. I know it will," Maya says. "It always does."

"I wish I were as optimistic." I sigh. "Do you ever feel the need to brace? Like you know something dark is on the horizon? I can't shake it. There is so much stacked against us…"

I let that thought trail off.

What's scarier is my support system doesn't argue. They exchange kind and sympathetic gazes with one another.

Well. It seems I'm not the only one who doesn't see rainbows and unicorns in my future. I guess reality is as bad as it seems.

"Let's get back to party planning," Addy quips. "Dinner needs to be a mix of both of you. What's your favorite food, Liyah? Do we do something Moroccan?"

I shake my head and tell them the truth. "Oh no. I'll take sushi or pizza any day. I'm seriously easy."

"Done. Sushi and pizza and apple pie for dessert. It's Ozzy's favorite at the holidays. I know if I ask him what he wants, he'll say he doesn't care," Addy says. "Tomorrow night in the Ordinary, ladies. I can't wait."

Tomorrow.

I'm with Gracie—these men need to hurry up. I'm anxious to know what normal will look like on Ozzy Graves.

I guess time flies when you're in hiding. I don't know how Ozzy's done this for years. There's nothing I want more than to shout to the world that I'm his.

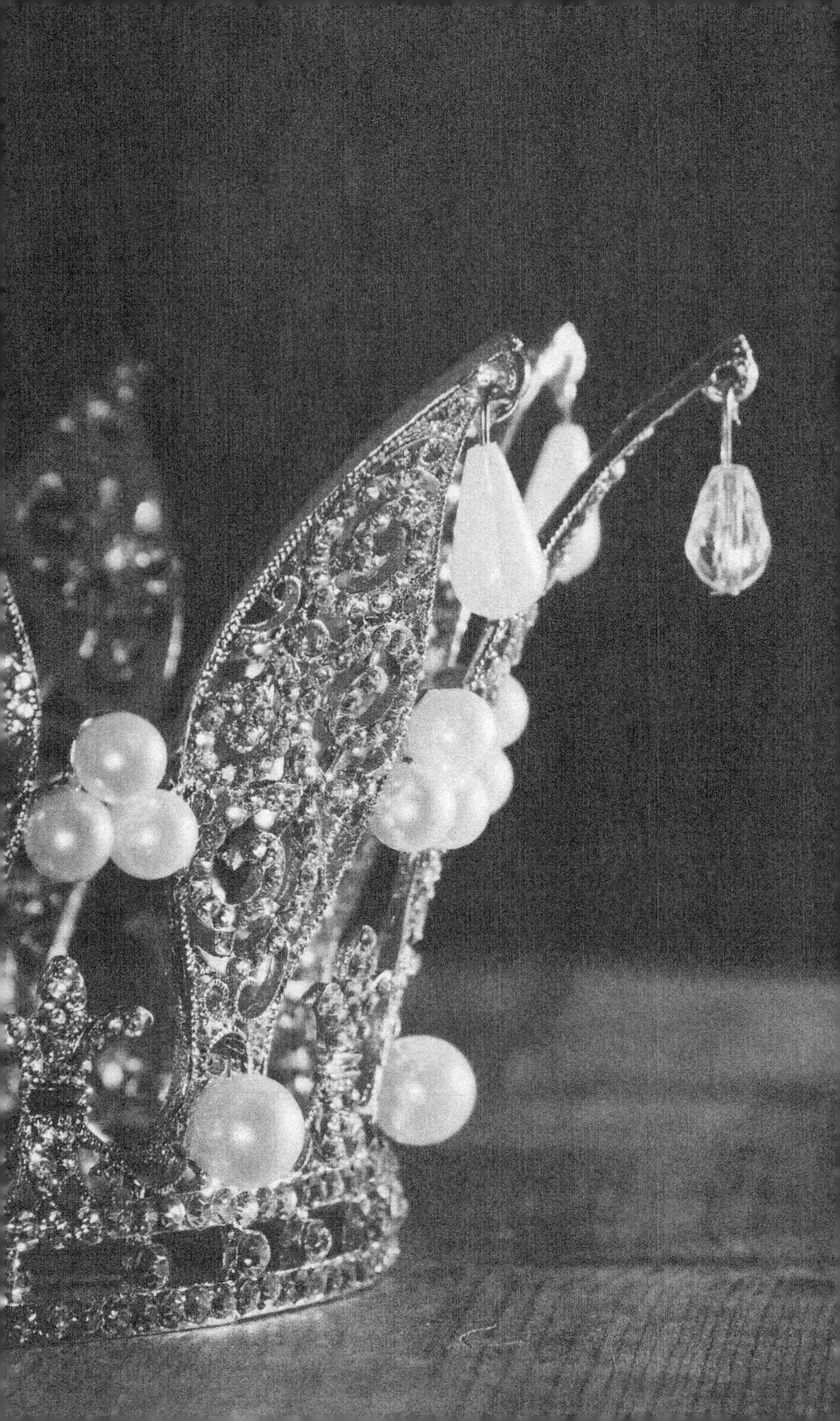

37

FINALE

Ozzy

Another day in my life.

Another day with no news of Liyah's mom.

Another day without anything worthwhile from the King.

There was one positive today. The traitorous assholes at the NSA got back to the fictitious me on the dark web. They even entered my private chat room to finalize our deal.

They'll have my information by the middle of next week. Carson is working it from his end. When they give me directions on where to send the money, we'll make our move.

Time hasn't been an issue for years since I had nothing to do but work. But recently, my days have meaning. I'm counting them down until Demaree and Cannon get me the goods on the old man who thought he could buy a princess.

My Princess.

Speaking of my Princess ... another Saturday, another dress.

This one couldn't be more different than the one from last week. It's only holding on by one strap on her right shoulder, which means I can see the swell of her left tit. It's longer and hits her below the knees, but I can see the skin of one thigh where it's slit up her leg. And that slit is required for her to move, because the damn thing is so tight, I'm worried about how she'll breathe.

Skin fucking tight.

And as red as the smoldering fire that burns in my gut for her.

I slide my hand down her hip and around to cup her ass. I love the way it fits in my hand. "You know, I've dressed up once in a matter of years before I met you. Is this going to be a weekly thing?"

She tips her face to me and smiles. Her hair is barely pulled up. It's intricate, but still falling in loose strands down her back and around her face. "You can't blame this on me. They're your friends."

I shake my head. "I think the people orchestrating this are very much in your court, Princess. They don't give a shit what I want but will bend over backward to make you happy."

She lifts her bare shoulder. "I don't know what to say. I like them."

"Pretty sure they're big fans of yours. Just like I am."

She slides a hand down my chest and over the T-shirt she insisted I wear under my sport coat. I did not argue.

"They're very sweet to do this for us."

I squeeze her ass. "They also use any excuse to get together."

"I think it's wonderful. They love you."

There's that word again.

The one I haven't spoken while she was coherent enough to hear it and the one she hasn't uttered again, with or without the word *might* in front of it.

I pull her up to meet me and take her mouth. I don't give two shits about her makeup. She could go to this party in her cutoffs and NASA shirt for all I care. She'd be no less beautiful.

Tipping my forehead to hers, I look into her dark eyes as they open for me. "We're close, baby. I feel it. Finales are on the horizon. A place where we can put shit behind us and make plans. Real plans. Hopefully out in the open for the world to see."

She pushes up on her toes and presses her lips to mine. "I hope so, Ozzy. There's nothing I want more."

I pull her into my chest and press my lips to the top of her head. "Let's go to our party so we can get back, and I can peel this tight-ass dress off you."

I feel her smile against my chest where my heart beats only for her.

"Why do you get to wear a T-shirt?"

I glance down at myself before putting my beer to my lips and shrug. I'm not about to admit it's because Liyah told me to. I don't need that kind of shit from the men.

"He's engaged to a model, a royal, and a sorority girl born in a different decade," Carson points out. "Our boy here has just leveled up big time. Pretty sure he can wear whatever the fuck he wants."

I slide my hand into my pocket, and glare at the CIA officer. "She's not in a sorority."

"She was last semester," the fucker points out, which I can't argue because it's the truth. "I'm just pointing out that your fiancée is a decade your junior, and if you don't know this by now, your wife-to-be over there will dress you for the rest of your days. You'll basically never have a say in anything ever again."

"He's right," Jarvis mutters. "Look at us? I can't remember the last time I had to wear a dress shirt twice in a year, let alone in one week."

"Bella's job is easy." Per usual, Carson won't stop talking. "I look good in anything."

"I remember the day Jarvis approached me about a friend who was in the worst bind he'd ever seen." Unlike Carson, when Crew speaks no one rolls their eyes. He doesn't waste words when he puts them into the world. He lifts his hand that's wrapped around the neck of a beer bottle and points it at me. "You were a risk, Oz. One I've never regretted and one I'm damn glad I took. Hate to say it, since you're only here because your life turned to shit, but we're lucky to have you. And all this," he motions around the Ordinary that's exploded into one big-ass party with flowers, balloons, and more food and drinks than our small group could think about finishing, "is just the beginning to you getting your life back. Happy for you."

"And just like that," Asa pipes in and looks at the leader of the group. "Crew's fucked-up family gets even bigger. Congrats."

Crew smirks.

"Maya reminded me your birthday is this week. If they try to pull this shit again for an excuse to throw a party, I refuse to wear another suit. I'll put my foot down," Grady complains.

I'd complain with the rest of them, but I can't as I take in my bride-to-be from across the small space. She's sipping a martini through a smile as Maya goes on and on about something that Liyah finds amusing. When Addy joins in, my fiancée puts a hand to her chest and laughs.

She laughs.

I'm not sure I've seen her laugh.

Damn.

It's a sight to see.

"I'm starving. I've had about all the cheese and veggies I can stand. I need real food. When are we going to eat?" Grady asks.

"Chill, man," Asa says. "There's an unwritten schedule for the evening."

"Fuck." I turn back and find Carson staring at his phone. His expression isn't cocky the way it normally is. It's concerned, grave, and not fucking good at all. He doesn't look away from the screen when he mutters, "Oz—"

That's when my cell vibrates in my pocket. I set my beer down and move to the side of the room.

Crew calls for me, but I don't answer. Hissed curse words and mutters bleed from the men behind me.

But I can't look away from my cell.

I read the article.

Then I read it again.

All of a sudden, I'm sick to my stomach, and my heart pounds heavy in my chest.

I turn and look across the centuries-old room.

Crew comes to my side. "What are you going to do?"

"Give me a minute." I hold my hand up to stop him and don't look away from Liyah. She's still laughing. Animated. Being herself—her real self. "Give her a minute. I just..."

Liyah's back is to us, and it's Addy who catches my eye first. Her face falls, and she turns her gaze to Crew and frowns.

"I've got to get her out of here."

I start to move and notice Bella. By the look etched on her face, she got the same news.

Fuck.

I put my hand to Liyah's hip and lean in to whisper, "Baby, we need to go."

She turns to me. For a split second her eyes are lit with joy, and a smile so natural takes over her face, my heart practically seizes.

I'm about to burst that bubble. And I have no fucking idea if I'll ever get her back to the way she is right now.

Her brows pinch, and she loses that happy buzz in an instant. "Are you okay?"

Just like that, I lost her.

I lower my voice. "Baby, we need to go."

She's confused. "Why? We haven't had dinner. I could eat my weight in sushi, I'm so hungry."

I sense the men at my back. The hum of laughter and chitchat come to a roaring halt. All attention is on us.

"Crew?" Addy moves to her husband.

He says nothing and pulls her to his side.

"Ozzy," Liyah clips. Perplexed, irritated, and firm. "What's going on?"

Bella brings a hand to her mouth and turns away from us.

Liyah looks back to me and widens her eyes. "Ozzy?"

"Let me take you back to the bungalow—"

"Stop it," she snaps, and looks around at our group before focusing her angry expression on me. Even so, her breaths come quickly. "Something has happened, and I demand that you tell me, dammit."

"Baby." I grip her biceps and lean down so I'm the only thing in her world. I want to be everything for her, so much it kills me, but I never prepared myself for this. I pull in a breath before I rock her world in a way it will never be the same. "We just learned the boat your mom was seen getting on in Algeria was found."

The room goes stagnant.

"What?" she whispers. "Where? And what do you mean *found?* Where is she?"

I bring one hand up and cup her face. "It was found offshore near the southeast coast of Spain near Almería by a fishing boat. It capsized. Baby, they looked. They couldn't find any passengers. I'm sorry, Princess."

Her gaze never leaves mine. "No."

I shake my head once. "There were no survivors. It's been confirmed by the company who owns the boat. Luciana Zahir's name was on the charter. The Spanish government put out a statement. So did your uncle."

"No." She shakes her head and tries to pull away from me, but I hold tight. "They made a mistake. It can't be."

"Baby—"

"I'm sorry, love. So sorry." Bella lays a gentle hand on

her arm. "My contact confirmed it's the boat she was seen boarding in Algeria."

"I'm getting the same reports from the office," Carson adds.

Tears mar her beautiful face. They might as well stain my soul. I'll never forget this moment.

"No," she repeats. "Ozzy, no."

Her hands go to her face as her legs give out.

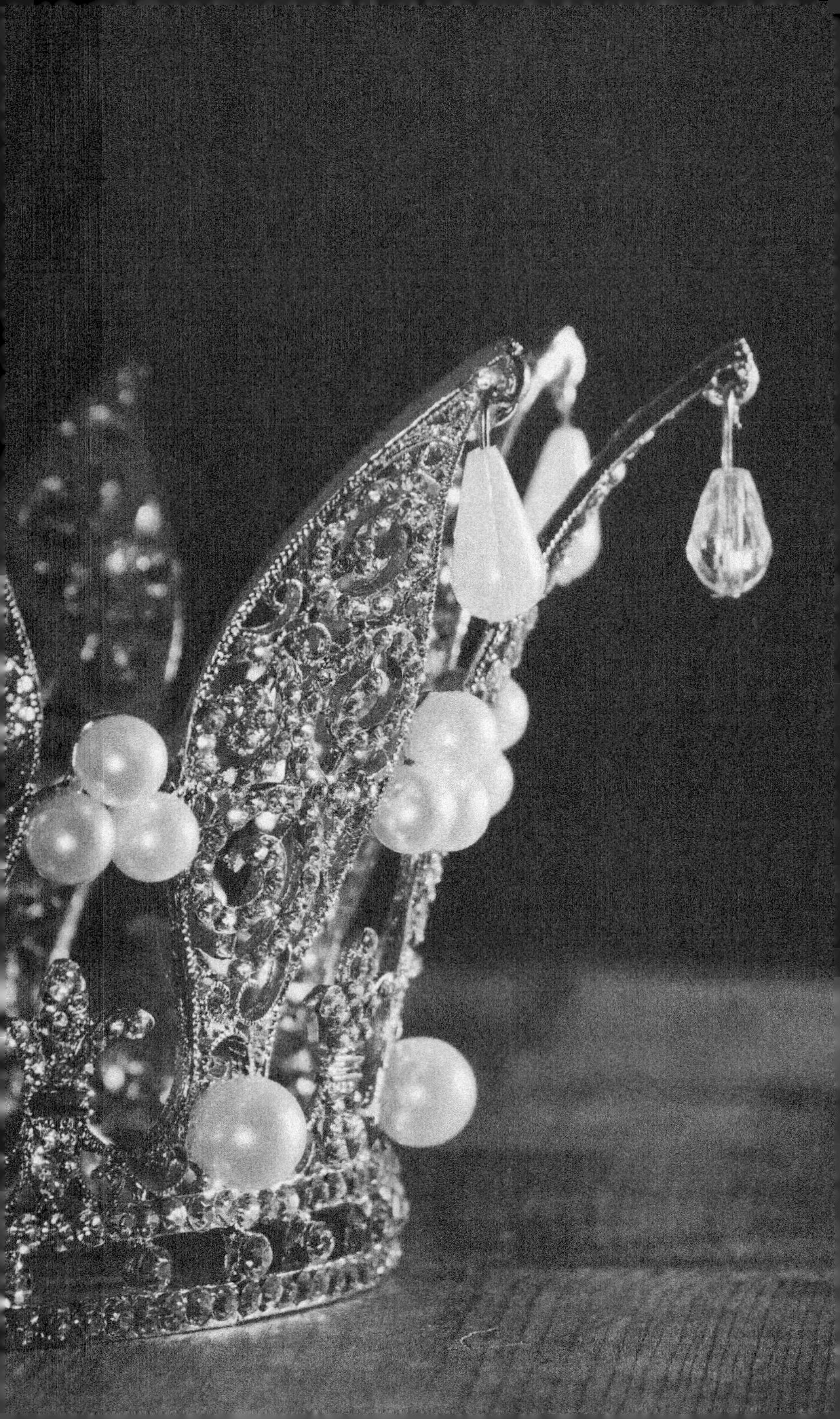

38

GONE

Liyah

"*I would sit in a dungeon for the rest of my days and never once think of trading you or my time with your father. Love has a way of getting you through the darkest of times. I'd do it all over again knowing my destiny.*"

Her words circle my mind and wrap themselves around my heart.

Regrets are the heaviest of all the burdens on the soul.

They're perpetual in the way they eat at you. They're everlasting with how you're forced to drag them around for the rest of your days. And they're heavy.

So damn heavy.

Regrets will weigh you down so you might never stand the same again.

My knees buckle under my regret.

But I don't hit the floor.

I'm up and in Ozzy's arms.

Scurrying and commotion are all around me, but I block it out. I'm clenching Ozzy's T-shirt with all the life I have left. My heart seizes, and pain bleeds into every cell in my body.

She's gone.

I can't believe she's gone.

She can't be gone.

Ozzy's arm angles up my back with his hand firm on the back of my head. His other is under my knees, holding me tight to his body. My tears become one with his skin and run down his neck.

Ozzy's words rumble through me. "Someone give us a ride. I'm not putting her down."

"I've got you. Let's go."

"What do you need?"

"Text. I can bring food later."

"I can't believe it."

"We'll be here for whatever she needs."

"Liyah, I'm so sorry."

I'm numb. The cool night air hardly registers as Ozzy whisks me from Crew and Addy's home.

"Ozzy—"

"I know, baby. I'm so sorry. Let me get you home."

Home.

That word means nothing to me.

"Hang on, Princess. I've got you."

A car door slams and an engine purrs beneath us.

"One minute, baby." Ozzy's lips press to the side of my head, and his grip on me tightens. "Hold on to me. I'll never let you go."

The ride is short as the car comes to a quick stop.

Ozzy has to shift me to dig for his keys, but he does as he said he would. He never lets me go.

It's Asa, and his words are low and as gravelly as the road that just brought us here. "We'll take care of everything in the control room. Take care of her, and tell us what you need."

Then, we're alone.

Like most of our time since we crashed into one another's lives. It's just me and Ozzy.

And he's taking care of me once again, like he's done since the beginning.

Ozzy puts me in the middle of the bed and only takes the time to throw my shoes to the floor. His sport jacket joins them before he joins me.

"Come here." He pulls me to his chest. "Fuck, I don't know what to do—what to say. If I could take this pain from you, I would."

I shake my head against his chest. We're on our sides, once again glued to one another, but this feels different. There's no yearning or desire. This is unlike anything I've experienced.

Ozzy is basic and necessary and vital. Like oxygen. Like water. If he peels himself away from me, I won't survive.

Because my mother is gone.

Just gone.

One moment I'm celebrating an engagement I had no idea I wanted, and the next...

She's gone.

I don't know what a world looks like without her in it.

I hold tight to Ozzy. He doesn't utter another word.

He strokes my hair, holds me close, and keeps his lips pressed to my forehead.

Time comes to a dead halt.

The night that started as a party for our future turned black in a heartbeat.

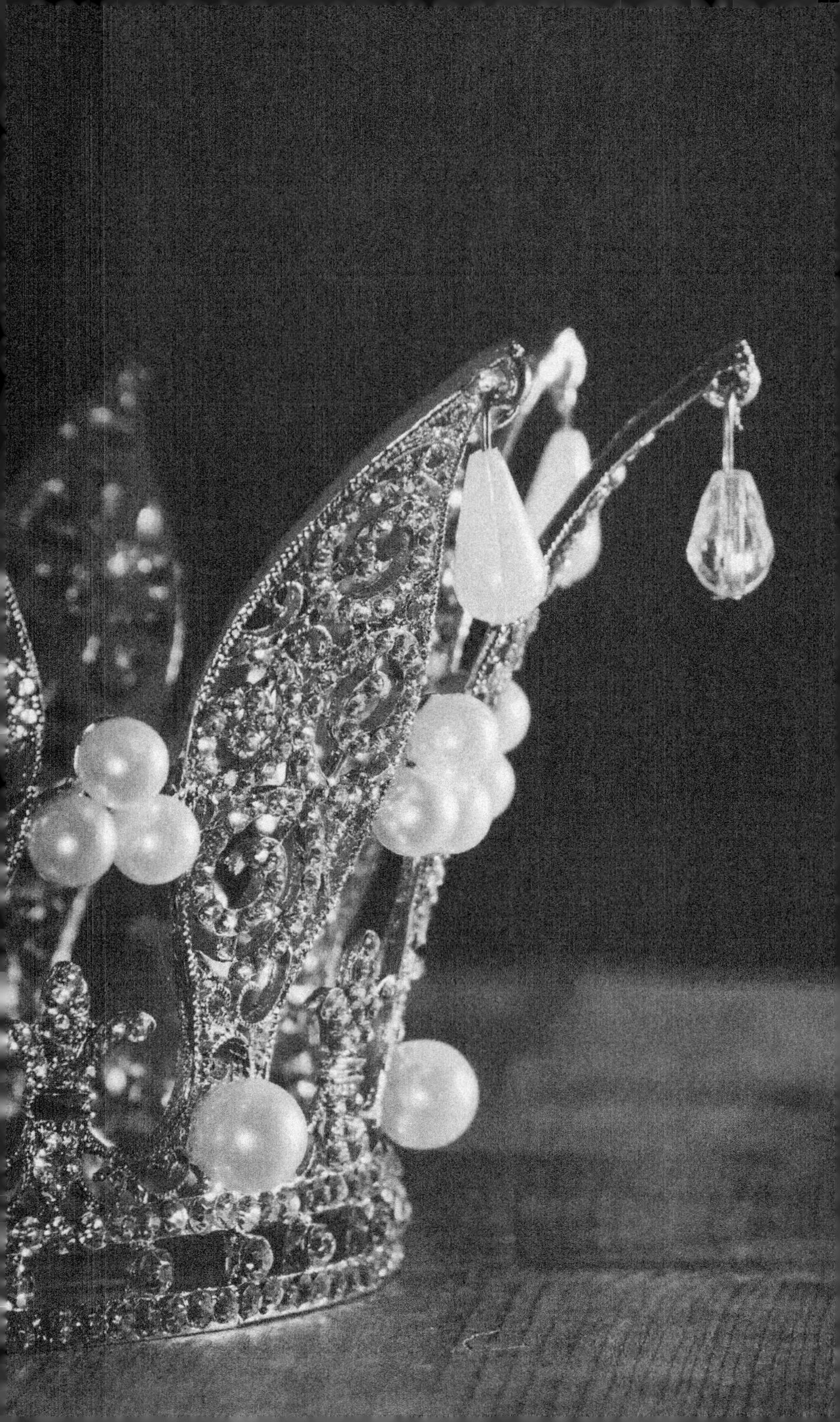

39

SUNDAY

Ozzy

Me – *Did the fucking King do this? I'm thinking of all the ways I'm going to torture that fucker before I kill him with my own hands.*

Grady – *I'm not saying the bastard doesn't deserve to be tortured, but we don't think he did this. We've read every piece of transcript since her death was announced. The King is pissed. He wants Liyah, and he knew his only pawn was Luciana. Without her, he knows he can't lure your Princess back to Morocco.*

Me – *What about Botros and the rest of his minions?*

Grady – *Same. They're pissed she's dead. They wanted her alive to use as a bargaining tool.*

Fuck.

Grady – *How's Liyah?*

I put my hand to her bare back where she's sprawled on top of me in only her panties.

It was a long night.

We shed our uncomfortable clothes sometime

between the hours of distraught and passed out. We only slept for a short time when the vibration of my phone woke me.

Me – She's carrying guilt she shouldn't. None of this is her fault. The fucking King was oppressive and controlling long before Liyah even came to the States.

Grady – Don't let her shoulder that. It'll eat her alive. I've done it.

I exhale and do everything I can not to wake her. When she opens her eyes to the first full day knowing her mother isn't living and breathing and walking the same earth she is, I have no clue what to do. Her tears and devastation cut through me last night.

Me – I'm not sure how to manage that, but I'll die trying. Any other news? Not sure what else I can handle today.

Grady – Listened to Cannon sing to himself all the way to the gym. It was painful. Besides that, nothing. Seems traitors take the weekend off too.

It's Sunday. I can't even keep my days straight anymore.

Me – Let me know if anyone gets chatty. As long as you're monitoring the feeds, I'm going to set my phone aside today for her.

Grady – I'll find you if the world blows up. Let us know if you need anything.

I power my cell down. My shit can wait. It kills me that the news we did get on Luciana is final. More confirmations came later in the evening.

I won't be connected to anyone but Liyah today.

My stomach is growling, I'm hot, and I have to take a leak, but as long as she sleeps, I'll act as her bed.

At this point, there's nothing I won't do.

But it would be nice to know what she needs so I can do it.

She stirs on my chest.

Shit. I'm going to need to figure it out sooner rather than later.

I feel it everywhere when she sighs. She's awake. I bring my hand to her hair and start to run my fingers through it to the ends where I pulled the pins out of it last night before she fell asleep.

Her feet fidget, and her lashes flutter on my pec.

"Baby?"

She says nothing and pulls in a deep breath.

"Are you hungry? I can make you breakfast. Or if something else sounds good, I can call one of the wives."

She shakes her head as she rests on me.

"Liyah, you need to eat. You skipped dinner."

Her only response is to press her face into my chest.

I sigh and rest my hand on the back of her head. "Okay, Princess. We'll get up when you're ready."

She presses her lips to my pec. "Thank you."

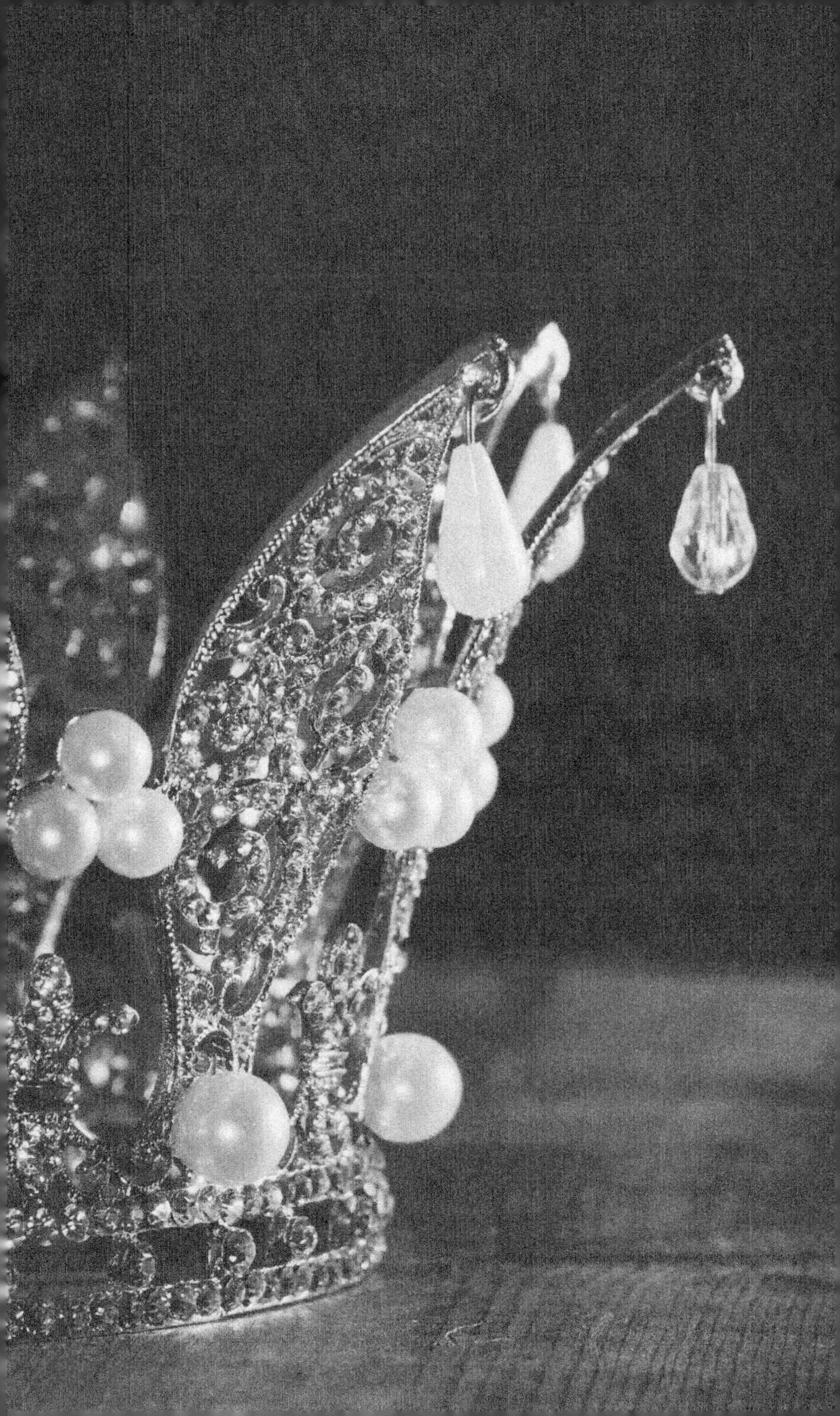

40

MONDAY

Ozzy

I wrap a blanket around her shoulders.

She's been sitting here for hours in the deafening silence, besides the rustle of the leaves, and my mom's chimes.

The chimes that were as loud as a gong when she first hung them. Now they're a part of the landscape, singing to the beat of my heart.

A reminder.

There's nothing like death to remind you how alive you truly are.

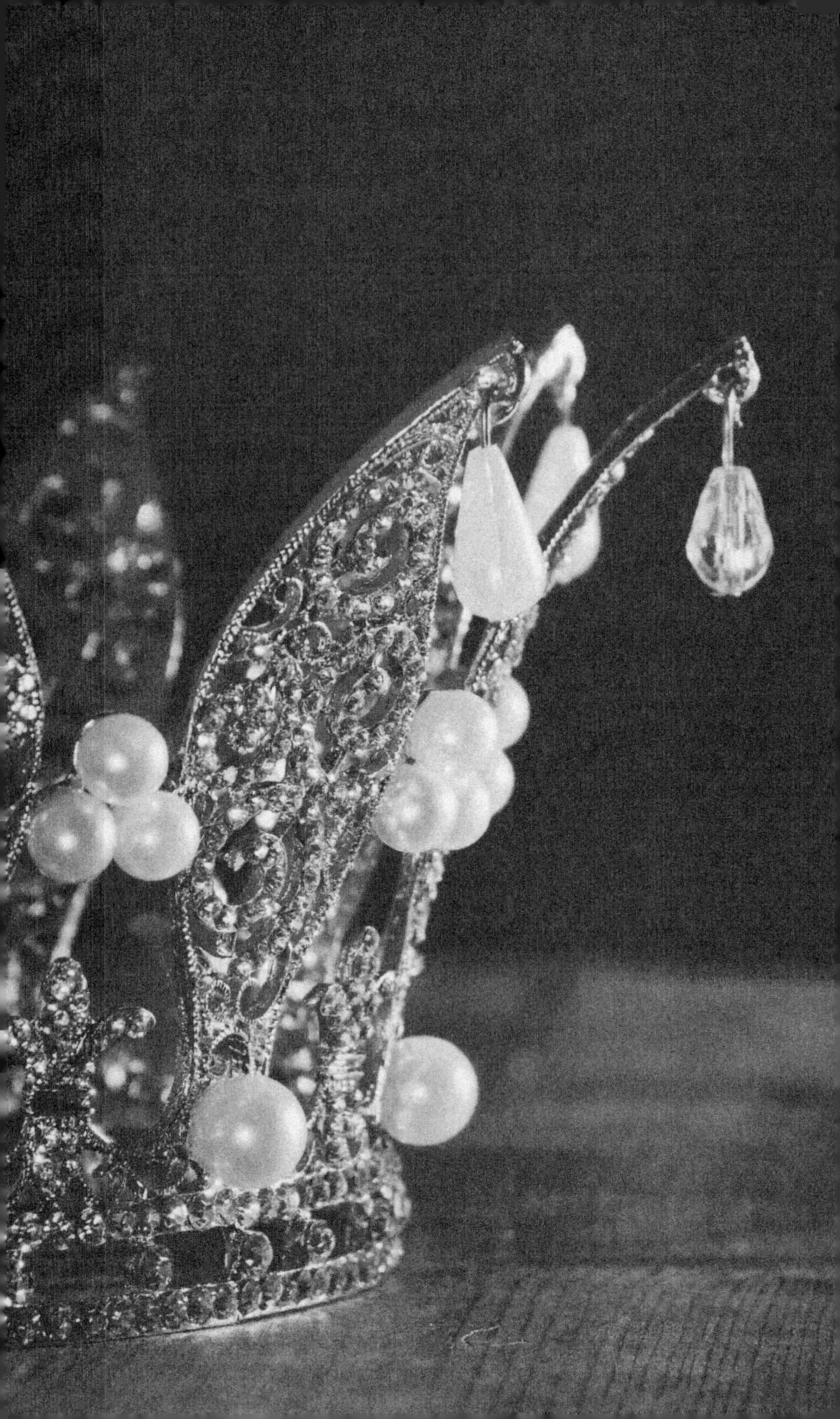

41

TUESDAY

Ozzy

I never knew time could be subjective.
    I thought time was time.
    A measure of life. The more that passes, the less there is in front of you.
    Living in the moment is bullshit.
    Or so I thought.
    I've pondered time a great deal in the last few years. I came to the conclusion that there's a future and there's a past. That the present—right now—is barely a blink.
    Fleeting.
    I've never been more wrong.
    Since we got the news about Luciana, time has stood still in the bungalow in the middle of the forest.
    We are unequivocally stuck in the present.
    Present is hell.

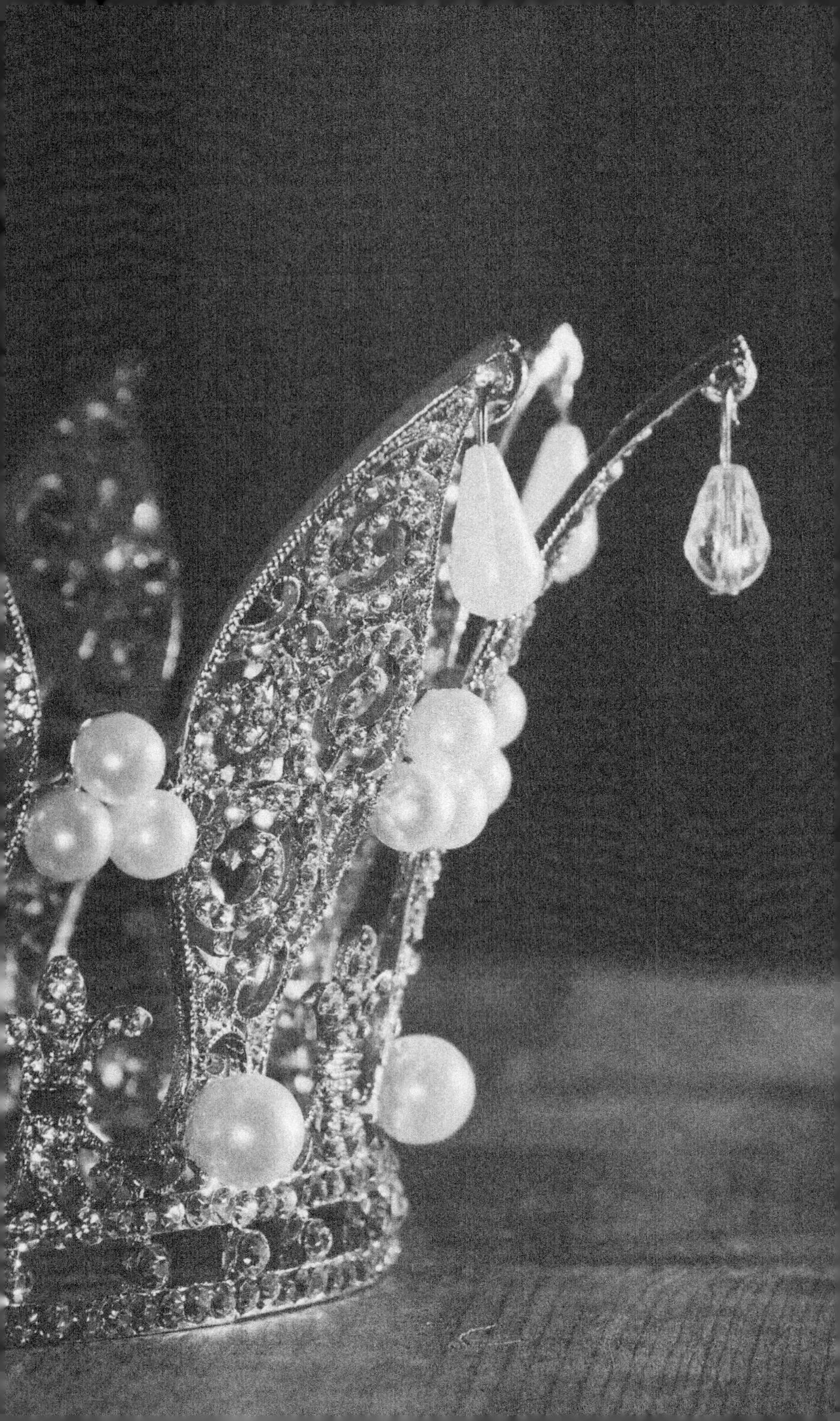

42

WEDNESDAY

Ozzy

I've only checked my phone while she's slept.
My laptop is collecting dust.
I don't recognize myself.

I've waited for years for a chance to corner Don Demaree and Bobby Cannon. There were times I was so desperate for it, I would've been willing to sell my soul to the devil to make it happen. My so-called life was hedged on shining a light on them so they'd never see the sun again.

Perspective is a powerful and intangible weight that's knocked me on my ass.

Don't get me wrong. I still plan on annihilating those fuckers. It's just not my first priority anymore.

Liyah is.

Very few words have been said in the last few days. Only ones necessary to communicate life's basic requirements.

"Are you hungry?"

"Are you cold?"

"Are you tired?"

Silence requires a whole other level of communication between two people. Liyah hasn't been out of my sight since Saturday night.

But it's not one-sided.

If I thought the mysterious draw only happened in our sleep, I was wrong. My Princess has been glued to me.

With very few words and no sex, all that was left was a different type of connection—one I didn't know existed.

Silent.

Deep.

Purposeful.

I sound like an Instagram poet.

Hell, I didn't even know Instagram had poets until Liyah sat on the island reading them to me when I was making her a sandwich last week. Poem after poem. She went on to explain that the fewer the words, the more beautiful they are.

She didn't know how right she was.

Her fingertips trace my abs, every inch slow and painful, as they make their way south.

This hasn't happened in days.

We barely opened our eyes. Just because there hasn't been anything remotely close to sex doesn't mean I haven't woken hard as a rock every morning.

I am me.

And I am waking up next to Liyah daily.

It doesn't matter who died—I can't help what I can't help.

I've touched Liyah in a million ways while time has stood still, but not like this.

Her finger drags across the waistband of my boxers.

"Baby." I reach to lift her face to mine. Her eyes are no less weary, distraught, or tortured. The tears stopped a day and a half ago, so they're at least not swollen like they were.

She pushes up my body and presses her lips to mine. I've kissed her countless times since we got the news of her mom, but not like this.

This is different.

This is desperate.

She needs me.

I roll her to her back and take over.

Her nails dig into my skin. Her grip on me is telling, but I still tear my lips away from hers, and lift two inches to look down at her. "You want this?"

Her eyes flare. "I want to lose myself in you. Even if it's only for a short time. Please. Give me an escape."

I take her mouth at the same time I fist her panties at her hip. They're on the floor and her tank follows in no time.

I cup her pussy. Drenched.

Spearing her with two fingers, I wrap my lips around her nipple and suck. She moans, pressing her head into the pillow, arching into me for more.

My Princess has given new meaning to dead in the last few days. I lost her spirit, the light in her eyes, and the hope that's kept her going since we met.

She's been dead, but she's just come alive for me.

Her fingers dig into my hair and pull. Despair and anguish are gone. Her body is needy and alive.

I don't take my time. Liyah broke a levee this morning. Her body is wired and ready for whatever I'll give it.

And I don't waste any time.

The days being with her, but not being with her, have built up in both of us. Working my way down her body, I wrap my lips around her clit for a quick suck. Fuck, I've missed this. My Princess has shed her innocence and hesitation. She plants her feet flat to the mattress and lifts her hips, pressing her pussy into my mouth.

Her moans feed my need for her and wrap us up in a way that blocks out reality. "Yes."

I fuck her with my tongue, licking her from her sex to her clit—I could do this all day. If this is what Liyah needs to lose herself from reality, I'm in no hurry to take her back to real life.

I palm her ass and hold her to me. I'm hungry. So fucking hungry. I'll never have my fill. It's not possible.

I want every inch of her.

My tongue circles her clit and I drag my finger from her pussy to her ass. When I touch her there for the first time, her thighs tense on my face, and her gasp interrupts her moans.

I don't stop.

Because ... her firsts.

They're all mine.

Liyah

Rage.

I woke up this morning so fucking angry.

My uncle.

The dynasty.

The kingdom.

The force that pushed my mother to flee a country she came to love while standing at my father's side. I'm hurt and angry she had to escape the life that slowly became a prison.

The only being in the world who can give me the escape I need is Ozzy.

His tongue teases my sex, my clit. He's spinning me into a frenzy as he rips reality out from beneath me, taking me to a place only he can.

That only he ever has. A place that will only be his.

Ours.

He spears me with a finger before shocking me.

All the air leaves my body when his wet finger circles my ass. Every muscle in my body constricts, but he doesn't stop, and he doesn't wait to see my reaction.

He presses in.

Oh, Lord.

Then he presses in farther, giving me something new.

But then again, everything is new when it comes to Ozzy.

My arms come up and I grip my pillow to hang on. His thumb from the same hand fills my sex, at the same moment he wraps his lips around my clit.

So full. He's everywhere.

Pumping me. Sucking. He's fucking me with his fingers and his tongue. I can't concentrate on any one thing. It's too much. Yet not enough.

I want more. I need more.

I press into his mouth, and that feeling only he's

given me starts to bubble low in my gut and travels up, wrapping itself around my heart and my soul.

He gives me the escape I need at the same time I'm grounded in Ozzy's reality.

I never want to leave it.

My ears tunnel, and I barely hear myself call out when I come. Between his finger, his thumb, and his lips, Ozzy takes me to a place I've never been before.

I come hard.

Just when I think I can't take another moment, I lose his hand and mouth. From a faraway place, I hear a condom rip, and the bed dips.

I open my eyes, and Ozzy is up on his knees. Naked and strong and rolling a condom onto his cock. "Can't wait to get rid of these, Princess."

His eyes drag over my body before his gaze meets mine. All the unspoken words between us in the last few days hang silently in the air. Ozzy has been ever present, constant, and a balm to my pain.

Finality, as tragic and excruciating as it is, has done nothing but ground me. The future is no longer teetering on a tightrope. Nothing is hanging in the balance.

My heart will be forever broken.

It will never look the same.

The future is no longer in question. Ozzy is my everything ... forever.

His eyes are warm with lust and promise and other things that have gone unsaid.

A hand lands on my hip. "Roll over."

I'm flipped to my stomach, and he drags a heavy hand over my ass before cupping me between the legs, lifting. My ass is in the air, and my knees are nudged apart. His thighs bump mine, and I'm even wider.

His knees are planted within mine, his cock resting hard and heavy on the crack of my ass. With my cheek to the mattress, he's everywhere, surrounding me. Not too different than he's been since I learned the news of my mother.

Present.

Supportive.

Devoted.

Ozzy is a dream during a nightmare.

The last few days have been beyond painful. Had I gone back when Hasim demanded, this wouldn't have happened. No matter how much my mother told me not to.

My mother was selfless for me. In the end, it was her demise.

And that thought suffocates me.

But when I opened my eyes this morning, I was able to breathe like the anvil was lifted. And what replaced it has empowered me. I'm ready to take my life back. Be in control of my choices. Be free of my uncle, the dynasty, and everything that oppressed my mother, and pushed her to her death.

"So fucking beautiful. I'll never get my fill of you. A lifetime won't be enough." His heat sinks into my skin when his chest presses into my back, his teeth nip the lobe of my ear. "Arch, Princess. This will be different."

I arch.

With one firm thrust, he fills me to the root. I pull in a breath, and my eyes fall shut. Every time is better than the one before, and he's right. This is different, deeper in a way I had no idea was possible.

He stays where he is, his lips trail the curve of my ear, over my hair, and land on my forehead. "I'd give anything to take your pain."

He pulls out and slides back in.

"I'm sorry, baby."

My eyes fly open. I'm still trying to catch my breath from my orgasm. "For what?"

"For not finding her. For not doing more."

My eyes sting at the same time I fall deeper.

"Your family will never hurt you again—in any way. I'll make sure of it."

I swallow hard and arch farther. Wanting more of him, as much as I can take. I'll never have my fill.

He starts to move. Really move. "Nothing bad will ever touch you again."

I lose his heat. I thought he was deep before. Ozzy's fingers bite into my hips and he's up, straight on his knees behind me.

He was right. This is different. And so good. He pulls me to him, to meet his every thrust. I want more, and for the first time since I gave myself to him, I move. Before now, Ozzy led, and I was here for it.

"My Princess likes this. Move, baby. Make it what you want."

Just like that, I'm an active participant.

I groan.

"There you go. Fuck yourself on my cock."

This isn't like before. This is eager, frantic, even desperate—and it's all me.

Because I've never needed anyone like I need Ozzy.

Every time we collide, it's beautifully brutal, and exactly what I didn't know I needed.

Ozzy's grip on my hips tighten, and he takes over. He

tenses, the way he gets right before he comes. I hear him suck in a lungful of air before he groans, holding me to him, impaled so deeply on his cock, I know I'll feel this tomorrow.

And I love it. I want every reminder of him, every minute of the day. Ozzy has become a security blanket. I know it won't always be this way, that we won't always be inseparable.

No matter how much I might yearn for him.

He gives me his heat again, and we're both working to slow our hearts and steady our breaths. His large frame presses my small one to the mattress, and he gives me his weight, still inside me.

He wraps me up and presses his lips to the side of my head. "You okay?"

I tip my head to him. "I'm better now."

His lips tip on one side, but it's not a happy smile. It's a sad one. "I'm glad, baby."

"I know there's going to come a point when you can't babysit me twenty-four seven. I'm sure Crew and the rest of the men are ready to have you back at work."

"Don't worry about them. And I'm handling work in my own way."

Now is as good a time as any. I've been contemplating it for days. When I woke up this morning, I made my decision. "Ozzy—"

His phone vibrates on the nightstand. He frowns. "Hold that thought, Princess. Everyone knows I'm off-limits right now unless it's critical."

Ozzy pulls out and reaches for his cell. I roll to my side, and yank the sheet over me as he flops down on his back, still half-hard and gorgeously naked.

It's his expression that pulls my attention away from his sculpted body. "What is it?"

A frown hardens on his square jaw.

"Ozzy," I demand.

His face turns to mine, and all I see is regret. "There's only one thing that can tear me away from you right now, Liyah, and it happened. I need to get to the control room, and you need to get dressed. Addy is on her way to hang out with you."

I reach for his forearm and squeeze. "What happened?"

He shakes his head before leaning in to kiss me quicker than I like. "About the worst thing that could happen, baby. I'll explain when I get back. This can't wait."

He rips the condom off and climbs out of bed.

And just like that, reality is back in all its ugly force.

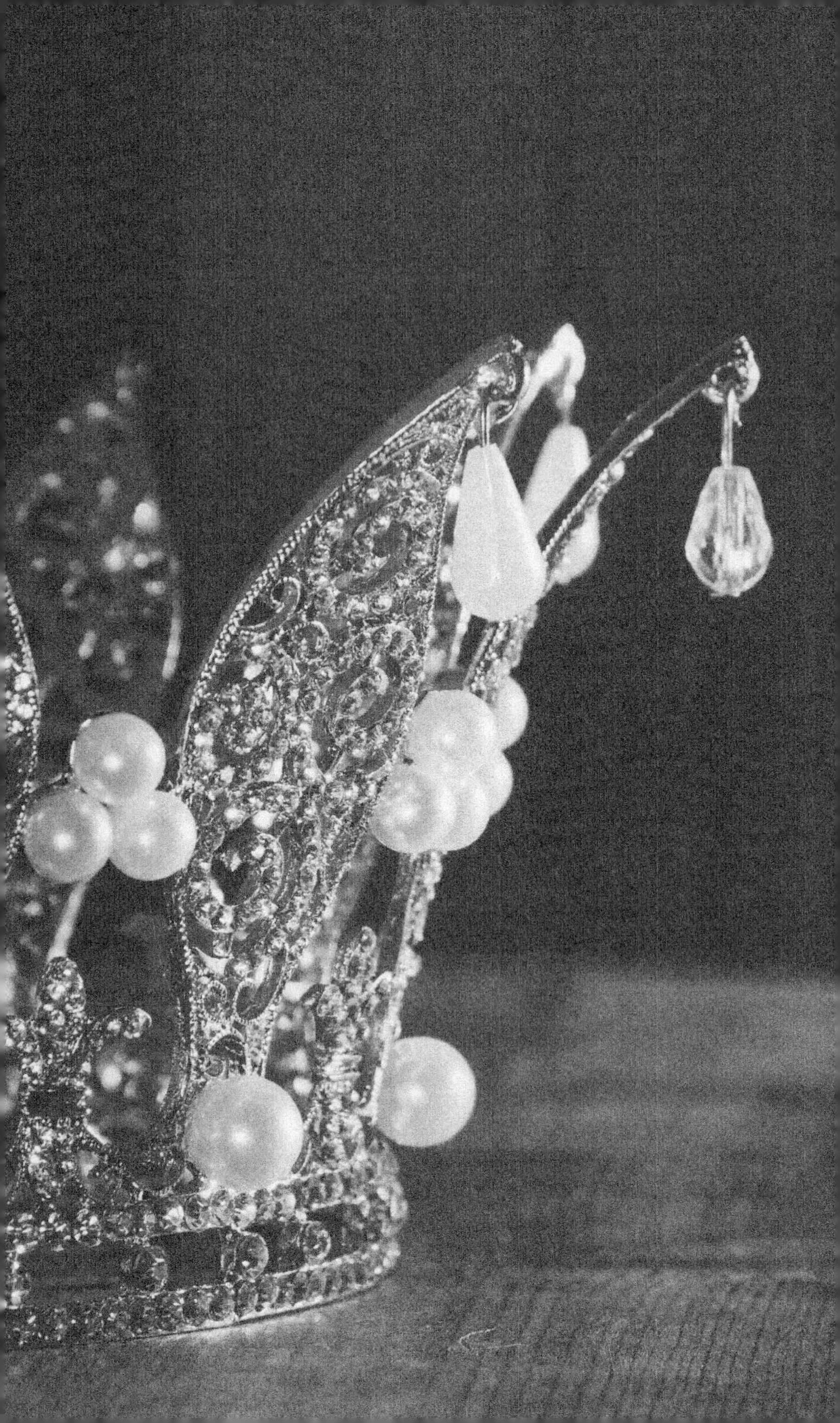

43

IT'S TIME

Ozzy

"Motherfucker. You cannot get to me, do you understand? You can try and try and try again to weasel your way into my life, but I'm right on your heels, asshole. And I'm going to find you. When I do, you'll wish you died years ago in that fucking inferno you somehow orchestrated. That would've been an easy death compared to what I have planned for you. It's only a matter of time."

A hand lands on my shoulder from behind, but I don't turn to see who it is. It's not a hand offering support. It's to control me for when I flip the fuck out as I listen to the recording that was taken twenty minutes ago from inside Bobby Cannon's car.

I'm staring at the voice recording on the screen that looks more like a hospital machine monitoring my erratic heart.

Fuck me. Cannon intercepted my tap in his car.

Besides his grating voice, the silence is thick in the control room.

"Until I find your sorry ass, Oz, I might take a little trip up to horse and buggy country, visit your family."

"Fuck." I scrape my hands down my face, and the hand on my shoulder tightens and presses down.

Bobby goes on. "I never got the chance to offer my condolences after you faked your fucking death. I might have to go up and see how Mama and Daddy Graves are doing."

Every cell in my body comes alive.

"And guess what else, cocksucker? I burned the taps you have on your family too. Too bad you won't know if your little brother's wife has a boy or girl. I hear you'll be an uncle again soon. Too bad you won't..." He spits his words, every single one of them getting louder and more livid with each syllable, until he screams the car down. "...live to find out, because I'm going to fucking kill you with my own fucking hands!"

That's it. That's when he cut the tap.

My heartbeat might as well be a gong in my own ears, and if I thought the silence in the control room was deafening before, it's painful now.

Crew moves in front of me, and Jarvis slides in behind him. The grasp on my shoulder must be Asa. I get a squeeze when he asks, "You going to lose it, or can I let go?"

I shake my head. I have no fucking idea what I'm going to do.

"We heard it happen live. So did Carson. He's monitoring the private network from the office." Crew explains. "He already scrambled units to your parents farm and your mom's store. We've got an eye on your brothers. Carson called his contacts at the FBI too."

My eyes go wide. "The FBI cannot be involved."

Crew shakes his head. "They won't. No one knows what's going on. Carson manages a shitload of cases at once, and filed their surveillance under another one. It's only surveillance. That's it."

I nod and exhale. That's good.

For now.

Crew is irritatingly cool and collected like normal. Like *I* normally am. But these assholes have their hands wrapped around my throat—I'm suffocating. Crew keeps filling me in. "Carson is close to having what he needs on Kruglov, but not close enough. There hasn't been a money transfer. And before Bobby dropped that bomb of a message in his own fucking car, we found out Don and Bobby are having a lovers spat. Seems Don is the brains behind the technology and put his foot down—refused to get the goods you asked for on the Moroccan President."

"Fuck," I hiss. I knew they were dragging their feet with my offer, but I thought they were waiting it out to see if I'd shell out more. Which I did. Bobby took the bait, but Crew's right. Don is beyond skilled compared to Bobby.

Crew juts his thumb over his shoulder to the screens. "This might not be what we normally do, but I'm not sure how much longer we can drag this out. Not when they're threatening you and your family. You need to decide how patient you're willing to be."

I know what that means. If we need to move in on these two and take care of shit the way we normally do, I won't be able to clear my name. Everything we've done to corner them, we've done illegally. I'll live just like this for the rest of my very dead life on earth.

But they threatened my family. How long will it be until they figure out where I am, and who I work for? I can't put Crew's entire organization at risk.

This is a balancing act none of us are used to. What I do know is, either side this drama ends up falling on, Don and Bobby will be in prison or dead.

And I'll sleep a hell of a lot better if it's the latter. But fuck, the fact that I have to make this decision is depressing.

I look up at Crew. "It's time. But I'll be the one to do it."

Jarvis's stare darts to Crew, but Crew doesn't look away from me. "You can't risk that."

"I'm the only one who *can* risk it," I argue.

"No." Crew tries to put his foot down. "I won't allow it."

I stand my ground. "You know you have my respect, and I literally owe you my life for helping me at a time when I needed it. But this is not a contract. This is on me, and I'm going to be the one to finish it. There's no other option."

Everyone in the room stands silent while Crew contemplates me. His intense gaze shifts over my shoulder to Asa, then to Jarvis. I have no clue what Asa's response is, but he must trust me not to fuck up the control room, because he drops his hand. Jarvis nods. Crew looks back to me. "When is it going to happen?"

This is easy.

I've contemplated a million ways to end this—end them—since the day I stood in the next field, and watched my family bury ashes they thought were mine.

Don Demaree and Bobby Cannon are going to pay. And the price will be steep.

This will be a dream come true.

And it can't happen soon enough.

"I need to talk to Liyah about what this means. But I'm done waiting on them to fuck up. The stakes are too high—it's happening tomorrow."

"Give it another few days. The pressure is on, one of them will slip," Jarvis says.

"I'm done waiting. I'll let you know my plan, but that's it."

Crew exhales. He knows he has no choice. He also knows he'd do the same thing if he were in my shoes. "Tell us everything. You might not be giving us a choice in this, but we'll be at your back. *That* you don't have a say on, Oz. I don't give a shit what you think. You can deal."

I lift my chin. I was counting on that, but don't say it aloud.

"Let's get this done. I want to get back to Liyah. I have a feeling she's not going to like this."

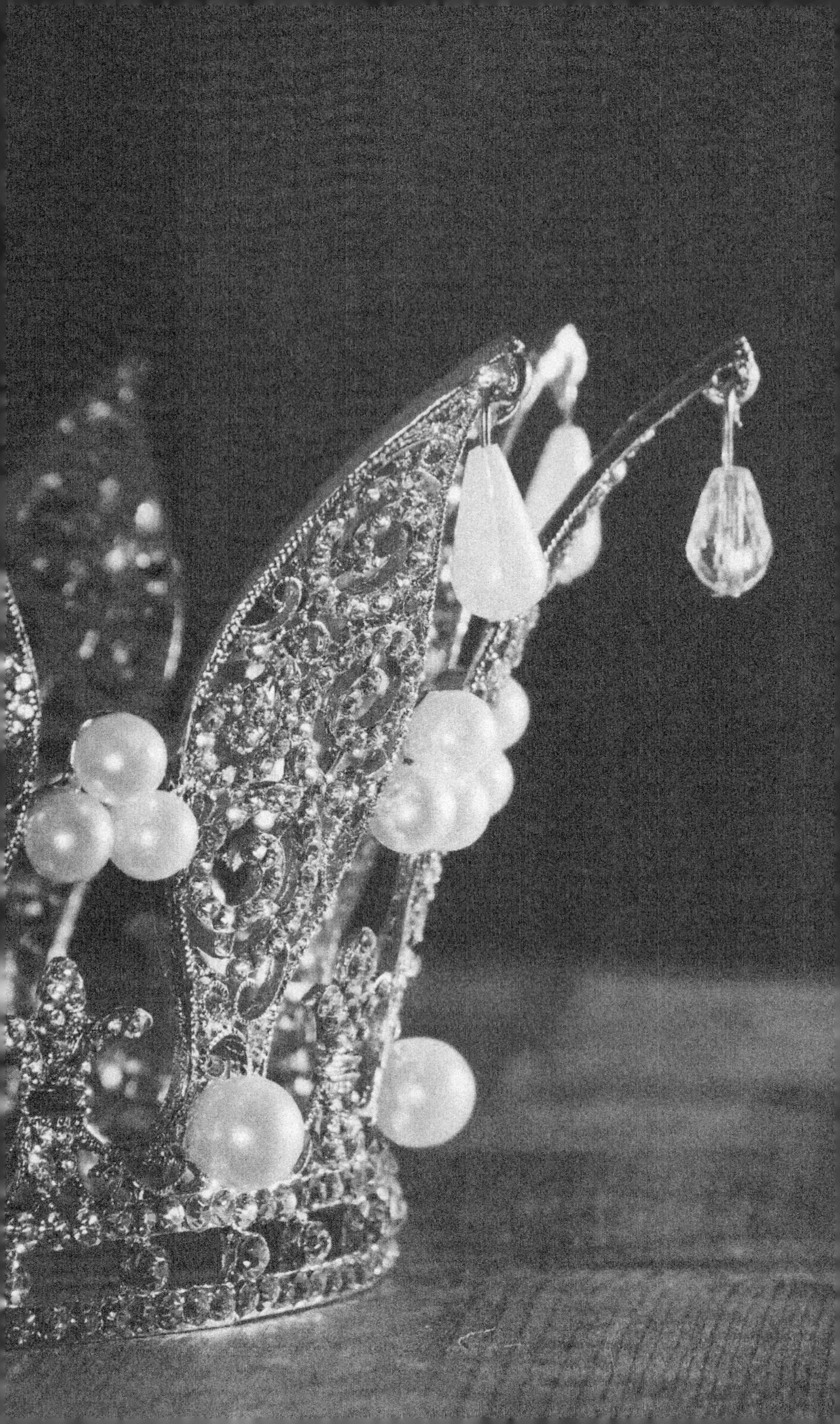

44

TWIST

Liyah

I stare at the man I plan to tie myself to for the rest of my days.

There's nothing in this world I want more. If losing my mother has proven anything, it's that.

Ozzy has been gone for hours, and I spent my first time away from him since learning about my mother's death. Addy continues to demonstrate what a sweet, caring woman she's been since I first stepped foot onto her vineyard. If I had an older sister, Addy is exactly who I'd want.

"Well?" Ozzy clips. "You haven't said anything."

I haven't.

His plan is ruthless, vindictive, and not at all what I've come to expect from the man I'm going to marry.

And, still, I respect it. I'd like to say I love it, but it doesn't go in line with who I am.

But seeing as I'm not the same woman I was before I received the dreaded voicemail from my mother and left my easy life in California, I go with the new me, because it's the truth. "I love it."

He frowns. "You love it?"

"I do." I close the two feet separating us where we stand in the bedroom. "I'm not sure if it's the emotions I've lived through since we met, or my anger toward my uncle. But yes, I love that the men who dragged you through hell will pay. They threatened you and your family. Nothing is too horrible or violent. Not even torture or an incinerator. Though, I'm not sure where you have access to one of those, but I won't question it."

He pulls me flush to him. "No shit, Princess. That was not what I expected you to say when I came in here and explained my plans in detail. I'll never lie or sugarcoat anything with you. Ever. But I sure as hell didn't expect you to *love it*."

I look down at my fingers that are playing with the buttons on his shirt. "It might be a bit selfish. I need you to do something for me."

He lifts my chin. "I'll do anything for you. You know that."

I look into his impossibly blue eyes. "I'm counting on it."

His brows pinch. "What do you need me to do?"

"After you take care of your NSA associates," I pull in a big breath, "I want you to do the same to me."

His hold on me tightens in an instant. "What?"

"Fictionally speaking, of course," I amend, licking my lips, because saying the words aloud stir my insides. "I want you to do to me what you did for yourself, Ozzy. My mother is gone. I'll never return to the palace or my home country. I refuse to on principle alone, even if I were safe, no matter how much my parents loved it and the memories I have of them there. And I have no desire to return to my life in California—"

Ozzy interrupts me. "No fucking way."

I press on. "I was about to ask you this morning, but you were called away. Now, it makes even more sense. You say you won't be able to clear your name before you take those men down. If you plan on living in the shadows for the rest of time, that's what I want too."

He shakes his head. His expression is hard when he echoes his own words with deep underlying emotion this time. "No. Fucking. Way."

"I've thought about it, Ozzy. And I have more than enough money to live a thousand lives. For *us* to live a thousand lives together."

"I don't care about your money, baby," he grits. "I might not have royal fortunes, but I could stop working today and never have to lift a finger again. That's not the point. The point is, I refuse to make you live in the shadows. There are implications you cannot fathom. I'm always looking over my shoulder, worried I'll run into some idiot from my freshman year of high school who meant nothing to me, but could ruin it all. And I don't have a face like yours. Even if I would consider it, there's no way to make it work unless I take you to the middle of nowhere to live for the rest of our lives."

I grip his shirt in my hands. "Please. That sounds perfect."

"You don't know what you're saying."

"I do. It's what I want."

His jaw goes tense. "Then, Princess, we just found the one and only thing I will not do for you. It's not happening."

"Ozzy—"

"No. Ask me for anything else but that."

My teeth grip the skin inside my mouth to keep tears from forming.

Ozzy lowers his voice. "Don't do that, baby. Trust me, the selfish move for me would be to orchestrate your death for the world. To keep you as mine and only mine. But I care about you too much to do that."

A lump forms in my throat, and my voice is low and gravelly. "There's nothing *might* about my love for you."

Ozzy freezes.

"I'm going to marry you, Ozzy, and it's not for protection or convenience. It's because I want to spend the rest of my life with you. Give you babies and grow old together. There's nothing I want more. And as crazy as this sounds, I want to be dead to the rest of the world. There's nothing more for me to live for than you."

He doesn't move a muscle other than his lips that I've become obsessed with. "You dropped the *might*."

I wrap my arms around him. "Yes. No more *might*."

He turns me in his arms and the next thing I know, I'm tossed on the bed.

"What did you do that for?"

He comes down next to me and reaches under the long dress I threw on this morning. His fingers grip at the panties at my hips. "That's a shitty way to finally admit that you love me, Princess."

My panties land on the floor and he rips at the buttons on his shirt. "It's not like you've exactly expressed your undying love for me either."

His shirt is gone, and he stands over me barechested, wearing a smirk. "I have. You were asleep."

My face falls. "Why would you tell me in my sleep?"

"Why would you tell me you *might* love me?" He rips

his jeans open, and my gaze wanders south to his cock, already hard, and ready for me.

I squeeze my thighs together, as wetness instantly pools between my legs. "Ours has hardly been a normal relationship."

He pushes my dress up to my breasts, leaving me mostly bare to him. "Baby, I knew you loved me. Hell, you agreed to marry me."

I part my legs to make room for him as his forearms land on the bed next to my head. The tip of his bare cock teases my sex. He feels different without a condom, and I like it. But I can't think about that right now. I place my hand on the side of his face. "You told me you loved me for the first time, and I missed it."

His blue eyes roam my face. "You still haven't told me you love me. I figure we're even."

I suck in a breath when he slides his cock inside me with nothing between us for the second time. "Ozzy."

"Want to take you bare, baby," he murmurs against my lips, before kissing me. Then he pulls out, rubbing the underside of his cock against my clit. Up and down, up and down. Delicious pressure, making me want more. With my feet to the bed, I lift my hips to meet him. "I don't care about the consequences. Hell, what am I saying? I care a shit ton about the consequences. I want everything with you. My life has been on hold for too long. I'm done waiting."

Between his words and the storm he's stirring between my legs, there's nothing I want more than to throw caution to the wind when it comes to anything and everything with him. If the last week has taught me anything, it's that life is too short, too delicate. I don't want to wait for anything. "There's no more might, Ozzy. I love you with everything I am."

He stills for a moment before sliding into me again in one firm thrust. I wrap my legs around his waist to hold him to me, and he takes my mouth, his tongue pressing in, tasting me. All I can think about right now are him and the consequences. And I want both more than anything.

"I think I loved you when you fell asleep on me the first time in the plane. The moment you accepted me for who I am and what I do. Hell, probably before that. Falling in love with you has been the easiest thing I've ever done, no matter what's been swirling around us in the process."

My arms and legs constrict as he takes me harder.

His lips brush my ear. "Love you, Princess. There's nothing I want more than to live a life with you. Be normal with you. Watch our babies grow. Get old with you."

From the moment I met him, nothing has stirred me as much as this. His words, his love, his emotion. They all touch me somewhere so deep, they'll be entrenched in my soul forever.

Every time he takes me, he hits my clit, pushing me to the edge that has me begging for more. I dip my fingers into his hair and hold tight. "Please, Ozzy. Don't stop. I'm close. So close."

He gives me more. More of his strength, more of his words. "I'm not stopping, baby. And I'm not pulling out."

My only answer is to hold on tighter.

Ozzy's answer is to give me what I want.

His thrusts become erratic, forceful. His intensity bleeds into me as we become one for the first time...

With nothing between us.

I press my head to the mattress, and my mouth falls open. I gasp when it comes over me, and I didn't think it was possible for Ozzy to take me harder, but he does.

And he pushes me off my edge.

"Fuck, I feel you everywhere, Princess. Don't stop."

My orgasm strangles me on a whole other level with him inside me. Ozzy is relentless, drawing it out until he comes too.

And, for the first time, he comes inside me, with nothing between us.

He might as well secure a noose around my heart—I've never felt so right. Being tied to him forever is the only thing I want in life.

He gives me his weight, and his heart races against my chest, in unison with mine, as we catch our breaths. Ozzy's words are hot and heavy on my skin. "Love you, Princess."

I tip my face to his. "I never knew love would stir a desperation in me, and that's what I am. Desperate for anything and everything when it comes to you."

"I'm right here, baby. I'd tell you there's no need for desperation, but that's exactly how I feel. Especially now." He presses his still-hard and very bare cock into me.

"So you'll do it?" My tone is full of hope. "You'll make me dead, just like you?"

His gaze drags over my face, slow and methodical. As if he's memorizing me. My heart stirs when his lips meet mine in a soft and languid kiss. So slow and so careful, excitement bubbles inside me for our future.

Privacy.

Off the grid.

Living a life that's only us and what we create.

His connection lingers with one last swipe of his tongue on my bottom lip. He pulls in a deep breath that I feel everywhere since we're still connected in the most basic and carnal way possible. "No, baby. I'll never do that."

My expression falls, but he doesn't allow me to respond.

"Love you too much. If anything, this." He presses into me one more time. "Has given me every reason not to give you what you want."

He loses the sad smile, and something else replaces it. An expression so intense, so filled with determination, it's close to scary.

"I'll find it, Princess. If it's the last thing I do on this earth, I'll find a way. But I'm not stealing your life from you. I'll never do that. And that means one thing."

My hold on him tightens, because I'm afraid of what he's about to say. "What?"

"It means torture and the incinerator are off the table for now. I'm going to clear my name, Liyah. I'm going to do it for you and for us and for our future. I'll find a way to make it happen."

"But—"

"Sorry, no buts. I need to talk to Carson. Already had that planned. With all the shit that's gone down, I'll only do that in person. Bella turned that meeting into dinner. Do you think you're up for more company?"

"I guess. It was nice to spend time with Addy today."

"Good." I get one more kiss before he pulls out and makes one more promise. "We just took a big step, baby.

One I'm fucking thrilled about. This step has made me even more determined—I want my life back, and I can't fucking wait to shout to the world that you're mine."

He presses a firm kiss to my lips before I lose his weight.

And my head spins from yet another twist in the cyclone we can't seem to escape.

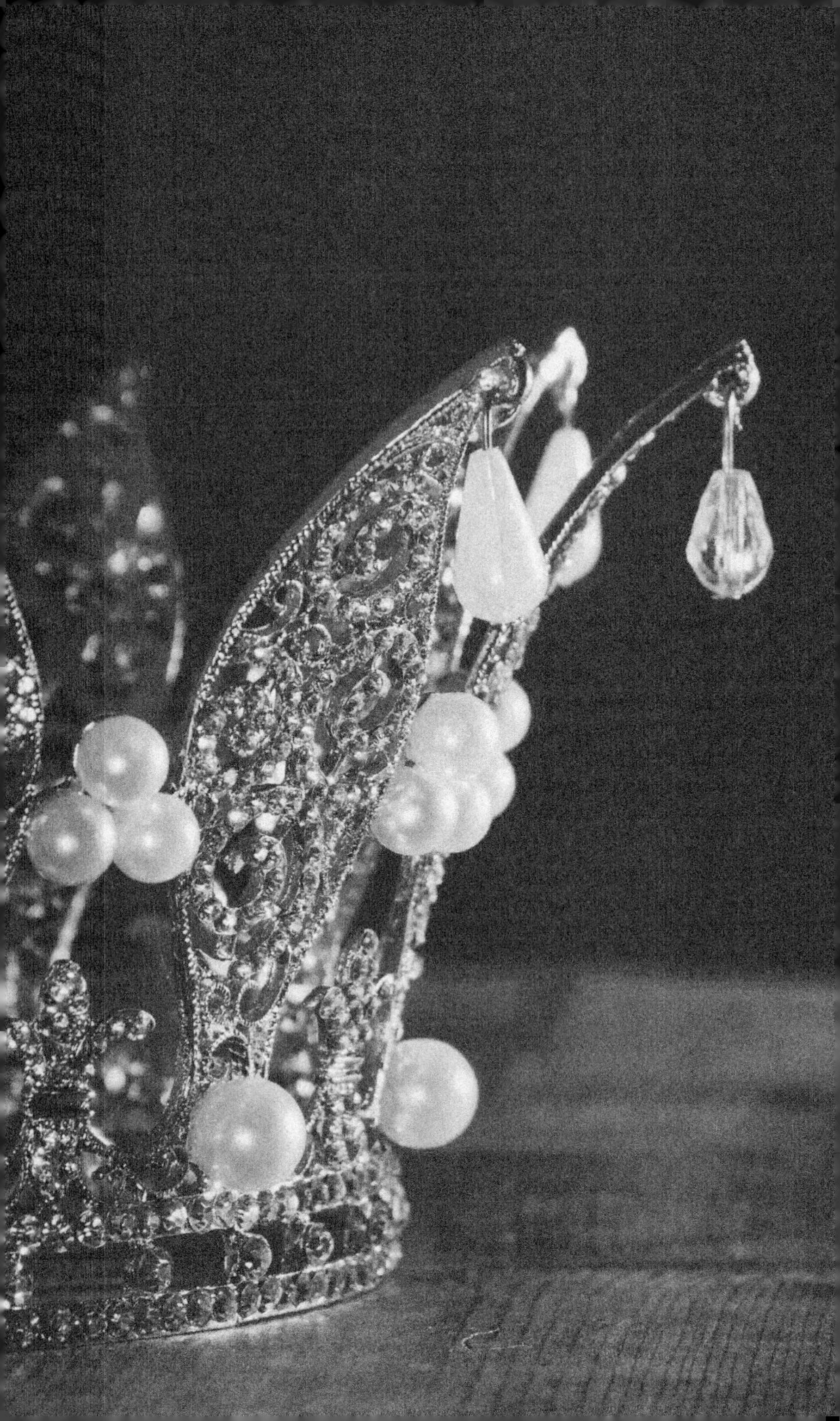

45

FAST TRACK

Ozzy

Carson crosses his arms. "Why the sudden change? Gotta say, I'm a little bummed. As messy as it sounded, the incinerator intrigued me."

I'm not about to tell anyone why the sudden change. Not the real reason.

Unprotected sex has a way of putting things into perspective. Liyah and I put ourselves on the fast track—or, the faster track—this afternoon. That wasn't something I had planned or contemplated.

But when she asked me to fake her death...

The fact she even thought that was an option pissed me off.

And when she told me she loved me?

I wonder if the overwhelming need to tie her to me will ever subside. She didn't balk when I told her I was taking her bare. In fact, I think she wanted it as much as I did.

"I'm glad you changed your mind," Jarvis says. "Carson has your family under surveillance—they're safe. We need to get these fuckers and clear your name. It's gone on too long."

"As long as my family is taken care of, I can be patient. I'm not happy about it, but I've waited this long." I check my phone for what feels like the millionth time.

I put more taps on Don and Bobby this afternoon. They know I'm alive, and I have the capability to be a fly on their walls. There's no hiding either fact any longer. They have jobs—real jobs—and lives and families. They can't spend every moment of the day running counter-programs to make sure their lines are clean.

That's the problem with being a treasonous asshole—you have two lives to balance. There's not always time to watch your back when Uncle Sam expects you to do your day job, and your wife wants you to take out the trash and mow the fucking yard.

"Still nothing?" Grady asks.

I shake my head. "They're in a standoff. Don won't pull the information I requested on Botros. I entered our private chat room this afternoon and told them if they can't produce what I need, I'll take my offer elsewhere. Bobby assured me they'd get it. What they don't know is I also have the text from Don telling Bobby to fuck off and find a way to get the information himself."

"They're going to slip up, Oz." I look to my boss, just as stoic as he was this morning, but less intense since I backed off the notion to take these assholes down on our homeland. "They're pissed and scared, but I've seen these guys on surveillance. Unless they're coming at you with another bomb, they're not you—a computer geek inside a warrior's body."

I slide my phone back into my pocket. "I'm not sure whether to be offended by that or not. I prefer computer *genius*, by the way."

Asa laughs before cracking open another beer. "Seriously, though. How's Liyah? It hasn't even been a week since she found out about her mom."

We've been here for almost two hours. We ate dinner, and the women cracked open a couple bottles of wine. But when I find my bride-to-be across the room, she's deep in conversation with Keelie with a glass of water in front of her.

I have no desire to tell the men about our days since we found out her mom died. Our time together is private, sacred. I hate the reason we endured it—and I might sound like a chick—but we're different because of it.

Instead, I shrug, and go for vague. "It's been tough—but she's tough. She'll be okay in time. I'll make sure of it."

As if she has supersonic hearing from across the huge open space, her gaze darts to me. She glances at her watch before biting her lip and hiking a brow.

I don't need to understand sign language to know what that means. "I think we're going to get out of here. Thanks for dinner."

"No problem." Carson slaps me on the back. "Bella is infatuated with your Princess. I'm only a little envious."

Asa ignores Carson, but adds, "We've got to go too. Everyone has school in the morning."

I move across the room to the women, where Liyah

has re-engaged herself into conversation. When I reach her, I wrap my hand around her hair and give it a gentle tug. When she tips her head to look at me upside down, her small smile screams relief. I kiss her forehead. "Let's go, Princess."

Maya sighs. "I want someone to call me Princess."

Grady smirks at his wife. "I'll call you anything you want, baby."

Maya shakes her head. "No. From here on out, no one can call anyone anything that has to do with royalty. It won't be the same—Liyah is an actual princess."

"I'm just putting it out there, I was crowned Homecoming King," Carson announces.

I ignore the crowd and look back to my fiancée. "Let's go."

Liyah wastes no time. She's up, at my side, and we've said our goodbyes and thank-yous to everyone.

I wrap my arm around her neck and pull her to me as we walk to my truck. "We stayed too long. You okay?"

She leans her head on my shoulder. "I'm good. I'm not sure how I can be tired after days of lazing around, but I'm exhausted. I'm sorry we're leaving so early."

"I'm not complaining. That group gets together so often, I wouldn't be surprised if someone steals you away from me before breakfast.

She looks up at me. "Tomorrow is your birthday. Don't think that it will go by unseen, Ozzy. I'll make sure you're thoroughly celebrated."

I pull her head to me and press my lips to the top of it. "Baby, as long as it's you and me, I'm willing to celebrate anything."

"No way. If you haven't celebrated your birthday in

years, we're doing it up right. It will be nice to focus on something happy, you know?"

The door to my rusty truck complains as I yank it open for her. "I guess I can't argue with that."

She climbs in, and I slam the door. When I get in, she's buckled and turns to me. "You have the most wonderful friends. I've never had that kind of love outside of my mother and father. I thought my friends in California were fine, but it's not the same."

I lean on the old bench seat of my pickup and pull her to me for a kiss. "Baby, I promise, you're the draw here, not me."

We settle in our seats. "You don't see it. They love you. Do you know how many times they've called you the little brother of the group?"

"That's because they want to take care of everyone. I'm older than Bella and Gracie." I roll my eyes. "I'm no one's little brother."

I pull out onto the two-lane highway that leads us back to the vineyard. Liyah keeps arguing how much the women of Whitetail want to play big sister to me. "But they only call you that in a loving way. They want the best for you. The best for us."

I start to reach over and take her hand, but my cell vibrates. I pull it out of my pocket as I drive. It's Reskill.

Bobby might've killed the line I had on the nav system in his car, but they never thought to check their burner phones. I've been monitoring them, but Don has been giving Bobby the cold shoulder—there was nothing to hear.

"What is it?"

I put it on speaker and set my phone on the bench seat between us. "I don't know. Don is calling Bobby this time, which is interesting. He hasn't given him the time of day in a week."

Bobby answers. "Now you want to talk."

"Motherfucker. You emptied the accounts," Don grits.

Well, this is the first interesting thing that's happened in days. I sure would like to know where those accounts are at.

A call comes through on my phone.

"It's Carson," Liyah says.

"Ignore it. I need to hear this."

"You drained the motherfucking accounts, asshole. What the hell are you doing?" Don demands.

"You wanted out. You said it yourself." Bobby is smug and cocky. "You're out."

Don explodes. "You took my share! I wanted to cool it until we got rid of Graves. I took more risks than you. Without me, there's no way you'd be able to do any of this shit. You took my motherfucking money!"

"Bella is calling me." Liyah puts her cell on speaker. "Bella, we're listening to—"

"I know," Bella clips, all business. "Liyah, minutes after you two left, Cole got word that Marat Kruglov transferred money."

I look at Liyah, and hers is the happiest expression I've seen in days. This is what we needed, but now we need to catch them.

"Bobby drained the accounts, Bella. Are you listening?" I ask.

"I am. We all are. You're driving so you can't see, but we located the accounts. They're in Belize. Cole is working on it from his side and is informing the FBI as we speak."

"Where are you going?" Don demands, his voice bursting through the old cab of my truck.

"What makes you think I'm going anywhere?" Bobby asks.

"You piece of shit," Don growls. "You're leaving, aren't you?"

"You're tracking me?" Bobby screams into the phone.

"What did you expect me to do?" This is beyond a lover's spat—worse than I expected.

"Fuck," I hiss. "Bella, do not tell me the FBI is going to sit on this. We need to get to them now. If Bobby leaves the country..."

As much as I want to see these two assholes charged and thrown in prison for the rest of time, the killer in me is intrigued. He can't hide forever. I'll find him and do what I've been trained to do.

"Cole is managing it," Bella assures us. "Bobby transferred just under seventy million from their shared account. He left Don high and dry."

I pick up my phone and flip through the screens as I drive to see where Bobby is. If there was any time I needed to be in the control room, it's now.

"If they get Don in an interrogation room by himself, he'll flip. I'd bet my freedom on it. Bobby stabbing him in the back is the best thing that could've happened to us. Don is pissed and broke." My eyes flit between the dark road and my phone, and I mutter to myself, "Where in the hell are you going, Cannon?"

I come to a stoplight and stare at the blip on the screen that's Bobby's burner phone.

Bella keeps the information coming. "Grady and

Asa just left, they're headed back to the control room. Crew and Jarvis are on their way to Bobby."

"You fucked up, buddy," Bobby seethes. "You crossed me. You might have the skills when it comes to a keyboard, but I'm the brains of this operation. Don't think for a second you can try to put a stop to my plans. You cut me off. I cut you out."

"Fuck you. I want my money," Don demands.

I look at the map on my phone.

I look at Liyah.

She reaches over and grips my thigh.

"Yeah?" Bobby lowers his voice. "Fuck you too. Because you're not getting it."

The feed goes dead.

Bella calls for me. "Ozzy?"

I put my hand to Liyah's face and look her in the eyes. "Love you, Princess."

Her brows pucker. "I love you too."

"I can't let him get away."

"Ozzy," Bella interrupts. "Let Crew and Jarvis handle it. The FBI has already been contacted. You cannot be seen."

Liyah places her hand over mine. "Don't let him get away. Make him pay for what he did to you."

I lean in to kiss her much quicker than I want.

When I let go of her lips, she proves she's as strong as she was the moment I met her. "Go. I want to be there when you take him down. It will be something I'll never forget."

"Fuck, yeah, it will."

"Dammit," Bella bites.

Instead of turning left, I turn right.

I'm ready to take my life back.

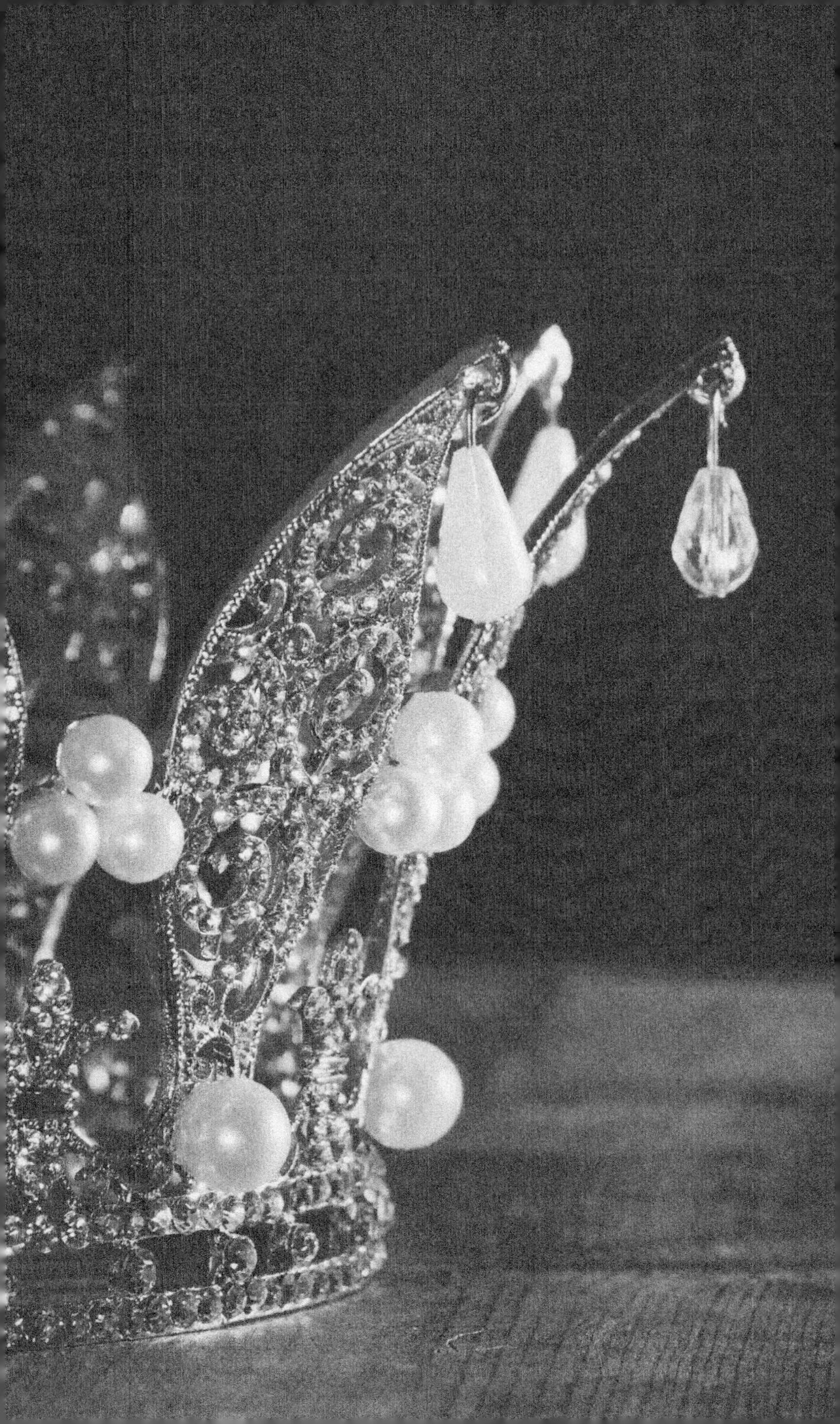

46

MAKE THEM PAY MANTRA

Liyah

I think back to the moment I left California to look for my mother. The need that drove me to make such a rash decision. I did it knowing I had no skills, no information, and no plan.

I had nothing other than my sheer desire to find her.

Ozzy has skills. He's proved it over and over again.

And Ozzy definitely has information. He's bursting with it.

But ask me if Ozzy has a plan. That answer would be...

I don't know.

His truck is old. The first time I saw it, Ozzy apologized, and said it wasn't fit for a royal.

I rolled my eyes.

He also explained how it was the first thing he bought when he started working for Crew, starting his life over as a dead man. That it reminded him of the truck his grandfather drove, and how it gave him a bit of his life back.

I immediately loved it.

This old, sky-blue pickup might scream sentimental on most days, but not today.

Old is the key word at the moment as we barrel down the highway. The engine complains, and I'm pretty sure Ozzy has the pedal to the metal in every literal sense of the word. We crossed the state line into Maryland fifteen minutes ago.

"Can you tell where he's going?"

Ozzy breaks all the rules when it comes to being on the phone while driving. He's flipped through screens, typed even more messages, all while talking to Bella, and answering my questions.

"He's heading north," he mutters, changing lanes and passing two more cars. "I have no idea, but he was far enough east, I might be able to cut him off. He's avoided the interstate."

I finally ask the one question I've evaded since I agreed that this man cannot get away. "Ozzy?"

He's too busy looking between his phone and the road to glance at me. "Yeah, baby?"

"Um, what are you going to do when you find him?"

"I'm going to stop him. Whatever I have to do, I'll do it. If he's not alive at the end of the night, that's not on me. He started this but I'm going to end it." He puts the phone to his ear. "Crew. Yeah, he's taking the back roads. Who the hell knows. He talks a big game, but my guess is he's skittish." He pauses. Whatever Crew is saying is meaningful—I see it bleed through Ozzy's features. He exhales what seems like a thousand pounds. "They're on their way? Good. Let me know when it's done."

He puts the phone down, and I'm upset he didn't put it on speaker for me to listen to. "What's done?"

"FBI is on their way to Don's house now. They're both flight risks. They've got probable cause to arrest without a warrant."

He turns right down a dark road flanked with forest on both sides. When he comes to a stop in the middle of the road, he throws it in park and switches off the tired engine, but leaves on his headlights. Then he reaches under his seat. My eyes widen when he produces a handgun. He does the whole thing—clicking and clacking, half-taking the gun apart, before snapping it back together. It's eerie and echoes in the quiet cab. Then he reaches behind the bench seat and produces a baseball bat.

He finally turns to me. "This is it, baby."

I look around the dark and deserted road. My feelings do not match his. I'm searching for my *make him pay* mantra I had just a bit ago, but it seems to have slithered away into the darkness. "I don't know..."

"Hey." He cups my cheek. "You'll be fine. There's no way on earth I'll let anything happen to you."

I shake my head. "I'm not worried about me. I'm worried about you."

He checks his phone again before pulling my face to his for a deep kiss. "No one is going to keep me from a future with you. Especially these assholes. Stay in the truck. If things get out of hand, hit the floor. Crew and Jarvis will be here soon. Carson said the FBI is on their way too."

He starts to climb out of the truck. "Wait! Where are you going?"

That's when headlights appear, coming at us from

over the hill where Ozzy parked right smack dab in the middle of the road. He climbs out of the cab, leaving me with the three little words my soul clings to.

"Love you, Princess."

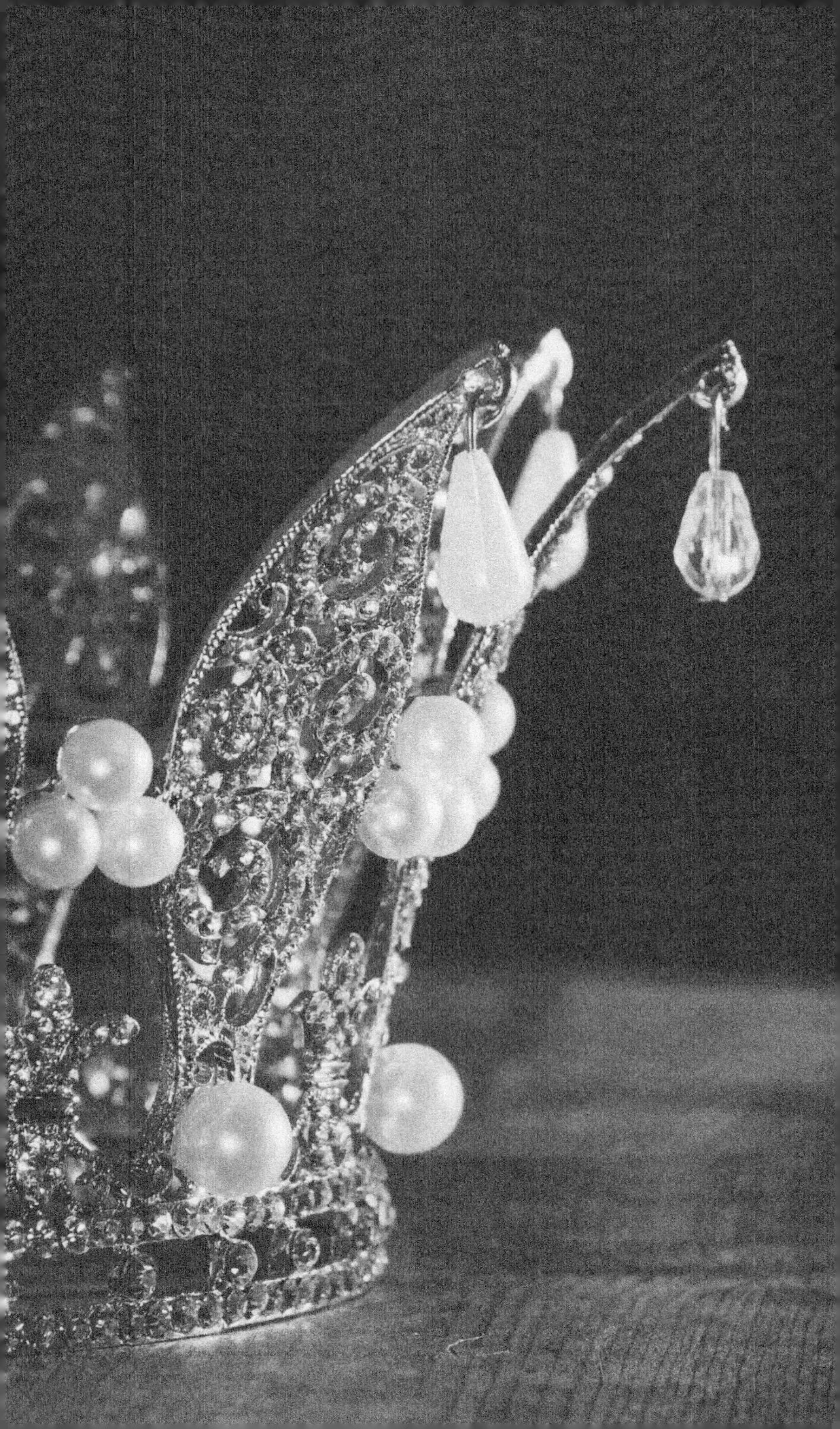

47

MANY LIVES

Ozzy

Headlights are at my back, lighting up the stretch of asphalt in front of me. I stand in the middle of the road, my back to the cab, where Liyah waits for me in the truck.

Waiting for me to finish this and get on with my fucking life. I can't believe just this morning I was willing to give up my shot at this.

I've dreamed of this for years.

The Mercedes comes to a screeching halt. I wish it weren't dark. I wish I could see the look in his fucking eyes when he sees it's me. That I found him in the middle of nowhere.

Just him and me.

The Mercedes, as dark as the night, is thrown immediately into reverse. There are ten yards between us when he starts to back up.

I don't hesitate.

I lift my Glock and two shots cut through the night.

A scream echoes from behind me, but I don't dare look back at Liyah. Bobby's front two tires might be blown out, but that doesn't stop him from trying to swing the car around on its rims.

I stalk forward and do the same to the rear driver's side.

Good luck getting anywhere on three rims and one tire, fuckwad.

"Get out of the car!" I stalk forward and put another shot through the grill.

Smoke hisses in the night air. The left headlight dies before the right one. It only takes a second for my eyes to adjust. Little does Bobby know, I'm used to working in the dark.

Since he fucked with my life, I've become a killer.

And I'll do it without a second thought.

Fuck, tonight, I look forward to it.

And when my eyes adjust, I see it. He lifts a hand, holding his own gun.

I don't flinch, but I do put a bullet straight through the windshield.

But I don't hit him. If I'd wanted to hit him, I would have. Putting a bullet through his head would be the easiest thing I've ever done.

He ducks, and I fire again. This bullet hits his roof.

"Fuck!" he yells.

I stalk toward the car, and before he can get his shit together, I pull my other arm back and aim for his window.

Glass shatters under my favorite bat before I drop it to the pavement at my feet.

Bobby is peppered with glass when he raises his gun again.

But I don't duck or shift.

Because he doesn't point his weapon at me. He turns it on himself.

No fucking way. There's no way I'm letting him off that easy.

I lurch through the broken window and point the gun away from both of us.

He pulls the trigger, but I have his wrist fisted in my hand. The bullet ricochets off the asphalt at my feet. Bending his arm back, I slam his hand on the side of the Merc until he drops the gun.

But I don't let go.

I put my boot to the side of his door and yank.

Bobby screams and writhes in pain as I pull him across broken glass and through the window, until he lands with a thud on the pavement.

My boot connects with his gun, and it disappears off the side of the road and into the dark forest.

"You leaving your family behind?" I demand, yanking him up by the collar and bring the butt of my gun to the side of his face. "You're an asshole on all levels."

"Don't utter a word about my family. You're the reason I have to do this. You're like the asshole with a million lives. Why can't you just fucking die for good!"

"Why me?" I ask, ignoring everything else. I have to know. However this night ends, I need finality on that.

"You really don't know, do you?" He sputters blood and tries to crawl away from me backward. "You were the best. Hell, they were fast-tracking you up the chain. You got all the best cases. That made you a perfect target. If they thought you could break into any foreign system, why wouldn't you do the same to steal? You were an easy fucking target, Oz."

My trigger finger is itchy again, and it doesn't feel like delivering warning shots. "You killed that family in WITSEC. Three kids. Innocent kids, you fucker! I was not going down for that. I wasn't going down for anything you did."

"I don't know how you did it." He proves he's not only ballsy, but stupid, too, because he climbs to his feet. No gun, no muscle, all ego—so stupid. "Who helped you? Your family is convinced you're dead. There's no way you could've done this on your own."

We're carrying out two separate conversations, because I keep pushing him. "You got Don to partner with you and do the dirty work because you don't have the fucking brains to pick apart the systems of the NSA on your own. You're the worst kind of human."

"You think this shit really matters?" He holds his arms out and goads me. "What are you going to do, Oz? Kill me out here in the middle of nowhere? Don knows about you. You'll have to come out to the world, and you'll still have nothing to prove your innocence. There's no fucking way. We made sure of it."

"That's where you're wrong. I've got it all. I know about your accounts in Belize. I've traced the transactions from Kruglov to you. And I have Don."

He pauses, and there's a tick in his clenched jaw. "You don't have Don."

"That's where you're wrong. Right this fucking minute, he's being taken into custody by the FBI. Do you know the sentence for treason against your country? Because I do. I have it fucking memorized. I thought I was going to serve it. The feds have the information they need, and I bet Don will be more than willing to cut a deal with them since you stole his blood money. My gut tells me he's not going to throw you under the bus but off the damn cliff."

Bobby does his best to look unaffected, but he's no actor. I've riled him. "I don't believe you."

"I don't give a shit what you believe. By my calculation, you have a very short time to live in your self-righteous world. Probably a few minutes. There's nothing I'm going to enjoy more than knowing you're rotting away in federal prison for the rest of your life."

His breaths come quicker in the cool, night air as his reality begins to sink in. His gaze darts around, as if he's going to find an escape.

I tip my head an inch. "Thought you were going to kill me. If I remember correctly, it was with your bare fucking hands. What happened to that?"

His stare jumps from me to the forest where his gun disappeared. His knuckles turn white.

"Look how the tables have turned. You went from cocky to desperate pretty damn fast."

"Motherfucker." The word barely escapes his lips when he moves.

He charges.

But Crew was right.

These guys sit in front of a computer all day. I know —that used to be me.

I lower my hand with the gun and grip him at the neck with my other.

He claws at my face.

I swing my arm around. The side of my Glock connects with his other temple.

"Fuck," he hisses, holding the side of his head, stumbling back. Blood seeps from the side of his face.

"With your bare hands, my ass. You needed Don to do your dirty work, and now you can't even finish me off. You can't do shit on your own, can you?"

That did it.

The fucker loses it and lunges for my bat.

If Crew taught me one thing, it's that if you lose control, you lose the upper hand. And having the upper hand is everything. There's no fucking way this guy is getting the upper hand with me ever again.

He grabs the bat, and I let him get close before I shift.

I duck when he swings and kick his feet out from under him. He's facedown on the pavement. I'm giving him another boot to the side when headlights fill the dark night from over the horizon.

I take my bat and move back to enjoy the image of him writhing at my feet, knowing his freedom is about to come to an end.

"You don't know how much I want to kill you," I spit. "Nothing would make me happier. And not a bullet through the head. I want to feel you die a slow, painful death under my fists. I want you to feel every bit of pain that family felt when you sold their souls on the black market. I want to hear you beg for me to kill you, because you can't take another second of it."

"Ozzy!" I look up and Liyah is climbing out of my truck. "They're here. I've been on the phone with Crew this whole time."

Shit, she needs to stay back.

Jarvis's car comes to a screeching halt next to the Mercedes. They're running to us.

"You okay?" Crew asks, but he doesn't sound concerned. He reaches in his back pocket and produces a zip tie as he fills me in. "Don is in custody. They secured an emergency warrant for his house—searching it now."

Bobby groans. I'm barely back two steps when Liyah collides with me. "That was amazing. I mean, I was scared to death until you dragged him out of the window, but after that, it was nothing but amazing."

I slide my gun into the back of my jeans.

She lifts up on her toes. "You're free, Ozzy. Free. You're no longer a dead man among the living."

"I'm sure there will be paperwork," Jarvis adds. "The FBI is raiding this guy's house as we speak. But your royal fiancée is right. Consider yourself a free man. Carson is all over it. Or, should I say, resuscitated and brought back from the dead."

Sirens ring, and my gut clenches. I'm not used to being around for anything official.

Liyah's fingers drag over my jaw. "We're going to Pennsylvania tomorrow. I can't wait."

I pull her to my chest and can't believe it's over.

How many lives can one man live?

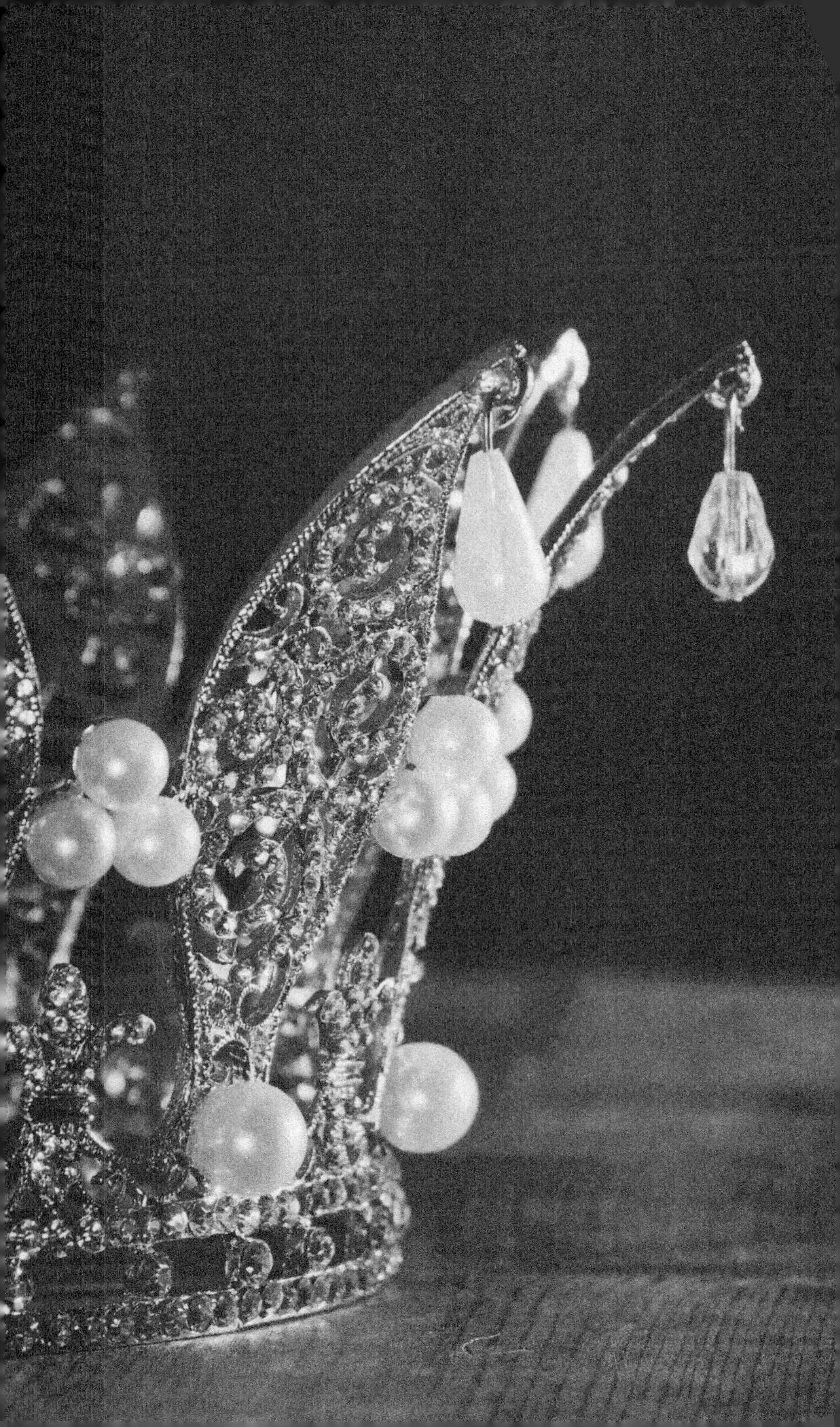

48

LIFE DAY

Liyah

My last happy memory with both my parents was when I was five.

They arrived home from a trip after having been gone for over a week. My father had many responsibilities as King. I had no idea then just how noble and authentic he was to his country and his people. Or how much care he took in serving them with his generous heart—not only Morocco, but Africa.

A five-year-old doesn't notice things like those. Especially not when it's all they know.

It was all I knew.

There was a reason my mother fell hard and fast for him.

But no matter how many ways he was pulled, or how much attention his position required of him, when he was home, I was his priority.

That following week was no different or remarkable.

It was the normal, loving family time I was used to my entire life.

Then a nagging cough turned into the worst diagnosis.

And that's when my life changed. Life changed for all of us. And it never returned to normal.

Normal.

That word is basic and rudimentary. It's simple, run-of-the-mill, and even boring. The measure of everything is based off of the average mean ... which is *normal*.

After that week, my family never had normal again.

I don't know many people whose life goal is to just be normal.

But the man I love, the man I plan to spend the rest of my life with ... it's all he wants.

And he's about to get his dream.

The last time I was this nervous was when I talked my way into an empty sleeper cabin on a train and the doorknob turned.

"Breathe, Liyah." Bella puts an arm around my shoulders and pulls me to her side. "It's going to be okay."

I don't take my eyes off Ozzy as he navigates the last two steps to the front door of his childhood home. We stand by the car parked down the drive. It's early, we hardly got a wink of sleep. The sunrise frames the quaint farmhouse from behind, and I force myself to memorize this moment. I want to pull out my phone and record it, but that feels like an invasion of their privacy.

Today is Ozzy's birthday. He's thirty-two. But I think I'll always refer to today as his Life Day.

Today is the day Austin Oswald Graves, III gets his life back.

Carson worked through the night to make sure the case on Bobby and Don is official and steadfast. He also prepared Ozzy for what to expect from the government. Faking your own death isn't illegal per se, but it doesn't come without its issues. There's no rulebook on how to bring a human back to life who was officially dead.

Bella and Carson came to Pennsylvania with us. It will only be a matter of time before the media descends upon my fiancé and the Graves family. Ozzy didn't want them to find out in any other way than him.

My love is about to get the normal he craves.

I just hope he doesn't give his parents a heart attack in the process.

Carson flanks my other side and mutters, "So happy for Oz. This will be something to see."

We don't utter another word. This moment is sacred.

Ozzy reaches for the doorbell.

Tears sting my eyes, and once again, the universe pauses.

The moment the door opens, a shrill yell fills the crisp, morning air.

Nettie screams and reaches for the door and turns the color of a ghost. But then again, she's looking at one.

Ozzy steps forward. I hear the low timbre of his voice, but can't make out his words. A man I only recognize from pictures Ozzy has shared, appears next to Nettie. He grips his wife.

Confusion slowly disintegrates as the couple take in their oldest son—the child they buried.

Or, thought they did.

My eyes swell as Nettie warily puts her hands on her

son's face. My tears are nothing compared to hers when she collapses into Ozzy's arms. His father joins them.

Carson sniffs and clears his throat. "Yeah, I'm glad I'm here for this."

Bella gives me a squeeze and her voice is thick. "Go to him, love."

I shake my head. "No. They need time."

"Trust me, he needs you."

"Go," Carson agrees. "He pushed boundaries for this. Bella's right, he needs you. Dammit, I'm all kinds of emotional today."

Bella doesn't wait for me to move on my own. She gives me a little shove, and I trip on my first two steps over the gravel until I find my footing.

Nettie's eyes open, and she freezes when her gaze meets mine. Ozzy turns. There's nothing on his face but pure joy and relief.

He holds out a hand for me.

As much as my heart breaks for my own mother, it's bursting for Ozzy.

He got his family back. And they have him.

Ozzy pulls me straight into his arms and turns us to them. "Princess, meet my parents." He presses his lips to my forehead, and I feel a smile there. "Officially."

Ozzy

"*THE NATIONAL SECURITY AGENCY had the tables turned on them in the last twenty-four hours, and they're reeling in the aftershock. High level security clearance employees Donald Demaree and Robert Cannon have been charged with theft of government materials and data. Demaree and Cannon are also facing multiple counts of conspiracy, aiding and abetting, and accessory to commit murder, related to the heinous deaths of a family of five, that have since been dubbed the WITSEC Murders. The NSA stolen data was sold to a Russian entity who is thought to have ties to top levels of the Russian government. Treason charges are not out of the question."*

Liyah is pressed to my side, glued to me from head to toe, as I finger the ends of her hair in a way that's become a habit.

Today has been surreal, but we're back in the bungalow, just her and me, like we've been since the beginning. It doesn't matter where we are, when we're like this, the world is balanced.

As balanced as it can be as I stare at the mugs of the assholes I only ever want to see when I testify against them in federal court, and again, when they're charged and thrown in a federal penitentiary for the rest of their miserable lives.

Liyah drags her leg over my thigh, entwining herself with me in every way possible as the national news correspondent continues reporting, but all I see is me, getting out of a CIA-escorted Suburban. Carson and my new attorney, who's the best in the District, because I'm done fucking around when it comes to the government, are at my side.

I was questioned for hours this afternoon and didn't get back to Whitetail until well after dinner.

"The NSA has not been immune to controversy over the years. Demaree and Cannon's case is directly tied to another NSA employee who was the main suspect in the WITSEC murders. Austin Oswald Graves, III was seen coming and

going from the FBI's Washington DC District Office today. Graves was pronounced dead years ago in an explosion from a single-car crash. Graves' death, at the time, was thought to be suicide since he was facing murder and treason charges. In a twist that has left the National Security Agency reeling, Graves is very much alive. It's rumored that he had a hand in clearing his own name. The CIA and FBI have taken over the case, and, given the magnitude of the security breach, the NSA is now being scrutinized from the top down. Sources say the WITSEC murders only scratch the surface compared to damage done by Demaree and Cannon over the years. This is an ongoing investigation, one we'll continue to follow closely."

I grab the remote and shut it down. That was hardly a blip of the real story. The NSA knows they fucked up. There are more internal investigations on them right now than they can keep track of. I gave the FBI ten percent of what I know, the portion I'm supposed to know legally. I'm officially Officer Cole Carson's CIA asset, leading him down the rabbit hole that blew up the lives of Don and Bobby.

No one knows I work for Crew Vega. No one knows I have access to a multi-million-dollar satellite system and have back-doored my way into more networks than Don and Bobby probably did the entire time they were fucking over our country.

Liyah's hand slides up my chest and lands on my jaw. "Are you okay?"

I look down at the woman who's been by my side other than during my interrogation with the FBI. That interrogation ended up being an info dump of me proving I didn't do what I was accused of. Carson filled in the dots.

Crew offered Carson a job years ago after Bella cleared her name. Little did I know that him staying at the CIA would help save my ass.

I roll to my side and pull Liyah into me. "I'm better than okay. I should ask the same thing about you. It's one thing to be tied to me privately, but now you're publicly engaged to a prior NSA employee who faked his death to avoid prison. You okay with that?"

"I'm more than okay. You forget that attention doesn't bother me. I'm accustomed to living my life and ignoring the world." She tucks her face into my neck, and I slide my hand over her ass to hold her to me. "I had a whole birthday celebration planned for you, but today was better than anything I could dream up. I'll never be able to top today."

I think about the best part of the day, showing up at my parents' house very much alive and breathing. Once my mom and dad got over the shock, it was better than I ever imagined, and it had everything to do with my royal fiancée at my side. "I told you I don't celebrate birthdays."

"You can forget about that." She yawns. "From now on, we're celebrating everything. Life is too precious not to. Leave that to me."

"It's been a long day, followed by a long night. I'm looking forward to a time when we aren't functioning on little-to-no sleep." I dip my hand in her hair and pull her lips to mine.

It hasn't been a week since she learned that she lost her mom. It doesn't matter how much my drama has been at the forefront the last twenty-four hours or how happy she might be for me, I know that loss is killing her inside. Being away from her today was hard.

Hell, who am I kidding? It would be hard without the loss of her mom. "How are you?"

She sighs. "It was a good day. The best day. I don't want to think about anything else."

"Okay, baby. Go to sleep. Tomorrow we'll work on being normal. It's going to take some getting used to."

"You being all over the international news because of the NSA is one thing. I'm sorry your picture is plastered all over social media and the entertainment news, as well. That's on me."

What I don't tell her is my days traveling the world for Crew as a killer are over. It would've been the case had I never hooked up with a princess and social media icon with millions of followers. My mug plastered all over the world as the dead man who came back to life is bad enough. I had that phone call with Crew on my way back from my meeting with the FBI. There's no way I can do that job and not be recognized. From now on, Reskill is my sole responsibility.

I'm happy to have my life back—my family, freedom, and normalcy. But I can't lie, I've gotten used to the privacy, and I like it. I wouldn't go back to a government job if they kissed my ass and offered me a fortune.

The story broke when we were in Pennsylvania this morning. It took about five minutes for the press to descend on my parents' farm. There are videos and pictures of Liyah and me walking from the house to the car, and when I saw them later, there's no question that we're together.

There are two types of media in this world. The ones that are interested in my shit and the ones interested in Liyah's.

Today, our stories collided and blew up. I'm not sure

which is bigger at this point—that I'm not dead or that I'm engaged to the elusive Moroccan Princess who effectively gave the King her middle finger on a world stage.

I'm getting calls from every media outlet for interviews, and Liyah is getting calls from photographers who are begging to shoot our wedding.

We're not taking anyone's calls at this point.

I pull the covers up and settle us onto the pillows. "I'm worried about you. The world can wait for everything else. If you want to get married tomorrow or next year, I'm good. Either way, life will be different, but as long as we end the day right here, I promise, everything will be okay."

She tips her face to mine. "I love you."

When I put my lips to hers, I feel settled for the first time in so long, I don't remember my soul ever being this content. Now I need Liyah to get there, as much as she can after losing her mom. "Love you, too, Princess."

For the first time since we met, Liyah and I close our eyes without wondering what will hit us tomorrow.

There's only one dangling thread out there in the universe that needs to be taken care of, but it can wait.

He can wait.

I'll take care of the King in my own way when the time is right—for what he tried to do to Liyah, and for what he did to her mom. But that can't happen while we're in the world spotlight.

The King and his asshole friend will pay. And I'll make sure their punishment fits the crime.

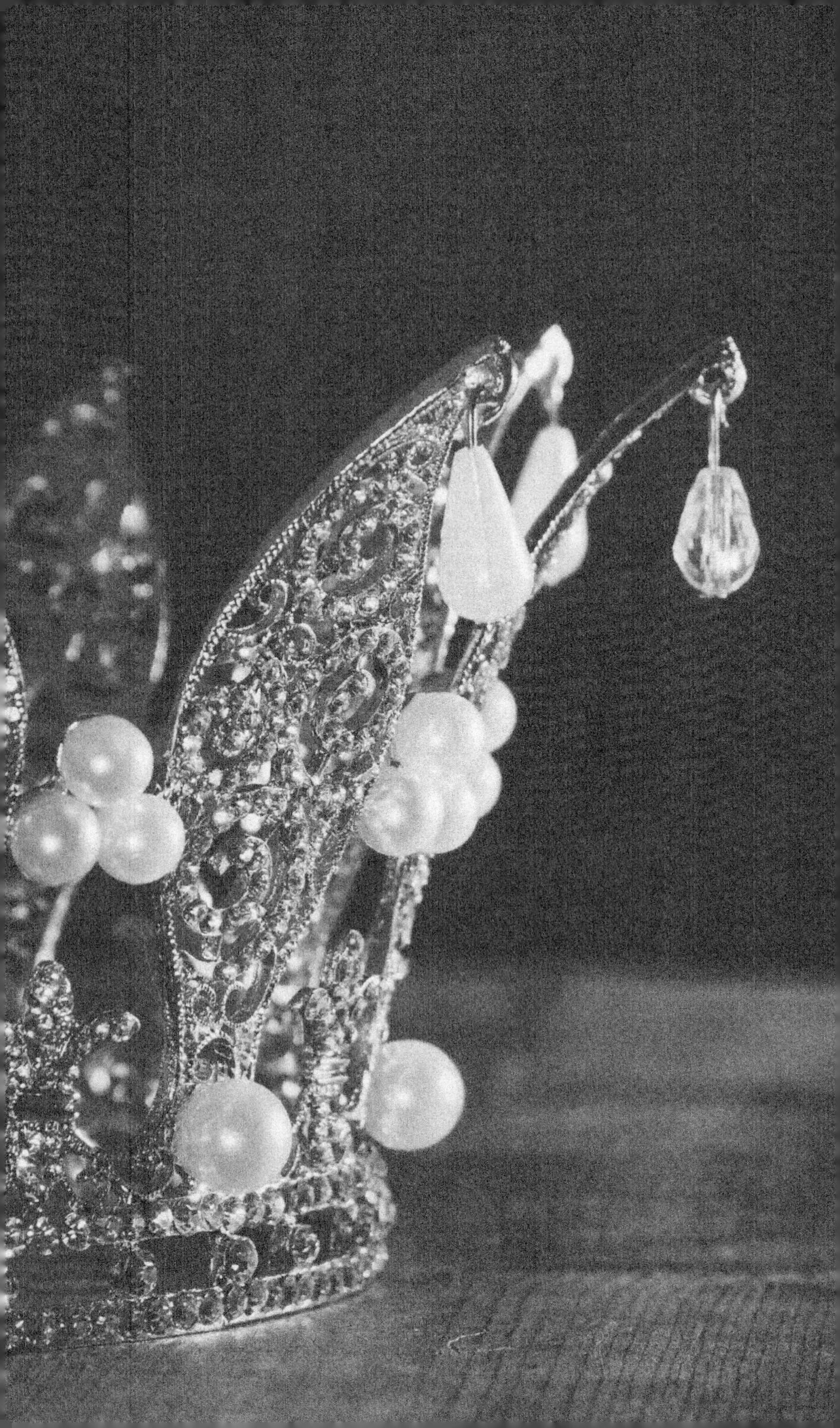

49

BIG AND BRIGHT AND FUCKING BEAUTIFUL

Ozzy
Two months later

"Baby, it's freezing. Come inside."

Liyah is wrapped in a blanket, sitting on the porch of the bungalow. Every time I cross the threshold to this place we've made a home, the chimes greet me. And the longer they're there, the less it feels like a ghost whispering from my past.

Maybe it's more that I feel less like a ghost.

Resuscitating yourself from death isn't the easiest of tasks since the government is a pain in the ass. I'm still knee-deep in paperwork, and there's no end in sight.

I started working with a realtor, but I can't get Liyah excited about a house. We've looked at over thirty and almost as many properties to build on.

I know she's used to a palace or a condo overlooking the Pacific, but every time we tour a property, she remains quiet. She states she loves it, that it will be perfect. She says she just wants me to be happy, so if I like it, it's good with her.

I've never been engaged, married, or bought a house before, let alone with the intent to live there forever with the woman I plan to spend the rest of my life with, but that sure isn't what I expected from the experience.

I put the realtor on hold and stopped asking Liyah about a wedding date. If she needs time, she'll get all she needs. She carries guilt for her mom's death. We talk about it daily.

There were unofficial memorials all over Morocco in the weeks following the news of Luciana Zahir. Liyah wasn't kidding when she said the people of her home country loved her parents. I keep tabs on the King daily. He not only didn't memorialize Luciana officially, but privately he was fucking angry by the outcry. At least he's given up on the notion he can auction Liyah off to the highest bidder. One less thing to piss me off.

I don't like guilt weighing heavy on the woman I love. Of all the problems I can fix, that one has eluded me.

Addy has taken to Liyah like an older sister, and Liyah has embraced her. While I manage Reskill for Crew, Liyah has immersed herself at Whitetail. She's not officially an employee, though. Addy offered her a job. Liyah refused but has worked in every area of the winery. So far, Liyah's followers know she's in Virginia, but not where. We've managed to live out of the public eye as much as possible and still live our lives.

Privacy and freedom...

A balanced combination we're embracing.

The sun set hours ago, and we're shrouded in the dark forest, lit only by the Christmas lights lining the bungalow. When Liyah mentioned how much she loved Christmas because of her mom, I turned into someone I do not recognize. The place looks like Santa threw up everywhere, but after we went shopping and lit the place up like the North Pole, she sported the most genuine smile I've seen on her since before we found out about Luciana—with the exception of meeting my parents. I may never take them down, since it seems we'll be here for a while.

"What are you doing out here?" I slide a hand into her hair and tip her head back to kiss her. When she looks up at me, her dark eyes are glassy.

She swipes a tear from her cheek. "I know why she did it. I mean, I knew, but now I know without a doubt."

I round the porch swing and squeeze in next to her. It's not hard to pull her to my side because the thing is so small. I put my finger to her chin and tilt her face to me. "Why who did what? And why is it making you cry?"

Her tears come quicker, and she puts a hand to my jaw. "My mother. She did everything she could to protect me. She fled because she knew if she remained, I'd do anything I could to get to her. She died trying to save me from a loveless life."

I pull her in tighter to keep her warm. "I know, Princess. We both know this."

She shakes her head. "But I didn't realize how much she loved me. I wonder about how she died. If she was hurt, if she suffered. But I know she'd die a hundred deaths, no matter how violent or painful, to keep me safe. That's how much she loved me."

I have no clue where she's going with this, so I trace

her bottom lip with my index finger and lower my voice. "I have no doubt."

"And now I have your family."

"You'll always have them. They love you, but how could they not?" Reuniting with my parents and brothers is something I never thought would happen. They haven't wasted time getting to know Liyah. To say they're obsessed with my Princess is an understatement. "Baby, it's cold. Let's go in—"

She puts a finger to my lips to shut me up. "Ozzy?"

I frown.

"I'm pregnant."

I pull her hand away from my face. "You're what?"

She nods. "I know. I'm surprised. Even though I'm not sure why, what with all the unprotected sex."

"You're pregnant." My insides tighten and tense and do a fucking backflip. After one conversation, we decided life is too short. We threw away the condoms and never looked back.

She nods and sinks into me. "I took a test this afternoon."

My frown deepens. "You've known since this afternoon and didn't tell me?"

She shows how little remorse she has, because her smile is as big as my frown. "I needed a minute to process it. I understand now. I understand why my mother did what she did. Why she took such risks. And how she did it so selflessly. Ozzy." She stands and shifts to climb on my lap. "We're going to have a baby."

I put my hand to her face and bring her lips to mine. Her tears, mixed with pure happiness, are sweet on my tongue. I thought I was grateful before for my freedom in the world, but it's nothing compared to now. This overwhelming need to shout out to the world that she's mine and carrying my child is unparalleled.

I stand with her in my arms and she wraps hers around my neck. "What are you doing?"

"It's freezing, and you're pregnant."

She has the nerve to laugh at me. "I'm not cold. Probably because I am pregnant."

I take her straight to the bedroom and have her undressed in under a minute. I rip off my hoodie and free myself. "Baby, I'm not sure you understand what this means to me."

She places a hand over her bare, flat stomach, and lowers her voice. "I know what it means to me, and I've only had hours to process it. Imagine a lifetime? I'll do anything to protect our child. Just like my mother did for me."

I lean on a forearm over her head and fill her with two fingers. She's already wet. "You're a dream I never thought possible. You've given me everything, Princess. Every damn thing in the world I never thought I'd get."

Her fingers dip in my hair. "I never knew I could love anyone like this. You and our baby. I'm overwhelmed."

I kiss her at the same time I slide inside, a place that's been a haven for me since I met her, but is now so much more.

Her eyes fall to half-mast, and her gaze connects with mine—with my soul—just like it does every time we're like this, from the first time I made her mine.

I reach between us and find her clit as I slide in and out. I circle her faster and thrust harder. "Feels like I've waited lifetimes for you. As long as we're right here, I don't give a shit where we live or when we get married. This is all that matters."

"Yes." She moans on an exhale. I know she's close.

I can't wait another moment. I really move. Her nails bite into the skin behind my neck, and all I can see is our future. Big and bright and fucking beautiful.

Her pussy spasms around my cock, and her body tenses under me. I slide an arm under the small of her back and angle my hips.

I'll never get enough of her.

My balls are about to explode when I come.

I don't dare give her any of my weight, and roll to my side, taking her with me, tucked to my chest. I think back to the first time I ever had her flush to my body, the moment she took a chance on me as I jumped out of a train window into the black of night. She had no idea I was a dead man, and I had no clue she was royalty.

We were just us.

And now we're three.

We stay like this for what seems like forever, my fingers roam her body, from her ass to her hair, over and over and over. I'm about to ask her what we do next. Doctor, vitamins.

I don't know ... is she hungry?

She must've read my mind. "I'm ready—a wedding, a house. I'm sorry I was paralyzed before."

I press my lips to hers. "Don't ever apologize, baby. Never be sorry, not with me."

Her eyes gloss over. "We're going to be parents."

My lips tip. "Hell, yeah we are. We're going to be fucking great parents."

"I want to get married soon. And I want it to be small. Your family and our friends here. That's it."

I roll to my back and pull her on top of me. "As soon as we can plan it, Princess. I can't wait to marry you."

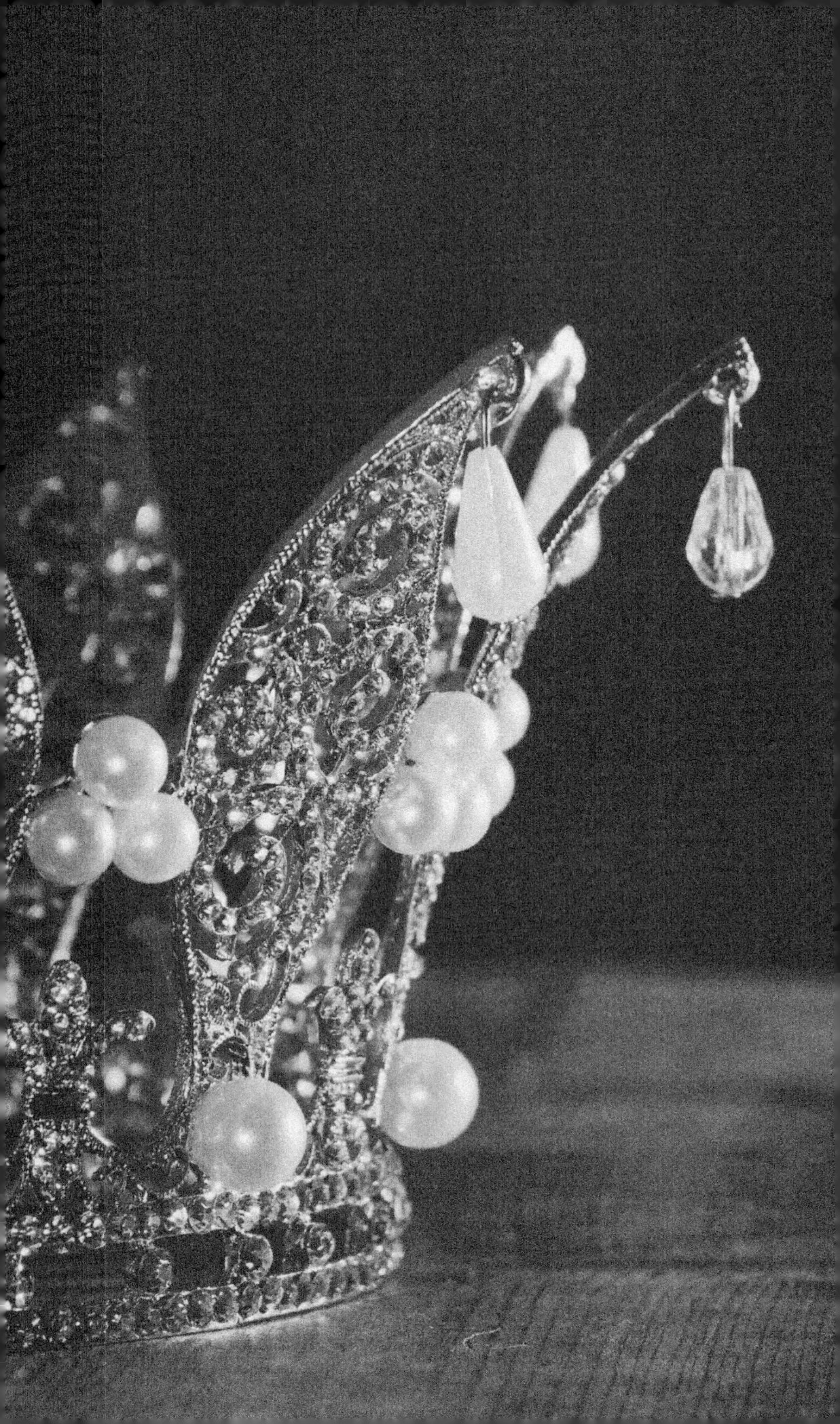

50

RESULTS

Ozzy
Three weeks later

I read the results.
    Then I read them again.
    I didn't believe it. Not once. I ignored the messages I got through my attorney until I couldn't ignore them any longer. I finally took the call, and I still didn't believe it.

I said it was bullshit. Millions follow Liyah on social media. Who knows how many more know of her in Africa and Europe alone.

She is a real-life princess. There aren't many of those. She gets attention that isn't good on a daily basis.

The press isn't the only reason I've done everything I can to maintain our privacy. The world knows my bride-to-be much differently than I do. They see a face, a body, skin.

Lots of skin.

I told Liyah if she wants to continue modeling, she should. She can do anything she wants. But I'll do background checks on everyone she works with, and she'll never be anywhere without me or someone I trust with my own life. Because hers is way more important than mine.

She said she's done modeling. Especially with the baby on the way. She can always go back to it later if she wants.

"Are you satisfied?"

I exhale and lean back to stare across the table. "I hope you understand my position. There's nothing I won't do to protect her. After the last few months, this…" I look down at the results, "is unbelievable."

"I know. But I'm not sorry."

I pull a hand down my face and try to figure out how I'm going to make this right. "No, I'd never expect you to be."

"I want to see her."

"I know. We're getting married tomorrow."

"That's why I'm here. And I know she's pregnant. That hasn't been made public."

"No, it hasn't." My mind is spinning, but as usual, my thoughts are centered on Liyah and our child. I hold the paper up. "So, you'll understand my caution with this."

"And I hope you'll understand my patience is thinning."

I nod, because I do get that. "Give me an hour. I need to manage this. This will change everything."

"I can't lie, I hope it does."

I pull in a breath and stand. "Stay here with Bella. I'll call. I won't be longer than an hour."

"I've waited this long. I can wait an hour, but that's it."

Un-fucking-believable.

There are no other words.

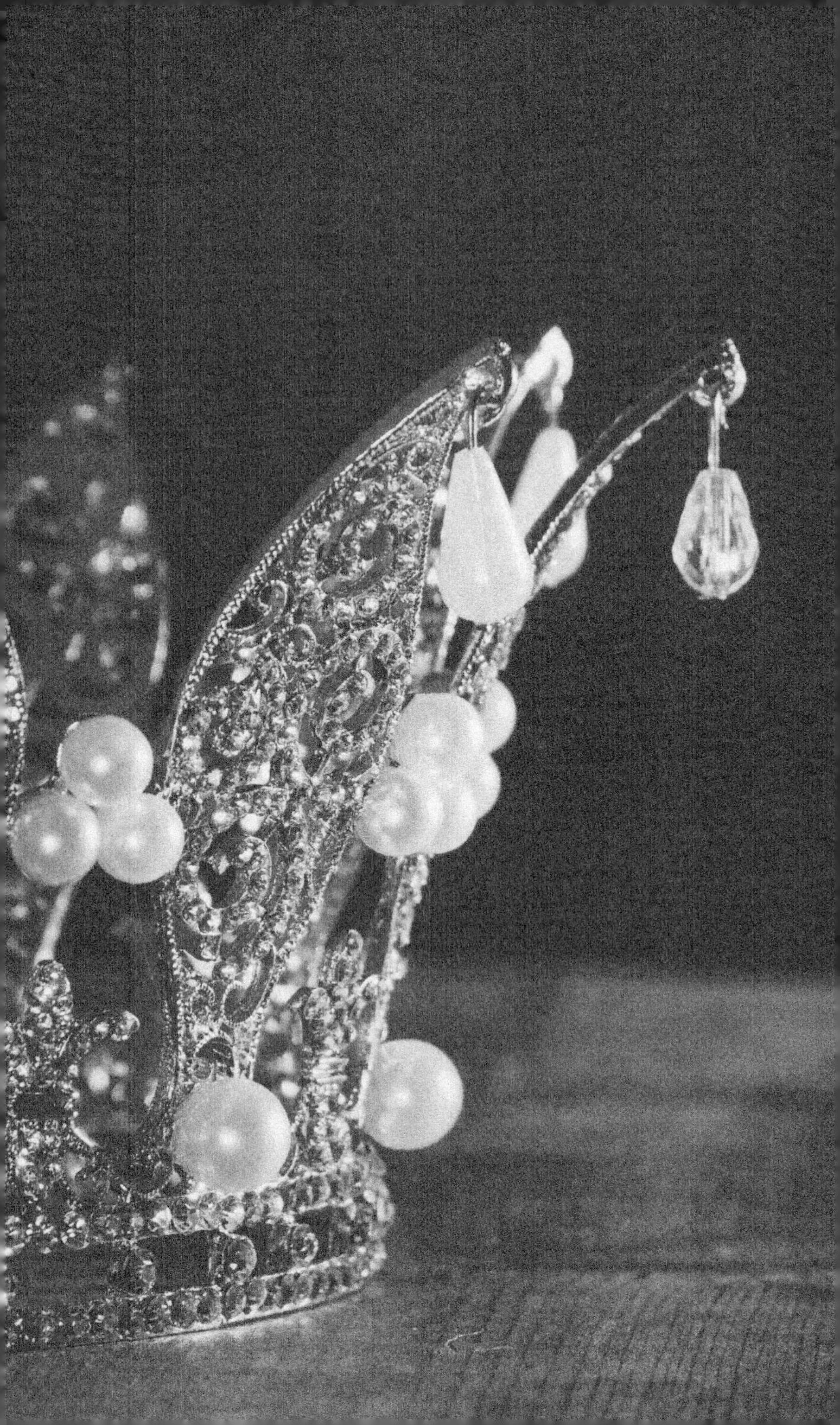

51

SOUL WRENCHING

Liyah

Ozzy puts the Porsche Cayenne in park. It still has the temporary tags on it. I've only had it a few days, but it's nice to be able to come and go as I like again.

The last three weeks have been a whirlwind. I never thought there would be this much to do for a wedding as small as ours.

Christmas was last week, and there's a fresh blanket of snow on the ground. As intriguing as a spring wedding sounded, once I decided I was ready, waiting even three weeks to become Ozzy's wife was painful.

We have a house under contract. Or, I should say, we have a dilapidated cabin on thirty acres under contract. The barn is nicer than the house. But the property has a creek running through it, it's fifteen minutes from Whitetail, and smack dab between the Carsons and the Jarvises. It's a property we looked at twice while I was too deep in mourning to process anything.

Not that the soul-wrenching pain will ever end. It never will.

We close on the property next week. The little cabin will be replaced with something big enough to fill with children and love, but not too big that we'll be lost in it. Being forced into proximity with Ozzy is something I have no desire to change.

But tomorrow we're getting married. It won't look anything like a royal wedding—not what my parents had, and not what I grew up thinking I'd experience someday because it was my right as the daughter of a king.

It will be better. So much better.

Since it's already safe and protected beyond measure, we will be married at Whitetail in an evening ceremony. Addy shut down the tasting room days ago to prepare.

I've never seen anything like it. The building has been transformed, and no expense has been spared.

Ozzy told me to make it what I wanted, and that's just what I've done.

I might not be getting married in a palace, but my father made sure I'd have fortunes to pass down for generations. My account balance doesn't start with an M; it starts with a B. To say that no expense has been spared is an understatement.

It's more beautiful than a dream.

I was meeting with the caterer when my hero came bursting through the door of the bungalow that we've made our home. He demanded that Addy take over, because he needed my full attention.

That it couldn't wait.

Not one minute.

In all the time I've known him, I've never seen him like this, and I've experienced a wide range of Ozzy's emotions after all we've been through. I've never seen him this agitated.

"You're making me nervous. What's wrong?"

He turns to me and takes my hand in both of his. The same one he put a ring on in Paris that hasn't budged since. "This isn't going to make sense, but I'm going to ask you to forgive me before we walk in there. No. I beg you to forgive me."

My eyes widen, and I try to pull my hand away, but he holds tight. "Forgive you for what?"

He shakes his head. "Baby, nothing should surprise me at this point. After everything we've been through, I had every reason to do what I did. There have been too many people who wanted to hurt you and me. My trust in general is thin at best."

Panic rises inside me. "Ozzy—"

But he doesn't waste another second. He's out of my new car, stalks around the front, and has my door open in no time. He holds a hand out. "Let's go."

I don't move. "You're scaring me."

He reaches in and gives me a tug. "I know, but trust me, the sooner we do this, the better."

We walk up the snow-shoveled drive to Carson and Bella's front door, but stop there. He turns me to him and frames my face in his hands. "I love you, Princess. This is going to be a shock, but I'm right here. I'll always be here to catch you."

Confusion courses through me, but I have no time to ask, demand, or scream at him for being elusive. He reaches for the handle and pushes the door open without another word.

Like every other moment since we met when we're this close, his touch never leaves me.

I thought I needed him in the past. His support, protection, love.

But I was wrong.

It's nothing compared to this moment.

Ozzy

I SLIDE my arm around her and splay my hand over our child, pulling her back to my front. Just like I thought, her knees buckle the moment she sees what I knew was a hoax, bait, or the most horrid prank one human could play on another.

Because people are shit, and I'll stand by that until the day I really die.

But today proves there are modern-day miracles. Experiencing this once was a wonder, but twice?

And to be on the receiving end?

Like I said, un-fucking-believable.

I didn't believe Bella when she called me two days ago, informing me the old priest found her source in Spain. The same one who questioned him months ago. The same priest who has badgered my attorney incessantly. Priests don't normally set up meetings with the dark underworld in which Bella Carson is tightly engrained or spam DC attorneys with more calls than a car insurance robot. Especially when that priest refused to speak to anyone but me.

And since I'm getting married tomorrow, and I don't trust anyone, a quick trip to Spain was not in the cards when his claims were so ridiculous, that all I could imagine was the damn dynasty was out to hurt Liyah.

Again.

I wasn't only put on this earth to protect her physically, but I'll lay down my life to guard her heart and her soul. She's been through too much to be toyed with.

But Bella cleared her schedule and insisted on making the trip. She's that nosey. And when they returned together, I was the asshole who demanded a DNA test.

You'd think after what I went through, I'd believe in the possibility of a miracle. But nothing will hurt Liyah ever again. I hope she'll forgive me. Hell, I hope, in time, my future mother-in-law will forgive me.

Because she's supposed to be dead.

But the former Princess of Morocco outsmarted the big, bad King, the dynasty, and all of Europe and Africa. With the help of an elderly priest, she faked her death. She knew it was the only way to protect her daughter and live her life out from under the confines of a prisoned palace.

And just like I thought, the moment my Princess set her gaze on her living and breathing mother, I had to support her weight.

Liyah's gasp falls somewhere between a yelp and a scream.

Tears stain Luciana's cheeks, and she holds her arms out.

Then I hand over my Princess to her mother and wonder if this is how Liyah felt when she stood back and watched me greet my parents.

Overcome.

Whole.

Elated.

Tears flow as they reunite in a way they will remember forever.

I say this to myself daily, but I'll never take life for granted. There were days I thought my soul would never be the same. But I'd happily relive it all because it brought me to her.

Liyah, my Princess, my lover. My child and the future children we get to raise. With our families intact and with us. Not to mention our army of friends.

My soul will never be the same.

I'm no longer dead. Liyah no longer seeks a ghost.

The Princess and the dead man, two lost souls no longer haunted by their pasts or fighting for their futures, but bound to one another with nothing but bliss on the horizon.

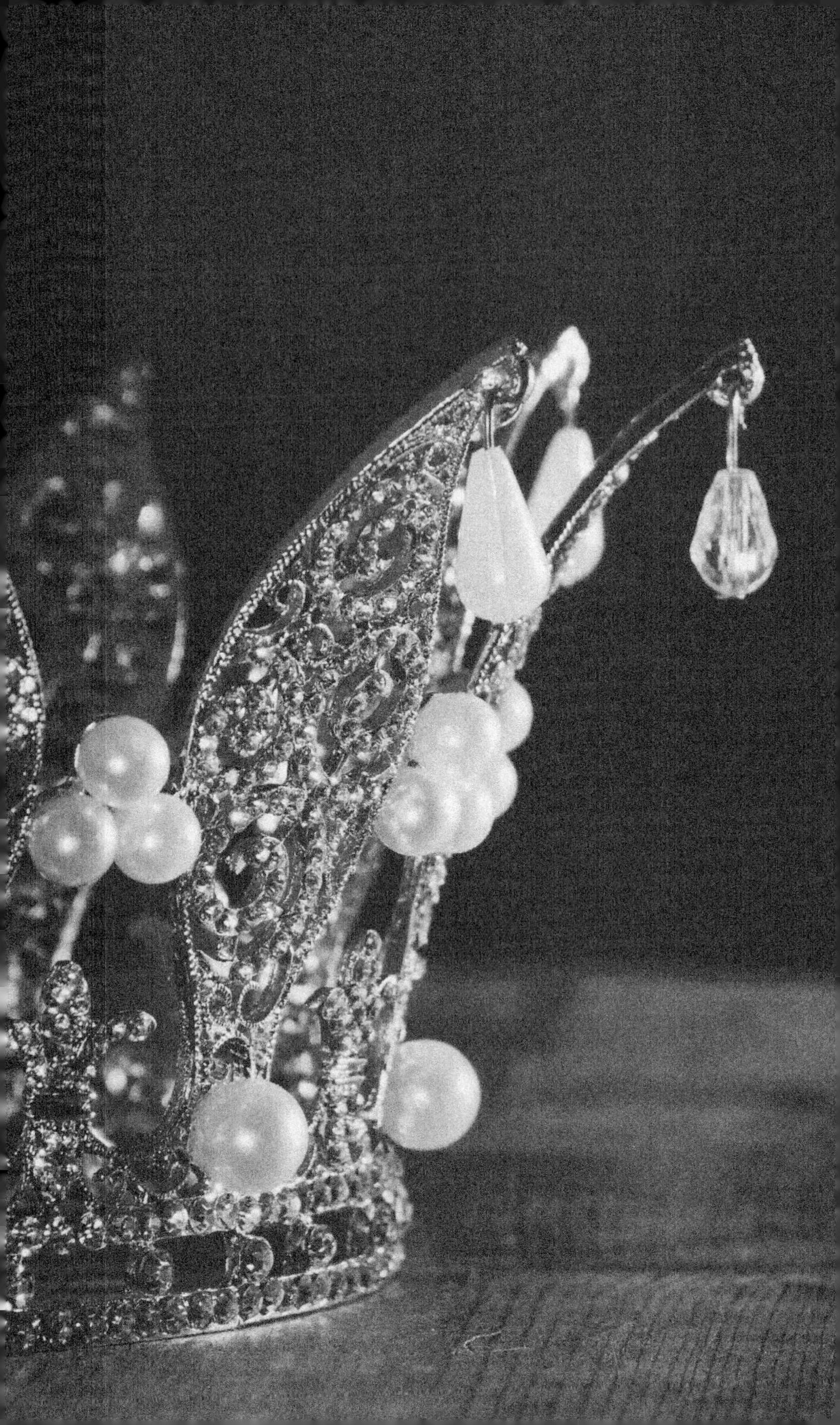

EPILOGUE

Liyah
Eight months later

I set my phone on the hospital table and return my attention to the scene in real life—my husband holding our daughter.

This is a memory I'll never forget. I've already videoed them endlessly, taken two million pictures, but posted only one to share with the world. It was only her tiny hand wrapped around Ozzy's finger.

That's all the world will ever get of our daughter.

I thought Ozzy was protective of me, but now that Ana is here, nothing holds a candle to how this child will be shielded. We agreed that, after today, her picture would never be shared again. Ozzy wasn't happy about even one picture, but he relented when I told him why it was important to me.

The precious image of her hand wrapped around Ozzy's finger is my last big, fat fuck you to my uncle and the President.

I don't give them much thought anymore. It took a while, but I realized the more mind space I gave them, the more control they had over me. But today, the best day of my life, I told Ozzy I wanted them to see how happy I am. The thought of what my life could have looked like had I not barged into Ozzy's cabin that fateful night shakes me to the core.

I wouldn't have Ozzy.

And I wouldn't have Ana.

Luciana Annette Graves.

Named after her grandmothers, but she'll go by Ana.

Our daughter's namesakes just left, along with Ozzy's entire family and all our friends who might as well be blood.

Family.

Ana will be loved beyond measure—grandparents, aunts, uncles, and cousins galore. Our family at Whitetail and Reskill round out our lives to perfection.

We don't need anything else and will stay nestled in our little corner of the world for the rest of time.

To the world, my mother is still dead. Ozzy and Carson said they could make her safe if she wanted to enter reality again, but it was her choice.

Because what she went through was...

Horrific.

Ozzy and I were married the day after she rocked my world, the same way Ozzy rocked his family's.

It wasn't until the following weeks that I finally coaxed the true story of what my mother endured—how she escaped.

Her story was not as clear as it first appeared. I consider it a miracle she's here today to meet her first grandchild. Just like Ozzy being here to make his family bigger.

Modern miracles.

"What are you thinking, Princess?"

My husband reclines in the beastly hospital chair looking like a dream. Had I not just given birth, I'd probably jump his bones. He's naked from the waist up and so is Ana besides her tiny diaper. They're bonding, skin-to-skin, covered only by a pink baby blanket. Though, I'm not sure anything could bring Ozzy closer to our child. He spent countless hours chatting with her while she was in my tummy. It's no wonder she prefers him already.

"I'm thinking about how lucky we are."

"You mean, you're lucky you picked my cabin. Beyond that, it has nothing to do with luck. We blazed our own trail, baby. You give too much credit to chance."

I rest my head on my pillow and do everything I can to keep my eyes open. Ana's delivery was not quick. Ozzy might be used to too little sleep from back in the day, but not me. I'm exhausted.

He looks up from Ana, who looks much smaller on his wide chest than her seven pounds, nine ounces. "Baby, go to sleep. I'll wake you when she's hungry."

"I love you, Ozzy. So much."

He supports Ana's head and her diaper-covered bottom in his big hands and stands. When his lips touch my forehead, he's about to say something, but my phone vibrates.

There aren't many people I'd interrupt this moment for, but she's one of them. "It's a text from my mother."

Mamá – Look at the news.

Mamá – Liyah, something happened in Morocco. A motorcade, it was attacked.

Me – What happened?

Mamá – President Botros was killed. The news said Hasim was with him, it was a motorcade from the palace, but there's no word on your uncle yet.

I stare at the screen.

"Is everything okay?"

I look up at Ozzy. "I don't know. You tell me. Botros is dead."

Ozzy hikes a brow. "You don't say."

"Yes," I drawl. "I say."

"Huh."

"Ozzy—"

"Baby, he wasn't just a disgusting old man, he was a pedophile. You saw the evidence. With his position, he'd never get charged with that."

He was. It's horrid and disgusting. It was only two weeks ago that Ozzy uncovered this bit of information.

"Ozzy—" I try again, but he's faster.

"Do you think I'm going to allow that bastard to walk the same planet as us after we brought a child into the world? I don't care what continent he's on. There was no fucking way he was going to live another day."

I shouldn't be surprised, nor should I be happy. And yet...

"And my uncle?"

He shrugs. "I'm too busy killing it as the world's best dad. I'll check during Ana's next feeding, but unless he grabbed an Uber instead of riding in his royal motorcade, then yes."

I try to bite back my smile.

Ozzy does not bite back his. "See? You're happy. Consider it your birthing present."

"So in addition to the diamond studs I'm wearing, you decided to add two dead bodies to my gift for giving you your firstborn?"

He leans in and presses his lips to mine. "You're welcome. And for your information, it wasn't easy."

I shake my head. "As long as you had to work for it, the gift means so much more."

Ana squeaks, and I forget all about my gift. I don't want to think about Botros or Hasim ever again.

I turn back to my phone.

Me – I just heard. Horrible.

Mamá – Yes, love. Just horrible ;-)

I turn back to my husband. "As I was saying, I love you. Now I might love you more. Are you happy?"

"Princess, we dropped the *might* a long time ago. And I love you more than I ever thought possible. But I'm warning you." He glances down at our daughter, a princess by blood, but she'll never know that life. "I'm going to want to do this a few more times."

A smile touches my lips as I settle in.

This reality is more than a dream. Fairy tales and the life of a princess are nothing compared to the life Ozzy has given me.

And since my husband wants to do this a few more times, it's only going to get better.

Ozzy

Five years later

I STAND under the red maple I used to climb as a child and stare at Ana and Kam as they play with their cousins.

The boys are tossing a football, and Kam just tackled his four-year-old cousin.

He just turned two, and he's a handful already. My mom said he's just like me, right before she told Liyah to brace.

This is the land I grew up on, and it will stay in my family. Axel is my youngest brother. He works for Dad, but he's also working hard so he can buy it from my parents.

I have no interest in farming, but I do have an interest in this land staying in my family. If for no other reason than I want my kids to celebrate every Fourth of July here, wake up on Christmas morning here, and bottle feed calves here.

I want them to raise hell like we did.

I also want my parents to be able to retire, and if my youngest brother's dream is to own a dairy farm, he's damn well going to get it.

It's going to happen next month. No one knows but Liyah and Drew, my middle brother.

I can't take complete credit. It was my wife's idea. She wanted to pay for the transaction with her royal billions, but I put my foot down. She usually gets her way, but not this time. Next month, I'm buying the farm and putting it in Axel's name.

Drew knows, and he's good with it. Of course he would be. He's the peacemaker. When we were kids, he was my shadow. He also did everything for Axel, which was why Axel couldn't tie his own fucking shoes until the second grade.

I look at Liyah and wonder if the youngest is babied in every family. No one knows she's pregnant besides me and her mom. We just found out last week.

Three.

Liyah wants four. She really took it to heart when I said I wanted to repeat this many times over.

I won't complain.

But four is a lot. We'll have to go into negotiations after that.

Drew hands me a fresh beer. "Dude, I thought you were done being a loner."

I take the bottle and put it to my lips. "Hard habit to break."

He huffs a laugh. "Like your wife would ever allow that. You know you'll do anything she wants."

I don't take my eyes off of Liyah, Luciana, my mom, and my brothers' wives in a female huddle. The sun is setting. Dad and Drew are getting fireworks ready for the kids.

A scene that might as well be on repeat since Liyah and I got married. Though it doesn't always involve fireworks. Sometimes Christmas trees, other times Easter eggs, but most of the time no one needs an excuse. To say my rebirth brought our family closer is an understatement. And Luciana is involved in every moment of it.

I thought we were tight before my fictional death. But when a miracle occurs, and you're given your life back, everything is different.

I wasn't only dead on paper. I felt dead in every other way that didn't involve a heartbeat.

I'll never take my miracle for granted.

"There are some days I can't believe it," Drew says.

"Believe what?"

"That you're back." I turn to him as he keeps talking. "Those were the worst years, Oz. Not gonna lie. It was like a black, wet blanket was thrown over the family." He takes a long pull of his beer and stares out at the kids. "Just saying, not many people get a second chance to appreciate what they had. Grateful to be one of them."

"You know, it's creepy when you say shit that I'm thinking."

He smirks. "I used to want to be just like you, but I don't think I can handle your kind of drama."

I slug him in the shoulder. "I wouldn't wish that kind of drama on anyone."

"Everyone knows Liyah's pregnant, by the way."

I turn to him fully. "What the hell?"

He lifts his hand holding a beer and points at the women. "The moment she turned down a margarita, everyone knew."

I sigh. There are no secrets in this family. But then again, I guess that's what makes us a family.

"Plus Liyah's talked about four kids ever since Ana was born. That'll be a shitshow, but congrats. You'd better not wait too long, you'll be chasing toddlers around when you're fifty."

"Fuck you. I'm not that old."

He laughs. "I guess your wife is just that young."

I ignore that. My brothers not only give me shit about leveling up, but marrying a royal. "Don't piss me off, Drew. I planned on paying off your mortgage next week, but I might reconsider."

He loses the smirk. "You what?"

"Do you think I'd buy a farm for Axel and not do anything for you?"

"Seriously?"

"Yeah. And there's the fact my very young wife insisted on it too."

"Dude. I don't know what to say."

"You're welcome."

"Thank you."

I tap the neck of his beer bottle with mine. "We should help Dad."

I'm about to move to the rest of my family when Drew grabs me by the bicep. "Not to get sappy and sound like a fucking Hallmark card, but you're the shit."

"I didn't know Hallmark cards cussed."

"I have no clue. If they don't, they should. It's more meaningful."

"Ozzy!"

I look back to the group, and Liyah is waving at me. Kam is climbing my dad like a tree. Not that Dad doesn't love it, but he's got his hands full with five grandkids and counting.

I slap Drew on the shoulder. "Come on. Let's drive Mom crazy and blow some shit up. After the kids go to bed, we'll play a game of Roman candle baseball."

"Fuck, yeah, we will. But if you aim for my shins, I'll jump your ass. I still have a scar from when I was twelve."

"You're such a middle child. You cried to Mom, and I had to shovel cow shit by myself for a week, asshole." I move toward Liyah. "Come on. I need to tell my wife everyone knows she's pregnant."

Drew falls in beside me. "You're living the dream, man."

He might be giving me shit, but he's right. Just when I think I can't be more content in my second life, I live another day to prove myself wrong.

Liyah

Ozzy climbs in behind me where I'm already half-asleep in his childhood bed. He's fresh from the shower, and his damp hair tickles my skin when he presses his lips to my neck.

"Please tell me everyone still has their eyesight after playing that horrid game."

"Roman candle baseball is not horrid. It's fun as hell. And we're not sixteen anymore—Drew brought his ski goggles. Safety first."

"Thank goodness for Drew. Do you think Kam will be as cautious as a middle child?"

Ozzy pulls me to his chest and smiles. "Kamal Graves is a tiny badass named after a king and is the son of an assassin. You really think he has one cautious bone in his body?"

I sigh and snuggle into his chest. "Stop. He's my baby, and he'll never play sports that involve fireworks."

Ozzy slides his hand to my ass. "Keep telling yourself that. Our kids might be part royal, but they're also American with Graves blood running through their veins. They'll raise Cain and drive you crazy for the rest of your life."

"Shut your mouth. We make precious and perfect humans."

"Okay, baby. Go to sleep. You need your rest if you're going to continue to make me perfect humans."

I yawn before brushing my lips over his collarbone. "Thank you."

He tips my face to his, and I drag my heavy eyelids open. "No, Princess. Thank you for making my second chance perfect."

He's right.

Perfection isn't a strong enough word.

My heart is happy and my soul is content.

Keep reading The Story of a Lost Soul, featuring Princess Luciana Zahir

Thank you for reading. If you enjoyed *Souls*, I would appreciate a review on Amazon.

Read Crew and Addy's story in *Vines*
Read Grady and Maya's story in *Paths*
Read Asa and Keelie's story in *Gifts*
Read Jarvis and Gracie's story in *Veils*
Read Cole and Bella's story in *Scars*
Read Evan and Mary's story in *The Tequila – A Killers Novella*

The Next Generation
Read *Levi*, Asa's son

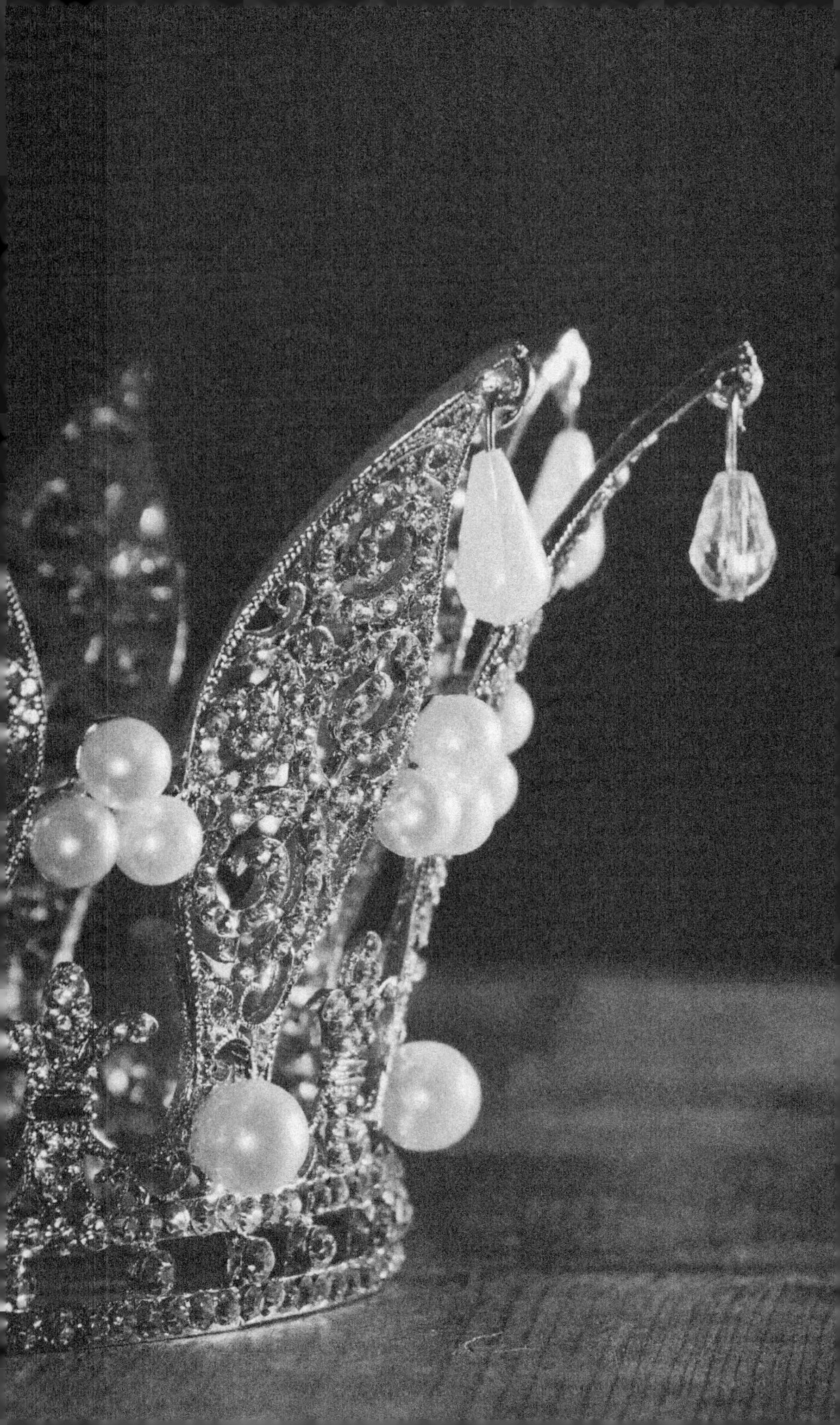

THE STORY OF A LOST SOUL
THE OTHER SIDE OF THE STORY...

Chapter 1

I've tried to be strong.

For her, I'll do anything.

Hasim took away my last form of communication to the outside world weeks ago. It was after my last call to Liyah, begging her to stay in California—that under no circumstance should she come to Morocco.

To say the situation at the palace is bleak would be the understatement of the century.

My staff, who has been with me since I married Kamal, was removed. Then I overheard whispers about Liyah. Hasim wants her back and is planning something. And since nothing he ever does is good or genuine or in the best interest of anyone but himself, I won't allow Liyah to be put in harm's way.

I was moved from the main living quarters of the palace to a basic room I didn't know existed, and this palace has been my home for a quarter of a century. It's not quite a jail cell, but it's damn close.

The thought of leaving the palace and Morocco cuts through me. Kamal brought me here to visit for the first time when I was eighteen. I was young, in love, and mesmerized by an older king. I gave him my heart and never looked back. Nothing mattered. Not our age difference, not our nationalities, nor the societies and traditions we were born into.

I was the daughter of a fisherman from a small Spanish village. Kamal was a king. We were separated only by the Alboran Sea, but our differences were vast. Our love story should not have been.

My parents were up in arms.

The dynasty hated me.

But Morocco loved me. I embraced the country as my own and did all I could for its people.

Until I lost Kamal.

I was only twenty-seven when he died. I was a young mother, and a princess who lost the love of her life.

I don't want to leave.

But this is my last chance. If I don't take it, I fear I'll never see my daughter again.

Faiz, Kamal's most loyal assistant and one of the last remaining from my husband's reign, stands before me. He and I have talked about this for weeks. This was our worst-case-scenario plan. It's by far the most dangerous for everyone. If I'm caught, this room is nothing compared to what I'll be subjected to by Hasim. Faiz will certainly face death.

And Liyah ... if she returns to Morocco to look for me, I fear for her fate.

"Princess," Faiz bites. "It's now or never. They've ordered me out of the palace—I'll never get back in."

I look around and realize this might be the last time

I ever see the inside of the palace, no matter if it is a jail cell. The toilet is shielded by a curtain, and the tub is dirty. Hasim has all but thrown me away and fed the key to dragons.

Faiz grabs my arm, and we're on our way.

There's no time to think, change my mind, or have regrets.

If this doesn't work, it will be because I'll be dead.

I'll die before anyone uses me to harm my daughter.

Chapter 2

I HAD A PLAN.

Escape.

Fake my death.

Find Liyah.

I stayed too long. Hasim stripped me of everything Kamal left me. But my husband made sure Liyah would be financially safe, and I moved her money out of the country long ago.

The only person I trust in Morocco is Faiz, and he said this is the only way. I'm out of choices. There's nothing to do but move forward.

"Princess," Faiz hisses. "We're close to the border. I see my contact.

All of a sudden the stifling air in the hidden compartment of this old sedan just got heavier. We're off-roading. If I don't have bumps and bruises from the drive, then I'm not a royal by marriage.

But they're the least of my worries, because Algeria

and Morocco don't play well—at all. The land border has been closed for years over a territory dispute.

My heart pounds in my ears as the rickety car slows to a rough stop. The door opens and slams before a sliver of light appears through the false compartment I'm hiding in.

I cringe and shield my face as the partition he wedged closed after we escaped is rattled open. A light shines in my face.

"That her?"

Faiz pushes the light away and offers me a hand. "Let's go, Princess. This is no place to hang out. The sooner you get out of Morocco, the better. It pains me to say it, but Algeria is safer for you. By now, the King knows you're gone. We can't risk sending you off from a Moroccan port. You'll go across from Algeria."

I take his hand and move, stretching my stiff muscles as I climb from the trunk to stand on the rocky terrain. The man holding the flashlight is huge, gripping an enormous semi-automatic rifle slung over his shoulder. My skin crawls as he studies me. "So she's still alive. There were rumors..."

"She was being kept alive to lure her daughter. I'm not sure what would have happened once Princess Aliyah returned."

I interrupt. "She can't return."

Faiz moves in front of me and takes my hand in both of his. "It was an honor serving you and King Kamal. I pray for your safe passage and for you to be reunited with Princess Aliyah. I trust this man to get you to your next destination."

"Thank you, Faiz. I owe you my life. If I make it back

to Liyah, I'll make sure you and everyone else who helped me are compensated."

Faiz bows his head, but I stop him when I pull him in my arms for an embrace. He's everything that's good about the country I came to love.

"Thank you, Faiz."

"Princess. Maybe one day I'll see you again."

I doubt that, but I don't admit it. As long as Hasim is in power, I'll never return.

The flashlight blinds me once again. "Let's go."

I swallow over the lump in my throat and turn to the strange man. "What's your name?"

He shakes his head and never lets go of his weapon. "You'll never know my name. Just know I hate your king and your country. This is my fuck you to the dynasty."

I'm not surprised, even though I'm grateful to have someone at my back with as much hatred for my brother-in-law as my own. I'm also accustomed to it. I've lived in the public eye since I was eighteen. Nothing surprises me anymore.

Faiz gives my hand one more squeeze. "Goodbye, Princess."

I choke back tears because now is not the time to be sentimental. I simply nod.

"Let's go." The nameless man points his flashlight to the ground in front of him and starts off.

I gather my dress and skip to catch up. Faiz told me the plan he arranged. This will not be easy.

We walk for hours when the man ends the eerie silence that's been broken only by the gravel crunching under our feet. "Say goodbye to Morocco, Princess. Our ride is waiting over the next ridge."

And the next ridge is a steep one. I'm huffing when

we get to the top of it. In the valley below are three armed trucks with more mounted guns and armed guards than I can count. I wonder if this man is from the Algerian military.

I'm thirsty. It's been hours since I've last eaten, not that I'd be able to stomach anything. The sight in front of me, coupled with the unknown, has my insides turning with nerves.

The incline is steep, and the rocks bite into my palms when I catch myself from sliding down the rocky terrain. The man stops for the first time since we headed off into the black night and turns to me, gruff with his words. "Hurry. We'll lose the dark and need to be far from the border when the sun rises."

It's at that moment it happens.

I'm on my bottom, trying to climb to my feet when shots ring through the night air.

And not just shots.

A barrage.

The man who led me to Algeria lands on top of me. Gunfire echoes through the canyon, and I couldn't move if I wanted to. The man doesn't move, shielding me from bullets flying and bouncing off the rocky earth around us.

Shouts follow as the shots come fewer and farther between.

I can't move from the weight of the man protecting me. I try to push him off, but pain shoots through my shoulder and down my arm.

He's dead weight.

Dead.

Feet hitting the ground get louder. I panic and try to scream, but I can't pull in enough oxygen.

A few more shots ricochet off the dirt.

And then, silence.

Low voices get closer, and I have trouble making out their words. I'm fluent in Arabic, but it's not my first or even my second language. Their dialect is heavy. But what I do hear is *Princess* and *woman* and *where is she*.

My lungs fill with air when the anvil is lifted. Or, more specifically, thrown to the side.

New faces—angry ones—stare down at me through the first rays of the day. "Fuck, they came out of nowhere."

"Were they from the palace?"

"I think so."

I bring my hand up to my shoulder. My fingers shake when I look down. Blood. So much blood.

They keep talking. "Is he dead?"

I look over at the man who led me out of Morocco. He's lying in a heap with his eyes open, staring blankly beyond me. Blood stains the dirt below him.

"He's dead."

My breath shallows, and my head spins. I'm dizzy despite being laid out flat on my back.

"She's been shot."

I look over at a man squatting next to me.

"We've got to get her out of here. They only said to deliver her—didn't say if she needed to be in one piece."

I'm roughly tugged into a set of arms and hardly recognize my own voice when I scream from the pain.

"Let's go. The boat is waiting."

Chapter 3

I TURN my head and hurl. The swells are enormous, and I was already woozy.

It's night again. A whole day has passed since Faiz rushed me out of an underground tunnel used only by groundskeepers. I knew they were there, but I never set foot in them. There was never a need until I was running from a place I once called home.

I've lost a good deal of blood. At least, that's what I've been told. And I still have a bullet lodged in my shoulder. I'm sure it could be worse. The poor man who took the brunt. Bless his soul.

Hasim's men from the palace—his henchmen, the ones who do his dirty work—caught wind of where I was headed. I just hope Faiz escaped. The thought that he might not have...

So many have risked themselves to help me.

But my biggest fear is that Liyah won't listen to me. She's hardheaded, willful, and loves me to a fault. I need her to realize I'm no longer at the palace, and I don't dare risk telling her my plan. Begging her not to come to Morocco was a last resort before I escaped. Faiz told me Hasim's people have intercepted her phone.

My life hasn't been grand for the last couple of years, but I've never been out of choices. And I've never felt so desperate that I've been willing to risk my life.

I have no idea who the men were who got me from the Algerian border to the coast, but they might as well be angels sent straight from Kamal. Within hours of the showdown, I was carried onto a small boat.

My father was waiting. I haven't seen him in years.

Barely large enough for the two of us, this vessel is not made to travel the Strait of Gibraltar, let alone the Alboran Sea.

I should know. I grew up on fishing boats.

But if anyone can do it, it's Papá.

Despite my loss of blood, motion sickness, and fearing for Liyah, a sense of peace fills me. One I haven't felt since before Kamal received the diagnosis that changed our lives forever.

"Drink, Luciana," Papá coaxes. "Just a few sips. You've already lost too much blood, you'll dehydrate."

I hardly have the energy to shake my head, there's no way I can manage picking up a bottle of water. My voice is hoarse and weak, and I don't recognize myself. "If I don't make it, you have to promise to find Liyah—"

He fights the whitecaps, saltwater spraying over the side of the boat. "You can tell her yourself. You're going to make it. We should've gotten you out of there years ago. You wouldn't listen to me."

He's right, but in my darkest nightmares, I never saw Hasim going as far as he did. I was determined to stay and carry out Kamal's wishes for his people.

I was blinded by love and grief.

The crackle of a radio cuts through the wind and the sounds of the sea. Papá can barely respond as he fights the tiller. I'm surprised the rudder hasn't snapped.

"We're close, love. So close."

I hope he's right. I need him to be right. All I have left is Liyah. I see Kamal in her eyes every time I look at her.

"What the hell happened to her, Emmanuel?"

Voices. So many voices.

"Bullet to the shoulder. She lost a lot of blood." I'm scooped into my father's arms. The pain is a dull constant in my subconscious. "You've got her?"

I'm jostled between bodies, and I wish I had the

strength to help. "Yeah. *Miedra*, it's rough today. Climb in, and we'll let it go."

The waves and winds are muted. I drag my eyes open and am immediately transported back to my childhood. I'm in the cabin of one of my father's fishing boats. I spent countless days here helping and playing and keeping him company as he worked.

"We need to get her to San Mateo. The Sisters will be able to take care of her." Papá pulls me into his arms and presses a drink of water to my lips. "Hold on, love. I'll make sure you're healthy and will never live in that prison again. I'll get you back to your baby…"

Chapter 4

"There she is. Welcome, Princess. Spain is happy to have you home."

I blink.

And blink again.

"What are you talking about? Spain doesn't know she's home. No one knows she's here but us."

"Shut up, Lola. She's been unconscious for two days. I'm trying to make her feel better."

"She's hiding from the world. Do you really think telling her that an entire country is happy to have her back is going to make her feel better?"

"You're always the bitter Sister. I'm going to pray that God will help you see the glass is half-full and bestow mercy on the rest of us so we don't have to listen to you."

I hear a gasp and have trouble focusing on the conversation. "Don't you dare pray for me."

"Oh, I'm going to pray for you. I'm going to pray hard. All. Day. Long. I'll even light candles."

"Enough!"

My eyes jump to the most wrinkled face of the bunch, since all I see are faces in habits. I'm surrounded by Sisters, and the only reason I'm sure I didn't die is because they're bickering. I'm pretty sure no one bickers in heaven. That's what I was taught in elementary school, anyway.

That, and there's the pain.

Lord, the pain.

A gentle hand lands on my good shoulder. "Ignore them. You're the most excitement we've had here in a long time."

I swallow and try to clear my throat. "Where am I?"

"The basement of the Rectory at San Mateo. Father Diego insisted you were safer here than at your parents' home. I'm afraid he was proven correct. The King of Morocco has sent his people to look for you. They came here, but the basement is hidden. Don't worry, you're safe."

Panic swells inside me. "My parents?"

"They're fine. I spoke with your father this morning, but it's too much of a risk for them to visit. Father will try to sneak them in as soon as it's safe."

It doesn't take much to remember being shot and the boat ride, traveling from one continent to another. The moment I move, the memories flood to the forefront of my brain.

"Get her medication now that she's awake," the older Sister demands before turning back to me. "Sister Mariana was a surgical nurse before she took her vows. She removed the bullet and did what she could. She, however, is not a plastic surgeon. I do think you'll sport a less-than-lovely scar for the rest of your days. But other than that, you should be fine."

Another Sister hands me a pill, and I don't question it. I open my lips and welcome the cool water on my dry throat.

"Sister Camila, go up to Father Diego's quarters and warm some soup. The princess needs to eat."

I shake my head. "Luciana, please. I'm not a princess anymore. I'm ready to be me again."

The older Sister smiles. "Very well. It's lovely to meet you, Luciana. I'm Sister Angelina."

She turns to leave, but I call for her. "Sister Angelina?"

"Yes?"

"My daughter. I need to check on her somehow. I can't contact her, but if there's a computer that I can check her social media? A cell I could borrow? Anything."

She gives me a small smile. "Of course. Let me see what I can do."

I sigh and try not to breathe too deeply. Moving in any way hurts.

My gaze flits around the basement of the church I grew up attending. San Mateo is centuries old and sits at the heart of Tarifa. It smells like history and its echoes sound like ghosts from the past. If I had to guess, the surgical removal of a bullet isn't the craziest act these walls have seen.

Even though I'm exhausted, in pain, and worried about Liyah, this is the most peace I've felt in years.

Once I reunite with Liyah, my soul will be intact. I'm

just afraid it's too much of a risk to happen anytime soon.

Chapter 5
Two weeks later

"Luciana, look! She posted. Princess Aliyah finally posted!"

My heart spasms as I watch Sister Camila rush to me. Time has crawled, and these Godly women are now as invested in Liyah's whereabouts as I am. It doesn't hurt they've been praying daily, and the church is ablaze with candles for her.

"Is she okay? Let me see."

"She's in Canada! The location is listed above the picture."

I take the cell phone from her. "Canada?"

"She's engaged, Luciana! Isn't it exciting?"

My expression drops as I take in the graphic on the small screen.

Liyah has always pushed boundaries. She's young, a natural beauty, and brave. She might have embraced the Western culture, but she's also smart, and has not only protected her heart, but her body.

However...

My daughter can be brazen, which was why I knew I had to do everything in my power to keep her from returning to Morocco.

And her bold bravery is proven by her posting a picture of herself naked, wrapped around a strange man.

Engaged?

"Forever with you can't come soon enough."

I can't look away from the image and repeat my thoughts aloud. "My daughter is wrapped naked around a strange man."

"He doesn't seem strange to her," Sister Camila says with a smile.

I turn to her and frown. "The last time I spoke to my daughter, she wasn't even dating. And now she's engaged?"

The young Sister's eyes widen. "Love is love. When you know, you know. It was the same way when I realized this was my calling."

But an engagement? There are no other posts of her with anyone. This has come out of nowhere.

I turn back to the image. She's right. I knew at the young age of eighteen that there would be no one for me but Kamal.

"You were eighteen." Sister Camila is now repeating my thoughts, with no apology in her tone.

I glare at her.

She stands, plucks the cell from my hands, and finally looks contrite as she winces. "Sorry. The moment you got here, we researched you. We'd never met a princess before."

I lean back into my pillows. My incision isn't as ugly as they warned it might be, and I've been off pain pills for over a week. "I'm not a princess anymore."

She sits on the edge of my bed. The makeshift hospital room has turned into my bedroom. It's where I'm still hiding in the basement. "Yes, but you were. At the young age of eighteen, may I point out again. How did your parents feel about that?"

I can't get the image of Liyah, naked and wrapped around that man, out of my head. And how she posted it for the world to see. I shut my eyes and mutter, "My parents were livid."

"Yet it was true love. A love you never regretted."

I open my eyes and glare at her. "Are you sure you're a Sister and not a therapist?"

Sister Camila shoots me a smug smile. "Rumor has it, a parishioner brought Father enough fresh ceviche to feed an army. I'll bring you some."

"Thank you, Sister."

I roll to rest on my good shoulder and wonder what my daughter is up to.

Chapter 6
Three days later

"Damn him! Damn him to hell!"

My pillow flies across the room, hitting a floor lamp. Sister Angelina proves she's as agile as ever, no matter her wrinkles. She lunges, catching it before it crashes to the stone floor.

"I can't believe him! How does he think he can do that to my daughter? Kamal's heir? He wants to hand Liyah off like some stray dog? If I were there, I'd strangle the bastard with my own hands."

An official announcement from the Palace was released today regarding my daughter's engagement to the fucking President of the Constitutional Court.

"He's married," I scream. Sister Angelina tries to shush me, but it's not happening. "And he's older than the hills! He wants to take her as a second wife. Second! My beautiful, smart, and charming daughter. A *second* wife? The man is disgusting and always has been. Hasim is going to die. Even if I have to hire it out after I gain access to money again. There's no way that man is touching my daughter. I'll come back from the dead if I have to and scream from the hilltops."

Sister Camila comes running down the stairs, but nothing can stop me. Kamal always said my temper would be the end of me, and he might be right. At this point, I want to swim back to Morocco and assassinate both Hasim and his fucking appointed President myself.

I drag my hands through my hair and continue my fit. "This is why he silenced me the way he did. He had this planned and knew if I had a public voice, I'd do just this. He'd have backlash from his people like he's never seen before. I know what he wants—he wants Liyah's money. For years he's tried to get back the billions Kamal put into a trust for Liyah, like he doesn't have his own fortune."

"Princess—"

I glare at Sister Camila.

"I mean, Luciana," she holds up her phone. "Princess Aliyah made another post!"

I stop in my tracks as I pace the stone floor beneath my feet. "She did? Where is she?"

Sister Camila shrugs. "It doesn't say this time. But she does have something to say to King Hasim."

I ignore the pain in my shoulder when I close the distance between us and grab the phone.

Well.

I pull in a deep breath.

When I exhale, my tension goes with it. And what it's replaced with is pride.

His Majesty is correct, I'll soon be married, though he has the wrong fiancé. My life will not be arranged, nor will I be sold for political gain. No one controls my happily ever after but me. If my parents taught me anything, it's that love will prevail.

With love,

Aliyah Zahir
Princess of Morocco
Heir of King Kamal and Princess Luciana

I ignore the picture of my daughter and the faceless man whose hand has disappeared down the back of her dress, gripping her bottom like it's his. Liyah knows what's going on and isn't taking it. Not only is she standing up for herself like the strong woman I raised, she's throwing it in Hasim's face publicly.

"Look at her," I whisper. "I'm so proud."

"Do you have any idea who she's engaged to?" Sister Angelina asks with a little frown set in her brow as she takes in the overtly sexual picture of my daughter.

I don't care what Sister thinks—hell, I don't care what the world thinks. Tears of joy prickle my eyes. "I have no idea. All I know is she's safe, and she knows. Somehow she knows what's going on. I'll find her when the time is right—when it's safe."

Sister Camila beams. "This is so exciting."

Sister Angelina sighs and places a hand on my good

shoulder. "You can rest knowing she's safe. You'll find her, Luciana. God will not keep you from your daughter. You've given so much to protect her. It might take time, but He has your path paved. I believe you'll be reunited."

I give her hand a squeeze and ignore the tear running down my cheek. "Thank you, Sister."

"That hand on her bum, though." Sister Angelina shakes her head. "Young people, I pray for them."

I ignore her comment. "I hope it's real. I hope she finds a love as deep and as powerful as I did."

I can't look away from Liyah.

I'll find her if it's the last thing I do.

Chapter 7

I STRETCH my arm as far as I can. I'm not sure what one is supposed to do after a bullet rips through one's shoulder, but moving it as much as possible seems like a good idea, even if it hurts like hell.

I haven't seen the sunlight since I arrived in Spain. The church bells, a small television, and frequent visits from the Sisters are my only connection to reality.

The days are dragging on as I wait for Liyah to post again. Her silence on social media has created as much of a flurry as her two latest posts announcing her engagement.

Soft steps echo off the stone surrounding me. It's not the excited patter of Sister Camila, or the efficient strides of Sister Angelina. When I turn, Father Diego appears.

He's been serving this parish as long as I can remember. I offered my first confession to him, I took my first communion from him, and I was confirmed under his blessing. He was also accepting, and even forgiving, when I announced I would be married in an Islamic ceremony in Morocco to the King.

Father Diego is in his eighties and still going strong. He visits me every evening, shares his dessert, and leaves me with a prayer for Liyah.

But it's the middle of the day, and he's not carrying a plate of cookies or cake in his shaky, wrinkled hands. It's midmorning, and his normally kind eyes are troubled.

My skin itches with anxiety. "What's wrong?"

He gets right to it. "I had a visitor. A man asking about you."

"Do you think it was someone from the dynasty?"

Father tips his head. "I don't know. He refused to tell me who he was, but it didn't feel that way."

I sit on the side of the bed. "I wonder if he went to my parents' home? I'm worried about them."

I haven't seen Mamá or Papá since I gained consciousness. Father said it was too risky. They don't want to come and go from the church and risk leading anyone to me. They've skipped mass out of an abundance of caution, and they never miss.

"I have word that your parents are fine. Do you think Liyah would send someone to look for you?"

"Nothing would surprise me when it comes to her. She has the resources to pay for whatever she wants. But the contacts to do such a thing? I'm not sure."

"We'll continue to be careful."

"Thank you, Father."

He gives me a small smile. "Gelato tonight."

"That sounds amazing."

He turns for the stairs. "I'm grateful for our time together, but these stairs ... hard on my knees."

Chapter 8

Well, then.

There's nothing like being a spectator to your own death to make you feel loved.

News that I've been lost at sea has traveled far and wide. Makeshift memorials and gatherings in my honor have popped up all across Morocco. It's touching and tugs at my heart. Kamal's love for his country and its people transferred easily to me. There's a finality about the situation that makes me sad. I never want to see Hasim again, but I will miss Morocco terribly.

The news has been out all day, but there's been nothing from Liyah. Not a post, not a statement, not a comment.

I'm sure she knows by now. Wherever in the world she is, she has to be shattered.

"You haven't touched your pie," Father says.

I stare at the TV. I'm only watching to see if Liyah is mentioned. "I'm not hungry."

"It was the only way, Luciana."

"I know."

"We will get you back to Liyah."

I shake my head. "Not anytime soon. This needs to die down, I don't want to put her at risk. But in time, maybe."

Father picks up his tea. "Whatever you think."

I sigh. "I'll know when the time is right."

The only people I trust are my parents, Father Diego, and the Sisters. Yes, I will reunite with Liyah, but not until my death fades like a distant memory.

Which could be a very long time.

Chapter 9
Almost three months later

Feet clomp down the stairs so loudly, their sense of urgency echoes off the narrow stairwell.

"Luciana! Luciana! She posted! For the first time since her fiancé had his hand down her dress. Liyah posted!"

It's not like I don't know what's going on in my daughter's life. It seems she tied herself to a man known worldwide in the intelligence community. Austin Oswald Graves, III has been in the news for the last three months. He was unjustly accused of murder a few years back and recently cleared his name. I've studied the pictures of him and my daughter that have been captured by the American press. Together they have caused a stir, for which I'm grateful, otherwise I would have been left wondering and worried.

What I still don't know is how Liyah met him.

I rush to Sister Camila. "What did she say?"

"It's a date."

The only thing on the graphic is Liyah's hand touching white lace.

A wedding dress.

My heart sinks.

She's getting married soon, and I'm going to miss it.

My beautiful girl ... a bride.

Sister Camila puts her arm around my shoulders for a side hug. I barely feel my wound anymore. "How patient are you feeling now?"

Patience is a virtue ... one that wanes with time.

Liyah is getting married.

"How do I get to her, Sister? It's a risk."

"Everything is a risk. You're here because you took a risk. You can't live in the basement of the rectory for the rest of your life. Let Father try to reach out to her fiancé. Maybe he can reach him somehow."

I stare at the lace I so dearly want to see Liyah wear in person. "Okay. Yes. Please have Father try to reach out to this man."

Sister jumps up and down, jostling me back and forth. "Yay! I'll be right back."

I cross my arms and turn in a slow circle, taking in the stone walls I've used as protection for months. It's been a long time since I've been out from under the thumb of Kamal's brother. I haven't seen Liyah since her eighteenth birthday.

It's a huge risk.

I'll always be the Spanish girl who caught the eye of the older Moroccan King in history books. That chapter of my life is over.

I'm ready to start a new one.

Chapter 10

I CLIMB the stairs for the first time since they brought me to San Mateo. So many stairs, and now I'm even more grateful Father managed them every evening to deliver me sweets and keep me company.

My parents have been visiting me weekly. Father sneaks them down after Mass. I've missed them so much over the last few years when I wasn't allowed to leave the palace. These last few months have made me realize how much life I still have to live.

I have a visitor—one Father insisted I meet in the sanctuary. Father Diego is waiting for me at the top of the stairs. "This is someone you should meet."

"You're sure?"

He nods. "I feel she's proven herself."

"She?"

"Come."

I follow, and we enter through a side door next to the confessionals. A tall, thin blonde is standing in the middle of the church with her back to us.

Father clears his throat.

The woman looks over her shoulder first, and our gazes meet in an instant before she slowly turns.

"Princess Luciana. Pictures don't do you justice. Liyah really is the best of you and your late husband."

My eyes shoot to Father before looking back at her. I answer in English. "I've officially dropped the title. It's Luciana."

She smiles. "Luciana. My name is Isabella Carson. Call me Bella. Your daughter has become a dear friend. I'm also an associate of her fiancé."

"You're a friend of Liyah's?"

"I am. I know you reached out to Ozzy—"

"Ozzy?"

"Your son-in-law-to-be. He goes by Ozzy. See, he and Liyah have had a time of it since they met. He's extremely protective, and they're to be married the day after tomorrow. When Father Diego reached out to Ozzy's attorney ... well, let's just say Ozzy was skeptical."

"How do I know you're telling me the truth?"

"I can show you pictures, if you'd like?" She pulls a cell out of her bag and brings it to life. I stay where I am, but she closes the distance and hands me the phone. My soul brightens as I flip through them.

Liyah, with a group of women I've never seen.

Liyah, with children I don't recognize.

Liyah, with a man I only know from the internet to be her future husband.

"Luciana, I'm more than happy to prove to you who I am, but I must warn you, Ozzy is questioning the fact you're actually alive."

I can't look away from the pictures. "I know, it's unbelievable—"

"Not that unbelievable, actually. If you can be patient enough to prove you're who you say you are, I can take you to Liyah."

I look from Bella to Father Diego when he says, "I think you should trust her, Luciana. She explained her background, and I've seen the pictures. There is no way she works for Hasim. I looked her up, and her story checks out."

"I have a plane waiting. You're officially dead, but it won't be an issue for you to travel. Trust me, my organization has some experience with that."

I look back at the phone. My daughter smiles back at me.

"Please, Luciana. I beg you to come with me. Liyah

has not been herself. When she learned of your death, she was lost in grief. I hope you can understand. She doesn't know I'm here. I would never raise her hopes just to crush them if you weren't who you said you are. Ozzy wants proof—DNA proof. But I know ... all it took was one look into your eyes. I see your daughter in you."

My throat thickens with emotion. "It breaks my heart knowing Liyah thinks I'm dead. But I had to do it to protect her and break away from the dynasty."

"I understand, but we can help you. And protect you."

"I want to see her get married. So much it hurts."

Bella's smile turns sly, and she hikes a brow. "Then allow me to dangle the golden carrot in front of you. Liyah is expecting."

My hand flies to my mouth. "Really?"

"Yes. She's going to be a mother, and you are going to be a grandmother." She reaches out to grasp my hand, and I'm instantly overjoyed Liyah has this kind woman as a friend. "I hope Liyah won't be angry I told you, but I have a plane waiting. I'll put my money on the hopes she's too happy I brought you back to life for her to care. She can tell you about the next one. She and Ozzy are so in love. I see many grandbabies in your future."

Grandchildren.

Bella blurs as tears fill my eyes.

I nod and swallow. "I'm ready. Let's go."

Bella's smile swells. "This is bloody brilliant. I feel like the happy police. I will not stop until everyone has their happily ever after."

Chapter 11

"Ozzy feels like shit for subjecting his future mother-in-law to a DNA test. Besides you escaping the evil King, reuniting with your daughter, and becoming a grandmother, that's the best part of this whole thing."

Cole Carson is something. I can say I've never met anyone quite like him.

I've been in Virginia long enough to nap, take a shower, and pick out an outfit from all the clothes Bella had waiting on me when we arrived.

"They're here." Bella pops up from the sofa, and tosses her phone on the coffee table. "I'm going to cry."

Cole sighs. "Fuck. I'll probably get something stuck in my eye again."

I follow Bella to the entryway. My heart is beating so hard, I hope I don't pass out.

My emotions grow thick as I watch the knob turn and the door open. I swipe my tears because I don't want to miss seeing her face for the first time in years.

There she is. For a blip of a moment, she doesn't register what's in front of her.

Then she screams.

The man who has proven he'll do anything in the world for her catches her.

I open my arms, and my future son hands me my baby.

And once again, my world is balanced.

Download a FREE *Souls* Bonus Scene - The Day I Healed by Nettie Graves

THOUGHTS AND ACKNOWLEDGEMENTS

When I stepped foot into a Virginia winery with Elle several years ago, I was inspired. All it took was one wine tasting to know that I had to write about a strong heroine, her quirky staff, pet cows, and the hot new neighbor next door. Just to make things more interesting, I decided to make that neighbor an assassin.

This was back in 2015. I didn't know what I was doing—there are still days I question myself—and thought, if readers like it, maybe I'd write a series of three books. I had no intention of writing six, a novella, and then start writing their kids.

There's nothing hotter than a hero out for revenge and a heroine on the run. Forced proximity might be my new favorite trope to write. Throw in a royal princess, an evil king, and a couple assholes who are stealing state secrets, and I had a romantic suspense delicious enough to stand with the rest of my Killers.

Emoji, the love of my life, thank you for putting up with my alarm going off at 4:45 a.m. to get this book written. Who knew that would be my magic hour? Your support and always having my back as I've made writing a career is everything. I can't wait for 2022 and all its changes. Life with you is sometimes like jumping out of a train window, and I wouldn't have it any other way.

Elle, it doesn't matter how many years pass, I will always look out my front door and miss seeing you across the street. You were my first supporter and lover of my words, and the longer I write, the more that means to me.

Writing a book is a solitary experience, but editing it is not. There's no way I could have done this without the superb editing of Hadley Finn and Karen Hrdlicka. And because it takes an army to clean up my errors, this book wouldn't be what it is without Carole, Beth, Carrie, Sarah, and Ivy. Thank you to Tracie at Dark Water Covers for putting up with all my cover changes.

Sarah Curtis and Layla Frost, your friendship and support means the world to me. I don't know what I'd do without you.

Annette Brignac and Michelle Clay of Book Nerd Services, I love you both. Thank you for your continued love, support, and help in navigating this crazy and ever-changing book industry.

To my street and review teams, your love and dedication to my work will forever be rooted in my soul.

And, finally, to my Beauties. Together, we've created one of the nicest places on the Freakybook. Most days, it's the only social media I invest in. Thank you for creating a vibe where people want to be, feel safe, and get that cows (the fluffy cute kind, not the medium-rare kind) and wine go together like an old friend and a good book. I'm the luckiest person on earth to have YOU in my life. And if you're reading this and you're not a Beauty ... like seriously? Why not?!

ALSO BY BRYNNE ASHER

Killers Series

Vines – A Killers Novel, Book 1

Paths – A Killers Novel, Book 2

Gifts – A Killers Novel, Book 3

Veils – A Killers Novel, Book 4

Scars – A Killers Novel, Book 5

Souls – A Killers Novel, Book 6

The Tequila – A Killers Novella

The Killers, The Next Generation

Levi, Asa's son

The Agents

Possession

Tapped

Exposed

Illicit

The Carpino Series

Overflow – The Carpino Series, Book 1

Beautiful Life – The Carpino Series, Book 2

Athica Lane – The Carpino Series, Book 3

Until Avery – A Carpino Series Crossover Novella

Force of Nature - A Carpino Christmas Novel

The Dillon Sisters
Deathly by Brynne Asher
Damaged by Layla Frost

The Montgomery Series
Bad Situation – The Montgomery Series, Book 1
Broken Halo – The Montgomery Series, Book 2
Betrayed Love - The Montgomery Series, Book 3

Standalones
Blackburn

ABOUT THE AUTHOR

Brynne Asher lives in the Midwest with her husband, three children, and her perfect dog. When she isn't creating pretend people and relationships in her head, she's running her kids around and doing laundry. She enjoys cooking, decorating, shopping at outlet malls and online, always seeking the best deal. A perfect day in Brynne World ends in front of an outdoor fire with family, friends, s'mores, and a delicious cocktail.

- facebook.com/brynneasherauthor
- instagram.com/brynneasher
- amazon.com/Brynne-Asher/e/B00VRULS58/ref=dp_by-line_cont_pop_ebooks_1
- bookbub.com/profile/brynne-asher

Printed in Great Britain
by Amazon